BURNING BRIGHT

BURNING BRIGHT

MICHELE KWASNIEWSKI

Rand-Smith LLC

BURNING BRIGHT: Book Two in the Rise and Fall of Dani Truehart Series

Copyright © 2021 by Michele Kwasniewski

Print ISBN: 978-1-950544-34-9 (paperback)
Digital ISBN: 987-1-950544-35-6

Rand-Smith Publishing
wwwRand-Smith.com
USA

First Printing, 2021

Contents

Contents ~ vii

Dedication

For My Sister, Christina – whenever I see a bird, I think of you.

I

I can't believe this is my life!

A warm, salty breeze stirs my senses. I gaze about my room bathed in early morning sunlight and take in the enormous television and piles of designer clothes oozing out of my overstuffed closet. Today is the first day in months that I have nowhere to be. I lazily stretch, enjoying a peaceful moment while I reflect on the past few months.

My first publicity trip to New York to promote my debut EP in November seems like a lifetime ago. Macy's showered my family and me with five-star treatment from the moment my private jet touched down. Limousines, suites at the Mandarin Hotel and a complimentary shopping spree were just the tip of the iceberg. For the first time in my life, my Mom Jodi was happy, reveling in the life of luxury she'd always dreamed of. I felt so proud that *I'd* achieved that for her. Any anger she had about being forced to hand over my legal guardianship to my vocal/dance coach Martin Fox seemed to evaporate while we were in New York.

Being a former member of REVOLUTION!, one of the biggest boy bands of the '80s, Martin had insisted the only way he would help me start my singing career was if he stepped in as my guardian. He didn't like how much pressure my mom put on me to succeed or how my dad, Don never stepped in to protect me from her. Martin also wanted to make sure any money I earned was kept safe in a trust. It's been learning process for us both but having him in charge of my career instead of my mom has reduced my stressed and made this whole process much more enjoyable.

After a decadent Thanksgiving dinner in my suite, my parents and sister returned home. I appeared on every daytime and late-night TV and radio show in the tri-state area. Then I spent three weeks traveling across the country, making as many appearances as my manager, Jenner Redman could schedule.

I was a little nervous that tensions would flare up between Martin and Jenner. Martin was so convinced I could be a star that he reached out to his former manager Jenner for help, even though they hadn't spoken since REVOLUTION! broke up. I don't think Martin's ever really forgiven Jenner for taking almost all the band's money with the lopsided contracts he offered the boys when he founded REVOLUTION!. But Martin believed in me enough to put his feelings about Jenner aside because despite the shady contracts, Martin felt Jenner was the only one who could send my career into orbit. For his part, Jenner's seems to feel really badly for how he acted in the past and has been working hard to prove to Martin that he's changed.

Throughout the tour, Martin and my sister Geena kept me updated on my boyfriend, Sean's grandfather, who'd had a stroke right before I left. I FaceTimed and texted Sean every spare moment I got. At least once a day, I broke down in tears, questioning how I could be traveling when I should be home supporting Sean. Martin and Jenner did their best to console me and repeatedly offered to fly me home. But there was always seemed to be an important show or big appearance I didn't want to miss that kept me on the road.

The time difference and my crazy schedule worked against Sean's limited availability to talk. I distracted myself by hanging out with Beau, the youngest backup dancer in the troupe. I was grateful to have someone near my own age to talk to. Martin worried that Beau was making a move on me. He eventually got Jenner involved, which seemed way over the top and pissed me off. But after a brief talk with Jenner, Beau assured everyone he had no romantic ideas and that he was just a friend.

Back at Jenner's compound where I'd been living since I signed my recording contract, we waited for Terrance Flemming, songwriter extraordinaire who'd written my EP, to polish the songs for my first full-length album. I spent my days rehearsing with legendary choreographer, Serena, training in the gym with my trainer Brett, and performing several times a week.

True to his word, Martin reimbursed my parents the $200,000 they had spent on my voice lessons. Remembering how money-hungry my mom was during that disastrous afternoon last fall when we'd reviewed my contract still makes me cringe. At least with the payoff, she can't expect any more money from me in the future. Of course, Mom immediately started spending it on herself, and her transformation was nothing short of shocking. By the time I got back from the tour, she had a new nose and new boobs. She'd ditched her no-nonsense shoulder-length hair, adding extensions and highlights. She looked like a different person.

But the biggest thing to happen since I got back, besides the creation of Jodi 2.0, was seeing my grandmother for the first time since I was a kid. I had spent ages agonizing over what to do after discovering my mom had schemed to keep us apart when my grandmother had dared question how much pressure our mother put on my sister and I to succeed. Geena got so sick of my stressing that she dropped by the compound one day with Grandma in tow. She looked just like I remembered—a helmet of permed white hair, slight frame, and velour tracksuit. I hesitated for a minute, racked with guilt. But Grandma flashed her loving smile and my guilt melted away. I flung myself into her arms and immediately felt like I was home.

Surprisingly, my mom didn't freak out when I told her that I'd reconnected with my grandma. I was thrilled when Mom invited her over for Christmas. If my singing career fails, I can honestly say that the best thing to come of all this is having Grandma back in my life.

After a quiet holiday with family and friends in Santa Clarita, I returned to the compound and jumped into recording my full-length album. The days were long and exhausting, but the songs were more of the same magic that had shot my EP to platinum status the first week it dropped. Each song made it into the top five on the charts. They play on radio stations across the globe, and the response has been incredible! Now, with only one song left to record, I'm enjoying a day off before the madness of the album release takes over my life.

Martin's voice comes through the intercom, tinny and small. "Good morning, Sunshine. Could you come down here? Just want to run something past you before I head out for the day."

"Be right down." I hop out of bed and get dressed. Martin and I have been joined at the hip these past few months. I don't make a move without consulting him. He consoled me on tour when I felt lonely and dispelled the last-minute stage fright that seemed to plague me before every live performance. He's always there to make me smile, wipe away my tears, or surprise me with a treat just when I need it most. My doubts about Martin's ability to manage my career were entirely dispelled during my three-week publicity blitz. Since then, I've felt secure knowing that Martin is at the helm, steering my career and protecting me from harm.

A few minutes later, I bounce into the kitchen in a bikini and shorts, my high pony swinging behind me. I plant a kiss on Magda's cheek as I pass, eliciting a blush and a flurry of Hungarian words from Jenner's housekeeper as she waves me away. Plopping onto a stool at the island, I smile expectantly at Martin.

"What's up, Captain?" Magda places a large mug of green tea in front of me.

"Brett and I are driving to Santa Barbara for lunch. Could you take care of something for me today?"

"Sure. I don't have any plans, just sitting by the pool."

"Good! Shouldn't interfere with your pool time." The doorbell rings and Martin snaps his fingers. "Right on time." He motions for me to follow him.

"Just let me know what you need. I'll take care of you for a change."

Martin pulls open the front door. There, with his dazzling smile and sun-kissed hair, is Sean.

Martin steps back, laughing, just in time to keep from being knocked over as I jump into Sean's arms. "I assume you don't need instructions from me!"

Sean puts me down and shakes Martin's hand. "Hi, Martin! Thanks for inviting me over. I didn't think I'd get to see Dani until next week."

"My pleasure. You two deserve a little one-on-one time together. Magda will prepare lunch and dinner, but if you decide to go out, just let her know. Anatoli can drive you." He looks at me. "Enjoy your day, eat what you want, and be home by ten. Text if you need me. We'll be back around nine."

I let go of Sean's arm long enough to give Martin a huge hug. "Thanks. You think of everything." He squeezes me and steps back as Brett appears in the doorway.

"Morning, guys!" Brett's eyes dance as they rest on Martin. "Hey, you."

Martin mouths "hey." Sean and I exchange smiles.

I chime in. "By the way, happy anniversary, you two. Six months now! Congratulations!"

Martin grins, and Brett smiles shyly. "Yeah, we're pretty excited about it. I guess we have you to thank for that."

I laugh. "I will accept nothing less than Maid of Honor at your wedding."

Brett turns red and Martin picks up his backpack by the door. "You're as bad as Mama!" He bows majestically as he steps out the door. "We're off. Oh, and I have another little surprise for you tomorrow." He winks as he closes the door. "See you tonight."

I lean into Sean, breathing him in deeply. "I can't believe you're here."

He kisses my hair. "Me, too. For the first time in months, I don't have school, practice, or grandpa-duty."

I smile. "We have the whole day to ourselves. The sky's the limit! What should we do first?"

The aroma of buttery waffles and bacon waft into the entryway and we both laugh. "Eat!"

***

An uninterrupted day alone with Sean is an absolute dream come true! We decide to stay at the compound where we swim, watch movies, walk on the beach, and nap. All the while we kiss, hug, and touch. It is a day of pure bliss, and I float through it on a cloud of sheer happiness.

With chapped lips and sea salt clinging to my skin, I reluctantly say goodbye to Sean just before Martin gets home. I sigh, replaying the day in my mind as I gaze into the glow of the fireplace in my bedroom. I'm grateful we're still on the same page about being intimate. It took the pressure off today and allowed us not to waste any of our precious time together debating about whether or not to go all the way.

A knock on the door rouses me from my thoughts. Martin pops his head into the room. "Hi, darlin'. Have a good day?"

I yawn, stretching. "The best! I can't thank you enough, Martin." I straighten up on the couch. "How was yours?" I give him a knowing look. "Did you two have fun?"

Martin beams. "Yeah, we did. It's such an amazing feeling to know we're in the same place about things. I feel so lucky that we found each other—thanks to you."

I pull my knees up to my chest, wrapping my arms around them. "I'm so happy for you two. He's a great guy." My eyes grow big, and my head pops up. "Do you think you're going to marry him?"

Martin looks away. "You know, I think I will. Not now, of course, but I really don't think I could do any better."

I squeal. "That's so exciting!"

Martin smiles. "It is." He glances at my bedside clock. "Big day tomorrow. Lights out at ten, OK?"

I yawn again. "If not sooner. I'm exhausted from relaxing!" I suddenly remember something. "Oh hey, what about your other surprise tomorrow? Is Sean coming back again?"

"Nope. I've been working on something for a while. I hope you like it."

My mind buzzes with possibilities and Martin laughs. "I don't think you're going to guess what it is. Night, love." He blows me a kiss and closes the door.

I get ready for bed, thinking about Sean and my surprise.

2

A restful night's sleep and a nutritious breakfast find Martin and me bouncing along in a golf cart toward the studio. Try as I might, I can't pry Martin's big surprise out of him. He looks mysterious and seems to be enjoying his secret far too much.

I'm still needling him for clues as we enter the studio. Terrance and Jenner are sitting in the lobby chatting. "Good morning! Enjoy your day off?"

I smile, dropping my bag on the floor and plonking down next to Terrance. "It was great. Martin's the best for arranging it!"

Jenner pats Martin on the back. "Well, looks like he's on fire these days with his surprises. I had my doubts when he first told me about this one, but it's truly phenomenal."

I can't contain myself. "Come *on*, guys! The suspense is killing me."

Martin laughs, dropping his bag onto the coffee table. "I'll put you out of your misery. I wrote you a song. I haven't thought about writing anything since my days in REVOLUTION! But being back in the studio with Jenner, seeing you perform, inspired me!"

It's the last thing I expect Martin to say. A weird stab of emotion grips my stomach. I'm suddenly keenly aware of the smile plastered onto my face. My cheeks quiver as I try to maintain my smile and my mouth goes dry. Everyone's staring at me expectantly. I utter a strangled "Oh, wow" as Martin excitedly continues.

"I've been working on it for months, but I didn't want to say anything because I wasn't sure if it was good enough. I also didn't want you to think I wasn't one hundred percent focused on you." Martin takes a breath. "But I finally got the nerve to play it for Jenner, who then played it for Terrance. They both agreed to put it on the album. Isn't that a kick in the pants? My first song *ever* on *your* first album?"

Jenner starts talking before Martin comes up for air. "Terrance and I agree that Martin's song is just what this album needs to be a smash. It has a killer pop beat and a hook that's contagious. It has a real shot at becoming this year's summer anthem."

Martin finally catches onto the change in me. He tries to speak, but Terrance jumps in, "You know, I wouldn't take a song of mine off an album for just any hacky number. Martin has a genuine ear for what works. Give it a listen, and I'm pretty sure you'll see what we mean."

I realize it has been way too long since I've said anything. *I don't want to make Martin feel bad, especially since he's done nothing but support me and protect me since becoming my manager.* Still, something nags at the pit of my stomach that I can't identify. *Discovering that Martin has secretly written a song and that Jenner and Terrance both knew about it before me seems more like an ambush than a surprise.* Shades of my self-interested mother come to mind, and I shake my head to dislodge them.

"Of course, I want to hear it," I pipe up half-heartedly. I exhale, trying to seem cool.

Terrance smiles. "Atta girl! Let's crank it up."

Jenner stares at me for a moment. "You sure you're OK?"

I nod and force a smile. "Yup. Can't wait."

Martin frantically searches his pockets. "Damn. Must have forgotten my phone up at the house. Why don't you get started? I'll be back in a minute."

I look at the ground, knowing damn well his phone is tucked into his messenger bag.

Jenner turns to Martin. "Are you sure?"

"Hell, yeah. Heard it a million times. Besides, I don't want Dani to feel any pressure listening to it with me hovering over her."

Martin addresses me directly, and I can barely meet his eyes. "Look,

D, if it doesn't curl your toes, let's just record Terrance's song as planned. It's more important that you're comfortable. A last-minute switch was probably a stupid idea anyway." He winks at me. "Be right back."

***

We move into the booth. I try to decipher my feelings as Terrance cranks up Martin's demo. Elbows on my knees, I stare at my sneakers when Martin's voice comes through the sound system, singing something about "try and stop me." I barely register the funky bassline that snakes out of the speakers, increasing its tempo to a crescendo only to be slammed by sharp trumpets peppering the air.

I look up and see Terrance bouncing his head, smiling. I sit up, extremely self-conscious about my lack of interest in the song. *I feel pressure to like it, which makes me immediately want to not like it.* I can't help but smile when Martin's falsetto voice belts out the quick-paced lyrics, weaving in and out of the music or sometimes stomping right on top of the beat, overpowering the music with his voice. I bounce my head as a smile creeps across my face. The song *is* infectious with its percussive lyrics, soaring vocals, and a nonstop groove that makes me want to get up and dance. When the song ends abruptly with a quick bass lick and horn flourish, I look at Terrance, stunned. "Martin did that?"

Terrance beams. "See what I mean? Pure gold."

"Totally!" I cringe, running my hand through my hair. "Ugh! I'm the worst. I don't really know where my reaction came from. I love Martin, and I know he'd do anything for me. I guess..." My words trail off as I try to verbalize my feelings.

Jenner scratches his head. "Do you think you might have been worried that Martin might be using you for his own advancement? I can see how us springing this on you might make you feel..."—Jenner pauses, searching for the right words—"like he's got a hidden agenda or something."

I consider that. "Yeah, maybe that's it. I mean, for years Mom was always pushing me to succeed and, well..." I shrug. "I learned she was more in it for herself than for me. Maybe I was afraid that Martin had the same idea."

Jenner nods. "I can honestly say that Martin puts you first and foremost in everything he does. If he thought for an instant that you would have been upset, he never would have pursued this. He was genuinely excited to create something special for you that would make your album a success. And I think he's done that."

Terrance flicks off the speakers. "Just imagine your voice on this track, plowing through those sassy lyrics. It's going to be epic!" Terrance turns to face me, crossing his arms as he leans against the counter. "But you've gotta listen to your gut. If you feel weird about this, it's not going to work."

I look around the room, half hoping I'll actually find the answer somewhere in the jumble of equipment. Finally, I shake my head. "This is stupid. Of course I'm going to record it."

Jenner and Terrance watch me with steady gazes. I smile slowly. "I really want to do this."

Terrance gives a fist pump. "All right then! Let's get to work."

3

By the time Martin returns, Terrace and I are in the isolation booth running over the lyrics while the band sets up. I want to talk to Martin about my awful reaction, but he gives me a wide berth and stays inside the booth.

Over the next ten hours, we craft a sure-fire number one hit bursting with funk and electricity. After our last take, I run over to Terrance at the piano and whisper into his ear.

Terrance calls out, "Martin, got a sec? I think we need one more pass before we can lock it down."

Martin sighs and closes his laptop. He comes into the studio looking annoyed. "So, what's missing that twenty takes haven't locked down?" Terrance crosses the room and steers Martin onto a wooden stool in front of the mic stand.

"Just you. Dani wants you to sing with her on this last take. Maybe release it as a bonus track on the album? I think a little of your George Michael falsetto is just what this baby needs to be white hot."

Martin pops up, knocking over the stool. "No way! I'm not out to steal her thunder, embarrass myself and her by singing a duet. I haven't sung in years. Absolutely not."

I up-right the stool and stand next to Martin. "First of all, no one calls it a duet anymore, grandpa. It's called a collaboration. And I'd like to make it up to you after I was such a brat this morning. I'm sorry."

He hugs me. "Nothing to be sorry for, darlin'. I was the idiot who sprung this on you. I'm sorry you thought for *one* second that I wasn't one hundred percent focused on you. You're my priority, not songwriting. We're cool."

I smile. "Good. Then let's get going."

Jenner's voice comes through the intercom. "It's no use, Martin. Might as well record the damned thing and get it over with." He smiles broadly, clearly enjoying Martin's discomfort. "Besides, you can show Dani how we did it back in the day."

I laugh, feigning shock. "Oh, now you're gonna school me, Martin? Show me how it was done back in the day? When was that, before cars and talkie pictures?"

Martin gives me heavy side-eye and removes his sweatshirt. "Challenge accepted. I'm about to show you what real soul is, sister. So, step aside and try not to hurt yourself. Terrance, give me a beat!"

4

With all the songs locked down, Jenner disappears into his office to haggle with my record label MEGA over which cuts will appear on the album and which cities we'll tour, and then manically plan a stellar drop party for the album.

When I'm not performing or going to publicity events, I rehearse with the dancers for the tour. I also work with a grad student Martin hired named Regina Williams, who is supposed to tutor me. Turns out I'm even less motivated by homeschooling than before. The only bonus is not having to see my arch-nemesis Zoe McFadden every day at school and witness her blatant attempts to steal Sean. I've barely touched my homework assignments, which seem so trivial compared with getting ready for my tour.

Before I know it, it's April and my sixteenth birthday! After a morning of phone calls, breakfast with my family, and gifts, I'm in the compound's wardrobe room dressing for the release party for my first full-length album, *Here I Am*. It feels like I've spent hours in the chair as my make-up artist Pauline, who also happens to be Martin's sister, does my hair and makeup. Now my costumer Petra is trying to maneuver me into a silvery-blue Ellie Saab couture gown. I'm nervous about the plunging neckline, but Petra assures me that she's used almost a whole roll of fashion tape to secure the dress in place. It's awkward to have Petra tape my boobs into position like I'm some weird art project. Martin says in time I'll get used to being handled by wardrobe people, but I can't imagine it will ever feel normal.

The deep halter neckline of my dress is balanced by a gossamer skirt that flounces in a million layers, with ostrich feathers sewn along the various hemlines. Silk flowers and rhinestones dot the bodice, giving the entire dress a whimsical look. Rhinestones sparkle in my swept-up hair. With pale blue eyeshadow and pale pink lipstick, I look like a garden nymph come to life.

My mom always forced me to wear makeup, but her pageant version and Pauline's are as different as night and day. Pauline taught me how to wear subtle colors to appear completely polished and natural.

And the clothes! I never really thought about fashion before because we never had enough money to buy anything nice. But now, every day the doorbell rings hailing the arrival of bags and boxes filled with dresses, shoes, purses, and everything else you could imagine. Martin says that designers love to send celebrities free stuff, hoping they'll get photographed wearing their designs. The wardrobe room is lined with piles of stuff that I haven't had time to look at. Petra comes in daily to catalog the new arrivals and put together outfits for me to wear. Sometimes I have mini-fashion shows during my lunch break where Petra snaps photos of me on the terrace or the beach, which she has Carlton, Jenner's totally creepy assistant, post on my Insta or Facebook. I've gifted more things to Geena, my best friend Lauren, and our moms than I can count. They all seem more than happy to have my designer cast-offs. I'm just glad I can share these perks with them.

There's a knock on the door and I shout, "Come in!" Sean enters wearing an incredible blue Armani suit, the collar of his white shirt open. He's carrying a bulky giftbox. His tousled blond hair is tamed into a heartbreakingly polished cut, and I melt a little just looking at him. *Every time I lay eyes on Sean, I'm still shocked that he's mine; that I am his!* I can't even move, I'm in such a daze watching him walk toward me, his broad smile mesmerizing.

"Happy birthday, Dani," he says as he sets down the box. I step into his arms, losing myself in his woody scent and his kiss.

"Whoa, girl. Let's remember all eyes will be on you in less than an hour. Can't have you looking like a rumpled blanket." Pauline leaps over and gently pries us apart. "I'm all for young love, but not right before launching your new album. Savvy?"

I utter a strangled "Savvy" while my eyes stay locked with Sean's. "Sean, you look...beautiful."

Sean chuckles and shoots his cuffs. "Martin convinced me jeans and a polo wouldn't cut it tonight. Petra sent this over yesterday and said it was on the house."

I whisper conspiratorially, "Everything I'm wearing right now is free. It's crazy."

"Man, I get why designers send you their stuff, though. You could make anything look good."

I blush madly as he picks up the gift and grabs my hand. "Can we talk for a few minutes before we go?"

Pauline shouts out, "No problem, we're all finished." She lays my clutch on the counter. "Lip gloss, blotting paper all inside. Have fun, sugar, and congratulations." She blows me a kiss and follows Petra out, shutting the door behind them.

Sean guides me toward the sofa and sits me down. He looks so nervous I start to worry.

"Is something wrong?"

He smiles. "Exact opposite, everything's perfect." He sets the box on my lap and takes a deep breath. "I know this might seem kind of old fashioned. But with you going on tour, I really wanted to give you something for your birthday that would make you think of me every time you looked at it. And something that would let the world know you were mine, even though we're not always together. You know that if I could drop everything and go with you, I'd do it in a heartbeat. But since I can't, I hope you take this with you and wear it every day and think of me."

Inside the box is Sean's letterman jacket nestled in a bed of pink tissue paper. Tears come to my eyes because I know how hard Sean worked for this jacket. He smiles at me as he lifts it out of the box and places it on my shoulders.

"I want the whole world to know that you're my girl. This is the most valuable thing I own, and I'm giving it to the most important person in my life." He crushes me in an embrace, and we kiss feverishly—wet, hot, and messy—until Martin barges in.

"Time to go, young lovers. We've got an album to debut." Martin takes one look at my tear-streaked, makeup-smeared face and sighs. "Pauline!" he shouts down the hall. "We need emergency repairs STAT!"

Pauline walks in, and minutes later, my makeup is fixed and Pauline hands me my clutch. She looks at Sean. "Next time, *you're* fixing her makeup. Got that, Romeo?" She laughs. "See you at the party."

Martin hustles us into a silver Maybach where Jenner is waiting. "You look wonderful, Dani." He smiles at Sean. "I'm glad you could ride over with us, Sean. You look terrific, too."

Sean smiles. "Thank you for the clothes. This is much better than anything I could have come up with on my own."

Jenner waves off Sean's thank you. "Happy to do it. It'll come in handy in the future. Never underestimate the value of a properly tailored suit, my boy."

5

We pull up to the Dream Hotel in Hollywood amidst a crush of limousines, spectators, and paparazzi. The front of the hotel is wrapped in white fabric and transformed with a wash of electric blue lighting, the two-story lobby windows glow warmly in contrast. Spotlights chase each other along the building's front, and my name and the album title are scrawled across the middle in hot pink script. The rooftop deck is illuminated with twinkly lights and colored floodlights. The dull thud of music can be heard through the closed car window. *It's all so surreal.* Sean squeezes my hand as we stare out the window.

"This is it, Dani," Jenner says. "All your hard work is about to pay off. And this is just the beginning. Wait and see what I have in store for you on tour. It's going to be spectacular everywhere you go. You deserve nothing less."

I'm at a loss for words. The pressure of his statement is unimaginable. *If people see something like this, they expect a performance, a personality, a voice to match it. I love everything we've recorded, but seeing this whole venue is making me wonder...am I enough? What if I can't match the hype?*

As if reading my mind, Martin leans over and gives my shoulder a squeeze before sliding Sean's letterman jacket off. "Jenner's right. You *are* worth all this fuss, and people are going to love you." He nudges my shoulder. "Look out that window—they already do. Get out of your head and get out of this car. Your future is waiting, sweetheart."

Throngs of people holding signs and cameras are staring at my limo, waiting. I take a deep breath. Sean gives my hand another squeeze, opens the door, and helps me onto the red carpet leading to the hotel. There's a deafening roar from the crowd when I emerge. So many blinding flashes go off at once that it feels like I'm stepping out onto the sun.

Sean folds my hand into the crook of his arm, and I grip him tightly as he escorts me to the step-and-repeat in front of the hotel. He's unphased by the noise and lights, acting as if he does a red carpet walk every Friday night. Girls are screaming and calling my name as I smile robotically, overwhelmed. I don't know where to look, and I can't understand what people are shouting at me, the noise and lights assaulting my senses. I try to look breezy and casual, but I feel like I'm failing miserably. After a few minutes of posing, Jenner has Sean step away, and I'm alone on the red carpet. My eyes dart from face to face until they settle on Sean, standing off to the side. He's smiling like crazy and nodding encouragingly. For the first time, I genuinely smile and take a deep breath. The paparazzi sense the change in me and start calling for Sean to kiss me, which he does. Eventually, Martin and Jenner join us for some photos. By the time we've taken every combination of photo possible, I'm totally relaxed. Martin gently pushes me to work the crowd, so I sign autographs and pose for selfies with fans. An hour passes before I make it upstairs to the party.

The open-air rooftop Highlight Room overlooking the Hollywood Hills has been transformed into a wonderland. A mix of friends and family rub elbows with entertainment legends, celebrities, and industry heavyweights amid passed hors d'oeuvres and cocktails. A DJ spins background music as the conversations of hundreds of people float on a gentle breeze that whispers in the trees growing about the venue. Paper lanterns, strings of globe lights, and moody accent floods flicker off the water of the glass-covered-pool-turned-dancefloor, creating a magical atmosphere. It feels like a fairyland forest in the sky.

Lauren, Geena, and Grandma are the first to greet us as we step off the elevator. I assume that Petra and Pauline have worked their way through my entire guestlist because they all look gorgeous, decked out in designer apparel with polished hair and makeup. I feel like this isn't just my debut but an accomplishment for everyone who has ever loved and supported me. It warms my heart to know that Jenner and Martin understand how I feel and have made sure that everyone is taken care of.

Geena screams when she sees me. "That dress is sick, sis!"

Lauren chimes in as she hugs me. "And your boobs—you're one sneeze away from breaking the internet!"

I self-consciously touch my cleavage. "I've got about twenty yards of tape keeping everything in place, so I think the internet is secure...for now, anyway. You guys look beautiful!"

Grandma leans in and pecks me on the cheek. "Those young women you sent over were wonderful! I've never had someone come to my house to do my hair and give me free clothes."

Mom charges over with Dad trailing behind. While she doesn't exactly knock my grandmother over, she does forcefully edge her out of the way. "This is *it*, chickadee! We've officially arrived! Did you see what Petra brought me today?"

Mom executes a wobbly turn; Martin and Jenner have to duck to avoid being smacked in the face by her outstretched arms. She's in a jeweled yellow satin MNM dress—gorgeous, but too tight in all the wrong places. Her dress strains to contain her new chest and it looks like she might have her own wardrobe malfunction if she isn't careful. She's wearing what can only be described as stripper shoes—clear platform stiletto heels that give her the gait of a new-born giraffe. Her spray tan is in full effect, and she's added at least another foot to her usual hair extensions, which cascade down her bronzed back like a washed-up mermaid.

I smile. "Wow, Mom, that's an amazing dress. But what's with the shoes?"

She grins wildly. "Well, apparently this dress is made for a six-foot twelve-year-old. There was no time to alter it, but I couldn't pass it up! I know it's kind of tight and about twelve inches too long, but I don't care. I made your father run out and grab these while I put on three pairs of Spanks. Petra tried to put me in some beige mother-of-the-bride number, but I said, 'No way, honey! This is my night to shine, and I only want the best!'" She elbows me sharply. "Do you know how much this dress costs?"

Her night to shine? Before I can respond, Martin envelopes my mother in a hug. "You look divine, Miss J! Tell me all about this ensemble. Who designed it?"

I heave a sigh of relief as Martin steers my chattering mother away, winking at me as they leave. My father, looking uncomfortable in his tailored suit, gives me a hug. "You look beautiful, Marie. Can't wait to hear you sing." He kisses my cheek before catching up with Mom and Martin.

Geena chuckles. "Martin is *really* earning his money tonight!"

Grandma gives her a reproaching tsk. "You need to be more respectful, Geena. She's still your mother."

I smother a laugh. Jenner clears his throat. "Dani, you should do a pass through the crowd before your performance."

I nod, grab Sean's hand, and say goodbye to everyone. We slowly progress through the party, Jenner networking and introducing us to dozens of people whose names I immediately forget. There's so much to take in—the decorations, noise, faces...I can barely keep up with what Jenner is saying. It takes us almost forty minutes to cross the room, and I'm relieved when we leave the crowd behind.

We take an elevator downstairs where we find Petra and Pauline waiting in a hotel room. Twenty minutes later, I'm sporting an unbelievable outfit that Petra designed herself. Tiny black leather biker shorts with a long flowing leather and tulle skirt that fastens over the shorts, leaving the front of the skirt open to allow the shorts to show. I look like a cross between Marie Antoinette and a spin instructor. A black, skintight, long-sleeve crop top with HERE I AM in white across the chest and combat boots finish the look. I don oversized black Gucci sunglasses, and my hair is slicked back into a high pony. My nymph-like makeup is replaced with minimal eye makeup and a stark red lip. I stare and pose in the mirror; my reflection looks like a bad ass with a flirty side. *I feel like such a boss in this outfit.* My usual pre-performance nerves are nowhere to be found. It's the perfect outfit for me to kick ass.

By the time we hustle into the elevator, Jenner is speaking on stage. Carlton keeps Martin, who is waiting backstage, updated via phone. Petra adjusts my costume while Pauline blots me within an inch of my life. I have no idea what happened to Sean, but the distraction from being ushered, poked, and prodded while reviewing my songs in my head keeps it from being anything more than a fleeting thought.

With Jenner's voice booming over the loudspeaker, we scoot down a curtained pathway toward backstage. I take a swig from a water bottle that Carlton hands me, nodding my head to the beat in my mind and silently singing the words to my first number. When we get backstage, Martin grabs my hand. "You look *fierce!*" He takes my water and hands me a bedazzled microphone. We crowd in among all the dancers who all whisper, "break a leg."

Standing in the shadows offstage, I'm relieved when I spot Sean by the front of the stage staring right at me. He gives me a thumbs up. It's the final thing I need to succeed. I pull down my glasses and blow him a kiss.

Jenner finishes his speech as the dancers take their positions on stage. "And now, without any further ado, singing songs from her debut album *Here I Am*, here's Dani Truehart!"

I take a deep breath.

With a bang of confetti cannons, the band slams into the first song. I leap onto the stage singing a song titled "Hit Me Up," and the crowd roars. *I have never felt more in command of myself and the crowd than at this moment!* The flirty lyrics pour out of me as I dance up and down the stage, touching people in the audience as they reach for me, gyrating to the music and interacting with the musicians like we're old friends. My voice soars. A few dancers hoist me above their heads and the song ends abruptly with a final chord. A triumphant feeling of accomplishment washes over me—*I've made it!* The crowd goes crazy with applause, and I beam back at them, sweat dripping down my face, while dancers settle me on my feet. Beau gives my hand a squeeze. With my blood racing and my heart pumping wildly, I turn and give the dancers and band a much-deserved hand.

I sing six songs off the album, and I'm flying by the time the set is finished. I spot Geena, Lauren, Magda, Anatoli, Terrance, Serena, and the rest of my loved ones in the audience. I make it a point to sing to each of them throughout the performance, though Sean is the one who I return to most often. I feel like I'm singing only for him, and I can feel my love for him coming off me in waves. The crowd is buzzing, and I quiet them down before the last song.

"You guys really know how to make a girl feel welcome!" The audience erupts in whistles and applause, and I can't stop smiling as I wait for the noise to die down. "I hope that all my concerts have an audience like you." Again, the crowd cheers, and it feels so wonderful to be up here, talking to this room full of people like we're friends.

"For my last song, I'm going to do something a little different, if that's OK with you?"

More applause and whistles and I smile. "Good! Because I want you to experience this song the way I like to hear it best. But I'm going to need your help."

I cover the mic and whisper to Beau. While he informs the dancers and band, I continue, "So, you might not know that my coach and one of my dearest friends is Martin Fox, the outstanding vocalist from the iconic '80s boyband, REVOLUTION!"

The crowd cheers. I glance off stage and see Martin shooting me a dirty look, shaking his head violently. I laugh and turn to the crowd. "Well, did you know that Martin is also an incredible songwriter and that he wrote this last song I'm about to sing? What do you say we give Martin a little encouragement and get him on stage to help me with this last number?"

Cameras start flashing and the stage lights start blinking as the crowd chants "Mar-tin, Mar-tin" over and over. I see Jenner and Terrance at their table in the back, laughing and falling over each other. It takes a minute, but Martin reluctantly appears on stage. I smile, holding the mic out to him, which he stares at for a few seconds before sighing and taking hold of it. The audience erupts in applause.

He turns to the audience and smiles. "You might regret this in a minute, but here we go…" Martin turns to the band and says, "On three."

He counts us in as I grab a mic from Beau and sassily say "Try and stop me!" as the funky bassline slaps the audience. We settle into the song just like we did in the studio, but the energy of the audience, along with the movement from the dancers, powers us forward with even more intensity. Martin's voice soars over the high notes and slams down onto the chorus as we harmonize and riff off each other. The song ends with a flourish of horns, and Martin picks me up and spins me as the audience loses it! Camera flashes and cell phones light up the rooftop as the air buzzes with excitement. Jenner charges onto stage and hugs us both, grabbing a mic.

"And there you have it, ladies and gentlemen, the first glimpse of what Dani Truehart has to offer. Trust me, you can't wait to hear what she does next! Thank you for coming out tonight. The party's just getting started here at the Highlight Room, so enjoy yourself. And don't forget to take a giftbag with you before you leave. From all of us at Redman Enterprises, thank you. Have an amazing night!"

Jenner gives the DJ a nod, and he cranks up another song from my album as the crowd cheers. We exit the stage, and it feels like my feet are barely touching the ground. I'm so hyped from my performance! We hug and high five each other, everyone talking a mile a minute.

"I could *kill* you, girl! Dragging me up on stage like that. What the *hell*?" Martin feigns anger but cracks a smile. "I almost died. But that was so much fun! Thank you for sharing your big night with me." He gives me another hug, and I smile.

"This isn't just my night. I wouldn't be here without you and Jenner."

Jenner laughs and holds up his hands. "Well, please don't go sharing the stage with me in the future. You do *not* want to hear me sing!"

We all laugh, and Carlton breathlessly rushes up with Sean and Brett. Sean picks me up and twirls me around as Brett embraces Martin.

"You were incredible! My God, Dani, it was unbelievable. Do you know how many people are watching you online right now? You've gone viral!"

I scream joyfully as Jenner looks at Carlton's outstretched phone. Jenner claps him proudly on the back. "Great job, Carlton! You just earned yourself a raise!"

Carlton beams as Jenner holds up his phone. "Apparently, Carlton livestreamed the whole damned thing AND arranged for a crew to record it. You already have fifty thousand likes."

Carlton blushes. "Well, I figured that you might want footage for future videos or something."

Excitement overshadows my usual discomfort surrounding Carlton, and I give him a hug. "Thank you, Carlton!"

He creepily holds me for a few seconds too long and I sink into his soft chest. Martin clears his throat and Carlton quickly releases me with a sheepish smile.

***

I change into a light pink and gold strapless cocktail dress with a tulle ballerina skirt and strappy gold heels. Pauline throws my hair up into a soft chignon and exchanges my red lips for a soft pink gloss.

Sean meets me outside the dressing room, and we head up to the party. My family and friends greet me with hugs as everyone talks over each other in excitement. Suddenly the lights on the rooftop dim, the music stops, and the crowd parts, revealing a towering pink eight-tier cake with flickering candles in the center of the dance floor. Cameras flash as everyone breaks out singing "Happy Birthday."

I'm beaming and take a moment to look around at all my loved ones. I had no idea that Jenner had planned a birthday celebration on such a big night—it's just like a movie! Sean leans in and whispers, "Make a wish."

Everything I've ever wanted has already come true, what's there left to wish for? Thoughts flash through my mind, and I feel rushed to blow out the candles before they melt all over the cake. So, I just blow out the candles, forgetting to make a wish.

6

The next few weeks speed by as we prep for the June kickoff of my world tour. Jenner had planned for me to open for a well-known band, but my EP and album have been so popular that MEGA wants me to be the main attraction, with several of their smaller artists opening for *me*. I'm headlining my first world tour!

I'm opening here in L.A. at the Staples Center tonight. *TONIGHT!* After we travel the U.S. and Canada, we move on to Europe and beyond. I've been booked almost every second since the party—interviewing, performing, promoting the album, or doing charity work. Any spare time is spent trapped in an endless loop of rehearsals, trying to iron out any wrinkles between the vocals, choreography, lighting, and video playback. We moved from the compound rehearsal studio to an old theater in downtown L.A. to get enough space to simulate a big arena stage. I've barely seen anyone since the release party because the school year is almost over and they're freaking about final exams and SAT testing. I'm stressing out because I leave tomorrow for my tour, and I really want to see Sean before I go. I barely had the chance to say hi to him at Geena's graduation party last night before I had to leave and finish packing. He has a final tomorrow and can't come to the concert tonight. I can't believe that he won't be there for my first big show. I know that finals are important, but this is a really big deal for me. I wish he could work it out.

Suitcases are scattered around my room. Martin keeps pulling things out of my suitcases, insisting that I don't need to take everything I own. He wants to keep things to a minimum because he says extra luggage means extra expense. He keeps reminding me that every penny we don't spend goes into my trust. While I appreciate his concern, I think my comfort while I'm away from home is worth way more than a few measly bucks.

I've also been in a fashion photo frenzy as Petra and Carlton load up on photos for Instagram. Petra wants to photograph as much as possible so that Carlton has a library of photos to post while we're traveling.

Thank God Carlton's in charge of all my social media! I know it's important to stay connected with my fans, but since I haven't had a phone for all that long, I find social media overwhelming. It's nuts the things Carlton comes up with to post, but my Insta is blowing up, so he must know what he's doing. Honestly, I'm a little weirded out by how much Carlton sounds like me when he posts. Jenner says it's an industry standard for celebrities to have someone handle their social media. I just wish that I had a girl closer to my age posting for me rather than creepy Carlton.

As I stuff more socks in a suitcase, my phone rings. I hit the speaker. "Hey, Laur, how're finals going? You coming tonight?"

A gut-wrenching cry comes across the line. I drop my socks and sit on the bed. "What's wrong?"

"I think Tom is cheating on me!" Lauren's words are lost in sniffles and sobs. I let her cry, murmuring a few comforting phrases while she calms down.

Once her weeping has slowed, I ask, "What happened?"

Lauren talks a mile a minute between sniffles. "I don't have any proof yet, but he's been super distant and acting weird. He keeps picking fights with me over nothing, and every time I try to get together with him, he says he's busy studying or helping his dad in the yard. Something just isn't right. *And* I've seen him hanging out with a few of Zoe's minions in the hall, which he's never done before!"

"The minions? That's *so* not like Tom. What does Sean say?"

"He doesn't know, either. He says that he hasn't really seen him lately because of studying for finals."

I'm trying to think of reasons why Lauren's longtime boyfriend is suddenly acting so different when there's a knock on the door. Martin pops his head in. "Almost ready? We have to leave in twenty minutes so we can get to Staples for sound check."

My stomach drops. *I can't keep all these people waiting because my friend is having boy trouble...but it's Lauren! I can't just hang up on her.*

"Do you have to go?" There's an edge to Lauren's voice.

I can't believe she's forgotten about my show, but she's probably only focusing on Tom at the moment.

I rack my brain for a sec before giving Martin a thumbs up. I pop in my ear buds. "No, we've got time to talk." I pull on Sean's letterman jacket, shove my feet into some flats, and grab my bag. "So, you haven't actually caught Tom doing anything wrong, right? He's just acting differently?"

Lauren sighs. "No, I haven't, but..." She continues to list her evidence of Tom's guilt as I clamber down the stairs and into the limo. Martin looks up from his laptop questioningly. I show him my screen and mouth "sorry" as Lauren rattles on.

An hour later, I'm *still* listening as we pull up into the Staples Center. Martin clears his throat and raises an eyebrow. "Um, Laur, I hate to do this to you, but I have to go. My first show's tonight, and I've got sound check right now. I hate to leave you when you're going through something like this."

Lauren groans. "Jecz, I'm an idiot! Of course, you have to go! I didn't even realize the date today. I should be calling you and wishing you luck, not whining on the phone like a pathetic loser."

I'm relieved that she's not mad. "I wish I didn't have to go." Martin grabs our bags, gets out, and taps his watch. I sigh, "But I do. Martin's giving me the stink-eye. Love you, Laur."

I hang up as I get out of the car. "Sorry about that. Lauren thinks Tom is cheating on her and she's a mess."

Martin shifts our bags to one hand and pats my arm. "I'm proud you took time to be there for your friend. Loyalty is an invaluable trait. Don't ever lose that."

"Now, let's put a pin in Lauren's drama and get focused on you. You're about to rock Los Angeles with your first arena concert. Are you ready?"

My stomach cramps at the thought, and I feel like I want to throw up. But I take a deep breath. "Yup, I'm ready!"

Martin chuckles and rubs my shoulder. "I wanted to vomit right before my first big show. And I did, too, right before I walked on stage. Felt so bad for that poor roadie whose shoe I yakked all over. Just push through the barf, honey, because what's on the other side is *so* worth it. Let's go!"

7

I thought it was crazy that we were getting to the arena six hours before the show, but I'm wondering now if that will be enough time! This is by far the largest venue I have ever performed in. There is a huge difference between performing in a nightclub and a twenty-one-thousand-seat arena! Just finding the entrance to the stage requires guidance from an arena staffer. Crew members are scrambling on catwalks adjusting lights. Graphics and video clips play erratically on huge screens as engineers run through media, checking to make sure everything is uploaded properly.

Tony, our production manager, walks us around the stage, pointing out where my marks for various songs have been taped down among all the cables and amps. We've been practicing our choreography in a rented theater, but it was nowhere near this big. Adding all these technical notes makes it seem like I've forgotten to learn a million new steps. If I move wrong, tripping is the *least* embarrassing thing I could do. I could knock out a cable to a guitar, cut the power to any number of amps, or end up performing in the dark because I've missed a pre-programmed cue.

I can barely contain my panic. "Why is this the first time I'm hearing about all of this? This is going to be impossible to remember!"

Martin adjusts the strap of his messenger bag. "You know all of this. We measured everything out in tape on the theater floor, remember?"

He smiles. "You've been practicing for months. This is just a bigger stage."

I wave my arm wildly at the empty seats. "It's massive!"

Martin takes a deep breath, indicating he wants me to do the same. He stares at me until I start to breathe deeply, which *does* calm my pounding heart.

"Better?" he asks. I nod sheepishly.

Martin smiles. "Tony, I think we're done for now. Let's run through sound check."

Tony turns away to address anxious crew members waiting with questions. Carlton, sweaty and wearing a crazy safari-type vest with a million pockets, rushes on stage with a wooden stool. "Here you go, Dani." He pulls a bottle of water from one of his vest pockets and hands it to me, smiling. He then pulls a walkie-talkie from another pocket and gives it to Martin, who clips it onto his belt.

I sit, concentrating on opening the bottle until Carlton slips back into the shadows. Martin hands me a mic and a pair of inner ear monitor buds, or IEMs, as the band files onstage and preps their instruments. He clips the IEM monitor onto the back of my jeans as I place the jeweled IEMs in my ears. When I first started performing, we used wedged-shaped speakers positioned along the front of the stage so I could hear the music. But the speakers cause a lot of feedback, not to mention the beating your eardrums take from all that music at max volume blasting into your face. And if you dance away from the speaker, you can't hear a thing. As soon as we could afford it, Jenner got me these custom-fitted IEMs, which have been a lifesaver. They keep me on key and in time with the music while letting me move freely about the stage.

The nasally voice of our no-nonsense stage manager, Carolina, booms over the sound system. "All right, Dani, you can sit for now, but eventually I'll have you move around the stage."

Martin hands me the playlist for tonight. We run through the beginning and end of each song and anything with a complicated audio sequence or video playback. I walk back and forth across the stage hitting my marks and testing out some dance moves. The longer I'm on stage, the more comfortable I start to feel. I take a moment to let everything sink in, imagining the arena filled with thousands of screaming fans. *I can't believe this is my first big concert tour.*

I'm pulled out of my reverie by a tap on my shoulder.

"Time for hair and makeup," Martin says. "I've got food coming in an hour, and your family will be here in two." He gives my arm a squeeze. "They'll have a private box complete with catering. Your mom will feel utterly pampered. You won't have to see them until after the show."

I heave a sigh of relief and silently thank God for the millionth time for sending me Martin.

***

A staffer leads us through a warren of tunnels backstage to my dressing room. It's huge and furnished with two gray couches, a couple of white-lacquered end tables, and a cloth-covered table laden with healthy snacks, teas, and water. Flower arrangements from MEGA and Jenner are scattered about the room. The CD Lauren made me as a going away gift back in the fall plays softly over the speakers. It's become a good luck charm to listen to before each performance.

Pauline greets me with a hug and guides me into a chair in front of a row of lit wall mirrors. Her table is covered with its usual array of hair and makeup supplies. "Let's get you gorgeous. I can't wait to see you out there tonight!" Martin grabs a seat on a couch and starts typing away on his computer, his walkie-talkie occasionally squawking softly.

Pauline keeps up an endless stream of chatter while she tackles my hair. She refers to photos taped to the mirror from hair and makeup tests we've done over the past few months. She and Petra came up with about fifteen different looks for the course of the tour, but I'll only be using one or two each night. Two video montages during the concert will allow a few minutes for costume changes. We've been practicing to make sure our changes are lightning fast, but we won't know until tonight whether all our practice will pay off!

She braids metal hoops into the front of my hair and then curls and teases the crown and back of my hair into a wild mane. I'm giving Mom and her extensions a run for her money.

I hear the dancers laughing in the room next door while I munch on chicken and veggies that Carlton brought me. *I wish I was in there hanging out with them!* They sound like they're headed out to a party rather than to perform for thousands of people. *I can't imagine ever being that relaxed before a show!* We've all gotten so close over the last few months. I don't feel like an outsider any longer, now I'm just one of the troupe. I feel like I'm hanging out with my friends, only they're older, raunchier, and have way more life experience than Sean and Lauren!

Once she finishes my hair, Pauline works on my makeup: heavy on the red lip, eyelashes, and flared-black eyeliner. It's bold but simple, built to withstand the epic amount of sweat expected to wash down my face over the next few hours.

Martin and Carlton leave as Petra enters to get me into my costume. I pull on pink fishnets, careful not to snag them on the outrageous gel nails Pauline applied yesterday. Next is a short, pink, high-waisted circle skirt that shows off a rhinestone-flecked booty-short when I spin. A sparkly white spaghetti-strap bralette peaks out from under a cropped jacket that matches the skirt. My shoes are these ridiculously awesome white thigh-high fabric boots with bows on the ankles; they look like classic heels had a baby with thigh-high boots. Petra describes this look as doe-eyed-sexy-chic, and I totally love it!

I hear a knock on the door and call "Come in!" as I fasten on a pair of killer rhinestone ear cuffs. They are the only jewelry I'm wearing so the quick costume changes go more smoothly. Martin pops his head in and gives me a wolf whistle.

"Damn, girl! You look all kinds of right in that outfit! Sean's going to be kicking himself that he couldn't make it tonight."

I groan, flopping onto a couch. I reach for Sean's letterman's jacket and hug it. "Don't remind me! I can't *believe* he's not coming. Or Lauren. It totally sucks!"

I sigh, pulling on his jacket as Petra slips out of the room. "Do I have time to call him?"

As if she's eavesdropping, Carolina's voice makes me jump. "Thirty minutes 'til curtain!" Martin runs over and lowers the volume on the loudspeaker mounted on the wall. "Guess we have thirty minutes." He smiles.

I FaceTime Sean. He picks up immediately. "I can't believe I'm not there! If this stupid final didn't count for half my grade, I'd blow it off. How are you?"

Seeing his face helps calm the butterflies in my stomach. "Do you know how *massive* this place is? It's freaking me out." I cover my face with my hand, careful not to smear Pauline's hard work.

Sean sighs. "I wish I were there. Tonight is going to be so epic, the first stop on your world tour! You've totally got this locked, D."

Sean stops talking, gives me a scrutinizing look, and smiles. I smile back. "What?" I look behind me in case Sean is smiling at someone behind me. "What's going on?"

"You! Do you know how effin' hot you are right now? God, now I'm really pissed I'm not there. Though, I gotta be honest, you might not stay that put-together for long if I was."

Martin loudly clears his throat and grabs the phone as I laugh. "Let me remind you that your girlfriend's guardian is sitting right here, m'kay? Keep it clean or keep it to yourself."

I grab my phone as Sean shouts an apology to Martin. I whip off Sean's jacket and prop the phone on the makeup table. I give Sean a full-length shot, twirling to show off my booty shorts. I pop a shoulder out of my crop jacket and give a sexy shimmy. Martin groans and throws a pillow at me when we hear a knock on the door.

"Come in and save me from these hormonal teens!" Martin shouts, covering his eyes with his hands.

The door opens, allowing distant music from the opening act on stage to wash over the room. Jenner enters, his neatly tailored black suit hugging his lean frame. He's dropped a lot of weight since the fall and he looks fit, as if he's thriving on all the stress from our impending tour.

"How are you doing, Dani? Ready for tonight?" He comes over and gives me a quick hug. "I hate to interrupt your call, but it's time to get psyched for the show and go huddle up with the dancers."

"Twenty minutes!" Carolina shouts.

The updates are starting to dial up my tension.

"OK. Be ready in a sec."

Jenner sits next to Martin, and they go over something on the computer. I turn away abruptly, seized by panic. Tears well up in my eyes. Suddenly I feel so *alone*. "I'm so nervous," I whisper into the screen. "This whole thing comes down to me...what if I don't have what it takes?"

Sean gives me a loving smile. "*You're Dani Truehart*. You've been working all your life for this. You're going to be amazing!"

I exhale loudly, nodding my head, trying to absorb Sean's encouragement. He continues. "My family and I will be watching Carlton's livestream. We're all so proud of you. Go out there and kick some ass."

I blow him a kiss and hang up, shakily stuffing my phone into his jacket pocket. I turn to Martin and Jenner, unable to speak.

Like clockwork, Carolina shouts. "Fifteen minutes to show time!"

My lip quivers, and I start to lose it.

Martin hops up and points his finger at me. "Get out of your head, Dani." He waves his hand at me. "Let's get you with the troupe. You need a dose of love STAT." He steers me into the hallway, encouraging me not to hyperventilate. The air feels thick with the pulsing music from stage, making me feel claustrophobic. My panic increases.

He ushers me into the dancers' dressing room, which is even larger than mine, filled with numerous wardrobe racks, makeup tables, and a jumble of mismatched furniture. No one notices our arrival because it's total chaos. Duffle bags, suitcases, and clothing are strewn everywhere, and the large space feels almost cramped with so many people rushing around. Some dancers are pulling on costumes, getting final touches on makeup and hair, others have already finished their prep and are warming up, eating, or horsing around. The energy is unmistakably vibrant and exciting, completely different from the quiet solitude of my lonely dressing room. I smile despite my nerves, and Martin gives my shoulder a squeeze.

Jenner claps his hands together and the dancers immediately snap to attention. They rush over and shower me with hugs. Everyone's speaking at once, and while I can't understand what anyone is saying, there seems to be a universal expression of love and excitement. Jenner gives us a few minutes before he hushes us.

"I want to thank each and every one of you—Dani, Martin, every single dancer, makeup artist, wardrobe person and crew member—for your hard work, your energy, and your heart. All of you have worked so hard to build this incredible show. Now that work is about to pay off. We've become a family over the past few months, and that love is going to show up on stage every night and make this tour the best thing the world has ever seen." Jenner motions with his hands. "Let's bring it in."

Jenner wraps an arm around me and the dancer next to him and everyone does the same, embracing whoever is next to them. I look around, tears of joy in my eyes. It's such an amazing moment. All my nerves have melted away. I feel *so empowered,* surrounded by all of these people who have worked so hard to make this show a success. I don't feel alone anymore, with the weight of the entire show resting solely upon my shoulders. *It's not just about me. I'm a part of this awesome team, and together there's nothing we can't accomplish.*

Overcome with emotion, Jenner clears his throat. "God bless every one of us tonight and always. May we always remember that with love and hard work, anything is possible."

We break into an epic round of hugs. Martin envelopes me in a bear hug. "Feeling better now?"

I grin. "I do. Thank you for always knowing what I need." I squeeze him hard.

"Dani!" Beau walks up expectantly.

Martin snorts softly. I give his arm a secret pinch.

"Hi, Martin," Beau says politely. "Can I steal Dani for a moment?"

"No problem, Beau." He musters a tight smile. "Break a leg tonight."

I make big eyes at Beau as Martin leaves. "He was almost nice to you this time."

"Or he was actually hoping I'll break my leg." He reaches into his pocket and pulls out a small box. "I got you a little something. I know you went to the mat for me with Martin and Jenner."

I pull off the pink ribbon and tear the thick black wrapping paper.

Inside the small box is a gold Sara Chloe diamond nameplate necklace. I can tell it's real gold because it is heavier than it looks, and the diamonds sparkle like only real ones can.

"Oh my God, Beau, I can't accept this! This is way too expensive."

He laughs as he takes the necklace and turns me around so he can fasten it. "It's custom-made, so you'd better take it. Besides, I have a friend who works at Nieman's, and I got an outrageously steep discount." He finishes with the necklace and turns me around to face him. "The only reason I can afford something like this is because of the job I have on your show."

I smile and touch the necklace. "Thank you, I love it." I hug him and catch Martin's unhappy reflection in the mirror watching us.

Carolina's voice booms over the loudspeaker. "Five minutes until show time. Places everyone!"

"Time to go to work!" Beau smiles as he runs to join the other dancers rushing out the door. "See you out there, Dani! Break a leg!"

Martin walks over, fighting the flood of people exiting the room. He picks up the nameplate with one finger, studies it, and lets it fall heavily.

"Nice necklace. It's real, too. Still think that kid's got no agenda?"

"All I'm thinking about right now is getting on stage without throwing up."

Martin snorts grudgingly. "Let's go, Princess. Time to shine!"

We enter the hall as Carlton scurries past us clutching a gray plastic bucket to his chest. I look at Martin, and he shrugs. "I suggested to Carlton he might want to be prepared. I certainly don't want you vomiting on *my* shoes."

I laugh in spite of my cramping stomach and take a few deep breaths as we head toward the stage. At the last minute, I have to pee and Martin radios for Petra, who rushes in to help me get dressed again. The backstage is lit with low blue lights, glow tape on the floor, and flashlights guiding me to my position just off stage next to the troupe. Martin hands me a mic as we wait for our cue. The audience whistles and cheers in the dark stadium, anticipating the start of the show. The air is electric. I clutch Beau's hand nervously as Carlton holds up his empty bucket to me with a questioning look. I shake my head.

A stage manager calls out "Go!" and in a surreal rush, we scurry to our positions in the dark. The pre-recorded opening audio package plays, and the glow from the video clips flashing on the wall of screens behind us light our way. I swallow bile as I take center stage, the dancers close behind me.

8

With a jolt of brightness that almost feels like a punch to the gut, lights flood the stage as the band plays the intro to "Nuthin' 2 Do!" The dancers and I move in formation, our steps second nature after hundreds of hours practicing our routines. We glide, thrust, and kick to the music. I clutch my mic and concentrate on singing, focusing only on the first few rows of seats, giving myself time to adjust to the vast audience sitting in the enormous arena. My nerves slowly disappear as I start to notice smiling faces and people singing along with me, waving signs and screaming. I steal a glance at the dancers, and I'm bolstered by their smiling faces and infectious confidence as they own each movement, reveling in the attention of thousands of people.

Above the music, I hear the audience shouting the chorus back to me, as fully engaged as I am in the song. Letting go of my last shred of doubt, I step to the front of the stage, the dancers following close behind me. I let my voice rip on a high note sequence, and the band pauses the music as I draw out the solo a few seconds longer than normal, my free hand fluttering in the air following the notes I sing. At last, I drop my hand and let the last note fade, surprised to hear a moment of pure silence in the arena before the crowd roars and the band slams back into the chorus. I punch the air and skip upstage, the dancers chasing behind me with leaps and flips. We all turn and freeze in the same instant that the music stops, and confetti cannons explode around the stadium. *What a kick-ass way to open the show!*

Breathing hard, I stare out into the arena as the deafening applause engulf me. *There's nothing that compares to the feeling of love and something like power I feel at this moment. There's no one that can sing these songs like me, dance like me, is me, and that's what they're all here for tonight. Everyone is here because of me, and I'm here because I am me. I've never felt this confident before.*

"Hello, Los Angeles!" I shout. A roar of cheers answers me. For weeks I'd been dreading this first little speech after my opening song. Both Jenner and Martin warned me how blasé L.A. audiences can be and that they often don't even get up and dance during a show. But after nailing that first song, the crowd is on fire. I'm psyched!

"Do you know that I was warned how subdued L.A. audiences are? Can you believe that?" The crowd roars again, stamping their feet. "Crazy, right?" I laugh as the audience cheers again. "I can't thank you enough for making me feel *so* welcome on the first stop on my world tour. I was a little nervous coming out here, there's so many of you and just one of me, but I can see now we're all friends here, and I have nothing to worry about."

The audience cheers again, and I continue. "In fact, since we're all friends, I think we should keep this party going and hang out at 'My Place!'"

The lights change as the audience roars again. The dancers and I jump into formation. We roll through that song and dozens more, the energy from the crowd, our seamless movements, and the pulsing beat from the live band powering the show. My costume changes go off without a hitch as I sing my way through my EP, my album, some of my favorite songs from other artists, and new material that Terrance created for my second album.

By the time I've sung two encores, I'm drenched with sweat! My entire body is as limp as a noodle, but my mind is racing like a rocket. The crowd cheers long after I leave the stage and head back to my dressing room, which is stuffed to capacity with dancers and crew members all popping champagne and celebrating.

Beau hands me a cold glass of champagne in passing. I'm so thirsty that I down it, not realizing what it is. I cough and sputter as the bubbles go up and out my nose, my eyes tearing. Martin pushes his way over to me and takes the glass out of my hand, replacing it with a bottle of water.

"You OK, darlin'?" he asks.

He hands the glass to Carlton whispering fiercely, "Tell Beau I want to see him *now*." Carlton scurries away.

Still coughing, I nod. "I'm just a little dizzy."

"No wonder. You downed a whole glass of champagne and shot half of it out your nose. Drink that, and I'll get you something to eat in a minute. You must be starving." He switches gears and grabs my shoulder. "Dani, you were *brilliant*! Those MEGA execs must be losing their minds right now. You are a goldmine, girl!"

Martin crushes me into a hug. I'm flying high, not from the champagne, but from his praise. Jenner joins us, sweaty and disheveled but beaming. He wraps his arms around both of us and gives us a squeeze. "Sheer perfection, Dani, that's what you are! The buzz online is phenomenal. We just sold out the next four stops on tour! Keep this up and we'll have to add more dates!"

Jenner smiles at me. "Did you have fun?"

I beam, looking from Jenner to Martin. "I can't believe I was so nervous. I feel like this is what I was born to do! It felt like the audience and I had this connection, you know? Like we were in it *together*." I shake my head, feeling like I'm failing trying to describe my emotions. "Does that make sense?"

Martin hugs me. "Totally! I had that same feeling whenever we had a great audience. It's the best feeling in the world."

I shiver. Martin claps his hands. "You need to shower and change before you get a chill from the A/C. Let's move this party to the dancer's room."

Carlton shoos the crowd into the next room while a sound tech removes my monitor pack and IEMs. As everyone files out, my energy starts to drop. Martin hands me a cup of hot tea. "Drink this to perk up. Food will be here by the time you're cleaned up."

Martin calls, "Jenner, a word?" Jenner huddles with Martin as they exit. I hear Martin fill him in on Beau's champagne fiasco. I shake my head as I take off my shoes, cringing at the trouble Beau just got himself into.

I shower quickly, slip into jeans, a worn REVOLUTION! tee that is my go-to comfy shirt, Sean's letterman jacket, and sneakers. By the time I'm finished, Martin knocks on the door and enters with Carlton, who sets down a huge tray filled with Pink's chili dogs, fries, and chocolate shakes.

"I couldn't let you eat alone after your first big performance!" He winks as we dive into our food. Hotdog in hand, I FaceTime Sean.

"That was sick, Dani! You were amazing!" Sean shouts into the phone.

"Sorry to call while I'm eating," I mumble. "I'm starving!"

Sean laughs. "No doubt! You were running all over that stage, singing your ass off. You've earned a hotdog! You too, Martin!"

"I must have lost twelve pounds in stress-sweat backstage. It's not easy to watch your baby bird soar for the first time."

There are loud voices out in the hall. Carlton comes in on Martin's walkie-talkie. "Martin, Dani's family is here. Can I let them in?"

Mom yells, "I'm her mother, you idiot! I don't need permission!" She pushes open the door, flattening Carlton against it as she barges in. Her demeanor instantly changes. "Baby, you were fantastic tonight! All our hard work has paid off. I'm so proud of you. Of *us*!" She yanks me up off the couch, chili flying everywhere from my hotdog, and smothers me in a hug.

Martin jumps up, dropping his dog. He peels Mom off me by enveloping her in a hug of his own. "She was amazing, wasn't she?"

The rest of my family files into the room, Grandma apologizing to Carlton. Mom barks at her. "Don't apologize for me, Marie. I did nothing wrong. It's not like this idiot doesn't know who we are, for Christ's sake!" She turns to my dad. "Give people a smidge of power and they run crazy with it."

My grandmother averts her eyes and says nothing. Geena scowls.

"*Mom!* You're being super rude. *Stop it!*" I complain.

Martin puts a hand on my arm. "Jodi, a few minutes ago Dani was changing. Carlton was making sure no one entered while she was undressed. He wasn't keeping you from seeing your daughter."

Mom adjusts her jean jacket huffily and stares at Carlton. "I've seen Dani undressed before, so it's not a big deal."

Martin patiently continues like he's talking to a child. "I know it's not a big deal to you, but Dani is growing up, so it might be a big deal to her. Now, tell me, how was your box?"

Martin deflects my mom's anger, distracting her by talking about her favorite subject—herself. While she rambles on about her luxury box, the rest of my family congratulates me. As we talk, I hear a faint "Dani!" shouted over and over. It takes me a minute to realize that I've completely forgotten about Sean! I grab the phone quickly, almost dropping it in the ketchup.

"I'm so sorry! My family just came in and my mom..."

Sean rolls his eyes. "I heard. Sounds like you've got your hands full. I'll let you go. What time do you leave tomorrow?"

I shout the question to Martin, and he holds up ten fingers. He can't answer because Mom has got him cornered.

"Ten a.m."

"My final isn't until eleven. I'll come over early to say goodbye."

Relief floods my body and tears come to my eyes. "I was worried I wouldn't be able to see you before I go."

"I'd never let that happen. See you tomorrow."

I smile and blow him a kiss. "Bye."

I visit with my family for a few minutes before going next door to enjoy the party. We all gather around a huge sheet cake with a picture of my album cover on it. Jenner gives another sentimental speech, and we dive into the cake. Soon, fatigue starts to catch up with me, so we gather our things to leave.

As we walk to the garage, I realize this is the last time I will see them for who knows how long. They're going to fly out and join me on tour at some point, but we haven't nailed down a date yet.

One by one, we hug goodbye. I cling to my grandmother and cry. *We just started talking again, and it is way too soon to be leaving her.* She shushes me and wipes away my tears. "It's not the end of the world, Dani. We can talk any time you want. I'll be waiting right here for you when you come home."

Dad has tears in his eyes as we say goodbye. He hugs me for so long that Mom elbows him to let me go. Mom gives me a quick fierce hug and a slap on the butt, her emotions firmly in check, as usual.

A final goodbye with Geena just about washes everyone away in a flood of tears. She promises to come out for several shows before she starts college in the fall. I can't believe that when I come back to L.A., Geena will be living a whole new life in Texas.

Martin wraps his arm around my shoulder as we watch my family drive away. Tears stream down my face. He hugs me and lets me cry.

Finally, Martin whispers, "I know it's not easy, sugar, but you won't be gone forever. I'll make sure you keep in touch, and we'll fly them out whenever you want." He wipes away my tears and puts a wild strand of hair behind my ear. "Leaving everyone behind is one of the really hard things about touring. But trust me, sweetie, soon you'll be so busy you won't notice this big hole in your chest so much. You'll get through this. I'm here to help you every step of the way."

I'm utterly drained—from the show, from crying, from my breaking heart as I realize how much I'm leaving behind. *Am I making a huge mistake? I feel so trapped—there's no way I can get out of this tour without costing Jenner and MEGA millions of dollars. How did I not see this coming?*

As we ride back to the compound in silence, I watch the city silently slip by. I feel like everyone I love is slipping out of my life at the same time. I trudge up the stairs to my room, too tired to change out of my clothes, and fall into a dreamless sleep.

9

I'm up at five a.m. I'm tired as hell, but I can't fall back to sleep. Knowing that I won't be in this room for months is making me anxious and sad. I take an extra-long shower, letting the hot water wash away the stiffness from my muscles. After I pull on leggings, a t-shirt, and Sean's jacket, I pack up pillow, and the last of my toiletries and leave them in a sad little stack by my bedroom door.

Time seems to be dragging and speeding up all at the same time. I can't wait to see Sean, but I know that when he arrives, we'll only have a short time together before he has to leave. I aimlessly wander the house, unable to find comfort. I end up in the kitchen picking at some egg whites as Magda hovers over me, trying to make me feel better.

At 6:45, the doorbell rings and I race to open it. Sean looks as disheveled as I feel, and I fall into his arms. We stand, silently embracing until we hear the front gates open. A black tour bus slowly navigates down the winding driveway.

I sigh. "Come on." Hand in hand, we walk down to the bluffs. The sun hasn't broken through the clouds yet, and the cold ocean breeze gives me goosebumps. We sit on a wooden bench, staring out at the choppy sea. Sean wraps his arm around me, and I burrow into him. I inhale his scent, wishing I could bottle it and take it with me for the long, lonely months ahead. The gray sky reflects my mood.

Sean kisses the top of my head. "Do you remember when we first found out you were moving into the compound? How we freaked out about not being able to see each other every day?" He shakes his head. "Man, if we only knew what was coming." His voice catches, and he clears his throat. "I wish you didn't have to go."

I burst into tears. My heart feels like it's being ripped apart. Sean squeezes me tighter and cries with me. After a while, it feels like we've cried all our tears. Silently, we cling to each other on the windy bench.

Sean looks at his watch. "I have to go soon." He stares at me, like he's memorizing my face. I'm doing the same, trying to etch his beautiful face in my mind. Staring at Sean's full lips, I'm overcome with a passionate urge not to waste any more of our precious time left together crying. I lean forward and kiss him deeply, our teeth banging together in my rush to show him how much I love him.

I climb onto Sean's lap; a low moan escapes his throat as I straddle him. We rock back and forth as we kiss, his hand frantically finding its way under my shirt. My lips move from his mouth to his ear and neck as I try to keep up with the building ache deep inside me. I feel Sean's hot breath on my neck as he lifts me up and lays me down on the grass, hovering above me.

I'm hungry for him, lost in a frenzy of love and sadness. But before we get too carried away, Martin's REVOLUTION! ringtone blares out. We freeze, our breath ragged and blood pulsing. My phone keeps ringing until I answer it, exasperated.

"Morning, Sunshine. Where are you?"

I try to calm my breathing and sound normal. "Taking a walk with Sean."

Sean sits up, taking deep breaths.

"The bus is here. We'll hit the road after Sean leaves. Be sure and come back to the house before he goes. Jenner and I want to say goodbye."

"We'll come up in a bit."

"Cool, bye."

I toss my phone onto the grass. I snuggle up to Sean, nuzzling his neck. "We still have time."

I lean in to kiss him, but he pulls away. "I never thought our first time would be a quickie in the grass right before you left on tour." He exhales. "As hard as it is to have you leave, it'll be impossible if we keep going."

The feeling of rejection is overwhelming, and I flash hot with embarrassment. My racing pulse makes it hard to think. Sean watches me intently, but I can't meet his gaze.

"You get where I'm coming from, right?" He reaches for my hand, holds it tightly. "This is such an important step for us."

I squeeze his hand. "I get it." I sigh and finally look at Sean. "Guess we should go up to the house."

He stands and pulls me up. As he studies my face, his eyes fall on my necklace. "Where'd you get this?" He runs a finger over it.

I gaze at the blowing grass. "From Beau. It's a thank you for hiring him."

Sean recoils. "He can't write a note?"

"It's nothing to worry about. We're just friends."

We walk back to the house in silence. Everyone is outside as Anatoli and the bus driver load our luggage. Martin waves us over.

"You two get a chance to say goodbye?"

Sean musters a smile. "Yeah, we took a walk. It wasn't nearly long enough, but I guess it was better than nothing." He looks at me, and I can tell he feels badly about what happened. He squeezes my hand, and I relax a little bit.

Jenner chimes in. "School will be over before you know it. We've got plenty of room on the bus, so just let us know when you can join us."

Sean smiles. "Thanks."

Martin waves at the bus. "Want to take a quick tour? It's pretty amazing what they can cram in such a small space." I notice for the first time that the bus has a big red heart on the side and "Here I Am" scrawled in white script on the side. It looks awesome.

Sean smiles ruefully. "I wish I could, but I'll be late if I don't leave now."

Martin gives Sean a warm hug. "No worries. Go kick some butt on that final and say hi to your family for me."

Sean takes my hand as we walk to his car. He leans against it and hugs me hard. "I love you more than anything. We'll definitely finish what we started when the time is right." He lets me go and his eyes fall on the necklace. I quickly tug my shirt over it.

I swallow all the embarrassment and rejection I'm feeling from our time on the bluff. My eyes tear. "I love you. I'm going to miss you so much."

We hug again, and Sean sighs as he lets me go. "We'll be fine."

I nod and give him one last kiss.

I wrap his jacket tightly around me and wave as he drives away. Long after his car is out of sight, I'm still looking up the driveway, hoping he'll come back. Eventually, I turn toward the house. I avoid everyone by checking my room to make sure that everything I want has been loaded onto the bus. A shout from out front lets me know that the bus is ready to depart.

Outside, I start to sob as a weepy Magda suffocates me in a tight hug. Anatoli helps disentangle me from his mother's embrace and she collects herself by reciting all the food she's stocked on the bus. She shoves a binder in my hand, which turns out to be a recipe book of all my favorite foods. Martin steps in to hug Magda while I escape. *I think I'm more devastated to leave Magda than I was to say goodbye to my own mother. How sad is that?*

Jenner calls us all over, and we take a few photos in front of the bus. More tears and hugs as we board the bus, and the driver shuts the door. We hang out the windows, waving to Anatoli and Magda as the driver slowly maneuvers the bus out of the compound.

10

I stare out the window long after everyone has pulled their heads in, the salty breeze blowing my hair around. As we pick up speed, the wind gets louder, intruding on my thoughts. I struggle to slide the window shut and slump on the leather couch I've been kneeling on. Never having been on a tour bus before, I look around, and my foul mood is slowly replaced with curiosity.

The front of the bus is set up as a lounge. Two cushy built-in gray leather couches face each other across a center aisle. The floor is a dark gray wood finish, and the walls and ceiling are shiny, white laminate. The ceiling is high with storage bins and inset lighting. There is a small closet behind the driver's seat, and a huge TV hangs on the outer closet wall. A built-in bookcase under the TV houses a stereo system, Blu-ray player, and several video game systems.

Martin sits down across from me. "Want to check out your new home? It's small but pretty incredible." He grabs an iPad from the bookcase. "Watch and be amazed." He taps the screen and a movie pops on the TV. "We have satellite TV and all the streaming platforms, so you should never get bored on the road. The bus is wired with surround-sound so you can hear the TV or music anywhere. And check this out."

With a swipe of a finger, the lights dim as music begins to play. Small star-like lights twinkle in the ceiling as the gray window shades begin to lower. Another swipe and the lights are replaced with multi-colored ones pulsing in time to the beat.

I smile. "Impressive! But where is everyone going to sleep?"

Martin chuckles. "We have ten bunks in this tin can, plus your bedroom. We've only got six people right now: you, me, Jenner, Carlton, Regina, and Ben, the driver. So, there are spare bunks for anyone that visits. Come on, check it out."

We walk into the snugly appointed kitchenette and eating area. Martin shows me how to open the safety cabinets that are stocked to the brim as Magda described.

We pass the bunks and stop before a closed door. "Voila!" Martin slides open an accordion door, and I squeeze past him into a tiny room. There's a small white furry rug underneath a full-sized bed with drawers built into its base. A closet is on the left side of the bed and a built-in bookshelf with drawers is on the right. A mirror hangs right behind the bed, reflecting the huge windows on either side of the room, making the compact space feel bigger. Built-in shelves and drawers line the walls underneath each window, and blackout window shades are ready to throw the room into complete darkness with the flick of a switch. A TV hangs to the left of the door. All of my photos and trinkets from my room at the compound fill this space. My favorite pillow, stuffed rabbit, and blanket lay invitingly on the bed, which is covered in a periwinkle blue comforter. A microscopic bathroom is to the right of the door. Martin hands me an iPad to control my room lights, temperature, etc.

"One too many burgers and I won't be able to fit in that bathroom." I laugh, sliding the bathroom's flimsy privacy panel shut.

Martin rolls his eyes. "Just be thankful you're not on the other two buses. All twelve bunks are filled, and within a matter of hours, those toilets will be, too! So, keep your complaints to yourself."

I nod, properly reprimanded. Martin smiles. "I know it's been rough, saying goodbye to everyone. Why don't you get settled, and we can watch a movie later?"

He slides the door closed as he leaves. I flop onto the bed, feeling crappy and sad. I glance at the iPad and I'm grateful to find all my music loaded onto it. I select a playlist of sad songs to match my mood. The music comes over the speakers, and I mope as I unpack my things.

With everything put away, I feel a bit more settled. I lower the shades and crawl under the comforter. The gentle rocking of the bus lulls me to sleep as I replay over and over those humiliating moments with Sean on the bluffs.

I I

I must have slept like a rock because I'm in a fog when Martin wakes me for lunch. Our concert is at the Chase Center tomorrow in San Francisco. Jenner has a meeting this afternoon with Tony and Carolina. They'll fly ahead of us to each venue to make sure things are set up before we arrive.

After lunch, Regina slides into the booth across from me. She looks like the ultimate nerd with her horn-rimmed glasses, short black hair, and gamer-chic clothes. I've been doing my best to avoid her for weeks because I'm so far behind on the homework. But it's hard to dodge someone when you're crammed together on a bus.

She smiles at me sweetly. "You all settled in?"

"Almost. I'm just trying to wrap my head around leaving home for so long. It's pretty overwhelming."

"Yes, it is. Soooo," she starts again. "I understand that today is probably not an ideal day to jump into studying. Probably not tomorrow, either, with your first gig on the road. But do you think you could manage some work on Thursday?" She whips out a folded sheet of paper and opens it.

Martin sees us talking and sits down next to me. "What's this?"

Regina smiles. "It's the schedule I emailed you last week. My plan for keeping Dani on track for graduation. This is just the first week. If she studies every day for two hours, she should be ready for graduation in two years. Mind you, it's two hours a day, six days a week, all year round, with a couple of weeks off at Christmas."

I open my mouth to protest, but Martin lays a hand on my arm. "Is that really necessary? Dani's already working several hours every night singing, and then she has promotional work before each concert. I don't want to wear her out."

Regina raises her hands in surrender. "I'm only doing what you hired me to do. You want Dani to graduate with her friends in two years. I've been giving her assignments since January. I haven't received anything from her since March." She looks pointedly at me.

Martin looks at me, annoyed. "Is this true?"

I shrug, embarrassed. "Well, yeah, but with so many rehearsals and appearances, and I had to see Sean and Lauren as much as I could before we left..." I look at Regina hopefully. "I'm sure I can't be that far behind?"

Regina sighs and pulls out another paper, which she hands to Martin. "This is the old schedule I emailed you back in January. Dani was originally slated to work two hours a day, five days a week, with longer breaks for holidays. This new schedule compensates for the months of time she's already lost. We can certainly ease up on schoolwork, but then Dani has to accept that she won't graduate with her friends."

I snap back, feeling defensive, "Well, then why didn't you get on me for all those missed assignments? Why am I just hearing about this now? Isn't it, like, your job to make sure I graduate?" I cringe slightly at the whiny edge in my voice. But I'm pissed I'm being treated like some delinquent when I've been working my butt off to prep for tour.

Regina's eyebrows rise in shock.

Martin shakes his head. "Don't get it twisted, girl. It's *your* job to make sure *you* graduate by doing the work Regina gives you. You don't get to blow off your work *and* cop an attitude because she's calling you on your crap."

Martin turns to Regina. "I apologize for not keeping an eye on this. Truth be told, it's my first time being a guardian, and I'm getting a crash course in taking care of a minor. It won't happen again. I'll make sure Dani gets back on track."

My outrage sufficiently checked; I realize I can't win this argument. "Sorry. I didn't mean to be a brat."

Regina exhales and forces smiles. "It's OK. You've got a lot on your plate. You're allowed to lose it every once in a while."

I'm a little relieved. *At least now everyone knows how far behind I am.*

Martin gathers up the papers. "Let me talk to Jenner. We need to carve out a little time every day for you two to work together."

I make a face, and Martin gives me the eye. "You're going to get your education one way or another, I promise you that. How fast depends on you."

I sigh. "Might as well do a little math now."

Regina gets up. "Give me a shout if you have any questions."

Martin smiles. "Great. We'll be in San Francisco in a couple of hours."

12

I spend an hour slogging through algebra. Regina has to help me a ton since I've forgotten most of the basics. If I'd kept up with doing a little bit every day, I wouldn't be starting from scratch again. I really hope I can stick with it, so I don't have to start all over a third time!

I notice we're pulling into San Francisco, so I abandon my work and open the window. Everyone joins me, and we watch the city roll by. The exhaust from the bus and surrounding cars on the freeway can't quite blot out the tangy salt breeze coming off the bay. June gloom clouds hang over the city, blocking out any chance of seeing the sunset.

A bunch of cars start honking, and I see people of all ages waving and shouting, taking photos of us. I look at Martin, puzzled. "How do they know it's me?"

Martin laughs and points down. I hang my head out and see my name scrawled across the bus. I laugh. "Duh!"

Carlton whips out his camera and starts recording it all to post later. I smile and wave at everyone, eliciting more honks and cheers. *What a great welcome to the city!* We pull up to the Chase Center, parking behind the other tour buses. Jenner grabs his bag. "I'm going to get up to speed with Tony and Carolina. Dani, why don't you get situated with your dressing room and grab a bite to eat. Be back here by eight, so we can ride over to our parking spot and get set up for the night."

I look questioningly at Jenner. "Parking spot?"

Martin waves Jenner on. "I'll remind her—you go ahead. I know you're chomping at the bit to get started." Jenner leaves, and Martin turns to me. "We went over this a few weeks ago. We're sleeping on the bus on the North American leg to save money."

I roll my eyes and Martin squints at me. "You're a little too diva-ish today for my liking. You've made it, yeah," he slides into a mock-impressed voice, "you're on tour." Martin points his index finger at me, "But you haven't *made it* just yet. Every penny counts right now. Once we see how long-term ticket and merch sales are doing, then we can start booking hotels. For now, we're sleeping on the bus. Just be grateful it's clean and warm. Got it?"

"Got it." I shove my hands in my jacket pockets. "Guess it's too late to argue about it now."

Martin ignores me and slings his messenger bag over his shoulder. "Let's go."

I grab some clothes, stuff them into a bag, and head out to the arena. It seats a few thousand less than the Staples Center, but it's no less impressive. A Chase Center rep greets us and escorts us inside.

The dancers are in a studio below, rehearsing our routines. The band is somewhere in the arena practicing. We can only travel with ten musicians, so we have to fill in the rest of the spots with local musicians.

The stage is a beehive of activity as crew members erect the screen wall, hang lights, and set up equipment. It's comforting to see the same stage setup in each new city. We have two stage sets that will leapfrog cities on tour so that they will always be ready by the time we arrive for each performance. Jenner, Carolina, and Tony are in a huddle with what I assume are the local stage managers going over their checklists. Our guide shows us to my dressing room and then to the deluxe work-out center where the Golden State Warriors train.

I call Sean while I'm in my dressing room, but he doesn't pick up. My phone buzzes with a text from my mom, but I hit ignore. Last thing I need on my first day on the road is a call from her.

After a quick workout and shower, we're ready for dinner. Jenner needs to stay at the arena, but Carlton and Regina join us. We stumble upon a cute dumpling restaurant nearby. We feast on tiny plates of garlicky green beans, crisp gyozas, and delicious steamed bao. We have a blast getting to know each other. Turns out Carlton's dad was bass player for one of the bands Jenner used to manage in the '70s. His tales of tagging along with his father on his summer tours cast him in a whole new light. He's still totally creepy, but now he's slightly cooler, if it's possible to be both creepy and cool at the same time.

Martin's phone buzzes at the end of dinner. "It's your mom." He stares at his screen, puzzled. "She wants us to send her a box of merch to sell it on her website?" He quickly taps at his phone. "Sweet Baby Jesus!"

I drop my chopsticks. "What?"

He shows me the screen and my stomach drops. Mom has started a website called "The Real Dani Truehart," which is more of a tribute to her than to me. Besides some basic publicity shots of me and a few childhood photos, it features photos of Mom as a baby, a high school cheerleader, and her pregnant with what I assume is me. There are also blog entries about everything from her childhood, parenting tips, and how she made me a star.

I gasp. "It says next week she's going to reveal the real truth about Dani Truehart. What the hell does that mean?"

Martin snatches the phone back. "Uh-uh." He growls, "This stops now." He furiously taps at his phone. "Let's go. I've got to meet with Jenner, STAT."

Back at the stadium, Martin stalks off to find Jenner. I grab a seat in the stadium and call Sean. My heart leaps when he picks up.

"Hey! How's your first day on the road?"

I muster a smile and try to get comfy on the hard stadium seat. "It was good until it wasn't, thanks to my mom. I swear her sole purpose is to mess with my life! Have you seen her website yet?" My words rush out as I fill Sean in on my mother's latest scheme. "I'll tell you one thing...I gotta give her credit for trying. Most people would think my iron-clad contract would prevent them from cashing in on a career that isn't their own. But not Jodi Truehart! She is truly in a class by herself."

"Holy crap, Dani. What's Jenner going to do?"

I nibble at my thumbnail, worried. "I don't know." My heart feels like it's going to pound out of my chest, and I take a few deep breaths. I slowly shake my head.

"This is not how I saw our first call from the road going. I'm sorry to make it all about my stupid mom once again." I stare at Sean and sigh. "I can't believe I saw you this morning and now I'm in San Francisco." A knot of anxiety develops in my stomach as I remember Sean pushing me away on the bluffs. "It makes me sad thinking that every day I'll be just a little bit further away from you."

Sean nods quietly.

I change the subject. "How was your final?"

Sean shrugs. "As good as can be expected when the love of my life leaves town. All I could think about was saying goodbye to you and what a disaster it was. I'm sorry it went down the way it did."

I exhale relieved, the knot in my stomach loosens. "Me, too. I was worried I came off as some sex-crazed nut or something. It's never felt that intense, and I guess I got carried away."

He smiles at me. It makes me wish I wasn't hundreds of miles away so he could wrap his arms around me. "Next time we'll be on the same page for sure."

I smile and nod. A text from Martin comes through telling me to meet him on stage. "I have to go. Call you tomorrow?"

"Can't wait."

I blow Sean a kiss and hang up.

I go find Martin.

"All set?" He smiles, shutting his laptop and stowing it into his bag.

I stare at him expectantly. "Well? What happened with my mom?"

Martin chuckles as he hops off the stage, settling his bag on his shoulder. "All taken care of. By the time we got back here, Jenner's lawyer had drafted a 'cease and desist.' She's threatening a lawsuit, but she doesn't have a case. The website should be taken down shortly since it uses your name, which Jenner holds the trademark to."

The news jolts me. "He holds the trademark to *my* name? MY name, like who I am?"

Martin sighs as we walk. "I didn't realize it myself until this came up. But since your name is a marketable asset, Jenner trademarked it and many different versions of it to prevent leeches and scammers from profiting off of you without your permission. It's pretty typical in the industry."

I stop short. "But he holds the trademark and didn't tell me. Doesn't that put him in the leech category?"

"Well, technically no, since he's splitting the profits with us." He gives me a hug. "Come on. You need to get some rest."

I shake my head. "I'm so pissed I don't think I'll sleep for weeks! I don't know if I'm angrier at Mom for being greedy or at Jenner for being shady and licensing my name without telling me. I feel like I'm a product everyone wants to sell to the highest bidder."

"It's not as bad as all that. Your mom's only being herself, and, truth be told, I expected something like this from her even if you didn't. And if Jenner hadn't bought the rights to your name, someone else would have, and *they'd* be earning big bucks off of you instead of all of us. I know it seems weird, but it is all perfectly normal."

He puts his arm around me as we walk. "Come on, my little trademark. Time for bed."

In spite of myself, I laugh as we exit the arena.

13

Spending the night on the bus isn't as bad as I thought it would be. The bed is comfy, and once the shades are down, my room is so dark I can't tell where I am anyway. I'm wrecked after saying goodbye to Sean, leaving home, and yesterday's concert. I don't budge until Martin taps on my door at six a.m.

I dress and head out for some publicity appearances. I argue with Petra about wearing Sean letterman's jacket, but Martin steps in and I finally get my way. *I don't want the first pics he sees of me on tour showing me not wearing his jacket!* A quick interview on a local radio show, a stop at an animal shelter, and a ride on a cable car posing in luxury sunglasses I've been sent. It's crazy how much Jenner crammed into a few hours, but Carlton snags tons of great stuff for my IG, and it's a fun way to see a new city. Everywhere we go, there are kids with signs cheering for me. I get stopped a lot to sign autographs, which is so cool! I can't believe Terrance thinks it's annoying, people gushing over you and wanting to meet you? I'll always make time for my fans!

My phone blows up all day with texts and phone calls from Mom, so I block her number to get some peace. I know it's an extreme move, but I can't deal with her crap right before a show.

After a quick lunch, we drive to the arena. We run through a few routines with the dancers, have sound check, and I take a nap. After a light meal, I warm up and go into hair and makeup. This time my look is a champagne colored, beaded and fringed, haltered hot-pants jumpsuit.

It's a cross between a flapper dress and a Las Vegas showgirl costume without the feathers. It's paired with strappy gold stilettos that have taken me months to learn how to dance in. Now I can run and hop in these shoes like a gazelle. My hair is curled into cascading ringlets and twisted into a high half-pony. Rhinestone lashes, cat-eye liner, white eyeshadow, and red lips finish my look.

I'm still nervous, but, having done a concert the day before, I now know what to expect. Carolina's countdown over the loudspeaker doesn't send me into a panic like it did yesterday. After a quick call to Sean, I head into the dancers' room to hang out.

Beau walks past me typing on his phone and my cell pings with a text.

B: *Martin's pissed b/c of the champagne. Not allowed 2 talk 2 U. Lame!*

I roll my eyes and text back.

D: *Totally! He'll get over it, tho*

I wink at Beau.

As if his Spidey-senses are going off, Martin enters and makes a bee-line for me. I see him eyeing Beau, and we quickly delete our texts.

"Full house tonight. Remember, after the show, we need to limit your talking. You've got an intense period of singing ahead of you. You've got to preserve your biggest asset."

We have a pre-show huddle in the dancers' room to get us amped before the show.

"Five minutes!"

There's a mad stampede to the door as everyone rushes into the hall. Carlton scurries before us, gray bucket in hand. I only have seconds to wait in the wings before the video package starts and the dancers and I run out on stage and get into position.

***

It's another mind-blowing performance if I do say so myself. The eighteen-thousand- seat venue goes wild from the moment the lights go up until long after we've played our second encore.

After the show, I stop by the dancers' room where the music is bumping. It's full-blown party mode with coolers of drinks and pizza boxes everywhere. Martin follows me, eyeing the room like a protective bulldog.

"What are you doing in here? You're supposed to be showering."

I smile and shrug. "I smelled pizza."

Bronwyn, a gorgeous Japanese girl with cascading black locks, half of which are shaved off on one side, and clad in a bra and sweatpants burps like a bullfrog as she walks by, chucking her beer bottle into the trash can next to us. "Oops, sorry Dani!"

Martin gives her the stink-eye. "Mm-hmm. This crew is a bit advanced for you, darlin'. I don't want you to pick up any bad habits." Martin speaks loudly, catching Bronwyn's eye. "I've known Bronwyn since she was twelve. I know her mama isn't going to truck with her walking around like that."

He shakes his head, puts his hands on my shoulders, and steers me out of the room, calling, "See you in Sacramento!"

He leaves me to shower and change into my sweats while he takes my bags to the bus.

Jenner has a huge sushi spread laid out on the kitchen counter. We all dive in and settle down to watch a movie as the bus rolls out of San Francisco. Exhaustion overtakes me, and I fall asleep as soon as I finish eating. I barely remember Martin nudging me awake or walking to my room.

14

The next morning, Martin wakes me up with a cup of tea. "Morning, darlin'! Breakfast will be ready in a minute."

I gratefully reach for the mug and sniff the air. "Is that bacon?"

Martin smiles. "Indeed! Chef Carlton is making breakfast. Apparently, he used to cook for his dad on tour, so a compact kitchen is no challenge for him. I'm sure whatever he comes up with will be much better than my famous peanut butter and banana toast."

I grab the iPad and roll up the blinds. We're parked in a litter-strewn lot, with trucks rumbling on an overpass above us. "Did we just spend the night camping under the freeway?"

Martin nods, grimacing. "Unfortunately, yes. It's actually a municipal parking lot that Golden 1 Center provided free of charge. Squatters can't be choosers."

I stare out the window as a homeless man passes by, pushing his overstuffed cart. *This is so not the "life of a rock star" that I'd envisioned.*

"I guess." I roll down the shades again, shutting out the depressing view. "Meet you in the kitchen."

***

Sacramento goes much the same as San Francisco, except with more homework and less talking, thanks to Martin's crusade to save my vocal cords. Publicity appearances at a food drive, the train museum, and the state capital building, followed by lunch and a round of bowling at the nearby Rock'n'Bowl restaurant fill the day. Rushed phone calls with Dad, Sean, and Lauren—who still suspects Tom is cheating—are squeezed in between naps, warmups, and pre-show prep. I still have Mom on block because I can't deal with her craziness right now. Dad told me how sorry she is for the misunderstanding and that she promises never to do something like that again. But I'm so pissed I don't even want to hear it. After another spectacular show, we're back on the bus and heading north.

Seattle, Vancouver, and Boise. Salt Lake City, Vegas, and Phoenix. The country rolls by as we drive, camping in KOA sites, arena parking lots, and the occasional Walmart. When the schedule permits, Jenner lets us stop to check out a few sights along the way, like the Hoover Dam, Capilano Suspension Bridge, and Donner Pass. Every scenic spot or hokey tourist trap is a nice break from the monotony of being cramped together on the bus.

Every day, Jenner pulls the bus over and Carlton takes a video of my workout with Martin. Over the past few months, Martin and Brett have developed a new exercise regime to get Martin into shape. It combines exercise bands, boxing, and a portable Pilates machine. Martin posts the videos to the REVOLUTIONIZE! YOUR BODY (RYB) channel on YouTube. Since we've been on tour, they've gotten over five hundred thousand hits. They plan on shooting proper videos and releasing the program once we get back from tour.

The best part is that Jenner gave Martin and his bandmates the rights to the REVOLUTION! name. Martin and Brett will get the bulk of the money for developing the program, and I'll get a small portion as the spokesperson. Martin's former band members will also get a cut of the proceeds. Kind of a payback for all the money Jenner stole from them. It feels good to be able to give something back to Martin for all he's done for me.

My fans have officially dubbed me "The Queen of Harts." A bunch of girls in Wichita came to the show dressed up in robes and crowns. They looked so cute in their royal outfits that I stopped for some photos after the concert. One of the girls gave me her tiara and the whole thing went viral when Carlton posted it on the Gram #TheQueenofHartsand-herTrueHartFans.

It's picked up steam, and now audiences chant "All Hail the Queen" before I walk on stage. If I make an appearance without my tiara, my fans freak out. Jenner has started selling tiaras at the concerts, and he can't keep them in stock! He's also having Serena choreograph royal-themed dance routines for the European leg of the tour.

Working and traveling in such tight quarters on the bus has given us a strong family bond, but after weeks on the road, we start to bicker like family, too. Jenner has this gross habit of flossing his teeth while he walks through the bus, and Carlton has a creepy fungus on his toes. Regina snores like a pug with a cold, and Martin spends so much time on the phone talking loudly to Brett that I've started putting on noise-canceling headphones anytime I see him pick up his cell. It's the same thing every day: wake up, eat together, homework, followed by publicity appearances and then sound check, maybe a nap, vocal warmups, dinner, show, shower, back on the bus, watch TV, blah, blah, blah. I'm about to lose my mind!

A few times a week after a show, I board the dancers' bus with either Martin, Regina, or Carlton as my chaperone so I can hang out for a few hours. At first, Martin refused to let me go, but I pitched such a fit about being bored hanging out with so many adults that Jenner finally allowed it. There's such a relaxed vibe on their bus—it's decorated with tons of pictures, a disco ball, and they have every kind of junk food imaginable. It's a total mess and smells kind of funky, but music is always bumping, and they watch way better shows than Jenner and Martin. The dancers' bus is like a mini vacation for all of us. Even Martin agrees that the change is doing us all some good.

***

We've been on the road for over six weeks, and Sean is finally flying out tomorrow with Brett! They're going to travel with us for a week, and I'm so excited I can't sit still.

I've been cleaning my room like a madwoman, letting fresh air pour in through the open windows, wiping away dust and putting away piles of clean clothes. Martin smiles at me from the hall. "Look at you, being all domestic goddess-like! Want to clean my bunk next? It could use a woman's touch."

"No, thanks. I've got my work cut out for me here."

"You got your homework done already?"

"Yes, and I did an extra hour, too. Think I can get a suspended sentence on homework while Sean is here?" I clasp my hands together, pleading.

Martin chuckles. "We can arrange that. But that means adding more time when he leaves."

I jump up and down. "I don't care if I have to do homework onstage, just as long as I can spend more time with Sean." I blow Martin a kiss. "Thanks!"

Martin lingers in the doorway, arms folded, and I get the feeling he has something else to say.

"Is there anything else?"

He shrugs nonchalantly. "Just confirming that you and Sean know he's sleeping in the bunk above Jenner." My face flashes hot, embarrassed, as I remember the uncomfortable 'birds and bees' lecture Martin gave me after the homecoming dance last fall.

Martin continues, "It should go without saying since you're only sixteen, but I wanted to make that clear before he arrives. And this door stays open at all times when you two are in here. Got that? I'll have a chat with him when he gets here."

I start to say something, but he interrupts me. "Don't worry, I won't embarrass you. But it's not up for negotiation."

I exhale and nod. *Guess that takes away the dilemma of sex for now. No danger of any time alone together with the warden making his rounds every few minutes.*

Martin looks relieved. "Good. Enough said about that then." He flops down on the bed. "So, are you excited to see Sean or what?"

I grin. "He *cannot* get here fast enough. This is the longest we've ever gone without seeing each other. I plan on spending every spare second together."

Martin chuckles and starts to fold a t-shirt. "It's important to stay in touch with people back home. Our routine is so intense, it's easy to get swept up in life on the road and lose yourself."

He finishes folding and looks at me. "How are you feeling about the tour? We've had great audiences every night, which makes it easier. And most of your songs have been in the top forty since your album dropped. But how are you coping with the fans? Not having any real alone time, the long hours...you OK?"

"Fine, I guess. I mean, at first, I loved all the fans at the shows asking for autographs and shouting for me. The whole Queen of Harts thing is amazing! But I see a little of Terrance's point, how fans can kinda bug, you know? I mean, there are a *lot* of them, and only one of me. Sometimes when I'm out, I just want to be *normal* and not mobbed by..."

A gross sensation in my stomach stops me from finishing my sentence and I groan. "I sound so ungrateful saying that...but it's how I feel sometimes. Adding those new dance routines for the European tour adds a lot to my daily schedule. And constantly worrying about what publicity stunt Mom will pull next is super stressful."

Martin nods. "I get it. Everything you're feeling is valid. I'm glad you told me. Jenner and I are in contact with your mother about her interviews. I've told her you refuse to talk to her while she's actively chasing publicity, so I'm hoping eventually she'll start missing you enough."

I pull a stack of tabloids off my bookshelf, reading the headlines aloud: "Jodi Truehart: A Mother's Sacrifice," "Raising a Star," "Dani Truehart: Daughter or Diva?" I fling down the magazines and give Martin a deadpan stare. "Give up the limelight? My mom doesn't love *anyone* that much. My not talking to her gives her the drama she needs to keep the press interested. She's addicted to fame, and she's gonna grab it wherever she can. It makes me sick."

Martin gathers the magazines. "You shouldn't be looking at this trash, darlin'. It'll only upset you." He pauses, considering. "How about I set up a call with Serena? She's toured the world and knows all about this stuff. She might be able to help you cope. Have you given any thought to developing your stage persona like she suggested last fall?

Audiences have been great so far, but eventually there's going to be one audience that's a nightmare. You need to start protecting yourself."

Fear, pressure, and anxiety swirl in my head as I imagine an entire stadium booing me. I start to feel dizzy. The panic must show on my face because Martin hurries to continue. "I'm not trying to scare you. I just want to prepare you. Even Dani Truehart is going to have an off night, and I don't want it to send you into a tailspin."

I take a deep breath, trying to slow the inner whirl of emotions. "It's been so amazing since my EP dropped. And my full-length album went platinum in like a second! Everyone except my mother has been so supportive and positive. I can't even imagine things changing, but everyone keeps saying they will at some point. The thought of the TrueHarts turning on me *totally* freaks me out."

Martin leans over and gives me a comforting hug. "Of course it does, darlin'. And we'll all be here to get you through it. That's why it's crucial to keep a part of yourself private. So, it isn't *your* heart and soul on that stage, absorbing all the hype and the shade. This is just your day job, like being an accountant, only with stunning costumes and much better perks!" His gaze turns serious. "But like any day job, you need to be able to walk away from it when the workday ends."

I sigh. "Maybe I should talk to Serena."

Martin stands up, taking the pile of tabloids with him. "I'll set it up." He looks around the disheveled room. "Thank God you sing like an angel, because your homemaking skills leave a lot to be desired."

He chuckles and leaves the room.

15

It's past four, and Martin and I are pacing the floor of my dressing room at the United Center in Chicago. Sean and Brett landed about thirty minutes ago while I was stuck here doing sound check. Martin sent Carlton to meet them at O'Hare.

I flop on the couch, whining. "I hope Sean gets here before I have to get into makeup." I cover my face with a pillow and groan while Pauline bustles around the makeup table. The dressing room door flings open.

"Sean!" I holler as I vault over the sofa into his arms. Everyone else in the room disappears. All that exists are Sean's lips on mine.

I don't know how long we're locked at the lips before I hear Pauline call out, "I'll let you all catch up. Back in a few." She chuckles as she leaves, turning Petra away at the door. "Not now, P." The door clicks closed behind them.

I come up for air and see Martin and Brett lost in an embrace of their own. A wave of pure joy envelopes me as I stare into Sean's deep green eyes and hug him close.

Our reunion is cut short by a knock at the door. Jenner's smiling face pops into the room.

"Welcome, gentlemen! Carlton put your bags on the bus, and we've got some food coming in for you shortly. Take a few more minutes to reconnect, but then you'll have to let Dani and Martin prep for the show. Dani should already be in hair and makeup by now."

I glance at the clock. "Oh crap, you're right."

Martin disentangles himself from Brett. "Sorry, Jenner, I got a little sidetracked. We'll get Dani into the chair in five and we'll be ready on time."

I wrap my arms tightly around Sean's waist. "Pauline can work around Sean, right?" I grin at Jenner.

Jenner gives me a tight smile. "Cute, Dani. But we've got some special guests, and I need you on point tonight." Jenner crosses his fingers. "So, get focused, OK? We have a couple of free days scheduled while Sean's here. Plenty of time to canoodle later. Tonight's important."

I straighten up as Jenner talks, his tone getting my back up. *Sold out concerts since we left L.A., and this is the first chance in two months I've had to see my boyfriend. Who does he think he is coming in here, talking to me like that...my boss?* I peel myself off of Sean, my temper flaring in pure imitation of my temperamental Texan mother.

"Wow, OK. I'll be focused. It would have been *nice* if you hadn't waited until the last minute to tell me you had special guests coming tonight, especially with Sean coming into town. But you don't have to remind *me* to be *professional*. I'm the one who's selling out stadiums across the country, not *you*." I cross my arms and scowl at Jenner.

I feel Sean's hand on my waist, almost as if he's restraining me.

Martin jumps in between Jenner and me. "Message received, Jenner. Dani will be ready on time and will amaze as usual. I think we're just hyped to have our boys here. We're all a bit thrown off." He pauses, turning to give me a pointed look, which Jenner can't see. "Right, Dani?"

With Sean's pleading grip on my waist and Martin's look, I nod and exhale. I don't want to ruin Sean's first few hours here by getting into it with Jenner. "Of course, Martin." I ignore the angry retorts buzzing in my brain, look at Jenner, and reluctantly say, "Sorry."

Jenner holds my gaze for a long moment before nodding. "Not a problem. Like I said, once you know more, I'm sure you'll understand."

He nods to the room as he leaves. Oblivious, Pauline hurries in and rushes me into the chair. She starts working on my hair, diving into her usual backstage gossip. Pressure and anger slowly build in my chest, making it hard to breathe, and Pauline's mindless chatter isn't helping. I'm struggling not to lose it.

Martin makes a beeline for me, the aggravated look on his face only adding to my stress. "What the hell was that? Jenner's been busting his butt to make this tour a success. You wouldn't be selling out a bathroom if he wasn't doing all the legwork he does. You can't cut the guy a little slack for a last-minute request?"

Pressed for time, Pauline yanks on my hair as she runs a braid down the top of my head. Irritated, I reflexively slap her hand and she gasps. The look on Martin's face brings me to my senses. I'm instantly mortified.

"Oh my God, Pauline, I am so sorry. I didn't mean to do that. I..."

I flounder for words, but Pauline quickly nods and murmurs "No problem" as she steps away to regain her composure.

Where is all this anger coming from? My stomach swirls with regret and shame. I feel out of control; like a stranger to myself. I'm intensely aware that Sean is watching my meltdown. Tears spring to my eyes. Martin gives me a serious look.

"What's going on, Dani? The last ten minutes are not who you are."

I take a deep breath but seeing Sean whispering with Brett only brings more tears. "I don't know. I was so excited to see Sean and then Jenner came in and was so rude, hassling me to get ready. He made me so mad, talking to me like that." I close my eyes and shake my head. "Oh God, I can't believe I slapped Pauline's hand! I'm so sorry." I look pleadingly at Martin, desperate for him to believe me. "I didn't mean to! I was annoyed by you talking and I was still mad at Jenner. I feel like every second of the day I have to appear here, interview there, and people are always pushing me and poking at me. I just wanted a few minutes alone with my boyfriend." I squeeze my eyes closed, shaking my head. "I just snapped."

I dissolve into tears. I feel Pauline's hand on my shoulder, giving me a comforting squeeze, and then I hear her clearing the room so I can cry in peace. Once my tears subside, the pressure in my chest eases. My anger evaporates, as does the overinflated sense of self that prompted my lashing out at Jenner. All that's left is guilt and embarrassment at what can only be described as an epic tantrum. I've never felt less like a star.

Martin hands me a tissue from the box on the makeup table. "Maybe this is a sign we have too much on your schedule." I clumsily blow my nose. "Clearly you're feeling a ton of pressure. So, we'll scale things back. I'm going to get that call scheduled with Serena, too. We've been playing phone tag, but this is clearly a priority."

Martin gently lifts my chin and stares at me solemnly. "You need to know that treating people like that is unacceptable. You are no better than *anyone* else on this tour, and you need to check your ego immediately. You got me?"

"I'm sorry. That's not who I want to be."

Martin squeezes my hand. "Good. Because if you aren't careful, that's who you'll become." He lets go of my hand. "One tantrum does not a diva make." He winks. "There's still hope for you yet."

When Pauline returns, I apologize again. She graciously accepts, and I close my eyes and concentrate on pulling myself together while she works her magic.

A hurried meal and a few cups of green tea have lifted my energy—if not my spirits—as show time approaches. With limited time to get ready, the best we can do is a jewel-encrusted black catsuit with an oversized white satin jacket and thigh-high red boots. My hair is in a high pony topped with my requisite tiara, and my makeup is heavy on the red lip and eye liner, with oversized Gucci sunglasses hiding my puffy eyes. *I feel more like a child playing dress up than a sexy pop star tonight. I hope I can get it together before the show starts.*

We huddle in the dancers' room for our pre-show pep talk. Jenner pulls me aside, reassuring me that we're good. I remember that Sean has never seen me perform in a large arena like this. As we race up the dark passages to the stage, my stomach knots into fresh twists, worrying if I can pull it together and deliver a performance amazing enough that he can forget my stupid outburst.

As we scramble into formation in the dark while the opening video package rolls, Beau whispers, "Did you hear that Kayla Spencer and Trey Connors are here tonight? Apparently, she's *obsessed* with you!" Brett squeals and squeezes my hand.

I almost drop my mic. *I wonder if that's what Jenner was talking about!* Kayla and Trey are two of Hollywood's hottest young actors, starring on the most popular series on Netflix. Even though they play brother and sister, they've been dating since the first day of shooting. Lauren and I are *obsessed* with their show and always watch it together, even now while I'm on the road. *She is going to pee her pants when she finds out that Kayla and Trey are here to see me!*

16

Knowing Sean, Kayla, and Trey are all in the audience only intensifies my desire to put on the best show possible. I shake off my shame, and when the lights come up, I'm in full-blown performance mode. I nail every high note, my exuberance coming through in every dance step. Whenever I address the audience, I focus on Sean, sitting in the front row with Brett. The intimate connection we share makes this show feel different from the previous ones. During "Without You," I sit on the edge of the stage and sing straight to Sean. The words really hit home about how much I miss him while I'm on the road. Tears pour down my face as I sing. The audience eats it up.

I'm so fired up that I even drag Martin on stage for my third encore and we belt out "Try and Stop Me." This has Brett jumping up and down, screaming like a crazed fan. The entire arena is on its feet. The applause echoes long after the lights are up, and we've left the stage. I'm riding high on the unbelievable wave of love that's vibrating throughout the building. My insecurity and shame from before are completely forgotten.

It's chaos backstage as fans jockey for a glimpse of me, screaming for autographs, snapping pics. As I hurry by, I grin and wave. Carlton trails behind me pulling pre-signed t-shirts, tiaras, and programs from his messenger bag, distracting the fans so I can escape.

I fall into my dressing room, the noise from the hall dulled by the closed door, grateful for a moment of quiet. But my relief quickly turns to annoyance when I notice Petra isn't waiting for me. *She knows I can't get out of this damn bodysuit without her!* A quick knock on the door, and I hurl it open, assuming it's Petra.

"Finally! Where were you?"

I stop dead, realizing I'm snarling straight into Kayla Spencer's gorgeous face! Jenner's eyes narrow. I sheepishly mouth, "sorry."

"Dani! I'm sure you recognize Kayla Spencer and Trey Connors. Kayla is a very big fan of yours."

Suddenly I'm not a famous pop star anymore, just another geeked-out fangirl who can't speak. "Oh my God, I cannot believe I'm meeting you guys! Come in! Come in!"

I hear myself babbling, so I stop talking and step out of the way, waving my arm to welcome them in. Like a pair of Norse gods, Kayla and Trey smile benevolently at me as Trey guides her inside, his arm draped over her shoulder.

Kayla pushes aside a lock of curling blonde hair, settling her piercing blue eyes on me. "I can't believe *you're so* excited to meet *me*! *This is insane!* I'm *obsessed* with you."

Kayla scans the room as she gushes, taking in my costumes, flowers, and tiaras. "You were on fire tonight! This seriously was one of the best shows I've ever seen." She shakes off Trey's arm and places a conspiratorial hand on my hand. "I threw a temper tantrum on set tonight. I wouldn't do another scene because I didn't want to miss your show." Kayla giggles and places a perfectly manicured hand over her mouth. "I'm going to have hell to pay later with my agent, but it was totally worth it." She whips out her phone and snaps a selfie of us before I'm even ready.

Jenner laughs. "Must be in the air tonight. Right, Dani?" A flash of anger and embarrassment seizes me, but Kayla laughs, oblivious to Jenner's jab. I have just enough time to smile as she snaps another pic of us.

Trey yawns and dramatically stretches out on the couch as he chimes in. "Yeah, it doesn't bother Kayla that we'll have to work overtime for the next two days because she just *had* to see the show tonight. If she had told the producers about your concert, they could have shot around her absence." Trey sighs loudly, sarcasm dripping off his words. "Yup, that's my girl, always thinking of other people."

Kayla rolls her eyes. "You'd think I'm completely self-obsessed by the way he talks about me." She turns to Trey. "I bet everyone was grateful that we left early tonight. They all got to go home early to see their families." She looks at me for support. "Wouldn't you like to leave early one night and get to spend time with your family?"

If she only knew...

I shrug, not sure what to say.

Trey bitterly chimes in. "Yeah, try explaining *that* to the prop department who spent all day filling up a bounce house with bubbles for the birthday party scene. They had to rent equipment, have extra safety officers on hand, not to mention all the child actors they hired. Do you know how many thousands of dollars you cost production because you just had to see Dani Truehart tonight? Christ, Kayla. You're so self-absorbed sometimes you make me sick."

I stand there frozen, embarrassed by the angry comments Trey is hurling at Kayla. But they seem to roll off her back as she browses my costume rack nonplussed, occasionally pulling off an outfit and holding it up to her Amazonian frame.

Next, she wanders over and helps herself to a tiara from my makeup table, settling it on her head. Eventually, she meanders over to Trey, snuggling next to him on the couch. I glance up at Jenner, who seems as puzzled by the unfolding drama as I am. They seem to have forgotten we're in the room.

"You're right, baby. I was so excited to see Dani, I completely lost my head and forgot about everyone else." She delicately fingers his blond hair, brushing it away from his furrowed brow.

"You know how carried away I get." In a small baby voice that I'm appalled to witness, she continues, "Would you fowgive me, Twey? I'm sowwy?" She bats her eyes seductively at him and I have a hard time muffling my laughter, certain he couldn't possibly be falling for this pathetic display.

But in a flash, his anger melts. He looks at Kayla and sighs. "You *gotta* start thinking of other people. It really makes you look bad when you disrespect everyone's hard work because you've gotta see a concert or go shopping or get your Botox done. And when you look bad, I look bad."

"Trey!" Kayla gasps, quickly looking around the room. "You know I don't get that stuff done. I'm too young to need Botox."

Kayla catches my eye and gives me a wink. "Us girls gotta keep the pretense up, right? Wouldn't do for America to know Kayla Spencer gets Botox at twenty-one. I've got a wholesome image to protect."

Laughing, she whips out a Juul and starts to puff away. "Another one of my hidden vices." She chuckles. "You don't mind, do you?"

Martin bursts through the door followed by Sean and Brett. His eyes bulge when he sees a thick cloud of vapor hovering in my dressing room, but he checks himself when he sees where it's coming from.

"Is that Miss Kayla Spencer? Only *the* most gorgeous actress today gracing this humble dressing room? What an honor! I'm Martin Fox, Dani's guardian."

Kayla jumps up, squealing, and throws her arms around Martin. "Of course, I know who you are! My mom was a REVOLUTION! groupie! I've been listening to your music since before I was born! Seriously, *in utero*! You *have* to call me Kayla. I insist!"

Martin takes advantage of the hug to grab Kayla's Juul, discretely passing it to Carlton, who immediately leaves the room before Kayla's even aware of what's happening.

"Thank you! Kayla, I'm so sorry, but we have a very strict no vaping rule around Dani. Her vocal cords are too precious. I hope you understand."

Kayla watches Carlton leave. "Oh, of course."

Martin straightens her tiara and smiles. He turns on the humidifier, waving the cloying stink out of the air as he walks. "How did you two enjoy the show?"

As Kayla loudly gushes about the show, Sean scoops me up in a hug. Over his shoulder, I catch Trey intensely watching us, like we're performing for his entertainment. *Doesn't he have the common decency to give us a moment of privacy?* A weird part of me is intrigued that he's watching us. A flash of excitement runs through my body as I wonder what he's thinking. But my thoughts turn back to Sean as I feel his arms tighten around me. I close my eyes, pushing Trey out of my mind.

"You were amazing up there." Sean puts me down and looks into my eyes. "I'm *so* proud of you!" He gives me a deep kiss, right there in front of everyone, and whispers, "Did I mention how unbelievably hot you were?"

My stomach melts and my body heats up as he kisses me again. But my mind shoots off in different directions: I'm hyper aware of Kayla squealing, partly wondering if Trey is still watching us, and self-conscious of Jenner and Martin being in the room, too.

Sean finally lets me go when Jenner chuckles. "Well, Sean, what do you think of your girl?"

Beet red with embarrassment, Sean grins. "The show was epic! I can't wait to see it again!"

Kayla pouts and kicks the floor. "Shoot! I wish I could see the show again, too. But you guys are leaving tonight, and we're stuck here shooting."

Jenner whispers to Carlton, who searches the pockets of his safari vest and pulls out a card. Jenner hands it to Kayla. "We just started touring. Plenty of opportunities. Just reach out to Carlton whenever you want to see a show. We'll have tickets ready for you and Trey."

"You're the best, Jenner. Thank you! You give my Sid a call whenever you want to do that guest spot thing. It'll be such a ratings boost!"

Martin and I exchange looks, wondering what she's talking about. Trey comes over. "Jenner's been talking to Kayla's agent about you doing a guest spot on *The Fleetwoods*."

My mouth drops open. *Me? On The Fleetwoods?!* I instantly switch into fangirl mode again. "Are you serious? That would be so awesome!" I turn to Sean, "Did you hear that? I'm going to be on *The Fleetwoods*!"

Sean laughs. "Yeah, I heard. I'm right here." He turns to Trey. "I'm Sean, by the way. Nice to meet you." They shake hands while I continue to freak out.

"Oh my God, Lauren is going to die, *die*, that I got to meet you two.

Wait." I look from Trey to Kayla. "Think I could get a photo with you two?"

Trey laughs. "Of course. We can call her if you want. Kayla loves talking to anyone who loves her." Trey chuckles and then sighs. "Look, sorry I was a jerk earlier." He pauses to find the right words. "It's just that Kayla can be *a lot* sometimes. She gets so wrapped up in herself, she forgets to think about other people. It wasn't cool to air our dirty laundry in front of you guys like that."

Trey turns around. "Hey, Kayla, you up for saying hi to Dani's best friend? Apparently, she's quite the fan!"

Kayla bounds over to us. She grabs my phone as I call Lauren on FaceTime. "I love calling fans and freaking them out!" Sean wraps his arm around me, and I sigh as I observe Kayla glancing in the mirror, adjusting my tiara on her head. *She isn't checking to see if she looks good...it's like she's just confirming that she's as beautiful as she remembers. Her confidence is amazing. Will I ever be that self-assured?*

Lauren's frenzied screams pull me out of my musing. I give Sean a squeeze, and I lose myself in Lauren's excitement.

17

The days rocket by while Sean is on the road with me. The only time we have alone is late at night when we cuddle up to watch a movie. But with everyone else sleeping fifteen feet away and only a thin partition separating us, we might as well be snuggled right next to them in their bunks.

Martin and I convinced Brett and Sean to appear in our daily *RYB* videos. Since they started, the RYB channel is blowing up! There's a whole #WeLoveYouMrTruehart community online. Sean can't believe he has a fan club of his own.

Unfortunately, Zoe is his most vocal follower. She's started a bit of a flap, trolling me. Her incessant putdowns have sparked the TrueHarts to clapback, and it's just short of an all-out feud! Carlton's been doing his best to calm it down, but my fans are over her shade. I have to admit that it's awesome to see them rush to my defense. I can't believe she's still dragging me after all this time. You'd think she'd be over me by now!

***

It's August and we're in New York. School starts soon, which means not only is Sean going home, but Geena is moving to Texas to attend Rice. We fly to London in two weeks to start the international tour, so I guess I won't see either Geena or Lauren until the tour is over.

I'm excited to go to Europe. Our Vancouver show was the first time I left the U.S. It was wild to see how everything was so similar, yet slightly different. I cannot wait to see the rest of the world now!

We spent last night in another luxurious parking lot, this time near the Barclay Center. Brett and Sean are out on a run while I meet with Jenner. I've barely seen him since Chicago. My behavior was pretty wretched, and I wouldn't blame him if he needed a break. But Martin assures me that Jenner's dealt with tantrums far worse than mine, and I shouldn't worry.

Jenner, Martin, and I are all sitting down at the kitchen table when there's a knock on the door. I hear a familiar voice and jump up.

"Terrance!" I run and give him a hug. Terrance grudgingly puts up with it for a few seconds before quickly disentangling himself.

"Yes, I've missed you, too, but let's not lose our minds, shall we?" He looks at me and laughs. "Oh, what the hell, come here." He gives me a quick hug. "I really have missed you." He looks around the table. "All of you. Congrats! You are crushing it on all fronts! This tour is the hottest ticket on the planet right now!"

Terrance's gaze rests on my tiara and he smirks. "All hail the queen, indeed!" He looks at Jenner. "That was a brilliant gimmick. The fans are eating it up. The public loves to be part of a squad these days. And the teeming masses pledging their oath to a supreme ruler is an idea that has never gone out of style. Just ask Mao or Stalin!"

Jenner chuckles. "Don't thank me—thank the Royal Court of True-Harts in Wichita. They were the brilliant innovators who came up with the concept, though I'm sad to report their high school economics teacher failed to teach them the value of filing for a trademark. Redman Enterprises proudly holds the license to The Queen of Harts, the True-Harts, and all the surrounding marketing possibilities. We're raking in a sizable amount of scratch with our side hustle."

Terrance pulls out his iPad and slings his messenger bag onto a sofa, narrowly missing Carlton. "I hope you're taking notes, Dani, because this man knows how to earn!" He smiles and sits next to Jenner at the kitchen table. "We don't have a ton of time this morning, so let's get down do it."

"Is everything OK?"

Terrance fires up his iPad and laughs. "It's more than OK, it's full-throttle amazing! We've had requests from songwriters and artists who want to collaborate with you! Artists from all across the globe. My phone has been blowing up and I know Jenner's has, too. We put a list together of potential projects to run past you. One of which we'd like to slot in tomorrow if you're up for it."

I can barely take in what he's saying. No words can capture the excitement that's building in my chest, so I just scream! Then the words start tumbling out. "Oh my God, who will I be working with? What will we be doing? I can't believe this is happening!"

Martin wraps his arm around me. "Another sign that you're in the big league now, girl! Everyone wants to hitch onto your rising star and get some of that glory for themselves. You're in an amazing position. You've got the chance to call the shots and make some really good choices. Enjoy it."

Martin rubs his hands together. "So, what are we talking about here?"

Terrance reads off a list of thirty performers interested in collaborating with me. Some are up-and-coming acts, and some are older stars who are on their way out but looking to grasp a few more seconds of the spotlight. But most of the names are not only people that I've heard of but huge stars currently dominating the pop chart. Boy bands, rappers, country musicians—the list is as diverse as it is long. It blows my mind that they all want to work with *me! ME!*

I laugh. "Not too shabby for a teen from Santa Clarita!"

Jenner shakes his head, grinning from ear to ear as he takes down notes. "Not too bad at all. What better time to work with international artists than when you're on tour? You can record a song every few days in another city. It's a great gimmick for your next album."

But even as I'm buzzing with excitement, imagining all of the musical idols I'll meet in the coming months, my heart begins to race. My vision narrows to a pinpoint and anxiety kicks in even before I can identify what's happening. *How am I going to find the time to record with all these artists when I barely have time to breathe as it is? Am I even good enough to sing with all these amazing people who have been doing this for years? What if everyone gets tired of me and all this goes away?* I break out into a cold sweat, trying to control the claustrophobic feeling that's suffocating me. Everyone is still smiling and talking, but Martin picks up on the change in me and places a cool hand over mine.

In a quiet voice, Martin says, "Carlton, please get Dani some water." To Jenner and Terrance, he adds, "Let's take it down for a minute, guys."

Carlton leaps up, shaking the entire bus as he bounds to the fridge, which does nothing to soothe my nerves. He returns in an instant with an opened bottle of icy water. My hands shake as I take the bottle, spilling water as I try to take a few sips. All the while, Martin is breathing deeply and exhaling with a shushing noise. Soon I'm unconsciously matching my breath with his, and I start to calm down.

Martin smiles. "Better?"

I continue breathing deeply. My vision returns to normal and the pressure in my chest eases. I nod. Jenner and Terrance look shocked, which doesn't make me feel any better. Martin pats my hand but addresses Jenner and Terrance.

"It's fantastic that everyone wants to work with Dani. I think it's a real tribute not only to her talent, but it's undeniable acknowledgment of how special this kid is and how amazing her connection is with her fans and everyone her music touches."

Jenner and Terrance both nod tentatively. I think we're all wondering where Martin is going with this.

"But I have to be honest. Dani's been struggling with the pressure of being on tour."

A small groan escapes me. *Ugh! Why did he have to say it that way? I sound like I'm some headcase who can't handle things.*

Martin squeezes my hand. "I'm not putting you down, sweetie. After your meltdown in Chicago, you told me that your daily schedule is too intense. I see it in the way you're snapping at everyone and how you treat the people around you when you're upset." He looks at Jenner and Terrance. "Heaping a ton of new collaborative projects on Dani while we're touring, doing daily publicity appearances, schoolwork, and rehearsing new numbers for the European tour...something's gotta to give, folks. And I don't want it to be Dani's sanity."

Jenner wipes his face wearily and then slowly nods. Terrance creeps his fingers across the table and gives my fingers a small, comforting stroke. I give him a quiet nod knowing what a big effort that is for him.

"I'm not saying she can't do these projects. But, as her guardian first and foremost, Dani's health and safety are my priority. As we move forward, I want to keep her stress levels in mind as we schedule these collaborations. And I think maybe a few sessions with a therapist might help."

"A therapist?" I bark, swiveling to face Martin. "I'm just a little stressed. I'm not crazy or anything."

Jenner looks at me reassuringly. "No one's saying that you are, Dani. We just want what's best for you."

He gives Martin a serious look. "Don't you think a therapist is a bit much? I think we just need to ease her schedule and reduce her stress. Serena's joining us in a few days before we head to London to oversee the new dance routines. She can meet with Dani and help her come up with a way to cope with everything. No need to call in a therapist just yet." He turns to Terrance. "Let's put a pin in tomorrow's recording session and schedule it later down the road."

Relieved, I nod. I'd much rather talk to Serena than to a therapist.

Terrance gives me a sincere smile. "No problem."

Jenner knocks on the table and points to Martin. "And don't forget you've got a valuable resource here. He's the only one on this tour who's been in your shoes, Dani. He handled it the right way. Talk to him. He's a good listener."

I nod at Jenner, suddenly exhausted.

Martin squeezes my hand. "Why don't you go lie down until Sean gets back?"

Suddenly a nap sounds like the perfect solution to all my problems. I drag myself back to my room and lie down. Martin follows me, closing my blinds and covering me with a blanket.

"Don't worry about a thing, darlin'. Just get some rest."
I'm asleep before he even shuts the door.

18

"Wake up, sleeping beauty." Sean plants a huge kiss on my lips.

Best alarm clock ever.

I feel much better after some rest. But it's almost noon. We have only a couple of hours before I have to be at rehearsal. I splash water onto my face and throw some clothes in a bag. A knock on the bus door and Alexi, our new head of security, appears. An ex-Israeli soldier, he's got closely cropped black hair and a chiseled face. He doesn't look or speak to me unless he has to, and, while that just might be part of his job, I suspect he doesn't like me very much. I never used to have security, but after Kayla started posting about her backstage visit on IG, my fans have tripled, and they always seem to be lurking about.

When we hop off the bus, I'm greeted by about a hundred fans and paparazzi screaming and holding signs, cameras flashing. I plaster a big smile on my face as Martin takes my bag. I spend a few minutes signing autographs, posing for photos, and hugging fans. Alexi then ushers me into a waiting town car, and we head into Manhattan.

Martin takes Sean and me to a diner within walking distance of the rehearsal space. He swears it has the best chicken pot pie this side of the Rockies. A chaperoned lunch date with Martin and Alexi isn't ideal, but Martin's convinced I'll get pregnant if Sean and I are left alone for more than ten seconds. So...a table for an awkward foursome, please!

Settled into our booth, Alexi sits at a table across from us so he can scan the room. I lean into Sean as Martin orders so I don't have to make eye contact with the frowsy middle-aged waitress, who clearly is trying to get my attention. After taking our order, she stands staring at me. Martin clears his throat. "Thank you, Greta." She scurries away.

"Sorry about that, sugar. I guess she's a fan of yours. I expect you'll have to sign an autograph before we leave."

I roll my eyes. "Remember the days when no one knew who I was, and we could eat in peace?"

I catch Martin and Sean sharing a quick look. I think about what I said and groan. I pull out a crumpled dollar bill from my letterman jacket and hand it to Martin. "Yeah, I realize how that sounds, and even *I* think I'm a jackass. Sorry." After my Chicago meltdown, Martin started charging me a dollar every time I'm rude, entitled, or have a tantrum. It hasn't stopped things entirely, but it has made me more self-aware. He plans on donating the money to charity when we get back from tour.

Martin shrugs his shoulders, pocketing the dollar. "At least you're catching yourself doing it now. If you don't reign it in, you'll be buying a whole grocery store of canned goods for the poor."

Chagrined, I glance at Sean.

"It's not a good look, D. I hate to say it, but it kinda makes you sound like your mom."

My stomach drops. "Really?"

Sean nods, looking like he would rather be anywhere but here having this conversation. "Yeah. I'm seeing a whole new side of you. It's freaking me out."

The sound of utensils and dishes clattering becomes deafening as I absorb the fact that Sean just told me that I'm acting like my psycho mother. *I want to curl up and disappear.* And *of course,* here comes Greta, the awkward waitress, stupidly smiling and taking years to place our drinks on the table. Only I can't be annoyed in front of Sean or Martin. I give Greta a tight smile. She startles, bumps into a passing waiter and knocks over his tray of food. Martin catches me rolling my eyes. Sean and Martin jump up to help pick up the dishes. Alexi stands up and hovers over the mess, scanning the room, and I glare at him. *Sure, don't do anything useful, Alexi, just watch the room as if an assassin was waiting for the stupid waitress to drop her tray to knife me in the back!* It's as if he can read my mind, because as soon as I finish my thought, he gives me a cold look and continues his watch. After a few seconds, I jump in to help, realizing how spoiled I look watching everyone on their knees, cleaning up.

As I grab broken plates and overturned cups, I see Greta on the verge of tears, and I feel awful about my earlier catty remarks. *I'm no better than Greta or anyone I meet. Why do I keep thinking that?* I reach out and grab Greta's hand and give it a squeeze. She looks up gratefully, and we quickly finish picking up the dishes.

The hostess rushes over, flustered. "Miss Truehart, I apologize. Normally Greta isn't this clumsy but having you here has really thrown our staff off."

Greta flinches as the hostess continues to grovel. I interrupt her, "Greta didn't do anything wrong. It was my fault that she backed into the waiter. I asked her where the ladies' room was, and she was kind enough to point me in the right direction."

"Oh, I see, well, from over there, I thought I saw..." The hostess looks from me to Greta and flounders for words. "I guess I owe you an apology, Greta."

We sit down and not two seconds later Greta re-appears with plates stacked up her arms. Her words rush out as she sets down our food. "Thanks for covering for me, Miss Truehart. I just want to tell you that my daughter is a huge fan of yours."

I smile. "I'm sorry I wasn't very friendly when we first sat down. What's your daughter's name?"

"Her name is Hannah and she's twelve. She wears a tiara like you do, and she practices your dance routines every chance she gets."

She quickly looks around before whipping out her phone. She shows me a photo of a cute redhead with a top-knot and a cheap sparkling tiara mugging at the camera.

"She's adorable!" I gush, genuinely touched. "Are you coming to the show tomorrow?"

Greta smiles and shakes her head as she puts her phone away. "All the tickets I can find are out of our budget. But we'll stroll by Barclay Center to check out the crowd anyway. She'll love seeing all the True-Harts dressed up."

Hannah is so lucky to have a mom like her. I look at Martin, and he reaches into his pocket and pulls out his wallet. "We can't have Miss Hannah missing out on her favorite singer! Here are four tickets and passes to get you backstage. We'll see you after the show and Hannah can show off her moves!"

We get up and take a few photos for Greta to show Hannah and then settle down to eat. I squeeze Martin's hand as we leave the restaurant, Alexi trailing behind us. "Thank you for keeping me on the right track. Seeing how happy we made Greta...it was so easy, and it cost me nothing." I shrug. "I don't know why my first reaction to everything lately is to be a jerk."

"You did a good job helping out that waitress back there." Letting me go, he slings my workout bag onto his other shoulder. "Come on. Let's get dancing so we can check out Manhattan!"

19

Rehearsal is quick and easy. We finally have all the new props for the show: a huge heart-shaped throne, a scepter, and a floor-length, red velvet, fur-trimmed cape for me to wear—which is incredibly hard to dance in. But that's nothing compared with the playing card costumes the backup dancers have to wear. Beau's the best dancer we've got, and even he's floundering in the large foam costume! The only thing we're missing is a huge crown that I'll ride on as it drops from the ceiling at the opening of the concert.

After a quick change, Sean looks amazing in light gray chinos and a short-sleeved button-down shirt. I'm summer-in-the-city ready in a swingy floral midi-dress, gladiator sandals, and a matching jeweled tiara peeking out of my hair. My phone buzzes with a Snapchat from Kayla and I glance at it.

Sean clears his throat and I look up. "All set?" he asks, eying my phone, which I quickly put away. "Let me guess, Kayla again with another fashion emergency or fight with Trey."

"Mm-hmm," I murmur as I stand on tiptoes and give him a kiss. "I know she's been texting a lot, but isn't it cool that we've become friends? I mean, she's only like the hottest celebrity out there and she wants to hang with *me*!"

"Don't you think it's a little odd that she's so much older than you? I mean, she can drink and vote. Why does she want to hang out with a sixteen-year-old? And when was the last time you talked to Lauren?"

His attitude totally throws me off—this is not how I expected to start tonight. I try not to sound annoyed. "Well, Kayla *is* a big fan of mine. Maybe she just wants to hang out with someone who gets the whole fame thing. I texted Lauren a few times, but she is still obsessing over Tom cheating on her, so it's been kind of a drag. But you're right. I'll give her a call tomorrow."

Sean gives me an odd look, his eyes wandering up to my hair. "Another tiara. I'm going to draw the line if you ask me to start wearing one of those things."

I laugh. "Don't tempt me! What the queen wants, the queen gets!" I spin on my toes, sending my skirt twirling out around me, giving Sean a flirty glimpse. "But if my king doesn't want to wear a crown, then I shall decree it so."

The joke falls flat, making me self-conscious. "Just kidding."

Sean shakes his head. "I don't think you making me do something because you're the queen is very funny. It's getting weird because a lot of your stage stuff is now how you are when you're offstage. It's like you're buying into all of it. Having you treat *me* like I'm one of your fans..." He struggles to find the right words. "It isn't cool. It's like you're forgetting who *we* are."

All of my fame, fans, everything I've been doing the past few months seem to fall away instantly. I feel like I've been caught naked in public. All my conceit, my flaws exposed. I'm reminded for the millionth time on this trip how much I'm messing up this relationship.

At a loss for words, I stand there, my eyes welling, the silence becoming heavier between us.

"All I'm saying is that I miss the old Dani. The girl who loved talking to me on the phone, who couldn't get enough of hanging out with me. You've got this whole new life...I feel left behind. And I don't recognize your temper. Your outbursts make me uncomfortable." He sighs and looks out the window at the Manhattan skyline. "I just want to get back to *us*."

I rest my head on his chest, and he wraps his arms around me. We stand there for a while, his words weighing heavily on my heart. *I can't argue with anything he's said. I'm the reason we're having these problems. If I were at home, going to school, we'd be fine.*

After a few minutes, Martin pops his head into the studio. "Car's here. See you downstairs." He disappears. Sean squeezes me hard before letting me go.

I sniff and wipe my eyes, looking at the ceiling. "Martin's been saying that I need to start separating myself from the show. Serena's coming tomorrow so I can talk to her about this stuff. Please let me try to fix this. I don't want to lose you."

I feel like my world is falling apart. Our phones buzz at the same time and Sean sighs, pulling his out of his pocket. "Martin's wondering where we are." He shakes his head. "I'm sorry I brought this up. I thought I could get through the trip without saying anything. Late at night when we're alone hanging, it's like we're back home and everything feels normal. But when we're with people, everything changes."

How long has he been feeling this way? How have I not noticed? "No, I'm sorry for being such a jerk. Being on tour is important, but so are you." I clutch at Sean's hand, desperate to convince him not to give up on us. "I can do better. Please give me a chance to show you."

Sean nods his head, but it doesn't make me feel any better. He sighs. "Let's go."

With heavy hearts, we clamber down the stairs. I pull my tiara off and slip it into my workout bag. *It feels important that I take it off tonight. Just be me for the next few hours and not The Queen of Harts.*

We climb into the limo, and it pulls away. Martin's eyes immediately focus on my bare head, and he gives me a questioning look. My hand self-consciously goes to my hair, smoothing it out as I look out the window.

Martin tries his best to ramp up our energy. "Last night together before our loved ones go back home. Let's turn it up! Show tired old New York how we do it, California-style!"

Brett gives an agreeing "Woo!" I don't even know where we're going tonight, and I don't care. All I want is for this sinking feeling in my heart to go away and for Sean and me to go back to how we were.

20

Thanks to Martin's action-packed itinerary, I make it through the night without bursting into tears. Alexi even cracks a smile once or twice during the evening. A trip to the Cloisters' gardens, dinner at Serendipity, video games at Family Fair Fun Center in Chinatown, and a chili dog from Gray's Papaya all help pull Sean and me out of our funk. For a few hours, we forget the stress of our uncertain relationship and make the most of our last hours together.

Saying goodbye to Sean is even worse than when I first left L.A., because at least back then I knew we were still together. I feel like I'm leaving a piece of my heart behind when we drop him off at JFK. We part with promises to work harder on communication, but I honestly don't know where his head is. Normally, I would text Lauren to find out. But since I've been so caught up in life on the road, I haven't been a very good friend to her this summer. I can hardly expect her to help me out with my relationship issues when I haven't been there for her issues with Tom.

The days blur together as I mope. We roll southward through Jersey, Connecticut, the Carolinas, and Georgia. Preoccupied and restless, I power through the concerts.

"You OK?" Martin plops down next to me as our bus maneuvers the parking lot of Disneyworld. Last night we drove all night from Atlanta for a day of photo ops at the Magic Kingdom before our show tomorrow at the Amway Center.

"I'm fine. Feels like it'll be forever before I see Sean again."

"We'll try to keep it under six weeks, but new tour buses, different show lineup...I want to get you used to all the changes before he comes out again." He pauses. "You ready for today?"

I adjust the Mickey ears Petra attached to my tiara and try to sound excited. "Of course! A few rides, a few photos, and a turkey leg—what's not to love?"

Martin gives me a sidelong look and I try again. "Seriously, I'm fine." I show off the front of the adorable off-the-shoulder black sweatshirt with a gold sequence Mickey silhouette I'm wearing. "I'm dressed and ready for fun!"

He puts on his own pair of colorful rainbow mouse ears and stands up. "Let's go, your highness. Fun awaits!"

We get off the bus. The dancers pour out of their bus outfitted in assorted Disney attire.

Jenner claps his hands loudly, but, like unruly teenagers, we all ignore him. Alexi puts his fingers to his lips and lets loose an ear-piercing whistle which silences us instantly.

Jenner clears his throat. "Thank you, Alexi. A park liaison will meet us at the gate, and we'll spend a few hours taking photos. We're slated to participate in the eleven o'clock parade, then the day is yours. Buses leave at closing to go back to the Amway Center where we'll be spending the night."

As Jenner drones on and the dancers chatter excitedly, I check my phone hoping to see a text from Sean. But my screen stares back at me, blank and accusing.

**

Though Jenner tried to keep my visit top secret, as usual, the True-Harts have somehow gotten word I'd be there. Our tram is mobbed as we pull up to the gates. Alexi flips into overdrive, keeping the crowds at bay as the park scrambles to find additional security. They end up having to rope off each section we visit to keep the crowd from getting out of hand. But we take our publicity shots on rides, with characters, and during the parade as promised. Eventually, Jenner and Carlton head to the arena to finalize details while we tour the park. After a few hours of fighting the crowds, signing autographs, and posing for selfies with fans, I'm done. I'm jealous that Beau and the rest of the dancers are staying until closing, but I can't enjoy myself with the constant pressure from my fans. Reluctantly, I board the bus with Martin and Alexi and head to Amway Center. Assured no one can jump me on a moving bus, Alexi takes a nap.

"I can't believe the TrueHarts showed up today," Martin says, "just like they mobbed that Boys & Girls Club appearance in Atlanta and the radio interview in Jersey. If I didn't know any better, I'd say someone's leaking your itinerary."

I flop onto the couch. "Someone from the Disney side probably told their daughter who told their friends." I kick off my shoes and stretch out. "What do you want to do for lunch?"

I grab the remote control and start changing channels. After a few minutes, Martin still hasn't answered me. I look over. "Earth to Martin. Did you hear me? What about lunch?"

Martin looks up from staring at his shoes. "Huh? Sorry, I was just thinking..."

"About...?" I ask as I continue flipping channels.

"I caught Beau alone in here last week."

"So? It's not like anything's missing, right?"

"Nothing's missing. But no one's allowed on the bus except for the seven of us." Martin turns to look at the kitchen table where Carlton keeps the tour calendar.

My stomach grumbles. "Come on, Martin, spit it out. I'm hungry."

"It's just weird that we keep getting mobbed by the TrueHarts despite the fact that only Jenner, myself, and Alexi know our itinerary."

I stare at Martin, incredulous. "You think Beau is tipping off the TrueHarts? Why would he do that?"

Martin shakes his head slowly, still thinking. "I'm not accusing him of anything. But it's something I'm going to keep an eye on." I give Martin the death stare and he shakes his head again. "Look, people pay big bucks for tip-offs about their favorite celebrities. The paparazzi are fighting to have the latest pics of you. There's big money to be made for someone with insider knowledge."

The seriousness of what we're discussing starts to sink in. The idea of someone possibly selling information about me gives me the creeps. *Could Beau really do something like that? We've been so close since he started working with us. It couldn't have been an act this whole time just to get close to me. Could it?*

"I get paid to worry about this, not you. It could all just be a weird coincidence. Now, how about we have Carlton order some Thai food? It'll be waiting for us when we get to the arena."

Martin texts Carlton while I play with the necklace Beau gave me. *All the time I've spent with Beau over the past few months, all the effort he's made to become my friend and earn my trust...was it all a game to him?* I'm seeing everything in a new light, and I'm not so sure I like it.

2 1

Carlton greets us in the Amway Center parking lot with a bag of Thai food. Martin immediately breaks his "leak" conspiracy theory to Carlton and Alexi, which starts to stress me out. So, I fix a plate and eat in my room.

I'm just finishing when there's a knock on my door. "Come in!"

"Dani!" Serena's deep, musical voice floats into the room, instantly changing the atmosphere. A subtle fragrance of vanilla and citrus wafts in with her. I feel relieved that help has arrived.

I burst into tears, and she folds me into a strong hug. "I should have come sooner."

We sit down on the bed, and I try to pull myself together. Martin slips in, whisks away my dirty dishes, and shuts the door behind him.

My tears eventually subside. "I don't know where to begin. Everything started out fine. The hours were long, and I never knew how hard being with people twenty-four-seven would be. But my stage fright seems to lessen the more shows I do, and I'm having a lot of fun meeting my fans and seeing the country."

I look up at Serena and she smiles warmly, waiting for me to continue. The silence stretches as I inwardly grimace at what I have to say next. "But I guess you know from Martin that things have been getting out of hand. I'm starting to get really stressed and short-tempered and, well, I've been saying and doing things I'm not proud of. Sean's visit was a disaster, and I've barely spoken to Lauren and Geena all summer because I haven't made the time. I've been avoiding Mom's calls and texts because I'm so mad at her for trying to cash in on my career that I don't even know what to say to her right now. I'm a mess and I don't know how I got this way."

Serena nods, smoothing out imaginary wrinkles in her long gray skirt. "That often happens in life. Your shows are fantastic, yes? Everything onstage is perfect. But off stage..." She pulls a face, "...not so much, correct? But since the shows are good, you overlook the little things." She takes a deep breath and continues. "But all those little things can pile up and become an avalanche if you don't take care of them."

Serena's words soothe me. Instead of feeling embarrassed by my behavior, I feel understood and even a little hopeful. Maybe she can help me fix this mess and make better decisions going forward.

Serena smiles. "So, where do you go from here? How can you stop feeling this way?"

I stare at her blankly, eager to know the secret to fixing my life.

"First—you slow down. You cannot do twenty things in a day. Interview, workout, homework, publicity, concerts, and calling home. You simply have to decide what your priorities are and build your day around them."

I stare at her, incredulous. "But that's impossible. I can't just *say* 'I'm not doing an interview or photo op.' That's my job."

A half smile plays on Serena's lips, making me wonder if she really understands what I'm up against.

"But you *can* say no, and you must. What would happen if you don't do everything on your list?"

It seems like an idiotic question. Just thinking about it makes my stomach cramp. I flounder for an answer. "Um, well, Jenner would get mad, for one. And the record label has expectations."

Serena shakes her head. "Jenner is extremely aware how important your health, both physical and emotional, are. He made that mistake in the past, and he's not willing to make that same mistake with you. He is very worried about you."

This revelation throws me for a loop. *Jenner worries about me? I've barely seen him on this tour except for the prayer circle right before the shows. He always seems so business-like. I never thought I had a choice to say no to his schedule...*

She continues to stare at me expectantly, so I search my mind, sifting through possibilities. "Well, what will the fans think if I don't make all these appearances? I can't let them down."

Serena reaches out, touches my tiara, and gives me a smile that makes it seem like she almost feels sorry for me. It's the worst feeling ever.

"You have to choose: your fans or yourself. The more you do for your fans, the more they're going to expect. Then demand. You *have* to set limits and stop trying to impress them. They're *already* impressed by you, which is why they're your fans in the first place. They will love you until they don't."

Rude! I gape at her and she pats my hand.

"Harsh, but true. Their love has nothing to do with *who you really are*. It is who they *think* you are—who you *let* them see. If you give them everything you are, you will be devastated when they turn away from you. And that will happen eventually. You will grow and change, and they will turn away. It is the cycle every performer experiences." She puts a warm hand on my arm and gives it a squeeze. "*Protect* yourself, Dani."

I think about the past few months. *I do seem to be prioritizing my fans, the press, and photo ops more than the people I love and my schoolwork. I never go anywhere without a tiara. I've become obsessed with checking Instagram and Twitter throughout the day, keeping tabs on my numbers when I never used to care before.* My stomach is heavy with regret, and I feel trapped.

"What can I do? The thought of negative feedback makes me panic."

Serena bends down to grab a notebook peeking out from my backpack. She opens it to a blank page. "We are going to separate you from 'Dani Truehart: Pop Star'. *You* are going to decide what your priorities are, and we'll build a schedule to accommodate those values. And then we discuss ways to safeguard your behavior, such as not spending hours on social media or reading articles about yourself. You've got a team to handle your publicity. Let them do their job. You stick to your job: singing and being a teenager."

I still don't quite understand how Serena expects me to make these changes. To be perfectly honest, what she's suggesting seems way out of touch with my reality. But I'm willing to try. I don't like who I'm becoming; but I don't know if I can make the changes she's asking for and still be The Queen of Harts.

22

It takes a couple of hours, but Serena and I break down every aspect of my life into lists: things that are important to me (*Sean and my friends*), things that aren't important (*social media and all the drama my mom causes*), and things I need to do but may not want to (*homework and working out*). In the end, we come up with a daily schedule that is much simpler: limiting publicity to a few days a week rather than every day, and more time for Lauren, Geena, and Sean. But unfortunately, no matter what I say, Serena leaves my allotted daily homework time exactly the same. Apparently, there is no escape from algebra!

"What's the point," I groan, tossing the lists up in the air. "I don't see how Jenner is going to accept this new schedule when it eliminates everything that he's made a priority in my life since last November." I flop back onto the bed, frustrated.

Serena calmly gathers the pages, flashing a reassuring smile. "Let me handle Jenner. He's willing to do anything it takes to keep you happy and healthy."

After she leaves, I decide to call Lauren. It's been weeks since we've talked, and it's all my fault. After Serena's pep talk about priorities, I feel like it's a good time to start implementing what we've discussed. My stomach twists in knots as the phone rings. I half hope she doesn't pick up so I can avoid this. *Wouldn't it be wonderful if I could have Martin smooth this over for me like he does everything else? But what kind of messed up friend would that make me if I can't even reach out and apologize when I've been a jerk?* Lauren picks up the phone, interrupting the argument I'm having with myself.

"Dani, what a surprise." Lauren's voice is flat, barely concealing her anger. But I find my courage and come clean.

"I'm *so* sorry, Lauren. It's my fault that we haven't talked all summer. I'm an idiot."

There's a long pause. "Keep talking."

I hope the fact that she didn't hang up on me means the door isn't slammed shut on our friendship. I take a deep breath and continue. "I can't even imagine what you've been going through with Tom. Me, not being there for you is inexcusable. I'm your *best friend* and I haven't been acting like it. I know I don't have the right to ask, but do you think you can ever forgive me?"

After another excruciating pause, Lauren sighs heavily. "You're a real jerk, Truehart, you know that?"

My heart sinks, and I brace myself.

"For years I've been there for you every step of the way, encouraging you, consoling you, doing everything I can to support you as you try to achieve your dreams. And the minute you do, you leave town and forget about me. You're all about your *new best friends*, Kayla and Trey, posting stupid pics on Insta and making appearances for all your stupid screaming fans." She exhales loudly. "You're the worst best friend ever!"

Tears pour down my face. "I know," I manage in a garbled voice. *I deserve every ounce of her anger. I wouldn't blame her if she never talks to me again.*

"But the thing that pisses me off more than anything is the fact that despite all the rotten stuff you've done, I still miss you."

"Really?"

"Every day. So *yes*, I forgive you, but you'd better bend over backward to make it up to me."

I'm almost dizzy as relief floods my body. "I swear I will!" I collapse onto the bed. "I don't know what I would have done if I lost your friendship."

"Yeah, well, I've been living that reality all summer and it sucks. Please don't put me through that again."

"I promise I won't. In fact, I'm working on easing my schedule, so I'll have a little more time to keep in touch. The tour's been crazy. The only time I have to myself is the few minutes I can grab in between events."

Lauren snorts. "And don't forget hanging out with Kayla and Trey. I'm sure that's such a nightmare obligation to deal with."

I feel a stab of guilt. Between Kayla and Carlton, there have been a lot of Insta posts and stuff in the tabloids. "It looks like we see each other way more than we actually do. Yes, they flew out for a few concerts, and we've hung out in my dressing room afterward. But they've been shooting a ton, so we've only seen each other for a few hours the entire summer. *But* I do have some good news..."

I can practically hear her eyes roll as Lauren grudgingly asks, "What?"

"I mentioned to Kayla that we're superfans of *The Fleetwoods*. I asked if I could bring you when I do the guest spot and she said *yes*! You and I are going to be on *The Fleetwoods* together!"

Lauren's scream is so piercing, I have to pull the phone away from my ear. I can't stop laughing as I listen to Lauren freak out. It feels like we're heading back to our old friendship, and it's a relief.

Martin pops his head in to see what the ruckus is about. "It's Lauren," I whisper, still laughing. He smiles but doesn't leave so I put my hand over the phone.

"Yeah?"

"Jenner agreed to give your new schedule a whirl."

I sit up. "That's great!"

I hear Lauren shouting on the phone. "What's great?"

Martin continues. "Yup. Hopefully, you'll start feeling a lot less stressed now. Nothing is slated for tomorrow except homework, sound check, and the show."

I victoriously punch the air as Martin leaves. "Sorry about that. Jenner's agreed to my new schedule, so I'll have more free time. I am so relieved!"

"That's awesome, D! Maybe you can start acting like your old self now."

I flinch. "Ouch! Is it going to be constant jabs from you for the foreseeable future, or can I expect you to let it go any time soon?"

Lauren snorts. "Well, it's been like ten minutes since you apologized, so I don't think I'll be pulling an Elsa and letting it go any time soon. Stop being a jackass long-term and then we can talk."

I grimace. "Point taken." I sigh, feeling truly lighthearted for the first time in a long while. "You know, I don't even care. I'm just grateful we're talking again."

"I'm just happy you called. I was beginning to feel like I'd been replaced."

"Never!" Apparently, I shout a little too loud because Martin pops his head in again, finger over his mouth to shush me, and pats his throat. I groan. "The voice police have informed me that I must rest my vocal cords now."

Martin nods, satisfied, and leaves the room.

"Already?" Lauren whines. "But we just started catching up!"

"I know, but since Jenner's agreed to alter my schedule, I kinda feel like I need to do this to show everyone I'm taking this seriously. Want to watch the new *Fleetwoods* episode tonight on FaceTime? There'll be minimal talking, but at least we can hang out."

"Absolutely! I've missed watching with you."

"Me, too."

"I'm glad you called, Dani."

I sigh happily. "Me, too, Laur. And thanks for forgiving me."

"Love you, D."

"Love you, Laur."

I hang up and stare at the hustle and bustle in the arena parking lot. It's the first time I've felt like my old self in a while. I think about texting Sean the good news, but things still haven't gotten back to normal with us yet, and I think of all the ways the texts could be misinterpreted. It'd be better to call than text, so I decide to wait until tomorrow. I lower the shades and settle in for a cat nap.

23

After dinner, everyone scatters. I prop my phone next to me on the couch to watch *The Fleetwoods* with Lauren. The show is just beginning when the bus door opens. I pause the TV as Jenner and Serena come inside. Jenner is grinning like I've never seen before.

"Hey, Dani!" He glances at my phone. "Is that Lauren?" He bends down and gives her a wave. "Great to see you!"

"Lauren and I are catching up on *The Fleetwoods*."

"Nice! Good research for when you two make your guest appearance." He bends down again. "You excited, Lauren?"

She squeals wildly, and Jenner chuckles. "It should be fun." He walks to his bunk, clapping Alexi's shoulder as he passes. He drops his bag onto his bunk and grabs a blazer from the closet. I turn to Serena, who is perched on the opposite sofa.

"Thanks for your help today," I say quietly.

"My pleasure, Dani." She looks at Jenner, a small smile spreading.

Serena continues to stare at Jenner. I follow her gaze. He sees us staring and gives us another goofy grin. "OK, we're all set." As he and Serena turn to leave, he places a hand on the small of Serena's back and guides her down the bus steps.

Lauren chimes in. "Are they going on a date?"

I grab the phone and look at her. "You got that vibe, too?"

Lauren clears her throat. "Not that I don't want Jenner to find love, but I'd much rather watch young hot people in love. So, press play already."

I laugh and remind myself to ask Martin about it when he gets back from the gym.

**

My new schedule is a dream. I have more time to stay in touch with people back home and I'm less stressed, which means less snapping, and I've got a better attitude. I even manage to get my homework done! The show goes phenomenally well in Orlando. After that, we make a quick run to New Orleans, Memphis, and Birmingham before coming back to our last two shows in Tallahassee and Miami.

On the drive from Memphis to Tallahassee, Jenner and Martin join me at the kitchen table as I struggle to solve the most impossible quadratic equation ever created.

"Got a sec?" Jenner slides into the booth opposite me and picks up my worksheet.

"Sure!" I sigh, shoving my notebook away. "Anything to get away from these stupid equations. When am I ever going to use this stuff?"

Martin chuckles. "...Said every teenager *ever*. No one uses this stuff except rocket scientists, engineers, and all the other smarty-pants out there. But famous singer or not, you've got to do your time in the prison of algebra just like everyone else. Consider it a rite of passage."

Jenner drops the worksheet. "I can figure out a multimillion-dollar budget down to the penny, but I can't make heads or tails of this junk."

"So, what's up?" I tap my pencil on the table. "You guys seem..." I look back and forth between them, picking up on a weird vibe. "...tense."

Martin pats my hand. "Not tense, darlin'. We just want your opinion on something. Remember how we talked about you collaborating with different artists while you're out on tour?"

I nod and Martin continues. "Well, we kinda stuck a pin in that, what with your outbursts and your new schedule. We were able to kick most of the collaborations down the road to our time in Europe, but there's one band that can't find another date to work. So, we want to see how you'd feel spending a day recording with The Trent Walker Posse while we're in Miami."

"What? That's my dad's favorite band!"

Jenner smiles. "Best Artist and Album awards at last year's CMAs, and Best Country Artist and Album awards at the Grammys, too. It'll open up a whole new audience for you. I don't want to add to your stress, but if we can swing it, it'd be a wonderful opportunity to lock down the first song for your next album."

I'm giddy with excitement. "That's awesome!"

Jenner pulls a CD from his jacket pocket. "Here's the track. We'll record it two ways. First, you singing backup on a version for their album, and then them singing backup for you for your album. Two songs on two different albums means double the profit for everyone."

I pick up the CD, turning it over in my hand as Jenner continues. "If you're up for it, we'll extend our stay in Miami by a day, so you'll have a day to rest after the show and then record the next day. Think you could get comfortable with the music in five days?"

Five days? I stare at the CD, trying to decide. *This would be a really great opportunity in so many ways. It goes against everything Serena and I've been doing for the past week, which has been working out really well. But if I lock down some songs on the road for my next album, doesn't that mean I'll be freer when I get home to spend time with everyone?*

As if reading my thoughts, Martin speaks up. "You don't have to do this, Dani. We can scrap the whole 'collaborations on the road' idea if it's too much. I'm going to tell Regina we're putting your homework on hold for today so you can listen to the song and decide. No pressure, Dani. Whatever you want to do is fine with us."

"OK."

Jenner gets up and leaves. I try to slide out of the booth, but Martin doesn't budge. "You OK?"

I consider it for a minute. "Yeah, I think I am."

I head back to my room and listen to the song.

24

Instead of another massive stadium, the Miami show takes place at BeauLiv at the Fontainebleau Resort, an iconic hotel and entertainment venue whose stage has been graced by the likes of Elvis, Frank Sinatra—and now me! The best part is that Jenner finagled us a suite at the resort as part of our contract. Our first hotel room on the tour! Jenner, Martin, Regina, Carlton, and I are all sharing a huge suite with two floors, five bedrooms, a private pool, and spa with a personal butler, too! In exchange for the free room, the hotel has a video crew following me around for a promotional video.

It's a beautiful fall morning, and I'm savoring a cup of green tea on the balcony overlooking the beach. The breeze ruffles the pages of my notebook. Martin comes out and sits next to me.

"Look at you doing homework first thing in the morning! If your name weren't on the side of the tour bus, I'd wonder who I was looking at."

I grin. "I don't want to waste such a gorgeous day stuck in here. I might as well get it out of the way while I take advantage of the beautiful view."

"That's very mature of you! When you're finished, want to go see the nesting turtles? I hear it's a pretty incredible sight. Or we could go check out Food Truck Wednesdays over in the harbor. I could really dig into some Cuban food right about now."

Martin's phone vibrates and he pulls it out, checking the screen. "It's your mama. What's she doing up so early?"

I groan and Martin holds out a finger to quiet me. "Good morning, Miss J. It's been a while. What are you doing up with the birds in California?"

I can't make out what she's saying. Martin listens, only managing to get in the occasional "Uh-huh."

"Well, you know earlier this year Dani paid you back. I can send you a copy of the document you signed when you received the $200,000 check."

She wants more money? "Are you serious?" I hiss. Ignoring me, Martin puts a finger to his ear as if he's having trouble hearing.

"I don't understand what you want Dani to do. She isn't responsible for paying Geena's tuition. I'm sorry you've gone through the money, but that's not her problem. And to be perfectly frank, she was under no legal obligation to give you that $200,000. That was a good faith thank you for everything that you and Don did to launch her career."

I can hear Mom yelling, and Martin gets up and leaves the balcony. I shove my chair back and stomp after him. I throw myself onto an armchair, jiggling my foot furiously as Martin paces the floor.

"No, I don't think that would be a good idea. You're too upset, and it's not fair to put Dani..."

Martin stops speaking; I can only assume Mom is in full Texas-tornado mode and is talking so fast he can't get a word in edgewise.

"Absolutely not! She has no say over that money anyway. It's in trust, and I..."

He is silenced again and then sighs, frustrated.

"I am *not* keeping you from talking to your daughter. I think..."

He pauses again and then shouts, "A lawyer? You're out of your mind! Dani is *not* being held against her will. You get Child Protective Services involved, and I guarantee they will *not* take kindly to you trying to bully me into giving you Dani's hard-earned money." He pauses again, exasperated. "Go ahead. Do what you have to do."

Fed up, I snatch the phone from Martin. "I'm not being held against my will. You and Dad signed the papers giving me permission to do this, remember?"

It's like a switch is flicked. My mom becomes a completely different person, her voice dripping with saccharine sweetness. "Finally! Martin wouldn't let me talk to you, which is ridiculous. Who does he think he is? *I'm your mother for Chrissakes.*"

I plop back into the chair. "I heard the whole conversation, Mom. Martin wasn't keeping you from talking to me." I sigh heavily. "What's the problem?"

"Well, I was just telling Martin that since Jenner blocked me from selling your merchandise on my website, I've been struggling to make ends meet with Geena in college now."

"You've been saving for Geena's college tuition since she was a baby, and you're not paying for my lessons anymore...why is money so tight all of a sudden?"

My mother clears her throat. "Well, when Geena was younger, we thought she'd become a gymnast, so we didn't really start saving for college until she quit. We started dipping into that account to pay for your lessons and coaches..."

She lets the sentence trail off, and I start to get impatient. "Yeah, but since *I* paid you back, you put that money *back* into her college account, right?"

"Uh, not exactly." Mom's words rush out as she works herself into a frenzy. "I've spent my whole life sacrificing for you kids. When we got that big check from you, I decided to treat myself a little bit. My mommy-makeover surgery cost a pretty penny. And those real hair extensions don't come cheap. Botox for all my appearances, and then I had to have a new car because I can't be pulling up to a television studio in that old jalopy."

When she begins to sob, my temper ignites and I explode, jumping out of the chair.

"*Appearances?* Please! I've seen all your trashy tabloid interviews. And I know you got paid for each one. You wasted *all* that money I gave you on yourself? You didn't put anything into Geena's college fund?"

She continues sobbing into the phone. Martin's eyes grow big, and he whispers, "Oh no!"

My heart feels like it is going to explode out of my chest. It's all I can do not to start cursing my mother. "Does Dad know?"

"I couldn't figure out how to tell him," she whimpers. "Dani, I don't know what to do. Please help me."

I can barely keep myself together, my hand shaking with fury as I clutch the phone. I take a deep breath and try to calm down. "I need to talk to Martin. You are too much! If ever I wondered about your motivations for pushing me into a singing career, I have no doubts now. You have about as much maternal instinct as a great white shark. Your days of cashing in on me are over. I don't want to hear or see you talk about me or say my name in public ever again. And you'd better tell Dad about all this because when I figure out if I can help Geena, I'm talking to him, not you."

Mom instantly switches gears, her hysterical blubbering replaced by her usual steely voice. "Now wait one second, missy. I gave birth to you, and I have every right to talk about you if I damn well please. I'm still..."

I hang up the phone and burst into tears. Martin rushes over and ushers me to the couch. "Oh sweetie, I'm sorry."

The door opens and Jenner comes in. "Martin, what happened?" Jenner hands me a handkerchief.

Martin answers while I blow my nose, completely ruining Jenner's handkerchief. "We just got off the phone with Jodi, and to say the call didn't go well is an understatement."

Jenner drops his briefcase and sits in an armchair. "Tell me everything."

Martin fills Jenner in, and Jenner can't hide his fury when he discovers what my mother has done.

"Is there any way I can pay for part of Geena's tuition?" I say. "It's my fault she's in this mess—it was my lessons my parents had to pay for. It's the least I can do."

Jenner points to me. "This is *not* your fault. Your mother took that money and used it for your lessons. You didn't ask her to do that. You even paid her back, which you didn't have to do and then she turned around and spent that money, *all of it,* on herself. You and Geena are completely innocent in this."

Jenner looks at Martin, who nods in agreement. "But I also think it would be a really nice gesture to pay for Geena's tuition. You certainly can afford it."

Jenner chimes in. "But that money is going into a trust in Geena's name, overseen by Martin and myself. We're not running the risk of this happening again."

"What is it, honey?" Martin looks at me, concerned.

"Well, aside from the fact that my mom is a lying, heartless thief, now I have to tell my dad about the money."

"I'd be happy to reach out to him, explain the situation," Jenner says. "Would that be OK with you?"

I nod.

"It's the least we can do." He reaches across and grabs my hand. "I'm sorry about your mom, Dani. I hope now that everything is out in the open, she realizes what she's done and works hard to fix everything, including your relationship. I'll get the ball rolling on Geena's trust. We're here for you. No matter what happens, you can always count on us."

But rather than comforting me, his words make me hollow inside. *Yeah, we're in it together where money is concerned. But I'm the only one whose mother has just shown her true colors. No one can take that burden away from me or make it better.* I sigh as I climb the stairs to my room, feeling empty and worn out.

25

Alexi stands guard over Martin and me on the white sands of the Fontainebleau's private beach. He looks ridiculous fully clothed and on high alert, but I'm too sad to laugh. After hours in the sun bouncing between listening to an endless loop of the Posse song I have to sing tomorrow, crying, fuming, and being numb, I spend the rest of my day in my suite napping and staring blankly at the television. Martin, Jenner, Regina, and Carlton all take turns hovering around me, trying to cheer me up.

My phone blows up all day with texts from everyone back home. Even Sean texts me a million times, which is about the only good thing to come of this nightmare—at least I know he still cares. I guess Geena spread the word about what happened once Jenner and Martin spoke to Dad. She must be furious. But I don't have the energy to talk to anyone right now, so eventually I turn off my phone.

Exhausted and emotionally spent, I slip into bed without saying goodnight to anyone, trusting someone will wake me up in time to get to the studio tomorrow.

***

Next morning, we take a limo to Criteria Studios, which has a mob of paparazzi and the TrueHarts outside. The crowd blocking the driveway is so thick that studio security has to push them back while the car inches forward, trying not to hit anyone. Jenner is furious. "How the hell did they know we'd be here?"

Alexi curses under his breath and surveys the scene as my hand wanders up to touch the necklace Beau gave me.

Martin heaves a frustrated sigh. "Now do you believe that we've got a leak in our organization, Jenner? We've got to find the rat and get rid of it. Fast!"

Alexi hops out of the car before it stops and scans the courtyard. We're greeted by one of the studio managers, who hustles us inside. The Trent Walker Posse is already warming up in the studio. Jenner shakes hands with their manager, and they make the introductions. It feels super awkward that I'll be singing with men who are twice my age, but they seem friendly enough. Trent is the epitome of a cowboy in his old flannel shirt, scuffed cowboy boots, and shaggy light brown hair peeking scruffily from underneath a worn red Posse trucker hat. He gives me a warm handshake, his Southern drawl slow and easy.

"It's nice to meet you, Dani! I really think this is going to be great for both of us. Not too many people your age know who we are. But with you on one of our tracks, it'll introduce us to a whole new generation of fans."

I blush. "Are you kidding me? You're like my dad's favorite band! I've been listening to you guys forever." I give Trent a squinchy smile. "Do you think maybe I could get your autograph? It would mean so much to my dad."

Trent laughs warmly. "Well, only if you do the same for me! I've got about six nieces who haven't stopped pestering me since they found out we'd be working with you. I don't dare show my face back home unless I get your autograph and a picture or two."

Jenner enters with a duffle bag. "Don't worry, Trent. I brought enough swag for everyone's daughters, nieces, and neighbors. We can have a little autograph sesh when we're finished."

Trent lets out a whoop and rubs his hands together. "Well, let's get to it, then. Don't want to keep those girls waiting!"

We run through the song a few times before we record it, first with me as backup and then with me as lead vocal. My voice isn't as smooth as it normally is, thanks to the crying I did yesterday. But the rough dimension adds something to the sad country vibe of the song, so I just roll with it.

The Trent Walker Posse has been working together for longer than I've been alive. They're so good at what they do that we're able to lock down both versions of the song before seven p.m. We're all exhausted by the end of the day, but we still take time to pose for photos and swap autographs and concert swag.

Martin touches my elbow as we take the last photograph. "Do you want to call your dad and have Trent say hi? I'm sure he'd love it."

I mull it over for a second, my stomach knotting the instant Martin suggests it. "I don't know. I don't want to talk to my mom, and you know she's going to be there."

"Then how about I record a quick video from Trent and send it to him?"

I tip my Trent Walker Posse hat. "You think of everything, Martin. Thanks!"

A few more photos and we're back in the limo, speeding to the airport.

Jenner clears his throat. "Not that I want to spoil you after your complimentary suite at the Fontainebleau, but MEGA's been so pleased with the tour and all the collaborations we've set up that they're sending us to London on a charter plane!"

Exhausted from singing all day, all I can do is grin and give Jenner a double thumbs-up.

We enter Miami airport from a private driveway, pulling up to a small building at the back of the airport. After security, we climb the stairs to a sumptuous Boeing jet that can seat our entire crew. A flight attendant escorts me to the master bedroom, which is outfitted with a large double bed, a marble en suite, and everything I could need on the flight to London.

"Dinner will be served shortly, Miss Truehart." She slides the door closed, and I lay down on the bed in awe. FaceTime rings and Sean's gorgeous face pops up on the screen.

"Lauren told me about your mom. Are you OK?"

We haven't really talked since we said goodbye in New York, and I don't know what to say, so I grimace.

"It's good to see you, Dani. I miss you."

I give him a shaky smile, relieved. "Sorry I didn't call you back yesterday...or in the last couple of weeks. I felt awful after you left New York and didn't really know how to fix things, so I just kept putting off calling you. And then yesterday happened and I really couldn't talk about it. I didn't mean to ignore you." I try to change the subject.

I circle the room with my phone. "Check this out."

Sean laughs. "That's sick."

"I know."

I look at Sean, take a deep breath, and exhale. "Thanks for calling. You're the only thing that's made me feel better."

"I didn't really know what to say after New York, either. But it doesn't matter much now after what your mom did. I'm here for you, Dani. Always."

"Thanks."

"Look, I've got to get to practice, but I just wanted to see how you are. Call me tomorrow. Love you."

"Will do. Love you, too." I say goodbye as the plane lifts off.

26

Martin wakes me around six a.m., and by the time I throw on some jeans and wrangle my hair into a ponytail, the plane is descending into London. I sit down in the main cabin next to Beau, and we look out at a blanket of wet clouds obscuring the city below.

Is he the rat?

The thought dissolves when he tears his eyes away from the window and throws me an excited smile. Every so often there's a break in the clouds, and we catch a glimpse of old buildings dotting the skyline.

"I can't wait to check out the clubs tonight!" Beau says, bouncing up and down in his seat. He grabs my hand and gives it a squeeze. "Have I thanked you lately for giving me this job and letting me see all these fantastic places?" He gives my hand another squeeze and turns back to the view outside.

It can't be him.

I chase the negative thoughts from my mind, latching onto his enthusiasm. "I never thought I'd be traveling the world, either. I mean, I know Mom always had these plans for me. But seeing everything actually happen—it's surreal."

My stomach drops as I suddenly remember all the crap Mom's pulled and how unsettled everything is with her. A lump develops in my throat, and I look out the window again, desperate for distraction.

Green parks, brick buildings, and the winding river look quaint and miniature as we come closer to landing. It feels like we're landing straight into a fairytale.

My phone pings as we land, and it's a message from Kayla.

K: Coming into see the show tomorrow. Have a surprise 4 u!!

Ugh! I stare at my screen, wondering how to reply. With everything going on, the last thing I need is Kayla hanging around. She's fun but she makes everything about herself, and I just don't know if I have the energy for it. But then again, maybe she'll be a nice distraction...

D: surprises. Can't wait 2 see u

I drop my phone into my bag. Watching the hustle and bustle on the tarmac, I realize *I'm in a foreign country! Oh My God!*

Security is quick at the private terminal and while the dancers load onto a sleek black bus, a Mercedes limo whisks Martin, Jenner, Regina, Carlton, Alexi, and me away to the Intercontinental O2 Hotel, which is just steps from the O2 arena where I'll be performing in two days.

I can barely sit still as the streets of London open up before us. Classic stone and brick buildings mix with modern shops and signs. "Oh my God, there's a double decker bus!" I squeal as the bus pulls up next to us. "Do people realize how cool that is?"

Jenner chuckles. "Well, to them it's probably just 'the bus.'"

I'm fascinated as we pass by parks and war monuments, museums, and churches. "Everything is so cool here—all the buildings have such style. It's unreal!"

We finally arrive at the hotel. Crowds of fans and press swarm the sidewalk, their screams penetrating the car as we pass. Hotel security has cleared the driveway for our arrival. I recognize one or two of the TrueHarts who have followed the tour in America, but there's a whole new British contingent, and they seem to have kicked up their royal costumes to the next level! A valet opens the door, and I'm hit with a brisk wind off the river that whips my hair around. The roar from the crowd increases when they see me, and I smile and wave as best I can with a face full of hair.

Jenner glides past us. "It's good to know your fan base is just as strong here as it is back home." He heads to the front desk, trailed by Carlton. They're intercepted by a tall man with a handful of cardboard envelopes. He's trailed by a hefty bald man in a matching suit and a waiter in a white jacket carrying a tray of assorted juices.

"Welcome to the Intercontinental O2 Hotel, Miss Truehart." The men bow.

I smile, taking a glass of orange juice. "Thank you. Your hotel is beautiful." Everyone else grabs a glass, and the waiter leaves.

The men straighten up, beaming. The tall man speaks. "My name is Gerald. I am the general manager of the Intercontinental O2." Indicating the bulkier man in black next to him. "This is Trevor. We are here to serve you throughout your stay. I will be on duty during the day, and Trevor will take over in the evenings. May I take you to your suite?"

As soon as the men turn away, I excitedly whisper, "Another suite?"

Trevor escorts Carlton and Regina into an elevator.

"Guess you're really blowing the socks off of MEGA," Martin says. "The poor dancers are stuck at the Holiday Inn Express—a nice hotel by any standards, but it's no Intercontinental, baby!"

He clinks his juice glass with mine as Jenner calls from the elevator. "Would you like to join us?"

"Sorry!" I squeak, and we rush into the elevator.

My suite is breathtaking, sumptuously decorated in hues of silver and blue, with plush velvet sofas, a glass dining table with mirrored chairs, and accents of wood and silver making the whole room appear decadently art deco in style. Panoramic views of the river and the city stretch out before us from a pair of large picture windows that dominate the lounge area.

An inviting array of breakfast foods are laid out on a black and silver sideboard, along with carafes of tea and coffee and juices. There must be ten flower arrangements scattered around the room, filling the suit with a heavenly scent of roses and lilies.

"Should you need anything during your stay, our office is at your service twenty-four hours a day." Gerald bows as he leaves. Alexi follows him out.

Jenner calls out, "Enjoy breakfast!" To Martin, he adds, "Give me a shout before you leave. I don't want you guys wandering around town without Alexi."

Martin wanders over to the buffet and puts together a plate as I stare down at the city.

"So, what do you want to do first, darlin'?" Martin asks through a mouthful of fruit as he sits down at the dining room table.

I tear my eyes away from the windows. "Everything! I want to ride the tube, see Abbey Road, the Tower of London, Buckingham Palace. Oh, and I want to have high tea! I want to see it all!"

Martin laughs, taking a sip of coffee. "Think I can finish my coffee before we storm the city?"

I roll my eyes dramatically. "I guess."

***

I change into something less conspicuous, abandoning my tiara for a plain black baseball cap, leggings, a t-shirt, and Sean's letterman jacket. Martin calls down to Gerald for some ideas while we wait for Alexi to arrive.

We hop on the tube at the station outside the hotel, and we might have gone unnoticed if it weren't for the three hotel beefy security guards hovering over me on the train. The London Police have to escort us off after a couple of stops because the crowd gets so huge that the train doors won't close. *So much for going incognito!*

Luckily, Alexi arranged a town car to follow the train route in case something like this happened. *I have to give it to the goon: he sure knows his job!*

In the town car, Martin looks pissed. Catching me watching him, he rearranges his face into a pleasant smile and shrugs. "Guess that knocks the double decker bus tour off my list today. Sorry, hon! But we can still see lots of things. We'll just have to outsmart the crowds."

Alexi breaks off from a call and shouts from the front seat, "Working on it. Harrods first."

"Alexi is reaching out to his contacts around town," Martin tells me. "He's getting you backdoor access and special security on all our stops today. We might not be able to hit everything we want this afternoon, but at least you'll get a taste of London."

I groan, frustrated, then realize I owe Martin another dollar. I reach into my jacket pocket, but he shakes his head. "That one's on the house, darlin'. Your frustration is justified today. I thought for sure we had a jump on the groupies by planning everything so last minute. That just proves someone's snitching on us." He nods toward the front seat. "Thank God Jenner brought Alexi on when he did. He'll sniff out the rat eventually."

The city slides by as my stomach churns uneasily when I consider the possibility of Beau selling me out to the press.

Martin looks out the window. "Oh crap." He points at a crowd blocking the front of Harrods, the hulking department store.

Alexi turns around. "When I open the door, step out of the car. Security will shield you with umbrellas, and we'll enter through a side door."

"Your fans are obsessed!" Martin says, incredulous. "I don't know whether to be impressed or scared."

A mix of fear and awe is roiling inside me as I see the TrueHarts swarm the sidewalk, running across the traffic-clogged main road to our car.

"Here we go!" Alexi barks from the front seat.

I pull my baseball down tight over my eyes, wrapping Sean's jacket around me like a suit of armor. Martin slings his messenger bag across his chest, and we get in position.

The car stops. Alexi hops out, snapping open a large black umbrella. He's joined by several more guards with umbrellas who appear out of nowhere. They create a protective pod for me to step into, shielding me from the flash of cameras, but not the intensity of the deafening screams.

I blindly shuffle as best I can, inching my way through the throng.

The whole experience is frightening. I know all these people are here because they love me, but their hysterical screams have me questioning if they want to hug me or rip me apart. The urge to run away is almost primal, and my breath turns ragged as sweat starts to pour down my face.

Finally, we make it inside and security wrestles the doors shut as the screaming mob tries to force their way inside. As the guards fold their umbrellas, I can't help but think how much bad luck I'm causing because of all these umbrellas opened indoors on my behalf. I hope it's not some sort of sign...

Martin puts his arm around me, dabbing my sweaty face with his scarf. "You OK? Should we just go back to the hotel?"

The thought of going back out into the crowd makes me nauseous. "God no, I can't go back out there, not yet." I look around at the dark marbled lobby. "We're already here. Might as well check it out."

Alexi agrees. "That gives me time to plan our exit." I jump as fans outside start banging on the doors, making them rattle and shake. Alexi waves his hand, urging us forward.

A man approaches, his voice as crisp and clipped as his brown hair. He is trailed by a neat young woman dressed in black with a bunch of bags hanging from her arm. "Welcome to Harrods, Miss Truehart." He bows and I smile as best I can. "My name is Claude. I'll escort you through the store. I apologize for the crowds. We thought we were prepared for your visit, but your fans are more exuberant than we anticipated." He waves his hands at the doors. "No matter; with three hundred and thirty departments over seven floors, I am sure we can find a way to fill the time until the crowd disperses." He smiles. "Allow me to show you some of the most interesting aspects of this historic English landmark. Come, let us start at the top with the Salon de Parfums."

He snaps his fingers and his assistant steps forward. She hands Martin and me canvas tote bags with the Harrods signature logo, filled with all kinds of store swag. The assistant tries to hand one to Alexi, but he glares at her.

I lean into Martin as we ride up the escalator in the dazzling Egyptian Hall. "Do we need to buy something? I mean, Claude isn't going to roll out this big reception for me for free, right?"

"Yup. This little spree is good publicity for both of us. Don't feel like you need to go nuts, but a few things won't break the budget." He pulls out a wad of colorful bills and shoves it into my hand. "Jenner gave us this for the day. Shop away."

For the next two hours we tour floor after floor of luxury goods from Alexander McQueen to Olivia von Halle, Channel to Givenchy. The price tags on each item are so astounding that Martin and I make a game of trying to guess the outrageous price on everything. A store photographer snaps photos the entire time.

Every few floors I make a purchase or two—a few t-shirts for Geena and a clutch for Lauren, a Christmas ornament for Grandma. That small list sets me back almost a thousand pounds. *I can't believe Martin let me spend that much!*

It's so nice shopping without the distraction of staring fans and flashing cameras that I'm sad to leave this gargantuan store. Claude escorts us through a maze of hallways that grow shabbier as we pass, ending with a large metal door. We pop out into a small alley where a silver G-wagon awaits, two guards keeping watch for press or fans.

We speed away in secret as my fans still swarm the front of the store. We slip into the swanky Ritz hotel using another of Alexi's secret agent connections and gorge on decadent finger sandwiches and petite desserts at high tea. We take a meandering drive through the city, passing Buckingham Palace, Big Ben, the Tower of London, and many more famous sites. Not as exciting as the double decker bus tour I wanted to take, but much less windy!

Hours later, we're back at the hotel. I get into my jammies and FaceTime Sean.

"Hey you!"

Sean answers as he walks down the hall, school bell ringing in the background. "How's London? I can't believe the TrueHarts mobs. It must be pretty crazy there."

"Yeah, and scary, too. But thank God Alexi's here. After the disaster on the tube, he worked some of his bodyguard voodoo and we dodged the mob for most of the day. I miss you!"

Sean smiles as the bell rings again. "I miss you, too."

The picture shakes. "Hey!" Sean shouts and Zoe's smug smirk fills the screen. "Don't you know Sean has class?"

"Give me the phone." The picture shakes again as Sean grabs the phone. Zoe's fingers trace Sean's chiseled shoulder.

"I'm always looking out for you, Sean. *Someone* has to." She giggles, snaking an arm around his waist. "See ya, Truehart." She blows a wet kiss at the screen and then kisses Sean on the cheek before walking away.

I'm about to erupt when Sean shushes me. "Don't give her the satisfaction of hearing you lose it. She's not worth it."

I take several deep breaths and concentrate on Sean's eyes rather than the red wave of rage washing over me. "Thanks. I don't want her to hear me lose it. But there's nothing I want more than to smack that evil smile off her nasty face. She hasn't stopped trolling me since I left. Have you seen the nasty comments she posted?"

Sean sighs. "Not to change the subject, but I'm totally late for class now. And you know Zoe is telling Ms. Prince that I'm on the phone with you. I'll be lucky if I don't get a detention for cutting class. Call you after school?"

I look at the clock. "It's already almost nine here and I'm dead tired."

"Get some rest. I'll try you tomorrow morning before school."

I blow him a kiss. "Love you."

"Love you, too. Bye."

I toss the phone on the bed and grab the silver framed photo of us that always sits next to my bed. I stare at Sean's face, remembering his strong arms wrapped around me as we took the photo, how good he smelled, how soft his lips were, and my thoughts wander to all sorts of heady and romantic memories as I slip into a blissful sleep, dreaming of Sean.

27

The next morning, I find a gourmet breakfast laid out on the sideboard. Martin is seated at the table in his gym clothes, working his way through an enormous plate of food.

"Morning, darlin'! Breakfast is served."

"Morning!" I fill a plate with eggs and fruit, grab a cup of tea, and sit next to him. "What's planned today?"

"Wuhl," Martin says through a mouthful of food. "Jenner and Carlton are checking out the arena and the new tour buses. Regina's picking up some school supplies, and we've got a quick run through of the show in about an hour. After that, we're free."

"Sounds good!" My phone buzzes with a text from Kayla.

> K: I'm here! When R U free??

Martin looks at me curiously. "It's the middle of the night back home. Who's that?"

I shrug, knowing Martin doesn't care for Kayla all that much. "It's Kayla, wondering what I'm doing."

He grimaces. "Of all the celebrities you have to befriend, you pick the vapid-est one of the bunch and her self-absorbed boyfriend. Honestly, I don't know which one I like less. Once you get past the looks, there's not much there for either of them."

"Hey!" I throw my napkin at him. "That's not the non-judgmental kindness you're always preaching to me."

"Those two are a cautionary tale if I ever saw one. Talk about not be-lieving your own hype. Those two idiots are the poster children for that cause."

Martin gets up to refill his coffee. "Sure am glad they're tied up film-ing in Chicago. I couldn't handle a dose of Kayla right now."

So, I guess I'll wait until Martin's in a better mood to tell him Kayla's in town?

"You OK?" Martin looks at me quizzically. "You seem stressed."

I smile. "I'm fine."

He winks at me. "Finish up and grab your bag. We'll head over when you're ready."

As soon as he leaves, I text Kayla.

D: *Welcome to London! Stuck in rehearsal today.*

She pings me back right away and my heart sinks.

K: *Ugh! Trey won't be here until tomorrow. Guess I'll hit the shops ALONE. Be by later. I'll drag U out if I have to!*

Stress builds in my chest and I abandon my plate of food. My brain whirs, trying to find a way out of this mess. Changed and packed, I long for a solution as I stare at the gray, foggy city below. I grab my bag and leave, hoping for a miracle.

Rehearsal flies by. The scariest and most exciting part is descending from the ceiling in a huge, bejeweled crown to open the show. Though I'm harnessed in, it still sends a terrifying thrill through my body as I look at the stage eighty feet below. It's such a shock that the first few times, I totally forget to sing and miss my cue. But Jenner makes us run it so many times that by the time we're finished, it's old hat.

Rehearsal runs longer than expected. I'm toweling off when I hear a commotion. I look up and see Kayla driving down the arena in a golf cart with Carlton chasing after her. She pulls up to the stage with a screech of tires and hops out. "Dani! Finally!"

She runs up the temporary steps at the front of the stage. "I thought I'd never find you. Thank God I saw Carlton milling around the lobby. He was kind enough to loan me his cart and show me the way." Kayla is runway ready in leather leggings, spiked Louboutins, and a sheer silk tank topped with a classic Channel black and white tweed jacket. Chunky gold jewelry accents her look. She throws her arms around me and kisses my cheeks.

Carlton comes to a sweaty, huffing halt at the foot of the stage. "You left without me, Kayla. Didn't you hear me calling after you?"

Kayla places her hand on her heart. "I did? I had no idea. I'm so sorry." She throws me a secret wink and walks to the front of the stage, bending strategically down, giving Carlton a glimpse down her shirt. He turns purple and looks away. "Please accept my apologies, Carlton."

She straightens up and throws me a devilish smile. I can feel Martin's disapproving glare. "Great to see you. It's so cool you're here!"

Martin chimes in flatly. "Yeah, super cool."

Oblivious, she gives everyone a dazzling smile. "I know, right? Trey had some boring charity appearance to do back in Chicago and can't come until tomorrow, so I thought, why not come to London early and spend some time with D?" She grabs my hand. "There are *so* many places I want to show you. First, we'll go to Floris to create bespoke scents like the royals do, then on to the Asprey flagship store where they're hosting an exclusive viewing of their fall collection just for us. We've got a table at eight at the Chiltern Firehouse for dinner. After that we'll check out Maddox or maybe Bonbonniere for some late-night fun." Kayla takes a breath and wrinkles her nose. "But God, you've got to shower. I can't take you anywhere smelling like that."

Martin steps forward. "I'm sorry, Kayla, but there's no way Dani can go out. She's been rehearsing for the last few hours. She needs to take it easy for the rest of the day." Martin turns to me. "And you know you need to limit your talking before the show tomorrow."

I think it's the first time anyone has ever said no to Kayla. She looks at Martin steadily for a second then bursts out laughing.

I want to melt into the floor and disappear. *This is not going to end well!*

"Dani's not a child, Martin! You can't tell her what to do. If she wants to go out for a few hours after a hard day's work, she has every right to. After all, her name isn't only on the front of the arena, it's on your paycheck as well." She smugly crosses her arms and looks at me. "Looks like someone needs to stay in their lane."

Mortified, I look at Martin, but he doesn't notice me. He is laser-focused on Kayla, and I cringe, waiting for him to start yelling. But instead, he speaks in a cold, clear voice. "Dani may not be a child, but she certainly is not an adult yet, either. I know for a fact those two clubs you mentioned are over twenty-one, so she cannot get in. I'm also *very much* in my lane because I'm Dani's legal guardian and *I* decide what is best for her health and well-being, not you."

Kayla's foot starts tapping angrily as Martin continues. "I have to wonder about the motivation of a twenty-one-year-old wanting to hang out with a sixteen-year-old. All I can guess is that you're bored and want to lead her down a bad path, and I'm *not* OK with that. If you can't respect my rules for Dani, then maybe you should find someone your own age to play with."

Jenner steps forward and places a restraining hand on Martin's shoulder. "Martin's right. Dani can't possibly go to an over twenty-one club. And she does need to rest her voice. But I'd be happy to arrange a spa afternoon for you two or maybe dinner in her suite? I know how much she loves hanging out with you."

Jenner squeezes Martin's shoulder. The look of frustration passing over Martin's face is painful to watch, but he remains silent. Tearing his gaze away from Kayla, he looks at the floor and takes a deep breath.

Kayla's eyes dart angrily from Jenner to Martin. She focuses on Martin, who glances up and meets her stare, looking like he'd like to squash her under his shoe. "I have never been spoken to like that before. How dare you question my intentions toward Dani. If you can't understand all the wonderful things about this girl, then maybe you have no business being her guardian."

She looks to Jenner, takes a deep breath, and flashes a brilliant smile. "I appreciate your offer, but I think I need to take a break from all this. I'll just see you at the concert tomorrow." Her smile snaps off like a light switch and she looks at Martin. "If that's OK with you?"

Martin doesn't take the bait. "Of course. See you tomorrow." He looks at me. "I'll grab our bags and we can go."

Jenner pats Martin on the back and leaves to answer his ringing cell. Kayla turns to me and winks deviously, whispering. "Be ready after the show. I'm busting you out."

"What?" I gasp.

Kayla turns to leave, springing down the steps. "Carlton, be a doll and fix my phone? I can't get the time to change." She tosses her phone at him as she passes, causing him to drop the clipboard he's holding, sending papers flying everywhere. She gets into the golf cart. Carlton abandons his papers, takes a seat in the cart, and taps away at her phone as Kayla peels out. "Ta!" she calls.

Finished with his call, Jenner exhales loudly. "That was a close one! I feel awful pulling Martin back like that because he was one hundred percent in the right. But I don't want to piss off Kayla, so we lose that *Fleetwoods* deal, either. I gotta go talk to Martin."

Jenner leaves and I pray everything blows over.

28

After a trip to the spa, a special room service dinner with dessert, and two movies, Martin is finally calm. At first, I thought he was mad at me, but turns out he's really angry with Kayla and worried that she's a bad influence.

I sleep fitfully that night, dreaming of Kayla stealing me away, Martin losing his temper, and my loyalty torn between them. When Martin shakes me awake the next morning, I'm exhausted, my mind as foggy as the London skyline outside my window. I try to reach out to Sean, Lauren, or Geena, but with the time change, they're all asleep. The sun is barely up, but I have to sit through five hours of Pauline redoing my hair extensions. My head is pounding by the time she's finished.

After lunch, we head to the arena for dance rehearsal and sound check. Before I know it, I'm back into my usual pre-show routine. Pauline throws my hair into a million curls as I cough my way through a cloud of hairspray. She gives me blood-red lips, rhinestone lashes with dramatic red and black eyeshadow and liner, and a cute rhinestone heart below my left eye.

My costume is a dream! It's kind of like one of those sexy Queen of Hearts costumes you'd see at a Halloween store, but a little more age appropriate. The bodice is a shiny red vinyl corset which narrows my waist to next to nothing. Red and black striped capped sleeves and a high, stiff red collar rises from the back of my neck, framing my face almost like the one on an old-fashioned vampire's cape. A micro red tulle skirt with gold hearts peaks out from the front of an overlay, floor-length black vinyl skirt that trails behind me, which will be removed for the second half of the show. Fingerless red and black arm cuffs go up to my elbows while black-and-white-striped stockings speckled with red and black sequins go past my knees. I'm wearing red bejeweled Mary Jane shoes, and the whole look is finished with a tiny, whimsical gold jeweled crown attached to a headband.

I'm busy checking myself out when there's a knock on the door. "Come in!" I holler, quickly spinning 'round.

Martin comes in. "All hail the queen! You look great, darlin.'"

Another knock at the door and Carlton enters with a gorgeous bouquet of flowers. I gasp. "Oh wow! Who are they from?"

Carlton artfully steps out of my way. "I'm sorry, Dani, but these are for Martin." Martin stands up with a look of surprise and buries his face in roses and lilies. "Me?"

I smile. "Aww, Brett is so romantic!" I sigh wistfully. "I wish Sean would send me flowers."

Martin chuckles. "That's one of the many perks of dating a man with a job." He fishes the card out and his smile fades. "Hmm."

He holds out the card to me and I grab it. "These are from Kayla?"

"Yeah. Apologizing for her outburst yesterday, blaming it on jetlag and PMS." He tosses the bouquet onto a chair and sniffs.

I give him a sidelong look. "OK, fine! It was a nice gesture, and she owned her crap, so I guess it's fine." I keep staring at him. "All right! I'll text her a thank you. Jeez, are you happy now?"

I clap. "Yes!"

Martin grudgingly picks up his phone and starts tapping. He makes a face when he hits send.

I pull a little baby face, all big eyes and pouty lips, imitating Kayla talking to Trey. "Thank you Mawtin!"

"Oh God, don't start with that!"

I laugh as Carolina's voice crackles over the intercom. "Twenty minutes!"

Martin stands. "OK, just enough time for a quick love huddle with the dancers before you get strapped into that flying crown. You're going to blow London's mind!" He slaps me a high five as we enter the corridor.

***

I know I keep saying it, but *tonight* really was the best show yet! The crowd went nuts when I floated down from the ceiling during the opening song. The stunt went off without a hitch, and it really set the mood for the whole show. Three encores later—and yes, I even dragged Martin out for the first one—I'm on cloud nine, soaring on the energy from the audience.

Back in my dressing room, Martin and I are gushing over the performance when there's a knock on the door. "Come in!" I shout. Kayla rushes in, decked out for a night of clubbing, and tackles me in a hug.

"Oh my God, you were on fire!" She jumps up and down, her off-the-shoulder sequined mini-dress threatening to fall right off, so I pull it up and stop her from jumping again.

Trey calls from the doorway. "Impressive, Dani." His eyes take me in. The way they linger on my body rather than my face makes me flash hot. Kayla doesn't seem to notice, but I catch Martin noticing and he's fuming.

"Uh, thanks, Trey," I say uncomfortably.

Martin clears his throat. "Thanks again for the flowers, Kayla. I'm sorry to rush you out, but Dani's got to get on the bus to Manchester. So..."

His words trail off and Kayla smiles. "Of course. I don't want to keep you guys. She turns to me. "I just wanted to stop in and say thanks for the tickets."

"Tickets?" I say. "Did I give you tickets?"

"Duh, of course. Carlton hooked me up. Remember Jenner said he'd give me tickets any time I wanted?"

Martin flinches as Kayla continues. "I won't be able to make Paris, but Madrid is looking pretty good." As she gives me a hug, she whispers. "Leave the door unlocked."

She blows Martin a kiss before sailing out of the room. "Ta!"

Trey looks me up and down once more and smirks. "See ya, Dani."

Following Kayla out, he glances back. "Martin."

Martin shakes his head. "That little leech is going to expect tickets for every stop on this tour!" He picks up his bag. "I'm heading to the bus. Alexi will escort you when you're ready. Muah." He blows a kiss as he leaves, shutting the door behind him. I flop onto the couch, waiting for Petra to come get me out of my costume.

A few minutes later, the doorknob rattles and I jump to open it. "Pet..."

Kayla shushes me and shoves me inside, closing the door. "I saw Petra coming down the hall and sent her to get your sweatpants. Trey is distracting your bodyguard, so we've got to get out of here, like, right now!"

I yank my arm out of Kayla's grasp. "I can't go! We're leaving for Manchester tonight." I wave a hand at my costume. "And it's not like I blend in with this outfit. I can't even get out of it without Petra. It's all laced up in the back."

Kayla looks at the back and groans. "We don't have time for this crap." She taps her foot on the ground. "*Think, Kayla.*"

My heart races as Kayla wanders the room, grumbling to herself. "Aha!" She grabs a bathrobe and towel. "Here, put this on." I argue with her as she wrestles me into the oversized robe and takes off my crown and wraps my hair in the towel.

I glance at myself in the mirror. "Now I'm just a jackass in a bathrobe."

Kayla smiles. "*Now* you're a superstar looking for a shower since yours doesn't work. We saw an empty dressing room down the hall across from an exit. Tell your guard you're going to use the one in there." She drags me toward the door. "Let's go."

Everything's going too fast for me to think.

Kayla steps out into the hall, shouting loudly. "Guess I left my phone at the hotel. See you, Dani." She calls down the hall. "Come on, Trey."

Trey hustles past.

I pop my head out into the hall. Alexi raises an eyebrow.

"My shower isn't working. I'm going to use the one down the hall. Be out in a few minutes."

Alexi nods and resumes scanning the hallway.

I walk as casually as I can, trying not to trip on the trailing bathrobe. When I round the corner, I see Kayla waiting at an open door. She waves me over, pulling me through and closing it as quietly as possible. Outside the arena, she pushes me into a waiting golf cart with Trey at the wheel. Trey whisks us away down a small path to a road that runs along the River Thames.

Once we're away from the arena, Trey asks, "So why all the cloak and dagger routine?" He looks in the mirror and fixes his hair. "This all a bit too double-oh-seven for me."

Kayla smiles sweetly at Trey. "I promised Dani a night out on the town, and Martin absolutely refused!" Kayla grins at me. "So, I busted her out for a few hours."

Trey slams on the brakes and we all slide forward in our seats. "Jenner's going to have the entire London Police Department looking for Dani. Unless we're spotted by the paparazzi first. How stupid are you, Kayla?"

Kayla pats Trey's cheek condescendingly. "Jenner's not going to tell a soul that Dani's missing. It won't be good PR for him *or* her if word gets out that he's lost control of his underage star and she's sneaking out at night. Trust me, I've thought this through. Drive another hundred feet and see what I mean."

Trey turns to look at me, furious. "Are you OK with this? Jenner and Martin are going to kill you."

Fear and excitement mix in my stomach and the rush of such an amazing show is still pulsing in my veins. "I know I'm going to be crucified over this, but dammit, I'm sixteen! I never get to do anything like this." I take the towel off my head and shake out my hair. "Let's go!"

Kayla lets out an ecstatic whoop. Trey shrugs, resigned. "Who am I to argue?"

After a minute, Kayla shouts, "Stop!"

As we get out, I start to untie my robe, but Kayla stops me. "You might want to keep that on." She grabs my hand and drags me down a pier ramp. Waiting at the dock is a beautiful wooden speedboat, sleek and elegant, its engine purring in the moonlight.

Glancing at Kayla, I gasp. "Are you kidding me?"

"Chartered just for you! Best way to avoid the London paparazzi. All aboard!"

Kayla graciously takes the captain's hand as he helps her onto the boat. I look at Trey, who offers me his hand to help me board. His other hand grazes my waist, and I feel a jolt of electricity. He boards and snuggles up to Kayla, making me think that the stress of sneaking out has my imagination working on overdrive.

A deckhand unties the boat, and we pull away from the dock. "To the club!" Kayla shouts and lets out a whoop as she snaps our picture. The engine roars to life and we snake our way through the city, the wind whipping our hair. I wrap my robe around me, grateful for the warmth.

29

Just as I'm about to turn into an icicle, we pull up to another dock. Shivering, we run up the pier into a waiting limousine. Trey cranks up the heat. As we slowly thaw out, I try to detangle my windblown hair.

Kayla reaches into her bag and, smiling wickedly, pulls out my crown and puts it on. "Now who's the queen of hearts?" She laughs, admiring herself in a mirror she pulls down from the ceiling.

My heart clenches, seeing my beautiful tiny crown on Kayla's head. Petra spent hours customizing it to match my costume perfectly. "Oh my God, I'm going to get into so much trouble if anything happens to that. Please be careful!"

Kayla pays no attention and continues to primp in front the mirror. "Not any more trouble than you're already in, sweetie. Besides, Petra probably has like twenty of these things. I'm sure she won't mind if I took this one."

Kayla's callous attitude is shocking. I start to feel sick. "I don't know if this is such a good idea. Maybe I'd better have Martin pick me up."

I reach into the robe pocket for my phone and realize I left it back in the dressing room. I start to panic. "Kayla, can I borrow your phone?"

Annoyed, she takes out a tube lip gloss. "What, so you can call Martin? No way. We haven't even gotten to Tableau yet. I had to pull strings to get a VIP table on such short notice." She points her lip gloss wand at me. "I don't appreciate you trying to bail on me before you've even seen the place. I've got a two-thousand-dollar bar minimum I need to meet tonight, so don't expect to run back home to Martin any time soon."

I look at Trey for help, but he looks out the window, refusing to meet my eye. After a few uncomfortable minutes, he finally speaks. "Look, Kayla, just let her go. The car can drop us off and take Dani back to the arena. I'll help you with the bar tab. You can't make Dani go if she doesn't want to."

Jamming her lip gloss back into her purse, Kayla slams the ceiling mirror closed. "Fine!" Her glare is so filled with rage, I'm a little scared. "I can't believe I spent hours planning a fun night out, and you've spent the whole time whining about getting into trouble." Kayla says the last few words in a high-pitched baby voice, making me flash hot with embarrassment. "You're not as mature as I thought you were, Truehart." Disgust transforms her face into an ugly mask. "Serves me right for trying to hang out with a high schooler."

"Easy, Kayla!" Trey lays a placating hand on Kayla's tanned shoulder. "Dani doesn't know how much work went into all of this. And if you really wanted Dani to have a carefree night, you would have made sure she didn't have to sneak out. It's not her fault. She's not used to stuff like this."

I give Trey a grateful smile as he continues. "Try to remember what it was like to be sixteen. You weren't always the power-clubber you are now. Remember the first time we snuck out to a club? You were practically in tears when your mom called you and made you come home."

Kayla's face softens. "I got grounded for a month." She sighs. "Yeah, I guess you're right."

She gives me a contrite look. "Sorry, Dani. Guess I got carried away. I'm just disappointed. This place is really off the chain, and I wanted to be the one to show it to you."

Relief floods my body. "I'm sorry, Kayla. I thought I'd be cool with it, but I'm really stressing out. I can totally pay you back for whatever you spend tonight."

Kayla waves her hand. "It's fine. Two bottles of champagne and a few appetizers and I'll meet the minimum." She sighs again. "We would've had a good time."

The limo stops in front of an old brick building with fancy scroll work over the arched doorway. The windows on the first few floors are covered with curtains. I can feel the music pulsing through the limo's windows. A line of people in club gear snakes down the sidewalk. Two burly, suited men guard the entrance.

"Wow, this place looks incredible." I feel a wistful tugging in my stomach. "Wish I could see inside."

Trey gets out of the car.

Kayla nods. "I know. It's a trip."

Trey pops his head back in. "Why don't you just do a quick walk through? Five minutes."

My mind races. I glance again at all the people tricked out in short, tight dresses, leather pants, and wild makeup. Kayla smiles encouragingly, and I feel pressure as the seconds tick past, knowing I have to decide.

"Um." *I should really go back. Martin's going to kill me as it is.*

A blast of electronica hits us as the door opens and three girls clad in skimpy dresses enter the club. I can't take my eyes off of the door, which seems to beckon me inside. *If I'm already in a lot of trouble, how much more can I get into if I just take a peek?*

I look at Kayla. "Five minutes."

She squeals and grabs my hand. "Yay! We'll have you back to Martin in no time. He won't even know you're gone!"

When we step out of the limousine, the line erupts in screams and flashing lights as everyone whips out their phones and starts snapping photos.

I wave at the crowd as we walk to the front door. One of the guards stops us, eyeing me. "That bird's not twenty-one."

Kayla smiles sexily and touches the guard's arm. "Technically, no, but she's just here for a peek. She just played a sold-out show at the O2, she's still wearing her costume! With all the hype she'll bring this place, you'd be a fool to turn her away."

The guard eyes me doubtfully, taking in my costume and windblown hair. Kayla shows him her phone and a TMZ article about my latest show. His eyes grow big, and he steps out of the way. Trey leads us inside.

It takes a few minutes for my eyes to adjust to the red lighting and the dizzying black-and-white-striped stairwell that leads up into the club. Upstairs, the vibe is like a nightmarish circus with a rainbow of lights providing more shadow than illumination. People in masks and wild clown makeup are dressed in everything from designer dresses and suits to athletic wear and costumes. Scantily clad girls in bright wigs parade through the crowd holding bottles of alcohol above their heads, flaming sparklers attached to the bottle tops. Neon signs, fun house mirrors, and circus posters cover the old brick walls. A fog of smoke, perfume, and the cloying aroma of cotton candy hang in the air, mixing with the heavy bass of electronica music making the atmosphere feel thick as I push through the crowd. Trey leads us to a roped-off alcove where a purple velvet booth faces the room. We sit down and a tall man in a black suit with slicked back blond hair immediately approaches.

"Miss Spencer, Mr. Connors. Lovely to see you again. Miss Truehart, welcome to Tableau."

I scan the scene, picking out the most random visions I could ever imagine: a goth ballerina in old fashioned aviator goggles sitting on a mushroom-shaped bar stool, a man in satin shorts and robe shadow boxing in a corner, burlesque dancers languidly oozing across the catwalk in the center of the club. It's hard to tell the performers from the customers. My costume seems tame in comparison.

Kayla smiles. "Thank you, Rolt. The crowd looks good tonight. Can you bring us over a bottle of Dom and a peach cooler?"

"Oh no, I can't stay!" I interject.

Rolt looks at Kayla, who smiles sweetly and nods her head. He hurries away.

"I know. Just a few minutes, then we'll get you on your way. Promise."

I groan, trapped in between Trey and Kayla in the booth. Rolt returns with a tray of glasses, followed by a waitress holding a flaming bottle of champagne above her head. The crowd oohs and ahhs, snapping photos as she pops the cork.

I hold out my hand as the girl starts to pour me a glass. "I don't drink!"

Kayla laughs. "That's why I got you a peach cooler." She hands me a tall glass with a sprig of mint floating on top. "Try it."

I hesitate, then take the glass, knowing she'll never let me leave if I don't at least take a sip. I bring it to my lips. "You're sure there's no alcohol in here?"

She smiles and crosses her heart. "Promise."

I take a sip. *It's delicious!* Cool and refreshing, like the taste of summer in this suffocating, tightly packed club. I take a deep drink and smile, feeling relaxed and a little heady. "Wow, that *is* good! Thanks, Kayla."

We clink glasses and sip our drinks as we watch the scene around us. Kayla snaps a million selfies. Before I know it, I've finished my juice, and Rolt places another one in front of me.

"I really should go." I smile at him, but he steps away as if he doesn't hear. Kayla's busy scrolling on her phone and Trey is talking on his. I sip my drink, waiting for them to finish.

A song comes on that I love, and it's never sounded *so good* as right this second! All of a sudden, I just *have* to dance. I grab Kayla. "This song is the *best!* Come on!"

I slurp down the rest of my drink and we get up to dance next to our table. A crowd gathers. I'm having the best time as the room spins around us. Camera lights flash, and I feel incredible! *I can't believe I was even worried about coming tonight!*

I close my eyes, swaying to the music, my head buzzing as Kayla steps away. She returns with Rolt trailing behind her, another peach cooler in hand. She hands it to me.

"Feel like singing a quick song? Rolt said he'd comp us the night if you do?"

"Really?" I jump up and down, spilling peach juice everywhere.

"Easy there, twinkle toes." Kayla laughs as Rolt hands her his hand-kerchief. She pats me dry. "So, you up for it? You can just sing over your normal track."

"Shure, I can doo thaa!" My words seem to come out slower than my mind anticipates. My lips feel numb and tingly. I press them together and give Kayla a lazy smile. "Thaan you woulgn't haf to pay fur yur baar taab." I down what's left in my glass and hand it to Kayla. "Let's gooo!"

Rolt ushers us over to the stage. A blinding spotlight comes on and he announces me. The club erupts in cheers that seem too loud and Kayla shoves me toward the stage. I trip up the steps, take the mic from Rolt, and smile at the crowd. My whole body feels slow and weightless, like I'm moving through water; my tongue feels dry and thick.

"Hello, Lond'n!" My words slur as I make my way downstage. A faint realization comes to my mind that I have no idea what I'm supposed to sing, but before I can grasp that thought, the DJ starts playing "My Place" and the crowd roars. Muscle memory takes over and I automatically stumble through dance steps as I sing. Sweat pours off me and my head starts to pound as I finish. I bow and the whole room spins. I swallow back bile that creeps up my throat. I wobble to standing and Kayla jumps onstage, waving to the crowd as she guides me off.

"I don feel sho good," I slur to Kayla and she takes my hand.

"Let's get you in the car."

Rolt clears a path for us. It's all I can do to put one foot in front of the other and I start to sink to the floor. *I just need to sit down for a minute.*

Strong arms wrap around my shoulder and waist. I flop my head over to see Trey helping me walk. I have to close my eyes so I don't throw up in the crazy striped stairwell.

"I don know wha's wrong wit me...I mus haf the flu."

Rolt snorts. "It's not the flu, babes, it's four peach coolers."

Outside, the driver opens the door as Trey lifts me into the limo. I try to smile and wave as cameras flash. He hands me a cold bottle of water and steps aside, closing the door. I struggle with the cap on the bottle, but finally give up and let it roll to the floor.

"You said it was juss fru juice." I turn to Kayla and discover that I'm alone in the car. I try to figure out where Kayla is as the city lights slip by in a nauseating blur. It seems like ages before we pull up to the hotel.

The valet has to hoist me out of the car. I weave my way to the front door, almost missing it and slamming into the glass wall. I hear faint shouts coming from behind me and camera lights strobe, adding to my queasiness.

"Miss Truehart!" I see a chubby guy in a black suit running toward me. *Wha's his name?* He snaps his fingers at the desk clerk. "Call Mr. Redman, NOW!"

They guide me into the elevator and hold me up as we speed up to my suite. My stomach flips and cramps. I must have fallen asleep because my eyes fly open when the elevator bell dings and the doors open. Martin, Jenner, and Alexi are waiting, looking angry as hell. I try to speak, but all that comes out of my mouth is four glasses of peach cooler mixed with my chicken dinner, soaking Martin's pajamas. He jumps back, cursing, and I feel instantly ashamed.

Tears stream down my face, but I can't seem to talk, just vomit. Alexi picks me up and races to the bathroom. He props me up in front of the toilet, where I continue to heave. Someone ties back my hair. The sickly sweet-sour taste of peach juice keeps me retching long after my stomach is empty. Exhausted, I rest my cheek on the seat of the toilet, unable to hold up my own head. I don't even have the energy to be disgusted that I'm using a toilet seat as a pillow.

30

I wake up hours later wrapped around the base of the toilet, shivering and achy from sleeping on the marble floor. My head's pounding like someone's taken a sledgehammer to it. I try to sit up, but the room spins so much I have to close my eyes and grab onto the toilet to keep from falling over. A tiny groan escapes my lips. The acrid taste of bile and peach juice coat my mouth.

"Morning, sunshine." Martin calls all too loudly from the bathtub where he's made a nest of blankets and pillows. I flinch, running a gummy tongue over my dry lips. He pulls out his ear buds and switches off his tablet. "How you feeling?"

It takes every last ounce of energy I have to whisper, "Like I want to die."

Martin squints at me, disgusted. "Serves you right." He sighs, gets out of the tub, and helps me up. "No sense in lecturing you now when you're too hungover to listen. As it is, you're going to be paying the price with that hangover."

I catch a glimpse of myself in the mirror. I look hideous. My costume is covered in vomit, the tulle skirt is torn, the collar is irreparably bent, and one sleeve hangs by a thread. My makeup is smeared, there's vomit in my hair, and my fishnets are all torn up.

Martin meets my eyes in the mirror, disappointment and anger staring me down. "I know you feel like crap, but that'll pass. In the meantime, get showered and changed. You can sleep on the bus. We've got to catch up to Jenner in Manchester."

I shake my head, which causes the room to spin again. I grab the counter as saliva pools in my mouth. "I can't perform tonight."

"You can, and you will. We're not losing hundreds of thousands of dollars because you can't hold your liquor. You want to party like a rock star, you're gonna have to pay the price."

Martin loosens my corset from the back. "You should be able to manage from here. Your clothes are on the chair."

He slams the door, and it takes me a long time to slip out of my ruined costume. I stand under the hot water, letting the steam revive me. Vague snatches of the night before flash before my eyes, but nothing makes much sense. After entering Tableau, everything is a blur. It's an unsettling feeling.

Thoughts swirl in my head as I get dressed. I'm clean but still feel dirty, ashamed of what happened even though I don't remember much. I move slower than usual, disoriented from the dizziness. I pack up my toiletries, gather my costume, trying not to get any vomit on myself, and walk into the living room where Alexi and Martin are waiting. Martin hands me a sports drink and two aspirin.

"This will help your headache." He grimaces as he takes my soiled costume and shoves it into a garbage bag. "How's your throat?"

I wince as I swallow the aspirin. "Raw. I hope I'm not getting sick."

"You barf for four hours, you're bound to have a sore throat. You might not be at your best, but you'll make it through."

He hands me the garbage bag and a pair of large sunglasses. We proceed downstairs in uncomfortable silence. There are no bowing staff members as we leave the hotel, and I can't help but feel that everyone but me knows what I fool I made of myself last night.

Outside, a crowd of press and fans scream. My head pounds as I attempt an energetic smile and wave. We climb onto the bus, and Martin hands me a bag of fast food. "This should soak up anything left in your system. After that, sleep. I'll wake you up when it's time to get ready."

No tour of the new bus, no excitement about the next series of concerts in new countries...I feel like this leg of the tour has started out cursed. I make my way to my room. This one is all dark wood and gold detail rather than the sleek gray and silver color palette of the last bus, but other than that, it looks exactly the same with all my things perfectly in place.

I flop onto the bed and reluctantly tear open the bag. At first, I don't think I can eat, but before long, the double burger, fries, and soda are gone, as is my sports drink. I down a few more glasses of water and feel less sick. I drift off into a troubled sleep, wishing I'd just stayed home last night.

***

I wake up and I make my way into the kitchen. I grab a bottle of water from the fridge and sit down at the table. Martin unfolds himself from his bunk and stretches.

"Feeling better?" he asks as he fills the kettle with water and turns on the stove.

"Yes, thank you. Everything you told me to do really helped." I pause, not knowing where to begin. Martin grabs two mugs and a box of green tea. He slices a lemon and minutes slide by, uncomfortably silent.

As the kettle whistles, he sighs and pours water in the mugs. "So, what do you have to say for yourself?" He brings the mugs over and sits across from me.

I swallow the lump forming in my throat. "I am so sorry, Martin. I never meant for that to happen. Kayla promised me it was just juice. I told everyone there that I don't drink. I'm so furious! I can't believe she lied to me!"

Nothing I say changes the hard look on his face. "You believe me, right? None of this is my fault. I didn't do anything wrong."

"I believe that you didn't order that drink or intend to get drunk. But you most definitely did do something wrong. You snuck out in a foreign country with two adults whom you barely know. You freely went into a club meant only for adults, where, yes, Kayla tricked you into drinking alcohol. But she could never have done that if you hadn't chosen to be there in the first place."

I shake my head, frustrated. "But I didn't want to go to that club. After we got off the boat, I kind of freaked out in the limo..."

He holds up a hand, interrupting me. "*When* were you on a boat?"

I flinch. "Uh, that's how we snuck away from the arena and avoided the paparazzi...which is pretty genius if you think about it." Martin doesn't seem impressed, so I rush on.

"The boat took us to a limo that drove us to the club. In the limo, I started to feel guilty about sneaking away. Kayla got mad when I said I wanted to go back the arena. Trey convinced me to stay for five minutes, and then Kayla gave me the drink and..."

My words trail off as Martin drums his fingers angrily on the table. "Did Kayla tie you up and carry you out of the arena?"

I whisper, "No."

"Didn't you dress in a robe and tell Alexi your dressing room shower was broken and that you were going down the hall to shower?"

Damn. "Um, yeah, but..."

Martin glares at me and waits.

My voice tiny. "Yes, I did."

"And did you know what Kayla had planned before she stopped by after the show yesterday?"

"No!" I say loudly.

Martin's eyes bore into me. I feel so guilty that I blurt out the truth. "OK, I didn't know *exactly* what she had planned, but I knew she wanted to take me out."

Martin gets up and grabs a plastic bag from the front of the bus. "Open it," he demands as he drops it on the table. I pull out stacks of magazines and newspapers with images of me from the night before dancing with Kayla, stumbling on the Tableau stage, falling down outside the limo. I look like a hot mess, and you can totally tell I'm drunk. Shame flashes hot over my body.

He thrusts his phone at me. Twitter and Instagram are full of photos and videos of me stumbling on stage, being carried out of the club, incoherent. There are hundreds of memes, all cruel, pathetic, and demeaning. The worst are the photos Kayla posted on her IG. *How could she betray me like that?* Tears spring up and blur the barrage of nasty comments, but words like "drunk," "jailbait," and "slut" still manage to swarm before my eyes. I shove the phone away. I feel so ashamed.

"I had no idea..."

"What? That anyone *noticed*? That they weren't all too happy to share pictures and videos of the hottest underage pop star today making a jackass out of herself, drunk at a club? That your dear friend Kayla would post all these photos?" He picks up the magazines and shakes them. "You're better than this, Dani! This isn't who you are! But now this one moment in time will be out there *forever*."

I cover my face and start to cry. Martin exhales, cursing under his breath. He gets up and sits next to me, putting his arm around me. "I'm sorry I lost my cool, OK?"

"No, you're right to get mad. You and Serena warned me about stuff like this for months, and then I go and do exactly what you told me not to. I'm such an idiot."

Martin gently wipes my tears away. "You're not a *total* idiot." I look up, shocked. "You're a teenager who just wanted to have a little fun. Everyone makes boneheaded decisions at your age. But unfortunately, the whole world is watching you, kiddo. Your fans are not just going to cheer your successes. They're also going to point and laugh when you mess up."

He shoves the pile of tabloids away. "It's not the end of the world. But you're definitely going to have to lay low for a while. And I'm taking away your phone for a month."

"What!"

He gives me a stern look. "If you did this at home, Jodi would skin you alive ten ways 'til Sunday. You're getting off easy. You can still Face-Time or text and use my phone while I supervise."

"Fine," I huff. Martin flashes an angry look and I lower my head, chastised. "Sorry."

"And it goes without saying that Kayla and Trey are off limits. You'll still do your guest appearance on *The Fleetwoods*, but there'll be no socializing. Got that?"

I nod.

Martin squeezes my shoulder and gets up, pushes the tabloids back into the bag, and shoves the bag into the trashcan under the sink. "Now I get the fun task of calling your parents and breaking the news to them. Thanks for *that*!"

I wince. "Oh God, Martin, I'm sorry. Let me talk to my dad. I'll explain it wasn't your fault."

Irritation passes over Martin's face, but he catches himself and takes a deep breath. "But Dani, it *is* my fault. I'm responsible for you. You snuck out on my watch. I have to convince your parents I'm not totally incompetent and that you're not on the brink of losing everything to drugs and drink." He walks to the front of the bus.

I go get my phone. I see a bunch of texts from Sean, Geena, and Lauren and I'm actually relieved I don't have to deal with them. I check a text from a number I don't recognize and instantly regret it when I see it's from Zoe.

Z: *This one's my fav*

It's a meme of me leaving the club, Trey struggling to hold me up. I look hideous—my eyes are half-closed, and I'm sweaty and drunk. The caption reads: "Another reason to stay in school, kids."

Humiliation complete.

I turn off my phone and force myself to listen while Martin speaks with my parents. I can hear Mom raging, but Martin takes it all in, letting her vent. After a while, he waves me over. I hand him my cell as I take his. "It's your dad."

Nervously, I put the phone to my ear. "Hi, Dad."

"Oh Dani, we're so disappointed."

Tears stream down my face again. "I'm sorry. It was stupid. I swear I just meant to have fun hanging out. I don't drink, honest."

"Martin explained how your friend tricked you. Though, to me, she doesn't sound like much of a friend."

Mustering up my courage, I finally ask the dreaded question. "How pissed is Mom?"

"She's terribly upset and embarrassed. The phone's been ringing off the hook with everyone wanting an interview about our drunk daughter. But she's standing by you and explaining how it was just a mistake." I roll my eyes, knowing my mother is probably overjoyed at the flurry of new interviews.

Dad continues. "If it happens again, we're going to have to consider bringing you home. Understand?"

My stomach drops. "I didn't think this would cause so much trouble. I can't believe this is happening." A fresh round of tears streams down my face.

"I hate to break it to you, Dani, but this isn't just a bad piece of luck that happened to you. This is all the result of the choices you've made. This doesn't have to be an issue if it doesn't happen again."

My tears subside, and I wipe my nose on my sleeve. "OK. I love you, Dad."

"Love you, too, Dani."

I hand Martin the phone, and he pockets it. "Let's go. Sound check time."

I wail. "I don't want to go out there. Everyone knows what happened last night."

Martin puts his arm around me as we exit the bus. "You've got a little walk of shame coming your way over the next few hours, but you'll survive. There's not one adult out there that hasn't been in your shoes. We've all just been lucky not to have it splashed across the tabloids."

I flinch. "Thanks for reminding me."

***

I feel awkward as hell when I enter the arena, but no one points and laughs at me. I get a few sympathetic smiles from the crew, but for the most part, it's business as usual at sound check. My voice is rough, and the high notes are a challenge. It's obvious tonight won't be my best show. Jenner approaches me as we wrap it up, looking serious and tired.

"Looks like last night has taken its toll."

I take the hot tea with honey Carlton hands me. "I'm sorry. It was stupid to..."

Jenner's face softens. "Martin filled me in. And it looks like you're already feeling pretty low about it, so we'll leave it at that for now. Martin said he spoke with your parents. You understand nothing like this can happen again?"

"Yes, I know."

"OK, then let's put this behind us. I've issued a press release that you had a bad reaction to some cold medicine last night, which should explain your behavior and cover any vocal imperfections in your performance tonight. I've spoken to Kayla and Trey's agents who are more than willing to back that story since it was Kayla who spiked your drinks and Trey is only nineteen and shouldn't have been drinking, either. They've already done some damage control on their end, and now it looks to everyone that you had an allergic reaction to OTC cold medicine. Disaster averted."

The tightness in my chest eases for the first time all day. But I pause when I see Jenner's steely look.

"Just because you dodged a bullet this time doesn't let you off the hook. We'll be watching you like a hawk from now on. Make sure this doesn't happen again, OK?"

My happiness moves down a notch. "I promise, Jenner."

I follow Martin offstage to my dressing room, trying to look appropriately sheepish.

I'm grateful Pauline ignores the elephant in the room and starts to work on my hair as soon as I enter. Petra helps me get dressed and brushes off my apology about trashing my costume. An identical costume to the one I wore last night hangs on the rack, ready for me to wear. *Crisis averted! My reputation is still intact, and no one seems to be too angry. As mad as I am at Kayla, I'm grateful she and Trey helped me fix this. It could have been a lot worse.* Only a tiny nagging feeling of guilt reveals the truth of how royally I screwed up last night. I take a deep breath and exhale slowly, trying to shake it off.

31

Looking like a carbon copy of last night but feeling like a shadow of myself, I sit on a huge gold and red throne backstage, waiting for the video package to roll. "Sounds like you had quite the adventure last night, rock star!" Beau elbows me playfully. I wince, grateful for the darkness that hides my burning cheeks.

"You wouldn't have thrown up on my watch. I'd never let you get that sloppy." He winks.

"Uh, thanks, I guess. But trust me, that whole scene won't be happening again. Jenner and Martin have me on lockdown, and my parents are threatening to pull me off tour if it does."

"Yeah, right. Like MEGA's going to let your *mom and dad* kill the cash cow that's raking in millions of dollars." He gives me a wry look, his features eerily highlighted by the dim blue stage safety light. "Not likely. They might talk a big game, but trust me, you could steal a car, rob a bank, or slap the president of the United States and you'd still find yourself on stage at curtain time."

Before I can respond, the video package rolls and the dancers scurry into position. As the music for "My Place" starts, the platform my throne is on spins around, revealing me to the audience. Still weighed down by the effects of last night, the stage lights are blinding rather than dazzling; I'm off my game. I sound throaty, like I've smoked a carton of cigarettes. My voice is coarse and the notes hard to sustain. I catch Beau give me a concerned look as I cross the stage for my first big vocal sequence.

I step forward and instead of unleashing the usual run of notes that ends in the ear-splitting "high C" that I've become famous for, my voice falters and I practically croak into the mic. I quickly switch to a lower octave and try to cover, but it's obvious to everyone with working ears that I've majorly screwed up. The change in the audience's vibe is palpable, but I do my best to soldier on, skipping upstage for the lift that ends the number. I catch looks of shock and pity from the dancers as I leap into their arms and manage to sing the last phrase of the song without incident as they lift me over their heads. I raise my arm with a flourish and smile more triumphantly than I feel. The applause from the audience is weak, certainly not the raucous cheering I'm used to. I shake my head as the dancers lower me back to the stage.

"What was that?" I shrug my shoulders and get a small laugh from the audience as I walk to the front of the stage. "I'm sure by now you've all heard I had a little cold yesterday. But I'm not going to let that stop me from putting on the amazing show you deserve." The crowd cheers loudly, and I feel encouraged. "So, if you can be patient with me, I'm going to make sure you enjoy yourselves tonight, despite my sore throat. Because you, Manchester, are totally worth it!"

The crowd roars to life and I hold my mic up to their cries, grateful they haven't given up on me. Part of me gets caught up in the applause and starts to believe that I really *did* have a cold last night and that I'm actually doing something heroic by performing.

I glimpse Jenner looking grim offstage, which brings me down to reality a little. Martin gives me an encouraging thumbs up. Carlton shuffles onstage with a mug of hot water and honey. I take a sip, which helps my raw throat.

I hand the mug back to Carlton, who places it on a stool on the side of the stage. "OK, Manchester, let's get this party started!" The crowd cheers again. I do my best to match their energy, but it's impossible. The entire concert is a sloppy effort at best, my voice cracking through every song, many notes either flat or missed. And I'm late on most of my dance sequences. The dancers do their best to cover for me, but there's only so much they can do when they're waiting to lift me and I'm not there.

Finally, Carlton comes out with a chair, which is no subtle hint that Jenner wants me to sit down and focus on my singing. Unprecedented, the dancers leave the stage. I sit and sing "Without You" relatively cleanly, but one whole octave lower than normal. It's still a beautiful song, but I know it's not the version the audience paid good money to hear, and their weak applause only confirms that. A few more songs from the comfort of the chair and I'm able to stumble through the closing number, my voice just a shadow of its usual powerhouse glory. It's been an excruciating concert, and my humiliation over last night is nothing compared with my shame of such an epic failure.

For the first time since I set off on tour, there is no encore. The lights come on after my last song, the applause dutiful but half-hearted.

I keep my eyes on the floor, tears welling up as Martin shepherds me to my dressing room. Instead of the usual high-fives from crew members and fans waiting backstage, no one approaches me. I collapse on the couch, bursting into tears as soon as the door closes. Martin grabs a box of tissues and sits down next to me.

"My voice was flat, I missed almost every dance cue...and Jenner sending out that chair? Oh my God, it was like being put in time-out! They're going to slay me online. I'm surprised no one is asking for their money back. It was mortifying."

Martin clucks and hands me a tissue. "OK, that's enough. Calm down, sweetie."

I blow my nose as he grabs a cold bottle of water off the table and hands it to me. The icy water soothes my raw throat.

Martin looks at me levelly. "Tonight was twelve shades of ugly, Dani." I wince. "But the good news is that if you lay off the partying, we won't have to slog through another show like tonight's."

I nod, wiping my tears. "You're right. And then I won't wake up clutching a stupid toilet again, either." I put my head back and groan. "God, Martin, what a crappy day!"

Martin laughs and I look up at him sharply. "Come on...toi-let...crappy? That's punny!"

I give him a death stare.

"So, you're not ready for puns just yet." He sighs. "This will be forgotten the more fabulous shows you put on. Let's get you showered, onto the bus, and leave Manchester behind us, OK? As Mama always says, you can't un-toast the toast, but you can sure as hell make sure you don't burn it the next time."

I laugh in spite of myself. He pats my hand. "I'll take a pity laugh any day of the week as long as it gets you to stop moping."

Martin gets up. "Hope you'll understand that I'll be waiting outside the door this time, and we'll walk to the bus together."

I nod sheepishly. "I understand."

"See you in a bit." Martin grabs his bag and a folding chair and settles himself in the hallway. I take an extra-long hot shower, hoping the water will wash away the remains of this disastrous day that cling to me.

32

We drive through the night to Paris. I decide to miss the wonder of our tour bus passing under the English Channel via a shuttle train and go to bed because I want to end one of the worst days of my life. When I wake up, I open the shades, expecting to gaze upon the romance and grandeur of Paris. Instead, I stare out at the dreary parking lot of the AccorHotels Arena. With nothing to look at but stage equipment and crew members scurrying past, my mood sinks even further. *We might as well be parking in Indiana for as much as this looks like Paris. So much for the glamorous life of a pop star. This sucks!* I go to the kitchen.

Corny accordion music and the heavenly scent of warm butter and sugar greet me as I enter. Martin dances around wearing a black-and-white-striped t-shirt with a ridiculously tiny beret precariously perched on his head while Regina and Jenner laugh and sip coffee.

Martin stops when he sees me, bowing with a flourish. "*Bonjour, mon ami! Bienvenu á Paris!*" He straightens up and grins. "We've got the whole day to sightsee." He tosses something to me. "Matching t-shirt. All the Parisians are wearing them." He winks, and I laugh.

Martin counts on his fingers. "Alexi's arranged a private tour of the Louvre and a walk through the Jardin des Tuileries, then lunch on the Champs-Elysées, a stop at the Eiffel Tower, and then dancers will join us for a river tour of the city on a bateau. I know it's barely a scratch on the surface of this amazing city, but it's all we have time for."

"Breakfast is served!" Carlton calls triumphantly as he sets down plates filled with hazelnut crepes, fluffy scrambled eggs, and mini buttery croissants.

I grin. "This almost makes up for the miserable view!"

"I know it's not the most luxurious place to stay," Jenner says, "but the more money we save on things like hotels and flights, the more money goes into our pockets."

I know deep down he's right, but I'm tired of traveling like some poor circus act. I look out the window. "All my life I've heard how beautiful and romantic Paris is...and here we are in the same ugly parking lot we've been sitting in all tour. After the hotels in Miami and London, it's disappointing."

"I get it," Martin says. "But we're going to soak up so much of that Paris atmosphere today that you'll be farting perfume by the time you go to sleep tonight. Promise!"

We all bust out laughing, and I'm grateful to Martin for lifting my mood.

***

Sporting a Marie Antoinette-inspired tiara, black cigarette pants, Martin's t-shirt, Sean's letterman jacket, and Chuck Taylors, I jump into a black Navigator, and we hit the town. I promise Martin I'll keep my talking at a minimum today to help my voice recover from London. Carlton is armed with several thermoses filled with tea with lemon and honey for my throat.

We spend over three hours in the Louvre. There are so many things to see there that we can't possibly take them all in, but I feel like we get the gist of it. It is totally amazing to think how old these pieces are. But let's be honest, how many pictures of pasty naked people or old-time battles do I need to look at before we can call it a day?

Security clears a path for us in the Jardin des Tuileries, but I can't lose myself in a peaceful walk when there's a mob of screaming fans and flashing cameras. My mood brightens when I spy a pack of TrueHarts decked out like Marie Antoinette. I run over to say hi with Alexi hot on my heels to save me from any terrorists disguised as fans. Carlton has a brilliant idea for me to take photos and videos with the TrueHarts riding on the antique carousel in the garden. It's splashed all over social media before we even leave the park, and any shade from my little "peach cooler" episode seems completely erased.

This is the first thing that has truly lifted my spirits since Tableau. Everything the TrueHarts have to say is so supportive it blows my mind. Not one of them blames me for what happened in London. They either talk about the dangers of OTC cold medicines or straight up blame Kayla for tricking me. They all say how much they're defending me against the trolls, and several of them even mention Zoe! I can't believe fans in Paris are talking about that cow back home who is still trying to take me down. She's officially a worldwide nuisance. *Get over me already, Zoe!*

After talking to the TrueHarts, I have come to believe that I didn't do anything wrong that night. I know Martin insists I did by sneaking out, and, while I agree that was an error in judgement, it doesn't compare to what Kayla did. So really, I'm the victim in all of this, and I know when Martin calms down, he'll come to see it my way. I'm grateful I can put all that misplaced guilt behind me. We say goodbye to the TrueHarts and head over to the Champs-Elysées.

We're finishing lunch when Martin gets up to take a call from Brett. "Be right back." As Jenner and Regina look over her museum guidebook, Carlton slides into the seat next to me. I jump, startled.

"Oh, hey! What's up, Carlton?"

He looks over nervously at Jenner, whose attention is completely absorbed. He leans in conspiratorially, and my first instinct is to lean back. "I have a message for you."

I look at him confused. "OK?"

He looks around again before whispering, "From Kayla."

Anger flares. "What does that traitor want?"

Carlton hands me his phone. "She feels awful. Look."

K: Carlton, Dani's not taking my calls. Tell her I'm SO sorry Tableau was such a disaster. I had no idea the coolers would affect her like that. Can she ever forgive me?

I stare at the message. "At least she cops to spiking my drinks. But what about all those embarrassing photos she posted?"

Carlton looks anxious. "What do you want me to say to her?"

"Tell her..." I try to think of something before Martin gets back. "Tell her that I'm glad she admits to lying about the drinks, but it would've meant a lot more if she hadn't posted all those pics from the club. Martin's furious with her and thinks she's a bad friend."

Carlton types furiously. Seconds later, his phone pings. "She says there aren't any pics of that night on her account. She has no idea what you're talking about."

I snort when Carlton pulls up her Instagram. Sure enough, any photos from that night have been scrubbed.

I jab my finger at his screen. "They were there! Martin showed them to me. How did they get on her feed if she didn't post them? Does she think I'm stupid?"

Before Carlton can answer, Martin walks in, triumphant. "RYB just secured major backing! Our first studio will be able to open this June!" Martin gives me a high five as Carlton scoots out of his chair.

I plaster a big smile on my face, trying to hide my anger. "That's awesome, Martin!"

"When we get back to L.A., we'll get cracking on our ad campaign. Your face is going to be plastered all over town as the face of RYB!"

***

My mood is pretty dark by the time we hit the shops. Jenner insists that we stop at several boutiques that have sent me promotional items such as Manoush, Valentino, and Gucci. He buys me something at each store telling me it is all good PR and that he can write everything off. *Who am I to stand in the way of a free gift?* He also buys me a wallet at Louis Vuitton and an adorable yellow dress at Nina Ricci. We wander into Osman Antiques, and I pick out this pair of outrageous gold and turquoise baroque armchairs. I match them with a gorgeous blue Turkish rug that will look amazing in my room back home. Carlton snaps photos and video of everything, as does the staff of each store. My IG blows up with praise for all my new swag. There's nothing like a little retail therapy to brighten up my mood!

Jenner's phone pings as we whizz over to the Eiffel Tower, and he lets out a triumphant yelp. "Nicely done, Dani and Carlton! All the Instagram buzz today just got you an invitation from Feu! He wants you to sing a riff for his new song. His manager says it'll only take you a couple of hours." Jenner turns around and beams at me. "You up for it? We can squeeze it in before we hit Barcelona." He turns around without waiting for an answer and taps on the screen. "Downloading your part now."

I look at Martin, and he shrugs. "The more exposure you can get in foreign markets, the better. I say go for it."

Jenner pipes up, "OK, here it is."

He plays the cut. My part is a funky refrain that rips through the hard rap, transforming Feu's harsh sounding lyrics into something playful.

I nod at Jenner and smile. "I'm in!"

Jenner gives me a thumbs up and taps at his phone.

Martin nudges me and smiles. "Collaboration number two! Your second album is going to be quite the eclectic mash-up of world music. It's gonna rock!"

* * *

Minutes later, our driver drops us off at the Eiffel Tower. A tour guide greets us and escorts us around the spindly structure, which looks insubstantial from far away but up close is a mind-numbing network of lacy but sturdy wrought iron.

I pose for publicity shots on the windy visitor platforms. In exchange for an hour of pictures, video, and interviews, the Parisian board of tourism is comping our visit at the tower and the boat tour later tonight. We're almost blown over by the gusty winds when we get to the top level. We rush inside to the restaurant so we can warm up. I ask Martin if I can FaceTime Sean. We sit at a small table, and he orders us a snack while I call Sean.

"Hey!" I shout when his gorgeous face fills the screen. I can tell he just woke up; his hair is all tousled, and he's not wearing a shirt. "Sorry to wake you!"

Sean rubs his eyes, his face filled with concern. "I've been waiting for you to call. How *are* you?"

I pan the phone around the room, Martin waving as it passes him, and the shot ends on the panoramic view outside the window. It's a clear day, and the bustling city stretches out for miles.

"Wow! Eiffel Tower, huh?"

It's been a couple of days since I spoke with Sean, and I start talking a mile a minute. "It's amazing! We have to come back together. Do you know the tower shrinks seven inches when it's cold? Insane, right? It's been VIP all day with a private tour this morning of a famous museum. I forget the name. Then Jenner took me shopping and bought me a ton of stuff, and now we're here for a free tour and lunch...well, second lunch, really, and then we've got a free boat tour of the city tonight with the dancers. And this super popular French rapper asked me to collaborate with him—can you believe that? I'm not even here twenty-four hours and I've already got French artists banging down my door! Oh, and I ran into a pack of TrueHarts today at the museum. They were totally calling Zoe out for the troll she is. Can you believe that people over here in Paris know what a troll Zoe is? That makes her an intercontinental troll!"

I stop to catch my breath and see the incredulous look on Sean's face. "What?" I ask.

"Um, the last thing I heard about you was that you were drunk in London and had to be carried out of a club. Geena said your parents, Martin, and Jenner are pissed at you. Martin said you've lost your phone privileges, and all you can talk about is all the free stuff you're getting and how your fans hate Zoe? I've been worried sick about you. And what are you even *doing* drinking anyway? You've never been into that stuff before! What's going on with you?"

Suddenly I'm aware we're talking on speaker phone. I look around, totally embarrassed. No one seems to have heard over the din of the busy restaurant except for Martin, who pushes his ear buds my way. I hastily slide them in.

"God, Sean, I *know* what happened in London. I would have talked to you about it sooner, but Martin took away my phone, *remember?* That was, like, the worst night of my life, and it's been torture ever since. I can't believe Kayla betrayed me like that. I'm having my first good day since it happened, so *excuse* me for feeling good about myself for the first time in a while and wanting to share that with you."

Sean stares at me. "It happened two days ago, Dani, it hasn't been weeks. And you seem to have gotten through the torture pretty unscathed, considering all the awful pictures that came out. No one seems to blame you at all. And even Kayla is getting away with giving alcohol to a minor. They're saying it was just a stupid party-girl misjudgment!" He exhales. "The Dani I know would never have snuck out in the first place, let alone go to a club and get drunk."

I fire back harsher than I intend to, feeling cornered and wrong. "What, you think I'm all self-centered and shallow now that I'm famous and not there to follow you around like a lost puppy?"

Sean looks at me in disbelief. "What the hell are you talking about? You *never* followed me around. Hell, when you were here, we barely saw each other because of all your lessons. But at least you made an effort back then. You used to *want* to talk to me, used to care what I thought. Now whenever we connect, all you talk about is yourself, your fans, what you're getting for free. Do you realize you haven't even asked how I am?"

Crap! The fire goes out of my anger when I realize he's right.

"I was sure when you finally called me, you'd be in tears over what happened. But you don't even think you did anything wrong! You're beginning to lose touch with reality. I don't even know if what I'm saying is coming across because I don't know how to relate to you anymore!"

I fight back tears, not wanting photos of me sobbing in public splashed all over the tabloids. "I'm still the same person, Sean. Maybe I'm a little mixed up being away from home, my schedule...just everything. But I'm still the same person. I swear."

Sean looks away from the phone. "Look, I gotta get ready for school. Let's talk about this later."

"But Sean, we need to finish this. I can't..."

He sighs, annoyed. "But the thing is Dani, *I* can't do this right now. You might have all afternoon to yourself, but it's morning here and I have to go to school."

I feel helpless, completely cut off by his anger. "OK. Call me later. I'm sor—"

He hangs up without even saying goodbye. I'm devastated, tears pour down my face.

"Here." Martin pushes my sunglasses across the table and takes back his phone. I put them on, the big frames hiding my eyes. I remove his ear buds as he stands up. "Let's get you out of here."

Martin signals to Alexi, who goes to call the elevator. We file in and scramble into the Navigator when we get to the street.

Minutes later, we pull up to the bateau pier. Martin hands me a black Moncler puffer as I get out. "Better put this on. Don't want you catching a chill on the water." I reluctantly take off Sean's jacket, almost feeling like I'm symbolically leaving behind our relationship, and pull on the puffer.

The bateau is a sleek double decker boat, the lower deck entirely encased in glass. As we board, I flinch when I see the same photographer from the Eiffel Tower snapping pictures of us stepping on board. *Thank God I'm still wearing my dark glasses.*

"Sorry, darlin'. He's the reason this whole tugboat experience is free." Martin hands me a tube of gloss. "Swipe some of this on and smile. I'll see what I can do to distract him."

As the sun goes down, the bateau pulls away. The dancers are already milling around the decks, enjoying wine and hors d'oeuvres. Over the loudspeakers, the captain welcomes us in a very thick French accent and drones on about the city sites. Feeling lonely and aggravated, I wander away from Martin and the photographer to find a spot where I can be alone and watch the city lights come on as the last streaks of daylight disappear from the sky.

"There you are!" Beau waves a plastic flute teasingly. "Should I get you a glass?" He stops when he sees my face and leans on the railing, nudging me. "You OK?"

I shake my head. "Sean's really mad at me." I look out at the dark river water, trying to find the words. "I get so wrapped up in all this...tour stuff. I forget what's going on back home, forget to be there for the people I love. I feel like I'm changing and so are they, but it's all happening at different speeds. I can't relate to their school stress, and they can't relate to what I'm going through. And then I make things worse with a boneheaded move like what happened in London."

I look at him, desperate to be understood. "I never would have done something like that back home. And now I'm doubting everything about myself on this tour..." A flash lights up the deck. I turn and give a fake smile to the photographer and wave, pretending to enjoy the view. After a few shots, he wanders away and I exhale, frustrated. "And I've got this idiot following me around all night."

"Sean isn't going to understand where you're coming from," Beau says, "because he's still in high school. His world is smaller, his stresses and pressures are different from yours. So yeah, you might never have snuck out back home, but that's because you weren't watched by thousands of fans, chased by paparazzi who document your every move for the tabloids. So you blew off a little steam," he adds. "What's the big deal? You didn't rob a bank, you took a break! Next time, you'll handle yourself better. Get over it already."

I look at Beau, grateful. "Thank you!"

"That's what friends are for!" He looks around and holds his champagne flute out to me. "Let's toast to no more guilt. It's a fruitless emotion and an utter waste of time."

I giggle and look around before I take the glass and down the champagne. It's bitter, and the bubbles make me gag. I accidentally snort half of it up my nose by laughing. I pull off my sunglasses and wipe my face. I instantly feel bubbly and lightheaded.

Beau winks and smiles encouragingly. "Stick with me and I'll make sure nothing like London happens again."

33

I stay by Beau's side on the cruise. He gives me another glass of champagne, but he makes sure I drink water and iced tea the rest of the evening. He doesn't want me to get "peach cooler crazy" again. The photographer gets some great shots, as does Carlton, who posts them on Insta and Twitter.

Martin steers clear while I'm with Beau. By the time the boat docks and we get back into the car, I am relaxed and calm, feeling like myself again but just the slightest bit fuzzy. The fight with Sean is just a distant nagging feeling.

I spend most of the next morning playing Feu's song on loop, memorizing my part and practicing in my head. I'm saving my voice for the show tonight, so I'm waiting to sing the piece until I'm actually in the studio.

I keep waiting to hear from Sean all day, but I never do. At first I'm sad, but as the day goes on, I get angry. The more I think about it, what Beau said about Sean not understanding what I'm going through makes sense. But I'm still hoping Sean will call, even while Pauline is piling my hair high on my head, supplementing it with additional wig pieces to match the overtop hairstyles of Louis XVI's court and topping it with an even more ornate tiara than I wore yesterday. My makeup is heavy on the white powder, exaggerated cupid-bow lips painted in blood red, and a red crystal heart below my left eye.

Since we're in Paris, Petra has created a Marie Antoinette-inspired costume. She laces me into a red and gold brocade corset so tight I can barely sing, my cleavage jiggling about suggestively despite yards of fashion tape. Three-quarter sleeves end in ruffled bells edged with gold lace, and one large gold silk bow is fastened at each elbow. A thick rope of rhinestones hangs around my neck and disappears down into my corset, and a wide gold silk bow is jauntily tied around my neck.

A micro birdcage skirt, wide at the hips, in the same red and gold brocade ends just below my bottom. Gold and white petticoats peek out below the hemline and lacy booty shorts can be seen whenever I spin. The look is complete with red silk over-the-knee platform stiletto boots with gold silk bows tied on the top of each boot. When I saw the costume on the hanger, I thought it was the most hideous thing I'd ever seen. It took two weeks of extra rehearsals for me to figure out how to dance and do the lifts with such a wide skirt. But seeing everything on, hugging my body, I feel hot as hell. *Eat your heart out, Sean!*

I'm checking myself out when there's a knock at the door. "Come in!" I holler, not taking my eyes off the mirror.

Martin whistles as he enters. "Let them eat cake, darlin'! You smoking tonight!"

As Pauline and Petra leave the room, I try to sit down on the couch, but my skirt makes it impossible. Martin grabs a stool and brings it over.

"Ready for tonight?"

"Yeah. I FaceTimed Terrance and ran through some scales. He said I'm totally fine for tonight and that if I stay quiet after the show, there's no problem for tomorrow's session with Feu."

"Good!" He pours a mug of hot water, floats a lemon slice in it, and hands it to me. "How's Sean?"

"You know I don't have my phone, so you also know he hasn't bothered to call."

Martin gives me a measured look. "He might be waiting for you to call him."

"*He* hung up on me! *In public*—it was *so* embarrassing. I'm surprised *that* didn't end up in the tabloids!"

"You called him from the Eiffel Tower on speaker phone! *Of course*, people are going to be listening. Clearly, you two need to work on your communication skills. Sean doesn't know what's going on with you right now, or did you not hear that? Seems like you were too busy losing your temper and screaming all kinds of nonsense. You almost reminded me of Jodi when she gets in a twist."

I gasp. "I can't believe you said that! I'm *nothing* like my mother!"

Martin holds up his hands and takes a deep breath. "I crossed a line with that comment. I'm sorry." He touches my elbow gently.

"Look, your relationship is none of my business. But I think you need to listen to what Sean said. In a long-distance relationship, you need to work hard on communicating or things can get misconstrued."

Carolina's nasally voice blares over the intercom. "Fifteen minutes."

Martin squeezes my hand. "The last thing I want is to upset you right before a show. Come in for the group hug when you're ready, and then we'll get you strapped into the crown up top. Everything else can wait."

He leaves, and I'm left stewing. *I wish Martin would just butt out sometimes! He's had a boyfriend for like a minute, but he's lecturing me about relationships like he's been married for twenty years. I know he was a pop star once, too, but that was ages ago. And he was just one kid in a huge band! It's not like he was a solo star like I am. He doesn't really know what it's like to be me or face the pressures I'm facing.*

I exhale deeply and shake off my anger. *I'm a professional, after all, and I've got to give my fans what they came for.* I head out of my dressing room to do what I do best.

***

The show is amazing! It's the exact opposite of the dumpster fire that the Manchester concert was. I take all my annoyance at Martin and my anger with Sean, and I shove them into my songs. From the moment that crown descends from the ceiling, I'm sassier, bolder, and more energized than ever and every flick of my hair or shake of my hips shows the audience just how in charge I am. Three encores, none of which include Martin (*suck on that Mr. "You Remind Me of Your Mom"*), and I feel invincible! No one can keep me down—not Sean or Martin or anyone on earth. This realization has all the dizzying excitement of a peach cooler but none of the vomit or hangover!

The next day, the session with Feu is a success despite the disastrous few minutes when we are first introduced. Apparently, Feu and his team barely speak English, and neither Jenner, Martin, nor I speak any French. We all just stand there like idiots wondering what we're going to do until Carlton enters the studio loaded down with our bags and saves the day! Apparently fluent in French, German, and Japanese, he translates for both our teams and the session goes off without a hitch. I'm telling you, the more I hang out with Carlton, the more impressive he gets. Doughy physique and stupid safari vest aside, he's got way more levels than I knew and is becoming the go-to problem-solver on this team!

34

After London, Martin put me on total lockdown—a steady schedule of homework, RYB videos, and shows. But soon we're all tired of being together, snapping at each other every chance we get. Somewhere near the French border as we're refueling, Martin plops down next to me on the couch. "Why don't you go over to the dancers' bus for a while?"

I look up from my history book. "Seriously?"

"Yeah. You still can't have your phone back, but even I have to admit that this is cruel and unusual punishment. Shows, riding on a bus, and doing homework—it's too much. I know it's only been a couple of days, but you need to socialize with young people. So ride with them to the arena."

"Thanks!" I leap up and head for the door.

"One more thing," Martin calls out.

I turn around and see Carlton lumbering down the aisle, adjusting his backpack. "She's in good hands, Martin. See you in a few hours!"

I shoot Martin a look, and he shrugs. "I'm easing up, but I'm not stupid."

Carlton gives me a creepy smile. "This should be fun!"

I nod politely and force a smile. "Yup!"

Martin chuckles. "Have fun!"

***

At first, I'm not too geeked to spend hours with Carlton hovering over me. But it turns out that Carlton has a huge crush on Bronwyn, so Beau uses that to our advantage. After Beau promises her a frontline spot in all the dance routines, Bronwyn keeps Carlton distracted enough that he doesn't notice the odd drink or two Beau slips me. I'm not getting sloppy drunk, but it's nice to have something to take the edge off of my day. And since Carlton has been passing along Kayla's denials of wrongdoing and apologies to me, the least I can do is be an excuse for him to get his flirt on. I spend a few happy hours on the bus every week, dancing or playing games. Carlton gets to flirt with Bronwyn more than he ever would in a normal situation. And Bronwyn gets more exposure on stage. Everyone wins, and no one gets in trouble.

Kayla's been shouting from the rooftops that she never posted the Tableau photos on her Insta. She even called Martin and Jenner. She's wasting her breath, though; no one believes her. Martin's happy because it's the perfect excuse to stop giving her free tickets to all the shows.

We roll into Barcelona, and it's all tapas and *fútbol*, museums, and publicity appearances. Then on to Madrid and Lisbon where, to be honest, it feels exactly the same. I know each city is different, with its own culture and history and blah, blah, blah...but seriously, when you come into town for thirty hours, it's hard to get a grasp on what makes each city unique.

The only real cultural insight I seem to get regularly is the costumes Petra designs. She and Regina work together to research each country and pull together a historic costume. In Spain, Petra modeled my costume off a painting of Queen Isabella welcoming Christopher Columbus to court. It's all pink silk and an ermine cape, and it's fly as hell.

After the Lisbon show, we drive to Milan via Monaco. I'm booked for some corporation's annual shareholders' meeting. It's weird that a bunch of businesspeople want to hear me sing. They're *so* not my demographic. But Jenner says they're paying $500,000 for four songs. I'll sing to anyone for that amount of money!

Taking a break from my pile of homework, I ask Martin if I can call home. I try Lauren first, but she doesn't pick up. So I try Geena, and she pops up on the screen. She's had a reverse reaction to her first year in college—she's lost the freshman fifteen instead of gaining it. She looks lean, healthy, and tan. Her hair is up in a ponytail, and I notice the lower half of her head is shaved.

"Howdy, sis! Where are you?"

"Driving to Monaco. What the hell happened to your hair?"

Geena grins and rubs her shorn head. "It's crockpot hot down here, so I shaved some off! It looks normal when I wear it down, but man, it's so much cooler!"

I'm amazed by Geena's bold new look. "I bet Mom flipped when she saw it!"

"Since she stole my college fund, I feel very little obligation to keep in touch. Besides, she's been busy doing a press tour since your hiccup in London. She's all over the tabloids talking about her 'at-risk daughter' and the pressures of being a star." Geena raises her eyebrows. "Dad seemed fine with it, and Grandma just looked exasperated."

At the mention of our grandmother, I flinch.

"Still haven't called her yet? Gotta face the music some time, sis. It's not like she's going to yell at you."

"But she'll be disappointed, and I swear that's so much worse than yelling."

"Just get it over with. Remember the story of how Dad got drunk at homecoming and threw up on the gym teacher? Now it's part of family lore! Just think of it as you carrying on the tradition of idiotic adolescent behavior. You and Sean can regale your kids with it." She laughs and then gets serious. "Speaking of Sean, what's going on there?"

"I haven't heard from him in a while."

Geena gives me a wry look. "Have you *called* him?"

All the bravado I've been cultivating with Beau flies out of the window. I look up and see Martin watching me. He mouths "Go ahead" and nods to my room at the back of the bus. I head back, sliding the door shut.

I flop on the bed and sigh. "I called him in Paris, and it was a disaster. He was so mad at me about London, saying I'm not acting like myself and I'm out of touch with reality. At first I was too pissed to call him back, but now it's been so long, I don't know what to say." I squint at

Geena. "And why is he being so judgmental? It feels like shades of Mom all over again, doesn't it?"

Geena guffaws. "Um, no! Don't try to twist it, D. Sean isn't being judgmental. He's concerned about you. You can't deny you've changed on the road, right?"

I groan. "Not you, too!"

Geena gives me a cutting look. "You've *totally* changed, and the fact that you can't even acknowledge it is part of the problem. Every time someone says something you disagree with, you throw a fit or give them the silent treatment. That might work with Martin and Jenner, but it's not gonna fly with anyone who's not on your payroll. Sean tried to talk to you about London and you blew up. And then you posted all these pictures showing you partying after the argument without a care in the world. How would you feel if Sean did that to you?"

"*I* didn't post those pictures. Carlton did. I was doing publicity, not partying."

Geena's deadpan stare needles me. I know she's not going to let me talk my way out of this one.

"I guess you're right," I admit reluctantly. "But what am I supposed to do now?"

"Time for you to eat some serious crow, sis. You gotta apologize and hope he can get over it."

"*Hope* he'll get over it? You don't think he'd break up with me over this, do you?"

Geena looks at me, shocked. "If Sean thinks you don't value his opinion or that you've changed so much that sneaking out and drinking aren't a big deal to you, *yeah*, he could break up with you."

Sneaking drinks with Beau on the dancers' bus flashes through my mind and anxiety grips me. It's like Geena's holding up a mirror and forcing me to look at how ugly I've been behaving these past few weeks. It's the worst feeling.

Geena continues, "I'm not trying to put you down. But I'm always going to be honest with you. Suck it up and call him. Jenner and Martin can't manage this away for you."

I nod, the lump in my throat so big I can't talk.

Geena gives me a sad smile. "Whatever happens with Sean, you'll be OK. Love you."

She ends the call. I stare at the ceiling, knowing what I have to do but not wanting to do it. Before I talk myself out of it, I sit up and FaceTime Sean, my stomach jumping with nerves. As soon as it starts to ring, the call is rejected.

That's not good. I try a few more times but all my calls are rejected. *Ugh! Now what?*

My mind races as I send Sean a text.

D: Hey, have time 2 talk? I owe U an apology 4 being such a nightmare

I wait a few minutes before trying again.

D: I'm sorry. I was wrong. I suck.

I give it another try.

D: It's OK if U don't want 2 talk. I understand.

Nothing. Not even those three annoying dots that show he's read the text and might be typing. I guess I deserve it. I keep thinking how awful I would feel if I saw pictures of Sean partying it up right after an argument. I feel ashamed of how I've been acting. As I try to figure out my next move, there's a knock on my door.

"Come in!"

Martin pops his head in. "How's Geena?" He leans against the doorway. "She snagged herself a fine cowboy down there in Texas?"

I laugh. "Not yet. She shaved part of her hair off, though, which is pretty bold."

He looks surprised. "Go Geena! Sounds like she's coming into her own. Good for her." He pauses. "So I heard you two talking about Sean...are you going to yell at me if I ask how it's going?"

I wince. "Sorry about that. I know I was a real B that night back in Paris."

"No argument there."

I ignore Martin's jab. "Geena got me thinking how, whether I agree with him or not, I owe him an apology for reacting the way I did...and for all those pictures posed on my Insta the night of the fight. I tried calling and texting, but he isn't picking up. It's been so long since we talked that I don't know how to start talking to him again."

Martin exhales loudly and rubs his scalp. "That sure is a pickle!" Martin taps his lip thoughtfully. "What to do, what to do? Hmm." I lie down, staring at the ceiling, my mind a total blank.

Suddenly he snaps his fingers! "I know!" Excitement spreads across his face. "How does a big star try to get someone's attention when they won't pick up their call?"

I look at Martin blankly.

"You use your star powers for good instead of evil!"

"Huh?" I sit up, intrigued by the scheming look on Martin's face.

He claps his hands. "Lucky you got some extra cash from this corporate gig. We're going to need to spend a little of it for love, honey. Come on! Let's go fight for your man!"

35

Martin's plan is complicated but brilliant. It banks on the TrueHarts and his and Jenner's star connections to inundate Sean with messages of love. We spend hours that day writing a song, begging Sean to forgive me. I've never written a song before, but with Martin's help, I'm able to put my emotions into a logical order and say exactly how I'm feeling. Martin sends it to Terrance before we go to sleep. By the next morning, Terrance has whipped up music to go with the lyrics. But instead of the melancholy tune I'd imagined, Terrance sends back this snappy upbeat song that is the equivalent of audio cotton candy. The first time I hear it, I absolutely *hate it*. But the more I hear it, the more it grows on me, and before I know it I'm *obsessed*. Within twenty-four hours, we have cobbled together a sassy pop tune written specifically for Sean called "Second Chance."

In Monaco, we record the song in a dinky little studio. The band members are elated to have a new piece of music to play. We leave for the corporate gig while Jenner stays behind to mix the song with Terrance weighing in over the phone.

The next day, with the dancers' help, we shoot a video around Monaco that Carlton films on his GoPro. Before we pull into the Mediolanum Forum in Milan the following day, the video is ready to be posted. I shoot a short video apology to Sean. Carlton posts my apology and the song on all my social media and blasts it to the entertainment websites. Everyone on the team starts tagging it and reposting it. Martin and Jenner pull out all the stops, contacting the biggest celebs in their phones to promote the song. I message a link to Sean and cross my fingers he'll click on it.

Jenner decides to throw "Second Chance" into the concert, hoping to generate some buzz. Beau comes up with a simple routine based on the steps we did in the video, and we run through it a few times before sound check. It's exciting to add a new number to the show, especially one that didn't exist forty-eight hours ago.

***

We blaze through the concert, invigorated by the new number. In honor of performing in the mecca of fashion, I'm wearing an ultra-couture costume with an electric-blue satin bodysuit that buckles up on the sides, with cut-outs exposing lots of flirty skin. I wear a matching see-through tulle mini skirt edged in black satin ribbon and white over-the-knee vinyl platform boots. I have a futuristic tiara with blue and white rhinestones, and my hair is slicked back in a sleek high pony. Makeup is shimmery blue eyeshadow with blue rhinestone lashes and blue shimmer lipstick.

"Second Chance" raises the roof on the arena! It must have really blown up online because the audience sings along with me. I rush backstage after a thirty-minute encore and the vibe is electric. For the first time in a while, I spend some time with the TrueHearts backstage, signing autographs and posing for pictures.

Martin pulls me away from the fans and we head to my dressing room where Jenner is waiting, beside himself with excitement. "Did you hear them singing 'Second Chance'? It's been online for six hours and it's already a hit! MEGA's blasting it on every radio around the globe. I definitely think you'll get Sean's attention."

Carlton shows me his computer which has a dozen windows open. I see hundreds of celebrities and fans posting pleas to Sean, begging for him to forgive me, celebrities and regular people singing or dancing along with my song—it's gone totally viral.

I look up at Jenner nervously. "Anything from Sean?"

Jenner sighs heavily. "Not yet, hon. But I'm sure it's just a matter of time. Have faith."

I try to swallow the lump in my throat. "Thanks, guys, for dropping everything to help me."

"We're all here for you," Martin says. "Let's get you changed so we can hit the road." He pulls out his phone to text Pauline and Petra, but they open the door before he hits send. "There you are!" He grabs his bag. "Take your time, D. I'll be in the hall."

All the men hustle out of the room as Pauline frees my hair from its headache-inducing ponytail and Petra unbuckles my costume. I try not to cry in the shower as I pray for Sean to get in touch.

Pulling on sweatpants, a tank top, and slides, I throw on Sean's jacket and head into the hall.

The dancers are blocking the way, talking excitedly. Feeling defeated, the last thing I want to do is hassle with a bunch of excited people on a concert high. But there's no way around them, and they *did* just help me shoot a video on their day off, so I suck up my irritation and approach them.

"Anyone seen Martin?" I ask. Suddenly, everyone erupts in excited cheers. The crowd parts and I see Martin at the center of the group. "OK, here she is, hold on a second."

Beaming, he hands me his phone. "It worked, darlin'!"

My mouth drops in disbelief as I see Sean staring back at me. The dancers all clap me on the back and start cheering and shouting things like "Awww!", "Forgive her, Sean!", and a bunch of other crap so I can barely hear what he is saying.

I bite my lip because, while everyone is excited that Sean's on the phone, the serious look on his face has me worried.

Martin sees my distress and claps his hands loudly. "All right, everyone! Get packed up and let's hit the road. Deutschland awaits!"

The dancers disperse and I look nervously at Sean. "Sorry about that. Thanks for calling me back." I look around for somewhere private to go, but there are people everywhere rushing to load out of the arena.

Martin waves for me to follow him, takes my bag, and hands me his ear buds.

"Well, you kinda didn't give me much choice. I've got half the Lakers, the cast of *The Fleetwoods*, and about a million TrueHarts blowing me up. I had to uninstall all my social media apps because they keep crashing my phone. Our house phone is ringing off the hook, and my parents are losing their minds. I don't want to be the jerk that doesn't call Dani Truehart back when she makes a worldwide spectacle of apologizing to me."

If he'd been smiling the tiniest bit when he said this, I'd feel better. But his face is so grave it scares the crap out of me. I'm grateful Martin gave me his ear buds so this entire conversation isn't blaring across the arena as we hurry toward the bus and climb aboard.

"Oh my God! I'm so sorry, Sean. I had no idea this would happen. I just wanted to get you to call me back." I dash back to my room and slide the door shut. Too worried to sit still, I pace and chew on a ragged cuticle.

Sean sighs heavily, a sound I've come to dread since I've been on tour...or maybe it goes all the way back to when I signed with Jenner. That quiet, weighty sound of disappointment.

"That's the thing, Dani. Lately you aren't thinking about me at all! This whole thing is a perfect example. Sure, who wouldn't want a song written for them, so the entire world knows how much you love me? It all looks really good from *your* side, because you've got people to answer your phone, deal with media, and keep the mob off your front doorstep. But I don't." He runs his hands through his hair. "I just had a fight with my girlfriend. I didn't want to become the center of attention and have a million people weighing in on our relationship."

My heart sinks. "I'll have Jenner and Martin pull everything immediately. We didn't think this through."

"Thanks." Voices in the background cause Sean to look up and cover the screen for a minute. Seconds drag by. "Look," he says, uncovering the screen. "Can you call me back in a half hour? I was supposed to get my grandpa's prescriptions, but the paparazzi's swarming my house and my parents won't let me go. I've got to hang out with him until they get back."

I cringe. "Yeah, of course. Please apologize to your parents. I'll work on getting everything taken down."

"Thanks. Bye." He hangs up, looking grim.

Now I feel even worse than before!

I find Martin in the kitchen unpacking a post-show Italian feast. The smell of garlic and cheese coming from the bags almost makes me nauseous.

Martin gives me a hopeful smile. "How'd it go? Was Sean surprised?"

"There are paparazzi gathering on his front lawn, and his parents are furious." Martin's eyes grow wide as I continue. "He's pissed that the world's now involved in our argument, and he feels if he doesn't accept my apology, he'll be labeled a jerk by millions of people."

"Oh my God, we made it so much worse! I'm so sorry, Dani." Martin slaps a palm to his forehead. "Me and my stupid ideas. I'll call Sean's parents and apologize. But first I gotta talk to Jenner." He picks up his phone and makes the call.

Martin wanders outside to break the whole thing down for Jenner. I sit down, then jump back up, feeling jittery. I make tea that I don't want and then flop back down at the kitchen table and shred a paper napkin into a million pieces. After a few minutes, Martin climbs back onto the bus.

Well, I've got some news and some bad news. What do you want first?"

I close my eyes and say a silent prayer. "Umm, news?"

"OK. Jenner is coming up with a plan to pull the virus out of this apology. But it's going to take a minute."

"That doesn't sound like much of anything. What's the bad news?"

Martin grimaces. "This video has gone worldwide in record time. Even if we delete Carlton's original posts, it's all over everyone's social media and downloaded to their devices. He'll ask, but he doesn't think MEGA will pull the song off the air because it's an instant hit. It's been downloaded almost half a million times since they posted it on iTunes."

I close my eyes. The weight of millions of strangers' opinions that I invited into our relationship feels suffocating. *How could I be so stupid?*

As if reading my mind, Martin sits down and holds my hand. "I don't know how I didn't see this coming. I guess part of me still thinks of you as that little girl in my studio trying to make her dreams come true. I keep forgetting that you've become an international star that tastemakers across the globe are watching. We've all got to start remembering that every second of our day."

***

My calls to Sean go straight to voicemail. It isn't until after midnight my time before I finally get through.

"Hey." His face pops up on the screen. "Sorry I couldn't pick up sooner. My parents were talking to Martin and Jenner. Then your mom came over and held a press conference on our lawn."

"Are you kidding me?" I screech, about to go off when Sean starts laughing.

"No, I'm not. I'll send you some video." A few seconds later a video comes through with my mother, looking like a poor man's Pamela Anderson, standing on the Mitchells' porch, fielding questions from the press. It is disgusting.

"Yup, she went full-blown 'media-Jodi.' At first my parents were totally pissed, thinking she was here to soak up the spotlight. And while I can't deny she wasn't eating up the attention, she did somehow convince the press it was inappropriate to swarm our house. She finally got them to leave about thirty minutes ago. My mom actually hugged your mom, which is a first." He laughs again, which is music to my ears. "Your mom might be a freak, but she's a paparazzi pied-piper!"

I don't know if it's shock from Mom's plastic appearance, her ability to charm the paparazzi, or the fact that Sean is laughing with me, but I am at a loss for words. I stare at Sean, dumbfounded. He clears his throat.

"So, I was talking to my grandpa while my parents were at the pharmacy. He pretty much told me I was an idiot for being mad at you. He said any girl who would go to such lengths to get my attention must really love me, and I'd be a jerk if I didn't forgive you."

Stunned, I stare at him as he continues. "Look, I don't want the world weighing in every time we have a fight, but I have to admit he's right. I'm sorry for blowing everything out of proportion. You didn't know this was going to happen. And if I'd just picked up the phone when you called, then you wouldn't have had to try something crazy to get my attention. So maybe can we just agree, no more crazy stunts in the future?"

I feel so grateful. "Absolutely!"

"Good. Let's just move on. No more talk about London or Paris, OK?"

Relieved, I nod my head vigorously. "Fine by me!"

He sighs. "This distance thing is really hard."

"I know." I pause and, remembering our conversation at the Eiffel Tower, change the subject. "So, frenzy of worldwide media attention aside, how are you?"

Sean gives me a big smile. "Thank you for asking." We both wait a beat, knowing how important it is that I am paying attention to him for a change. He catches me up on his basketball season (*he's started every game so far and sunk the winning shot last game*); he has three classes with Zoe this fall (*which is annoying, but whatever*); and his grandpa's speech has improved, but he still has trouble walking. He starts filling me in on what's happening with Lauren and Tom when there's a knock on my door.

"Come in!" I shout. Martin, dressed in sweatpants, enters. "Hey, Sean." Martin speaks into the screen. "Sorry about today. I'll keep my relationship advice to myself next time, I promise."

"No worries. The press is gone and everything's back to normal."

"Good." Martin pats my foot. "As much as I'd like to let you two talk all night, we've got an early RYB shoot in the Alps. Better get some rest, Dani."

"OK. I'll get off in a sec."

Martin gets up. "Night, Sean."

"Night, Martin!"

I look back at Sean, feeling as if we're on a new path...a fresh start. "Sorry I have to go."

"It's OK," he says, and my heart skips. "I'm glad we're talking again."

"Me, too. Give you a call tomorrow?"

He smiles, "Can't wait. Love you."

"Love you, too."

We hang up, and I climb under the covers. I want to fall asleep right away so I don't lose this feeling, hoping I dream about Sean. For the first time in a long time, I'm not stressed or angry. I'm happy.

36

After a chilly sunrise RYB workout with the beautiful aqua waters of Lake Lucerne in the background, we wind our way through the Alps.

With things back on track with Sean, life is good. For a while after London, I felt like I had to walk around on eggshells trying to keep Martin, Sean, and everyone else happy. But as the weeks pass and autumn takes a firm hold on the weather, I start to relax.

Hamburg, Antwerp, Prague, Vienna...the cities blur together, but we do see a few cool things along the way, like the enormous gothic Cologne Cathedral towering over the banks of the Rhine. Jenner sets up a free afternoon concert in the cathedral square, and so many people show up the police have to escort us back to the buses. We bike the storybook canals of Amsterdam, stopping to eat thin buttery Dutch pancakes smothered in lemon and sugar (*heaven!*), and Martin even convinces me to a try local delicacy—raw herring (*blech).* Everywhere we visit, history abounds with buildings older than America jumbled together with glass and metal structures and with scars and memorials of past wars visible in every city.

Sightseeing aside, my routine stays maddeningly the same. I slog away at schoolwork, though at this rate I don't really see the point—I'm making money hand over fist and don't think I'll ever graduate on time.

I've been locking down songs with artists every few weeks, slowly building my second album. MEGA wants to drop *Songs from the Road* as soon as I return from tour. It'll buy some time so we can crank out the third album, which they're pushing for as soon as possible. *Three albums!* It feels unreal that things are going this fast, but when you're hot, you're hot. Everybody seems to want a piece of me lately. It's nuts!

Even though Sean and I are doing great again, it's still really hard to stay in contact given the time difference and our schedules. Whenever I'm free to talk, he's asleep or in class. And when he's free, I'm usually asleep or busy. Same with Geena and Lauren. Thank God for Beau, who's been keeping me entertained! Carlton and I are still visiting the dancers' bus several times a week. A few times we've miscalculated how much I've had to drink, and it's taken a combination of pure luck and stellar acting skills not to get caught! But so far, so good!

One day Martin plops down across from me while I'm finishing up my chemistry homework at the kitchen table.

"Got a sec?"

I look up and Martin looks extremely nervous.

"Yeah. Is everything OK?" I close my textbook.

He rubs his head. "Jenner just got a call from a publishing house. Your mom has written a tell-all book about you: your childhood, her role in making you a star, and..."—Martin closes his eyes and exhales loudly—"Your struggle with sobriety."

"My *what*?" Furious, I pick up my book and hurl it across the bus.

Jenner hurries over and joins us. "The publisher contacted me to make sure you're on board with Jodi's authorized biography, *Growing Up Truehart*. I told him we knew nothing about it."

I look from Martin to Jenner, incredulous. "Authorized? By who? She can't tell everyone about my life without my permission, can she?"

"I made it very clear that before anything comes out, you and your guardian need to approve it," Jenner says. "Apparently your mom already turned in a signed release on your behalf and neglected to tell them Martin is your legal guardian, not her."

I kick the table leg, frustrated. "I *knew* she was up to something. She's been too quiet."

Martin shakes his head. "She pulled this crap before, trying to set up that website using your name as a springboard. We shut her down then, so I don't know how she rationalized that she'd get away with a book. It's the same thing!"

Jenner gets up, pulling out his phone. "I'll get my lawyers on this ASAP." He stalks down the hall to my room, slamming the door shut.

I feel like I'm about to explode. My hands are shaking, and my mind is racing. My mother never ceases to surprise me with her selfish under-handedness. *Thank God I'm nothing like her! I'd never lie to get what I want or hurt the ones I love for a big payoff.*

Martin reaches out and pats my hand. "You need to breathe, darlin'. You're turning purple."

I look at him and take a deep breath. I didn't realize I'd been holding it. "First, she stole Geena's college money to turn herself into some pathetic dime-store knockoff Barbie, then she's been on every trashy TV show and gossip magazine she can find talking about me and how she raised a star, and now she's pedaling a book, trying to put a positive spin on the fact that she stole my childhood in order to make money off of me? She's a monster!"

Martin lets me rage. After a while, my temper ebbs. Exhausted, I stare at the table; all my ranting hasn't changed anything. I lean into that realization, grasping for clarity. *Nothing has changed...that's what's bothering me.*

I try to piece it together out loud, "I feel like I'm attached to a bungee cord that's anchored to my mom. No matter how far away I go, no matter what I accomplish, sooner or later that cord snaps back and I'm hurled right back to my mother." Frustrated, I shake my fists. "I can't get away from her dysfunction. Nothing I do or say ever seems to change that. She just doesn't get it."

"I don't think she can see it, darlin'." Martin sighs. "This a difficult subject for me to discuss with you. I don't want you to think I'm badmouthing your mother. But her behavior isn't normal. She's been putting money and fame before your interests for quite a while. She'll never see that. You've achieved so much through your hard work and your talent, and your mother is jealous. She probably won't change. You need to hit the mute button on her when she does stuff like this."

I squint at Martin. "So I'm just supposed to let her get away with this and pretend that it doesn't bother me?"

"No, not at all. Jenner and I are here to make sure she doesn't get away with anything. Our job is to protect you. *You* have the hardest job of all—trying not to let your mom keep hurting you by being who she is. You have to accept that this is who she is and stop being so shocked every time she pulls a new stunt."

I stare at Martin, his face full of concern. "I'm sorry, Martin, but that's about the stupidest thing I've ever heard. There's no way I'm going to sit back and be quiet while my mom spews lies and twists the truth to make herself look like a saint. Turning the other cheek isn't something my mom gets. To her, it's a sign of weakness. I need to speak to her in terms she understands."

I pick up my phone and start typing madly. Martin slides into the booth next to me, trying to get a peek at my screen. "Don't do anything stupid that you're going to regret later."

I turn away from him and finish typing. "Done."

He grabs my phone and sees a photo of my mom and me from my album release party.

@therealdanitruehart It's come to my attention that an 'authorized' biography of my life will be coming out. Don't be fooled TrueHarts! I have NOT approved any book & my legal team is on the case. Don't believe the lies! *"The saddest thing about betrayal is that it never comes from your enemies."* The Godfather

Martin looks up, resigned. "Shots fired."

I stare Martin down and snatch my phone back. "No, shots returned. I didn't start this, but I'm finishing it. Thanks to my dad for making me watch *The Godfather* a million times. Let's see what my mom does when the TrueHart Nation comes after her."

My phone rings. I smirk as Mom's face pops up on the screen. "That was quick."

Martin rejects the call before I can pick up. "You'd better let the lawyers handle this one. No sense in throwing gas on a fire. You've done enough already."

My phone rings again. I grab it and slide off my seat, sitting under the table before Martin can reject the call again.

"Dani, stop!" he whispers as I take the call.

"Hello, Mother."

"What are you playing at, you little brat?" Her voice is so loud there's no need to put the call on speaker so Martin can hear it. "My publisher is talking about scrapping my book and asking me to return the advance. I've already spent it! What's your problem? I'm writing about *my* experience as your mother. *How* is that offensive to you?"

Martin is still whispering for me to stop, and I wave him off. He gets down on the floor, but I scoot further under the table away from him. *I have to get this off my chest.*

"You being my *mother* is very offensive to me. You're constantly trying to profit off my name, and I'm tired of it. If the publisher hadn't contacted Jenner today, I'd have never known about your book. Considering it's an 'authorized biography' about me, don't you think that you should at least ask my permission?"

My mother gasps, infuriated. "Your *permission*? You wouldn't be *alive* if it wasn't for me! I've sacrificed everything for you and your sister, and this is the thanks I get? I've never met two more spoiled brats in my life. If I want to write a hundred books about being your mother, you can't stop me. There are millions of moms out there who want to follow my path to success. Check your ego, missy, you weren't *born* a star. You were made one with my hard work and money."

"You're delusional, *Jodi*," I spit back. "I can't even bring myself to call you 'Mom' anymore, because you're nowhere near what a mother should be. You want to write a book about parenting? Fine! But you are *not* using my name to do it. If you do, I'll go on every radio and talk show and tell them what growing up Truehart was *really* like. And I'll sue you for every dime you make on this book. You'll have nothing after I'm done with you."

Mom lets loose an ugly guttural shriek that makes my muscles clench in terror. Martin and I look at each other, shocked.

Her anger is palpable, her volume increasing with every word. "What did I ever do to deserve such an ungrateful *bitch* of a daughter like you? I wish you'd never been born!"

Stunned, I freeze; my breath ragged, my vision pixelated. The hate pouring out of the phone is devastating. All my rage has evaporated. My mind can't comprehend the extent of the vile things my mother just said. I never dreamed the conversation would get this bad. I want to hang up, but something makes me continue. I feel it's important to say everything I have to say, because I'm not sure when or if we will speak again.

The hollowness in my chest feels all-encompassing. My eyes slide away from Martin's concerned face. Quietly, drained of the will to fight, I say, "I've only ever wanted you to love me for who I am. I realize now that you'll never be able to understand that because you have no heart. There's no way to fix this; you are who you are. Goodbye."

I end the call, dropping my phone as sobs wrack my body. I feel so alone, abandoned by my mother. The sense of loss is overwhelming. I scrunch myself against the wall, finding some small solace hiding in the dark, cramped space under the table, like a child hiding from a thunderstorm.

Unable to squeeze himself under the table, Martin lies on the floor and puts his hands on my arm. "Oh, Dani." I'm crying so hard I feel like I'm going to throw up. I start to gag, and Martin shushes me, trying to calm me.

"Come on, sweetie, let's get you out of there." He backs out from under the table, gently pulling me after him. He wraps his arms around me as I weep. I don't know how long we sit like that, but eventually I have no tears left, my body shudders. My eyes are so swollen from crying they barely open. My throat is raw from yelling.

A handkerchief appears. Jenner's big warm hand rests tenderly on my shoulder. I stare at the floor. My mind is a blank, overwrought. Minutes tick by.

Eventually, Jenner sits down in the booth. "I should have told you not to speak with your mom. My lawyers said the publisher is pulling the book. She was just unloading on you when she should have been directing everything at Martin and myself. Once she cools down, I'm sure everything will go back to normal."

Martin softly chimes in. "I don't think it'll be that easy. Jodi said some very hurtful things."

"Oh, I see..." Jenner flounders, "Should I try to smooth things over with your mom?"

Out of the corner of my eye, I see Martin give a small shake of his head. I squirm out of his arms and struggle to stand up.

"I'm going to lie down."

I drag myself to my room and collapse onto the bed. Martin follows me, gently covering me with a blanket, and then lowers the window shades.

"You rest, honey." He quietly slides the door closed. As Jodi's shrill voice continuously shrieks how she wishes I never was born, I fall into a fitful sleep.

37

I wake up with an intense headache. It's five a.m. I've been asleep for more than fourteen hours. I stumble into the kitchen to make some tea and find some aspirin. Martin is sitting at the kitchen table reading. He smiles and closes his book. "Can I get you some tea?"

I nod and slide gingerly into the booth. "And some aspirin? I have a killer headache."

"I'm not surprised. You cried your eyes out yesterday and slept through dinner. Here." He hands me two tablets and a glass of orange juice. "Take that and I'll have your tea in a second. Can I make you some toast?"

"Yeah, thanks."

He places a mug and a plate full of buttery sourdough in front of me and returns to his seat. "I'm so sorry, honey. I knew your mama would be upset, but I had no idea that would happen. Your dad, grandma, and sister called, and they're really worried about you."

"I'm worried about me, too," I say as I pick at the toast. Martin comes over and puts his arm around me. "How could she say those things? How could that book mean more to her than me?"

Martin shakes his head, "I don't know, honey."

I push the plate away. "I'm going back to bed."

"OK, darlin'. Whatever you need."

***

Hours later, hunger pangs wake me. I peel my eyes open and look at the clock. It's been more than twenty-four hours since I last ate. My heart aches, and all I want to do is sleep here in the dark. But the pains in my stomach are getting worse, so reluctantly I get up.

The bus isn't moving, but I don't have the energy to raise the shades to see where we are. I have no idea how I'm going to make it through the show tomorrow. Nothing really seems to matter after that conversation with Jodi.

Jodi. That's how I think of her now. I let the name roll around my mind, probing how it feels. It gives me a protective barrier, rather than thinking of her as Mom.

I hear muffled female voices coming from the kitchen. I slide open the door and see Grandma and Geena having coffee with Martin and Jenner at the table. I burst into tears when Geena rushes over and envelopes me in a hug.

Grandma lays a warm hand on my arm, patting me gently. "Martin thought you might need a visit from family right about now." She places her arms around Geena and me, her embrace surprisingly strong. After a while, we break from the embrace and I take a deep shuddering breath.

"I'm so glad you're here," I croak. "I...I..."

Grandma puts her arm around me and guides me to the table. "Plenty of time to talk later. But first, I understand you haven't eaten since yesterday. I brought you something special from home to cheer you up."

I slide into the booth as Geena places a thick slice of homemade chocolate fudge cake in front of me. Martin sets a cold glass of milk next to the plate. I stare at the cake, memories of when I was small flooding my mind. I look up at Grandma gratefully.

"Lucky for you I'd just finished icing this cake when Martin called. It was supposed to be for my bingo group, but I think you need it more than they do."

I take a bite of the rich cake. It's better than any other food on the planet, more healing than a thousand hours of therapy. I savor the fudgy frosting and feel the sugar hitting my system. "This is exactly what I needed!"

"I was pretty worried about you," Martin says. "Jenner got on the phone and convinced MEGA to loan us their plane. Your grandma was in a limo forty minutes after I called, cake in hand. She stopped in Texas to pick up Geena, and here they are."

I beam at Martin. "Thank you."

"Of course, darlin'." He slides my phone over to me. "Sean and Lauren have been texting you like crazy."

Reluctant to pick up my phone, I continue to eat my cake. "Can you tell them I'll call later? I really want to focus on Grandma and Geena right now."

"Sure thing." He picks up my phone and starts texting.

After I scrape my plate clean and down the last of the milk, Martin claps his hands. "OK, get your stuff together and let's go. Jenner sprung for a suite at the Grand Hotel in Oslo. They're only here for two nights, so he wanted you all to make the most of it."

I look out the window and see a gorgeous granite stone building with Juliet balconies and copper-topped gable windows. It looks classically European and very inviting.

"You're the best, Martin! I'll get packed."

I pull on jeans and a sweater and throw some stuff into a bag. Shoving my feet into flats, I put on a flower headband instead of my usual tiara. I grab Sean's jacket and exit the bus. Alexi carries our bags while Grandma carries her Tupperware container. "I figured we might want a snack later tonight."

Martin looks bereft and Grandma winks at him. "Don't worry, I left some cake on the counter for you and Jenner."

Our suite is incredible with three bedrooms and a terrace overlooking the city and the fjord.

Martin gives my hand a squeeze. "Well, as jelly as I am that I'm not joining the slumber party tonight, I've got to jet. Zoom meeting to review final contracts with RYB investors. Text me if you need anything," he says as he leaves.

Grandma looks around the room. "First a private jet to Norway, and now a penthouse suite. I never thought I'd see the day."

Geena yawns loudly. "Should we take a cat nap first? I'm sure you're exhausted, Grandma."

"Nonsense!" Grandma snaps on her fanny pack and adjusts her pink velour track jacket.

"I didn't fly halfway around the world to sleep." She hauls Geena up by her elbow. "Change your clothes, grab some more coffee, and be back here in five minutes. We've got the next forty-eight hours to see everything we can in Oslo. Let's go!"

***

You'd have thought that we would spend the day talking about Mom, but Grandma isn't someone who believes in wallowing in misery. Instead, she whisks us away on the ultimate tour of Oslo. Very few people approach me for autographs or selfies. I think my grandma and sister make the perfect disguise for me. I'm grateful for the anonymity; I don't think I could handle a huge fan circus right now.

Geena is dead on her feet by dinnertime, falling asleep on our drive back from touring the towering Olympic ski lift outside town. Grandma and I order room service while Geena goes to bed.

"Your grandfather would have loved to come here. He always wanted to travel, but that was put on hold when he was drafted for Vietnam. Once he came home, he'd lost the travel bug."

"I didn't know Grandpa was in Vietnam. I don't remember him very well."

"He died when you were very young." A slow smile spreads across her face as she reminisces. "You know you got your talent from him, don't you?"

I snuggle back into the soft cushions. "He was a singer, too?"

Grandma nods excitedly. "He had the most beautiful tenor voice. He was part of the Army Chorus after an injury ended his combat career. He would have been over the moon to know his granddaughter is making a living as a singer."

"Wow! I never knew any of that. Dad never told me."

A look flashes across Grandma's face, pain mixed with anger. "Well, I'm sure a lot of that has to do with what happened between your mom and me." She looks at me. "I wish that argument never happened, but I had to speak up for you girls. I'll always regret the time we lost together." She looks at me, her eyes full of love. "But we're here now, and that's what's most important."

I tug at a loose thread on one of the throw pillows, twisting it as I talk. "We've never fought like that before. I don't know if I can ever forgive her for the nasty things she said. Part of me keeps expecting this to blow over, like when she freaks out over losing car keys or getting cut off in traffic." I look plaintively at Grandma. "She's my *mother*. I can't just stop talking to my mother, can I?" The thread I've been playing at is destroyed and it looks how I feel. "But I can't go on with how things are now...and I don't see her changing or apologizing."

Grandma gives me a sympathetic look. "My heart just breaks for you, sweetheart. I might not be Jodi's biggest fan, but I know deep down she really does love you and Geena very much. She must be out of her mind to have talked to you like that." Grandma pauses for a moment, thinking. "I hope, in time, your mother will calm down and put things right."

We fall into silence, lost in our own thoughts.

Grandma gets up and stretches. "I think the time change is finally catching up to me." She gives me a big hug. "You'll get through this, Dani. Try not to close off your heart to your mom. She might surprise you."

We walk down the hall, arm in arm. As Grandma turns to enter her room, I give her another hug. "Thanks for coming. I don't know what I would have done without you."

She gives me a warm smile. I feel more comfort and love from that smile than I've ever gotten in my entire life with Jodi. "I'd fly to the moon for you, Dani. Nighty-night."

38

I'm up at five again—too much sleep from the day before. Geena's awake, drinking a cup of coffee at the table. A room service tray is spread out, and there's an open textbook next to her plate. "Morning! I was starving so I ordered breakfast. Hope you don't mind."

She pours me a cup of coffee and loads it with cream and sugar. "I know you don't normally drink this stuff, but once in a while it won't kill you." I take the cup, sit across from her, and look out the huge picture window at the dark city. We speak softly so we don't wake Grandma.

"How're you feeling?" Geena asks, offering me a warm croissant. I shrug my shoulders as I pull apart the buttery pastry, showering crispy flakes over the table.

"I don't know. I don't want to talk to her. And I'm sure she doesn't want to talk to me. She has to return the advance money and she said she already spent it. She stopped working at the hotel, so I don't know where she's going to get it." I take a sip of the overly sweet coffee and grimace.

Geena snorts. "And she can't dip into my college fund anymore, so she's really up a creek." She sighs. "I'm sure Dad will bail her out. Though he's totally pissed, trust me. He had no idea she was writing a book or that she forged the release form. Can you imagine your spouse writing a whole book in secret? Who *does* that?"

We look at each other at the same time and say "Mom." I smile. "At least we've still got our sense of humor."

"Not to sound like I'm siding with Mom, but it was pretty cold to sick the TrueHarts on her. She's getting pounded online, they showed up to the house, they're sending hate mail...it's a mess."

I gape at Geena. "So, it's OK for Jodi to write a book full of lies and forge my signature on a release, but I'm the monster because I tell my fans what she's done?"

"You know what your fans are like! You've let them troll Zoe for months because you think she's after Sean. They bombarded Sean and his family when you were trying to get his attention, so *of course* you had to know what they'd do to Mom when they found out about the book." She waits for me to respond, eyebrows raised.

It's all I can do not to lose it. I practically growl. "Traitor much, Geena?"

"I just *said* I'm not taking Mom's side. I'm trying to teach you how to fight fair. Something neither you nor Mom can do, apparently."

Her lecturing me like I'm a child is only making me more furious. But I know I'll seriously embarrass myself if I lose my temper like Jodi always does.

Geena continues. "You're the one with all the power here, Dani. We both know Mom's a total psycho and, yeah, she messed up royally, but you have the ear of the world. And you set the world on Mom for revenge. It's not a good look for you."

The caustic look I shoot Geena only makes her chuckle. "Or were you going for 'Squabbling Family Feud' as part of your new image? You look petty, while Mom looks money-hungry and deceitful. There are no winners in this fight, trust me."

"I don't look petty. I look strong." I hate the way my voice sounds high-pitched and peevish. I take a deep breath, trying to sound calm. "I'm standing up for myself and showing the TrueHarts it's not OK for people to lie about you."

"Did you already forget how Sean felt when you involved your fans in your relationship? You've got to stop hiding behind your fame and start dealing with your life without the help of your employees or your fans."

I stand up abruptly, causing the dishes to clatter on the table. My voice drips with forced control. "If you feel that way, why did you bother coming? I had no *idea* you were so close with Jodi, especially after she stole your tuition. You'd think you'd show a little loyalty to me, considering I was the one who swooped in and saved your education." I hold up my palms in surrender. "I'm the victim, Geena. Try and remember that."

I storm out, seething. *Who does she think she is defending that witch? Jodi's ruined both our childhoods and stole from Geena. But I'm the problem for telling my fans what she's doing wrong?*

I pace around my room. Finally, I FaceTime Lauren, hoping she will talk me off the ledge.

"Hey, D! Didn't think I'd hear from you with your family visiting."

"I'm so pissed, Lauren. I need someone to talk to."

"What's going on?"

I fling myself onto the bed. "Geena had the nerve to tell me *I* was out of line for telling the TrueHarts about Jodi's book stunt. She thinks it's unfair to bring them into it, even though I didn't start this whole thing and I'm just protecting them and myself from whatever lies Jodi put in that book."

"Huh, that sounds weird. I mean, I know the TrueHarts can be a bit extra at times, but you've got a right to let people know the book isn't authorized. Are you sure you understood what she said? It's not like Geena to take up for your mom."

"It is totally *not* like Geena. Maybe shaving her hair off has shaved some brain cells or something. God, this whole thing sucks start to finish."

"I know it does. Even if Geena didn't say what you wanted to hear, she flew out right before midterms...that's a pretty big ask for a college freshman."

I sit up. "Midterms?"

"Yeah, midterms, remember them?"

"Oh crap." I flop back down, my anger deflating. "Now who's the jackass? I got so caught up in everything with Jodi I didn't realize what's going on with Geena right now."

A heavy pause stretches between us, and I can feel what Lauren is thinking. "And I guess that I'm doing that to you, too?"

"Yup. I'm used to it now, I guess. But it still sucks. Being in a relationship with you is very one-sided these days. I only seem to hear from you when something amazing has happened or you're in tears."

Sheepishly, I reply. "Sorry."

"Thanks for apologizing. Maybe one day you'll even do it without people having to point it out." Lauren sighs. "I love you, D, but being your friend is exhausting."

I go from feeling justifiably wronged and angry to feeling like a self-centered idiot.

We spend a few more minutes talking; I make sure to ask Lauren lots of questions about Tom and her family. But I sense she knows it's something I'm trying to do rather than something instinctive, and the conversation feels stilted and unnatural. She begs off the call, saying she has a test to study for.

I drag myself down the hall and tap on Geena's door. When she calls out, I sit on the bed while she brushes her hair.

"I'm sorry, G. I overreacted."

She looks at me in the mirror. "You figure that all on your own or did someone have to tell you?"

I flash hot. Embarrassed, I cop to it. "I talked to Lauren."

Geena turns around, packing things into her purse. "It's OK. You're under a lot of pressure, and this whole Mom thing is a nightmare." She looks up at me. "But sooner or later you're going to have to realize that everyone around you is not here to serve you. Believe it or not, we all have lives that are important to us, even if they aren't that important to you."

"You're right. And I really appreciate your coming all the way here with midterms looming. I'm really sorry."

"Thank you. Love you, sis."

"Love you, too."

***

We squeeze in a few museums after breakfast before we drive to the Telenor Arena. Grandma and Geena insist on coming to soundcheck, and I realize they haven't seen me perform live since my album release party.

I'm digging tonight's costume, which is based on the traditional Norwegian folk dress. It has a red satin vest, heavily embroidered with colorful birds and flowers, coupled with a short black skirt with similar embroidery, lacy petticoats peeking out, and pair of red satin bootie shorts with the Norwegian flag on the butt. White over-the-knee tights with black embroidered ribbon up the sides paired with patent-leather platform Mary Janes complete the look. My hair is styled in two braids that are secured on top of my head, and Petra has created a tiara that looks like a flower crown.

Pauline is putting on the last touches of makeup when there's a knock at the door. "Come in!" I shout. The door flings open, and Martin leads Grandma and Geena inside.

Geena sits on the sofa. "I can't believe you do this every few days in a different city. This show is a monster to set up and take down! No wonder you're so wrapped in what's happening on the road." She dips her head. "Respect!"

"Thanks, G! I mean, it's not studying biochemistry at Rice, but for me, it's not too bad."

Geena scowls. "Don't go echoing back all that crap Mom stuffed into your head. You know you're smart. You just took a different path."

I catch Grandma giving me an appraising look. "Fine, I'm just as smart as you. Better?"

Grandma smiles at me. "It will be better when you start believing it." She turns to Martin. "So, when does this shindig get started? I want to make sure we have plenty of time to get to our seats."

"Why don't you stay for the pre-show huddle, Mrs. Truehart? Then Carlton can take you to your seats. He'll be sitting with you in case you need anything."

Grandma smiles. "I've told you a million times, call me Ardell."

Carolina's voice booms over the loudspeaker, "Thirty minutes!" Grandma and Geena jump.

Martin offers Grandma his arm. "That's our cue, Ardell. Shall we go?"

* * *

The show is a trip; the audience goes wild as I descend to the stage on my crown. Grandma insisted she wanted to sit in the front row instead of the luxury box Jenner had arranged. It is so cool to see her bobbing her head, surrounded by the TrueHarts, who give her and Geena tiaras to wear. I bring them onstage during the encore while Martin and I are belting out "Try and Stop Me." Grandma drives the crowd crazy with her dance moves. It's a show I'll never forget.

Backstage, we all pose for pictures with the TrueHarts. A few of the regulars hold up signs with "TrueHarts for Truth" and "Stop the Lies." I pose, thumbs up, as Martin and Geena look on, tight-lipped. I have Carlton immediately post them online.

Jenner's arranged for a buffet backstage, and we hang out with the dancers and the band as the crew dismantles the stage. Martin hurries over, my phone in his outstretched hand. "It's Sean!"

"Sean!" I duck into my dressing room and collapse on the couch.

"Hey, Swiss Miss!"

I laugh and feign seriousness. "It's Norwegian Miss, actually. We're in Oslo."

I remember what Lauren said about our friendship being one sided, so I immediately launch into a list of questions. "How are you? How's your family? What happened at the game yesterday?"

His smile fades into a look of concern, "While I appreciate the interest in my life, it's you I'm concerned about. I got Martin's text that you had a blow up with your mom. What happened?"

I sniff. "Nothing new other than Jodi sinking to the next level of selfish. She wrote a book on my life *in secret*, forged my signature on an authorization form, and lied to the publisher about having my permission for the book. When I confronted her, she said I was a bitch and she wished I'd never been born."

"Holy crap!"

The shock on Sean's face makes me feel awful. Every time I tell Sean some new drama with my family, it's humiliating. Sean's family is so normal.

"Dani, I'm so sorry. I'd be devastated if my mom said something like that to me. Are you OK?"

"Yeah. But don't you get tired of hearing about my messed-up family? Because I'm tired of telling you about it." A hard knot of tension builds up in my chest as I put my fear into words. "I worry that things with us are so complicated because of my family and my life that you're going to get tired of dealing with it all."

"It's not my favorite topic, but it's not like you're making this stuff up, either." He gives me a look that melts my heart. "I love you."

His love, pouring through the screen, calms the panic welling in my chest. "That's one worry you can take off your list," he says. "Let's face it, we haven't had a Jodi-fueled problem in a while, so it was about time she did something stupid."

I laugh, feeling instantly understood. "That's what I told Martin!"

"The TrueHarts are ripping her a new one. It's pretty savage."

"Geena said the same thing this morning. Look, I'm just protecting myself."

Sean scrubs his face and sighs. "I don't want to get into a big fight with you about this. Just watch out. I've been on the receiving end of the TrueHarts, and it's overwhelming. Who knows what it will drive your mom to do if she's as crazed as she sounds. It might make everything worse."

I sigh, remembering the huge blow out we had in Paris. "OK, fine." I rearrange my annoyed face and smile. "I promise I won't post any more about Jodi. Your opinion matters to me. If you think it's wrong, I'm going to listen to you."

Sean is taken aback. "Wow, really?" He looks relieved. "Thanks, D."

My eyes connect with Sean's. "It's important you know that I'm hearing you."

"Thank you. And I really am sorry about your mom."

"Thanks. I'm taking a break from all things Jodi for now. I can't waste any more time on her."

A knock on the door and Geena pops her head in. "Hey, we need to wrap things up. Grandma's tired, and we have a long trip home tomorrow." Geena waves at the phone. "Hi, Sean!"

"OK, let me get out of this costume. I'll shower back at the hotel. Can you send Petra over?"

Geena nods. "Sure."

I look at the phone as the door closes. "Gotta go. Thanks for calling. I'm sorry I didn't reach out sooner, things got a little crazy here with my family visiting."

"No problem. Take care of yourself. We'll talk after they leave."

"OK, bye."

"Bye."

I blow a kiss and hang up with mixed feelings. *I love that Sean wants to help, but I hate the fact he's always stuck dealing with my family drama.* Thankfully, Petra comes in and saves me from my thoughts.

39

Saying goodbye to Grandma and Geena is hard. They've made me feel so much better just by being here. Bags packed, we ride down to the lobby where the entire dance troupe is waiting.

Beau gives Grandma a hug and spins her around. "We couldn't let you leave without saying goodbye, Ardell!" He sets her down on her feet, keeping a steadying hand on her back. The small gesture warms my heart.

Grandma hugs each dancer, working her way through them like a celebrity. Geena and I watch her, amazed. Martin joins us. "Your grandma is incredible."

The dancers mill around as I tearfully hug Grandma. "I don't want you to go."

She rubs my back gently. "I know, sweetheart. But you'll be home before you know." She breaks the embrace and cups my face in her hands, smoothing the hair away from my eyes. "You're going to be OK."

I nod, and she steps away to hug Martin and Jenner. I turn to Geena. "Thanks again, sis. I love you."

Geena hugs me hard. "I love you, too." Arm-in-arm, we walk toward the street. Grandma and Geena climb into the limo and roll down the window.

"Safe travels, everyone!" Grandma calls, waving with both hands. "Lots of love. Bye!"

I sigh as the limo drives off. Martin puts his arm around me. We watch the dancers pile onto the bus. "Why don't you ride with them for a while? I'll tell Regina you're skipping school today."

"Really?" Sadness is replaced with excitement as I imagine a day filled with music, movies, and a few cocktails.

Martin smiles ruefully. "You're already so behind I can't see how one more day will make a difference."

I jump up and down as Martin waves Carlton over and fills him in. "See you in Stockholm!" Martin calls as he gets onto his bus.

Carlton and I climb aboard the dancers' bus. Beau lets out a whoop when he sees me. The bus is a mess as usual—people, clothes, and trash on every surface and the funk of old food and unwashed clothes fills the air. Music blares over the speakers, competing with the movie playing on the big screen. The dancers talk loudly, trying to be heard over all the noise. It seems like heaven right now.

Carlton makes a beeline for Bronwyn. He plops down next to her on the crowded couch. "It's great to see you, Bronwyn! I can't wait to show you the pictures of a Viking ship I took yesterday. The craftsmanship is stunning when you consider the crude tools they had." He scrolls on his phone. "Just a minute and I'll pull them up."

Bronwyn gives him a pained smile and tries to scoot away from him, but a napping dancer blocks her escape. I wink at her as I walk back to the kitchen.

"Can't wait! I just need to grab something in the back." Bronwyn follows me and grabs Beau by the hood of his sweatshirt as she passes, dragging him behind her.

"Hey!" Beau barks, "Watch the drinks!" He juggles two red plastic cups, trying not to spill their contents. With a yank, Bronwyn closes the curtain that separates the kitchen from the lounge. Beau hands me a cup, and I take a deep pull of the fruity drink, leaving a little red mustache on my face. He points and laughs as I try in vain to wipe it off.

"I've had it!" Bronwyn cries. Beau and I try to shush her, but she ignores us. "I've been putting up with that nerd for weeks, fawning all over me, leaning in with his rank breath, touching me with his sweaty hands." She shivers, grimacing at the memory. "I'm done! I can't look at one more space documentary or nature photo. You're going to have to find another stooge to take that freak off your hands so you two can party." She turns and stomps to the back of the bus.

Beau and I look at each other, wide-eyed. After a few seconds, we notice the unnatural silence on the bus. We pull the curtain back and see Carlton standing in the aisle, a crushed look on his face.

"Carlton!" Beau says, surprised. "What's up, bro?"

"What did she mean, 'take that freak off your hands'?" Carlton stutters painfully, "She was the one...she said she...I thought..."

Beau holds up his hands. "Don't worry, Carlton, she's just a little moody today. You know how us dancers are. Emotional, flighty...just give her a few minutes, she'll be fine."

Carlton's eyes widen, realization dawning. "You've been partying together *all* this time? While I've been talking with Bronwyn?"

I shake my head vigorously. "Not that kind of partying. Just hanging out, you know?" As I watch Carlton's eyes move down to my hand, I realize too late that I'm still holding my cup. I try to hide it behind my back, but he grabs it, sloshing sticky red liquid everywhere. He sniffs the contents, and his face grows dark.

"Just hanging out, huh?" he says accusingly. "You must really think I'm stupid!"

My mouth runs dry as I imagine my parents finding out about this. Spiteful Jodi will surely demand I come home. I can't think of anything to say. I look at Beau desperately.

Cool as a cucumber, Beau gives Carlton an appraising look and plucks my cup from his hand, talking as he pours the contents into his own cup. "I don't know what you're talking about. I'm sorry Bronwyn rejected you, but that doesn't give you the right to yell at Dani and make up lies." He tosses my empty cup on top of the overflowing garbage can, but it falls and rolls under the table.

Carlton and I both stare at Beau, dumbfounded.

Beau shouts down the bus. "Anyone ever see Dani drink anything other than soda here on the bus?"

In unison, every dancer looks at Beau, shaking their heads. Some shout out "no." As friendly as Beau is, the dancers know how vengeful he can be and prefer to keep on his good side. Beau looks back at Carlton smugly. "There you have it."

Carlton turns purple. He sputters at Beau, spittle flying everywhere, losing his last scrap of dignity. "Ever since you got hired, you've been acting like you're invincible. You may have Dani fooled, but Martin is already onto you. He knows you're undermining his guardianship; he's just never had any proof it *until now*. What do you think Jenner will say when he finds out you've been providing alcohol to Dani regularly? Think she'll be able to save your job then?"

Beau coolly wipes his face. "Say it, don't spray it, Carlton." A few dancers giggle uncomfortably as Beau continues. "I guarantee no matter what you say, *I'll* be fine. After all, what do you think Jenner would say if he found out you were too busy pathetically trying to cop a feel on Bronwyn to do your job and chaperone Dani properly?"

Carlton clenches his fists, which makes Beau laugh.

"What? You're going to hit me now, dough boy?" Beau raises his hands in surrender and taunts, "Go ahead? Try it."

I cringe at Beau's mocking tone and try to give Carlton a sympathetic look. Beau's no better than a schoolyard bully right now, and he seems to be enjoying embarrassing Carlton a little too much for my taste. But my fate is pinned to his scaring Carlton into staying silent.

Carlton raises a fist halfway but drops it. An evil smile draws across his mottled face. "Fists are the weapons of ignorance." He spins on his heels and stalks down to the driver.

I glance at Beau. The confidence drains from his face and my heart sinks. All his bravery was a front, and it looks like Carlton is going to call his bluff.

We watch as the driver and Carlton argue. Carlton whips out his phone and makes a call.

"Beau!" I turn and whisper fiercely. "How did this get so out of control! I'm dead if my parents find out."

He keeps an eye on Carlton and runs his hand through his hair. "I thought he'd back down if I just leaned in. Christ, this is out of hand!"

We wait for a few minutes and watch Carlton hang up the phone triumphantly and whisper to the driver. He plops on the seat right behind him and gives us a smug stare.

I take a deep breath. "Let me see if I can talk to him. We've always gotten along."

Beau gives me a questioning look and I mutter, "Well, kinda." I hurry down the aisle, conscious of all the dancers watching me. I sit next to Carlton.

"I am *so* sorry things got so out of hand. Beau didn't really mean any of that. He was just trying to keep me from getting into trouble. If my parents find out I was drinking today, they might pull me off the tour."

I search Carlton's eyes for a spark of compassion. But the hard, stubborn stare I receive extinguishes all hope. Carlton's pride has been beyond bruised. I can tell he's not going to let this go, no matter how much I beg.

"All my life, Dani, I've had guys like that..." he looks down at Beau hatefully, "macho idiots treat me like dirt, like I'm invisible. Their insults they think *I'm too stupid* to get." He snorts and shoots me a cynical look. "What, like a *dancer* can pull one over on me? I'm in Mensa, for Christ's sake. That dolt didn't even finish high school."

I put a hand on Carlton's arm. "You're right. Beau was insulting and condescending and totally out of line. But if you take him down, you're going to be taking me down, too. My mom is already pissed at me, and Martin and Jenner are still upset about London. You're the only one who can save me, Carlton."

His eyes soften for a moment and my heart soars. But then he looks up again, spies Beau, and his compassion evaporates. "I'm sorry, Dani. But you have to be more careful about the company you keep. I can't let Beau continue to be a bad influence on you or the rest of the troupe." He looks away and folds his arms resolutely.

I trudge back to the kitchen, utterly defeated. "He won't budge."

Beau curses. After a minute, he snaps his fingers. "Give me your phone."

"What?"

"Give me your phone!" He grabs for it as I fumble it out of my pocket. "Just follow my lead," he whispers as he dials. He holds up a finger to silence me.

"Martin? No, it's Beau."

Carlton stares at us. Beau turns away, closing the curtain behind him. I follow him to the table and listen.

"Look, I hope I'm not overstepping the bounds." He speaks urgently into the phone. "Dani's been confiding in me for the past few weeks, and I really think you need to know something. Gosh, this is so awkward..."

My stomach drops. *Where is Beau going with this? How did this get so messed up! Just a tiny white lie about Bronwyn liking Carlton so we could have a few secret cocktails, and now people might get fired? I might get pulled off the tour. Sean's going to break up with me if he finds out I've been lying to him.* My mind reels with all the awful possibilities.

"It's Carlton. He's been making Dani feel, well, *uncomfortable*." Beau pauses meaningfully.

"No, nothing like that. It's all those long staring looks, always *being* there, hovering in the background. I mean, I know he's Jenner's assistant, but it's almost like he's stalking her. He's always *there*, you know? Haven't you noticed it before?"

I'm mortified! *The accusations Beau is making are serious! Carlton's an adult! And while he's creepy as hell, and yeah, he stares a lot, he's never touched me or done anything inappropriate. This could ruin him if it got out. I wish we could rewind the day and be back at the hotel in Oslo. I'd never get on this stupid bus.*

I wave my hand furiously at Beau, but he avoids making eye contact.

"He did? Well, then I think he may have overheard Dani talking to me about it, and he might be trying to save himself. Look, I don't want to get in the middle of this. And if I've overstepped, I'm sorry. I just thought, as Dani's guardian, you needed to know." Beau listens. "He's up front with the bus driver. OK, I'll keep her back here with me. See you in a few minutes."

Beau hangs up, looking queasy. "Well, it's done. I think Carlton's lost all credibility with Martin."

I stare at Beau, shaken at the enormity of his lie. *Our lie.* "I can't go through with this, Beau. It's wrong."

"I know. But if we don't, you'll probably be pulled off tour and we're all out of a job."

"But you said after London MEGA would never let my parents do that."

"I was just trying to make you feel better. Now come on." He gets up. "We need to get Bronwyn on board."

I have the same sinking feeling that I had in the limo when Kayla freaked out on me for not wanting to go into the club. *Is Beau saving me or himself? Was he lying before about my parents pulling me from tour after London or is he lying now?* I wish I had someone I could ask, but I've backed myself into a corner. I'm all alone on this one.

Bronwyn needs no convincing to join our plot. Since Martin is friends with her mom, she'll do anything to keep her part in our scheme from getting back to her mother.

Soon we pull over at a rest stop in the middle of nowhere, and Carlton darts off the bus. Beau and I watch Jenner approach him. Carlton gesticulates wildly as he speaks. My whole body is tense as I imagine what he is saying.

Beau nudges my shoulder and whispers as we watch the scene outside. "All you have to do is say you don't want to talk about it. If Martin asks why you never told him, say you know how much Jenner relies on Carlton and you didn't want to cause any trouble. Don't get detailed. The less said, the better."

Martin rushes onto our bus, his expression serious, and sits across from me at the kitchen table. "Can we have a few minutes alone, Beau?"

"Sure." Beau gets up. As he walks behind Martin, he gives me an intense "don't screw this up" stare.

Martin gives me a sympathetic look. "Beau told me how uncomfortable Carlton's been making you feel. I had no idea. Why didn't you tell me?"

I shrug and parrot back what Beau told me. I'm so nervous, I speak in starts and stops, which gives Martin the impression that I'm extremely uncomfortable talking about this. *Which I am.* The idea I'm lying never crosses his mind; it crushes me that I am so unworthy of his faith in me. Desperate to make this better somehow without coming clean, I grasp at a straw.

"Look, touring is making everyone act a little weird because we're all together constantly. We've both always thought Carlton is a little creepy...but he's never *touched* me or anything gross. Maybe we just need a little space? Could he maybe just go back home?" I gulp, saying with more meaning than Martin can imagine, "I don't want to be the reason he loses his job."

Martin stares at me. "You are something else, Dani Truehart." He pauses, and I glance at Beau standing down the aisle, all color draining from his face. Tears well up in my eyes and I open my mouth to confess.

"Who else would worry about someone's job when they've been causing so much trouble? You are one in a million. I'll have Jenner send him home." He gets up. "Sit tight and I'll be right back."

Beau nods at Martin as he passes. Martin turns around and holds out his hand. "I know we've had our differences, but coming forward to help Dani..." Martin shakes Beau's hand. "Dani's lucky to have a friend like you. Thank you."

Stunned, Beau slides into Martin's seat. "Well, that makes me feel like garbage."

"I know."

Beau squeezes my hand. "At least you saved Carlton's job. That's something. And now he won't be watching you all the time, threatening to turn you in to Martin. He'll always have this shadow over him, so anything he says or does in the future won't hold much weight."

I stare into the distance, contemplating everything that just happened. "I don't know if that makes me feel any better."

40

Jenner questions everyone, and they all seem to have had their own uncomfortable experiences with Carlton's stares or his crowding their personal space when talking to them. Martin suggests that the problem could best be solved by sending Carlton home. Jenner agrees with mixed feelings. He'd do anything to keep me happy but losing his right-hand man on tour is tough.

When we reach Stockholm, Alexi drives Carlton to the airport. Jenner tasks him with preparing the compound for our return and locking down details for my next album. I wish I'd been able to apologize to Carlton and let him know everything I did to save his job. But I can't talk to him privately after publicly accusing him of being a creeper. Guilt dogs me throughout the days that follow. I'd never planned on telling Sean, Lauren, or Geena about what happened because I didn't want to lie to them. But since Oslo, Geena and Beau have been texting each other and he accidentally let it slip that Carlton left. So, I end up having to go into the whole made-up saga with everyone, which just makes me feel worse. It reminds me of Grandma's adage: "Lies are like potato chips; you can't have just one."

Preoccupied with remorse and worried that somehow my dirty secret will be revealed, I'm irritable and find myself snapping at everyone. The repetitive schedule and close quarters only add to my bad mood. As much as I want to distance myself from Beau, I find myself spending even more time on the dancers' bus, downing drinks to quiet my mind.

Martin's so enamored with Beau's trustworthiness, he's been assigned chaperone duty. I can't believe how stupid Martin can be sometimes.

The excitement of new cities and foreign countries has worn thin, and I long for the simplicity of home. I miss Magda's cooking, the compound, and my friends. I long for time alone and convince myself that once I'm back at the compound, I'll have the time and space to make better decisions, be more honest, and drink less.

More than once I've had Beau bring me a secret cocktail before a show to settle my mind and nerves. Never more than a few sips, but it does the trick to loosen me up and get me stage-ready.

One bright spot is being nominated for three Grammys: Best New Artist, Best Album, and Martin and I are nominated for Best Pop Duo Performance. For a few days while we're in Japan, I'm able to forget my guilt and revel in the honor of being recognized for my voice. It reminds me that all the other stuff I'm dealing with pales in comparison to the gift I've been given and the opportunity I have to share it with the world.

Before I know it, we've wrapped the tour in Auckland, and I'm on a private plane home. RYB and *Songs from the Road* publicity will start up as soon as I'm back while I somehow have to squeeze in Christmas shopping and catch up on school. I'm miles behind where I should be, and I don't know how I'll find the motivation to catch up. After Christmas, Lauren and I will fly to Chicago to film our *Fleetwoods* appearance, and then it's back into the studio for the new album, which Jenner wants to drop on my seventeenth birthday. It's no wonder that all I want to do on the flight home is sleep. The demands on me are overwhelming, and the secret guilt I carry is suffocating.

***

Pedazo de Cielo truly lives up to its name and the compound feels like a little piece of heaven. Nothing has changed, and it feels spacious and uncomplicated after the strenuous tour. I fall into my bed after the flight and sleep like the dead.

Martin comes into my room the next morning and opens the curtains. Weak December light floods my room and I groan. "What the hell, Martin!" I struggle to sit up, the huge king bed feeling enormous compared with the cramped tour bus bed. I rub my eyes, trying to wake up.

Martin, still in his pajamas, sits on the foot of the bed. "Sorry, I know you wanted to sleep in, but I didn't want you to hear this from anyone but me."

"What?"

He turns on the TV above the fireplace and Jodi, in a garish tangerine suit, face shiny and tight, beams at the camera, full Texas twang in effect. "Well, Kelly, I've watched this show every morning for years. Who'd have thought that a nobody from Texas like me would ever be here? Thank you for having me!"

The host holds up a book. "Your book *Truehart, True Home* has been an instant sensation! The entire world wants to know how you raised such an amazing and talented young woman."

Jodi smiles benevolently. "I'm happy to share my secret with anyone who's interested. In fact, I'm hosting a series of parenting seminars across the country starting tomorrow. We've already sold out in almost every city. Being a mother has been the greatest joy of my life, and my daughters mean everything to me. If I can help families achieve a fraction of what my girls have, I'd be honored to do it. I really feel like being a mother has been my calling, and I'm blessed to be able to share what I've learned along the way."

I scream and throw a pillow at the TV. "How can she get away with that? I thought Jenner stopped her book from being published."

Martin frowns. "He did. But clearly, she's changed the book's focus. And this whole seminar thing...I checked out the website. She states only that she's your mother. As long as she doesn't lie, use your name to promote the book, or sell merchandise with your face on it, we can't stop her."

"But what about what she says in the book?"

"That's what we need to find out. Jenner's trying to get a copy of it, but it's sold out everywhere." He looks at me pointedly. "Your mom's not stupid. She made sure it dropped while we were on the plane home, and she didn't do any advance publicity. Now all we can do is play catchup. Even if we get it pulled from the shelves, copies are out there. There's nothing we can do about it."

I grab my phone and start searching for the book. Martin pulls it out of my hand. "Uh-uh. We are not having another public feud. You need to stay radio silent while Jenner figures out our next move."

I start to argue, but he cuts me off.

"That's not a request, that's an *order* from Jenner and MEGA. The TrueHarts are nothing compared with MEGA's legal team. You sit back, keep your mouth shut, and let the adults handle this one."

I jump out of bed and pace the room, restless as a caged lion. "I can't believe this."

"Your mother's not one to lose graciously. Brace yourself, and do not, under *any* circumstances, talk to her. She is going to be calling you as soon as she hears from MEGA, which should be as soon as she finishes this interview."

I stare at the TV, my breath ragged, and Martin clicks it off. "Get dressed. We're going for a run."

I continue to stare at the blank screen, seething. Martin pushes a stack of workout clothes into my arms and nudges me toward the bathroom. "I'm serious. You need to run it off."

***

I'm so pissed that we end up we running for more than an hour, pounding along the hard-packed sand. I use my rage to push myself as hard as I can, my lungs burning. I'm exhausted by the time we return, but much calmer. We sit on the stools at the kitchen island as Magda lays out a breakfast feast before us.

Welcome home, *lanv.*" She places a glass of water and a mug of tea in front of me.

Magda's Hungarian term of endearment makes me smile and I stand up to give her a sweaty hug. "I've missed you!"

She beams. "I make special burgers for you tonight. You're too skinny." She pats my arm, and seeing Jenner storm in, bustles away.

Jenner pours himself a cup of coffee. "Your mother is one slippery fish. Since she's changed the book from your 'authorized biography' to her *experience* being your mother, we don't have a leg to stand on."

"So that's it? It's out there and there's nothing I can do about it?"

"Unfortunately, yes. If we find anything slanderous in the book, we can take her to court, but I think she was very careful this time around."

I hit the counter. "Well, she got her dream! A spot in the limelight with a built-in fan base, thanks to me. God, I wish she showed this much dedication to loving me rather than trying to make a profit off me."

Martin squeezes my hand. "I'm sorry, sweetie. She's just gone plumb-crazy."

The doorbell rings, and Jenner slaps his forehead. "Damn! I completely forgot to tell you. Your dad called while you were out. He's coming over."

Jenner winces when he sees my angry face. "I mean, he's here."

Martin gives me another squeeze and lets me go. "I think you should see him, Dani. I'd bet money he had no idea what your mom was up to."

I want to run upstairs. *I can't imagine how Dad is going to try to spin this to deflect blame from Jodi. He always takes her side, and I just don't want to hear it this time.*

Martin holds my gaze and eventually I relent. "Fine! But if all he does is defend her and tell me I need to forgive her, I'm out."

Jenner goes to the door while I take a sip of my tea and try to calm down. Dad rushes in and folds me into a hug.

"I am sorry, Dani. I had no idea what she was up to." He continues, "She said she had to go to New York for an interview...I didn't really pay attention. I had a big deadline at work, and I thought it was just another one of those stupid tabloid shows. When I turned it on today at work and I saw her..." His sentence trails off and he frowns. "It was the last straw."

He looks up at Martin and Jenner. "Any chance I could have a few minutes alone with my daughter?"

Martin looks at me. "Sure, if that's OK with Dani."

I give a small nod, and he gets up.

Dad sits on Martin's stool and takes a deep breath. "I don't know how to say this." He looks straight into my eyes, and I brace myself for awful news. "I'm leaving your mother."

"What!"

He sighs. "Ever since the day we reviewed your contract, when you pointed out how I always side with your mom, I started noticing things. Stealing Geena's college fund, wasting all that money you gave us on cars and plastic surgery...it made me see your mom in a new light. But I loved her, despite it all." He gets a wistful look in his eyes. "She was still my Jodi."

His expression grows darker. "But when I discovered she wrote an entire book in secret, forged your signature, and said those horrible things to you, it nearly broke us. She begged me to stay, and I did because part of me still loved her. I warned her if she ever did anything like that again, we'd be through

"After this," he says bitterly, "she's blatantly disregarded everything I said and turned her back on her own children for money." He looks at me, and my heart breaks because I see how painful this has been for him. "She's not the woman I fell in love with, not anymore."

He hugs me. "I'm sorry that I've let it go on for as long as I did. I should have stood up to her years ago." He looks at me. "Maybe if I did, none of this would have happened." He sighs, "I'm just sorry it took me so long to realize what was happening."

He looks so bereft, I hug hm. "It's OK." I pause. "Well, it's not OK, but...I'm glad you realize it now. What are you going to do?"

"Well, I'll be moving in with Grandma for a while." He sighs. "How pathetic is that? I'm almost forty years old and I'm living with my mom."

"Can't you get an apartment on your own?"

"Your mom's destroyed our finances and maxed out all our cards. We can't afford to run two households on my salary. I think the best move is for me to stay with Grandma for now." He waves his hand dismissively. "Sweetheart, this is stuff you don't need to worry about. Most important is that you and Geena know how much your mom and I love you."

I stare back at him cynically. "Did you read that in the divorced parent's handbook?"

"I read it online before I came here," he says sheepishly. "But I know deep down your mom does love you. She'll come around."

I smirk. "Like mother, like son. Grandma said the same thing."

He chuckles. "Good old Mom. One good thing to come out of all of this is that I'll get my fill of chocolate fudge cake and all the casseroles I can eat. What more could a middle-aged divorcée want?"

He sees the clock and jumps off the stool. "I hate to break bad news and run, but I've got to get to my lawyer's office to sign some papers." He stops and gives me a serious look. "You sure you're OK?"

I pause. *Lying about Carlton to save myself, drinking in secret to cope with life, my parents getting a divorce, having my own mother hate me then launch a career as a parenting coach for money...what could possibly be wrong?*

I plaster a smile on my face. "I'm fine."

I walk him out, grimacing once the door closes. I pull out my phone and text Beau.

> D: *Emergency! Any chance you can bring me some relief today?*
> B: *Be there shortly.*

So much for drinking less.

41

Beau keeps me sane and supplied the first few days I'm home. Our secret cocktails take the edge off my family chaos, and I'm grateful for them. Ever since Martin's newfound trust in Beau, he's a regular at the compound.

Jodi had a meltdown when she found out Dad left her. The neighbors called the cops because she was tearing the house apart, and they for sure thought someone was being murdered. The publicity did her no good as far as her parenting seminars were concerned, and her book sales have plummeted. She's close to broke, publicly humiliated, and insane with rage.

Logically, Jodi places all blame on me. Not her lying, thieving, or heartless self; but *me*, her teenage daughter who's been gone for the better part of a year. Every chance she gets, she's on some cheap tabloid show or magazine, moaning how my selfishness tore her family apart. Not quite the advice millions of moms would want to follow.

Dad's settled into his new routine with Grandma, and he seems to be having a sort of renaissance. He's not growing a ponytail or getting his ear pierced or anything stupid. But he seems more...relaxed. He smiles more, expresses his opinion freely now, and seems more confident.

Jenner and MEGA are doing their best to spin this mess away from me. They've killed any promotional interviews for *Songs from the Road* because, after the first few reporters kept bringing up Jodi, I'd either get angry or burst into tears. Now I only do step and repeats or other publicity that doesn't require speaking. Whatever statements they need to get out to the fans gets tweeted or IG'd. All the drama has boosted sales, and it's the number one album this holiday season!

I'm doing my best to keep my head down and walk the straight and narrow. Other than the occasional cocktail to soothe my nerves, I'm the picture of a good girl acing my homework, studying for my driving test, and killing it in the gym and at vocal practice.

While it's awesome to be home again, it's kind of a pain because I have to make sure I haven't had a drink before I see anyone. For the most part it's been manageable, but a few times, people have wanted to come over for a spontaneous visit and I've had to find an excuse to keep them away. Lying to Sean is weighing heavy on me. So many times, I've come close to blurting out the truth about Carlton and my drinking just to relieve my conscience. But then I remember the hurt look in his eyes during our argument in Paris and I bury that instinct.

If I just keep my mouth shut, everything will be fine.

Martin and Brett are in full-throttle RYB mode and they've bumped up the grand opening date. Once the investors were secured, they started constructions on the gyms and locked down my spokeswoman contract. We're set to launch the gyms around the time my third album drops in April.

We're already rehearsing songs for my next album, *Queen of Harts*. The vibe across the whole album is heavy synthesizer and electronic drums, like an homage to the '80s. MEGA wants to capitalize on the popularity of the last two albums and get this one out ASAP. It's like they're scared people will lose interest if I don't release new music every few months. It seems like a stress for nothing. If I've learned anything this past year, it's that I have the most loyal fans out there, and there's nothing they wouldn't do for me.

Christmas is here before I know it, and my family decides to spend it at the compound. Of course, Jodi isn't invited. I feel a stab of guilt on Christmas morning and almost call her. But then I remember all the hateful things she's done, and I hang up the phone.

***

It's New Year's Eve and Alexi is driving me to Sean's house. We're going to a party at Tom's, and I'm furious Martin made Alexi come with me.

"This is so embarrassing! It's not like there are going to be any terrorists or paparazzi there! It's just a stupid house party in Santa Clarita. I'm going to look like the biggest idiot with you walking in behind me."

"It is no matter to me if you are happy, I am here. Martin and Jenner want me to look out for you, and that is what I am going to do." He smiles at me as he parks the car. "I'll try not to cramp your style."

I throw him a murderous look. "I'll be back in a second." I slam the door and stomp to the porch, punching the doorbell. I adjust my tiara. The rest of my outfit is casual—skinny jeans, silver tank top, and Sean's jacket.

"Dani!" Sean's mom opens the door and gives me a hug. "So good to see you, sweetheart!" She looks out the door and says jokingly, "You don't have any paparazzi following you, do you?"

She grins like she's the funniest person on the planet, and I play along. "Nope, looks like I lost 'em."

She invites me in. I give Mr. Mitchell a hug, and then I hug Sean's grandfather. He holds my hand, beaming. "P-P-Pretty as a p-p-picture!"

I give him a big smile. "You're looking very handsome yourself! Your speech has gotten so much better."

Sean enters, and, after giving his grandfather a kiss on the cheek, grabs my hand. "Bye guys, see you later. Happy New Year!"

"One o'clock, Sean. Not one minute later!" his dad calls out.

Sean rolls his eyes. "'K Dad!"

We leave and pause on the porch. "Now we can say hi properly." He pulls me in for a kiss, and it's a few moments before I remember Alexi. I tear myself away and glance at the car where Alexi smiles and gives me a goofy wave, like some nerdy father.

Sean cocks his head. "Are you serious?"

I nod grimly. "Martin and Jenner insisted. Sorry."

"Awkward, but what can we do? Guess it's a G-rated evening for us."

We get in the car and Sean is a better sport than I am, making small talk with Alexi as he drives. Alexi parks the car at Tom's house, and we make our way to the front door.

"Are you sure you have to come inside?" I ask, not bothering to look at Alexi.

"You won't even know I'm there. Quiet as a mouse."

"A six-foot-four combat-trained mouse." Sean snorts.

Inside, the party is packed. We can barely move.

"I thought Tom was just having a few people over?" I shout at Sean.

We shove our way through the crowd, but soon it begins to part for us as people see the mountain of a man walking behind us.

"I was hoping to blend in," I whisper to Sean, annoyed by all the people watching us, snapping photos and videos.

"The chances of that were slim to none no matter how many people Tom invited. You kinda stick out like a sore thumb, even without the tiara." My hand reflexively touches my tiara, and I do a double take, spying Zoe draped across an armchair, her shapely legs kicking in time to the music.

Sean follows my gaze and throws a nod to Zoe. "'Sup, Z!"

"What's *she* doing here?" I glare at Sean, who lets out a sigh.

"She's Tom's lab partner now and, well, with the way the TrueHarts have been going after her online, we all feel kind of bad for her. It's been pretty brutal. She's not the same as she was before. If you give her a chance, you'll see that."

"Are you effing kidding me? That girl has been a nightmare since I started high school, and now you're all buddies? Am I losing my mind? Are you?"

Sean snorts. "Forget it, D." I knew it'd be a long shot asking you to talk to her. He grabs my hand. "Come on, let's find Tom."

He tosses a wave at Zoe who smiles back. I'm confused when I realize she's holding the smile while she looks at me. She doesn't grimace or sneer like she used to.

What the hell is happening here?

We find Lauren and Tom in the kitchen. Alexi settles himself in the corner, arms crossed, not bothering to blend in. Several beer-drinking teens scuttle out of the room.

"Daaani!" Lauren shouts, waving a champagne bottle. "Let's toasht the new year!"

"It's eight o'clock." I laugh, dodging champagne that slops out of the bottle. "We've got some time."

Sean leans in and eyes Alexi. "And besides, I don't think her babysitter will approve."

Lauren blows a raspberry at Alexi, who raises an eyebrow.

"You're no fun!" she slurs.

"I think you might have had too much fun already." I look at Tom. "Is she going to make it to midnight?"

He takes a sip of his beer. "Who knows?"

I secretly long for a pull from that champagne bottle. "Since when do you drink, Lauren? Coffee, that's what you need."

Tom points to a cupboard. "Thanks, Dani. Everything you need is right there. I'm going to do a round and make sure the house isn't being destroyed." He hits Sean's arm. "Come on."

I set Lauren down in a chair and start making coffee. Lauren's body is like liquid, constantly threatening to spill out of the chair. "Seriously, when did you start hitting the bottle?"

"You're alwaysh on the road. Things here are not eashy. Sometimes a girl needs a lil pick me up."

She grabs for the bottle, and I lift it out of her hand, replacing it with a bottle of water.

"Sorry, Laur."

She rests her chin on her chest, eyes fluttering closed. I clear my throat. "So when did Zoe become everyone's best friend?"

Lauren slurs, "Af'r she chimed in about the whole London mess, the TrueHarts deshtroy'd her. It wass awful. I know she'sh been a total jerk to you but shtill, she didn't desserve to be lit up like tha'. Even the minions turn'd on her, afraid to defend her. She became a pirannah."

I look questioningly at Lauren. "A fish with teeth?"

She looks confused. "A purina?"

Alexi chimes in. "A pariah."

Lauren nods. "Thank you, babysidder! A pur, a pir...wha' he said."

I hand her a cup of coffee.

"Sean knew what it wash like to haf them go af'r him so he step'd up and befriended her when school started. We all kinda followed."

I look out into the living room and see Tom lean over Zoe's chair, talking intently and rubbing her shoulder. "Um, looks like Zoe's just switched focus is all."

She looks up and waves her hand. "They're jusht friens." She looks at me as seriously as one can when totally wasted. "He says I need to work on bein' a better friend to Zoe and trushting him more."

I look at Alexi, who shakes his head at me.

"I can't believe I missed all that. I'm sorry, Laur."

She shrugs. "It ish wha' it ish."

I glance back in the living room and catch Tom whispering into Zoe's ear as she laughs.

Doesn't look like just friends to me.

***

The rest of the evening is a total bust. We end up taking Lauren home at eleven because she has a killer headache from the champagne. We ring in the New Year at Sean's house with his parents, his grandpa, and Alexi.

The first weeks of the new year find me juggling RYB shoots, vocal rehearsals for the album, study sessions with Regina, obsessively going over my lines for *The Fleetwoods*, and driving practice with Martin. There is not one minute of the day when I'm not expected to be somewhere, fulfilling a publicity obligation for MEGA, preparing for an upcoming event, or learning something new. I'm exhausted, harried, and constantly annoyed.

It isn't until I start packing for Chicago that I realize how long it's been since I spoke with Kayla. She tags me occasionally on Insta and Twitter. I always respond, but we aren't as close as we were. Lauren and I are scheduled to shoot *The Fleetwoods* next week, so I reach out to Kayla to make sure things aren't awkward when we get there.

D: Hey Stranger! How's it going?
K: Good! Excited to see you. Was worried you'd cancel
D: Just needed some time. Things got weird
K: I understand. We good?

I think about it for a few minutes. London seems like a lifetime ago, and I feel like I've aged ten years. I think we can be friends if I don't put too much trust in Kayla.

D: Yeah, we're good

42

Martin, Alexi, Lauren, and I leave for Chicago; I've forgotten how easy traveling can be when you're not traveling with fifty people and huge set pieces. Lauren practically has kittens when she finds out we're taking Kayla's private jet. She barely sits still on the flight, snapping pics of everything on board, including the crew. Her excitement is infectious; I've forgotten how exciting traveling like this can be.

Production booked us a suite at the Langman, which is a hop, skip, and jump from the studio. A beautiful flower arrangement and a basket of treats, compliments of Kayla and Trey, greet us in our suite when we arrive. We get in early enough for the three of us to go to the spa for manis. We're in terry cloth robes having our nails done, and it feels like we're starring in our very own chick flick.

"You nervous about tomorrow?" Martin asks, examining his freshly cut cuticles.

Lauren gasps, "Petrified!"

I chuckle. "Lauren, you have one line. I think you'll be fine."

She sticks out her tongue at me. "Excuse me, Meryl Streep!"

"How hard can it be? I'm playing a waitress. I take an order, carry a plate of food. It's not *Citizen Kane*."

Martin scoffs. "Don't let her fool you. She's been practicing carrying glasses of water on a tray for weeks."

I blush. "Well, I don't want to look like a total idiot."

Martin pats my hand. "You have a nice little walk-on part. Could open the door for more if things go well. You'll both do fine."

***

The next morning we're up at the crack of dawn to take a limo to the studio. Lauren and I share a dressing room. It's a trip watching how excited Lauren is as she goes through wardrobe, hair, and makeup. By the time we're finished, she's been transformed into an ordinary high school student, and I look like a waitress in my blue polyester uniform and apron. They even gave me one of those little white waitress hats as a nod to my tiara!

As we chat in our dressing room, there's a knock on the door. I shout, "Come in!"

"Dani!" Kayla cries, rushing over to air kiss me. "So glad you're here."

I air kiss back. "Thanks for the flowers and gift basket."

Spying Lauren, Kayla rushes over and air kisses her, too. She looks like she might die from happiness. "You must be Laura." Lauren nods stupidly.

"Lauren," I gently correct her.

"Lauren! Of course, you are!"

Oh my God, I can't believe I ever fell for that act! How did I not see she's so fake?

"OhmygodIcan'tbelievei'mmeetingyouI'myou'rebiggestfan!" Lauren's words rush together and Kayla, well-versed in fangirl speak, is instantly charmed.

"You are *adorable*!" she cries. "I can't wait to show you the set."

I have to keep myself from rolling my eyes. Martin enters the doorway and grimaces.

Kayla grabs Lauren's hand and sets off for the door, but Martin blocks her way.

"Kayla," he says, his words dripping with disdain. "And I thought you were avoiding me."

Kayla smiles. "I was just giving you some space. I know after London I'm not your favorite person. I'm grateful you let Dani come to the show."

"As much as I would have liked to cancel, I know it's too good an opportunity for Dani to pass up. And I appreciate your reaching out to apologize to me personally, as does Jenner. Just understand that nothing like that will be happening on this trip." He gives Kayla a level stare.

"Understood." She salutes him, grinning, and heads to the door with Lauren.

"The girls are wanted on set to go over blocking for their scene," Martin says stiffly.

"Of course." She lets go of Lauren's hand. "Well, maybe later today I can give you that tour, introduce you to the cast."

"That'd be amazing!" Lauren gushes.

"Done. Ta!" She waggles her fingers at us as she leaves.

Martin turns toward me, steely-eyed. I hold up my hands. "You can put an ankle monitor on me if you want. I won't sneak out again, I promise."

***

Acting is harder than it looks! It takes a lot of effort to look so natural, but after a few takes, I pull off my lines somewhat genuinely and manage not to spill food all over Trey. The director seems super happy with what I've done and says she'd like to expand the part and have me back in the future. *Cool!*

Martin beams at me when I take a seat next to him off-camera. "Look at you, Miss Triple Threat. First singing and dancing. Now acting. Must be nice to be good at everything you do!"

I giggle and toss my hair dramatically. "It's a burden, but my talent must be shared!"

We watch Lauren do her line. She's just supposed to ask the cashier for her check, but she's really nervous. I'll give it to Kayla, though. She works her magic and has Lauren calm after a few takes. When Lauren finishes, the director officially wraps us and everyone on set applauds. We take photos with all the actors, and we're both buzzing with excitement as we head back to the dressing room.

Kayla pops her head in. "You two were amazing today." She looks at

Lauren. "I can't believe you haven't acted before! You should seriously consider acting professionally."

Lauren is glowing. "Coming from Kayla Spencer, that means everything. I've always wanted to be an actress, but I never thought I'd have the chance."

I look at Lauren suspiciously. "I thought you said you wanted to be a stylist?"

Lauren ignores me. "What do you think I should do? Could you give me any advice?"

"Oh my God! I have a brilliant idea." Kayla claps her hands. "I'll be your mentor! You can be my protégé." She wraps her arms around Lauren. "Let's go to my dressing room and map this thing out."

Martin jumps up. "Wait for me, Lauren. I promised your mom I'd keep an eye on you." He grabs his bag, muttering under his breath, "Help me, Jesus!" He hurries out after them.

I close the door and start to change out of my costume when the door bursts open. Trey barges in. I quickly pull up my dress, grateful my back is to the door.

"Jesus! Sorry!" Trey runs out, slamming the door. I quickly throw on clothes and open the door.

Trey is bright red. "Sorry, I thought Kayla was here."

I wave my arm to invite him in. "Kayla was here, but she just left to open up a talent agency with Lauren as her first client."

Trey laughs. "Well, looks like Kayla's fallen off your pedestal! No surprise after London, but I wasn't sure since you agreed to come here." He plops on the couch, putting his feet on the cushions.

I walk over and shove them off. "Didn't your mother teach you any manners? No feet on the couch. Especially if it isn't your own." I sit in an armchair. "You're sounding a little bitter yourself? Trouble in paradise?"

He exhales, sounding more like my middle-aged father than a young Hollywood idol. "I've been dating Kayla since I was fifteen. She's hot and we have a good time, but"—he rakes his fingers through his hair—"we shoot, we party, we make appearances. I'm starting to wonder if this is all there is." He gazes at me, a lost look in his eyes. "I guess I'm just bored with it all and not sure what to do about it."

I put all my acting skills to use trying not to react to the bombshell Trey just dropped.

He looks at me intently. "You know what I really want to do? Hike the Appalachian Trail. Strap on a backpack, walk all day until I can't move my legs, sit by a campfire and sleep under the stars." He snorts. "But Kayla doesn't like dirt or bugs or carrying anything heavy."

"I had no idea, Trey." I flounder, totally unprepared to deal with anything this heavy. "You two always seem so in sync, so together."

He smiles bitterly. "Thanks to the Kayla Spencer PR Machine! She has an image consultant on staff whose sole job is to find every mention of our names. They review everything in a daily conference call, and she either promotes or refutes posts to curate our image as the perfect couple. A break up would tear apart everything that she's built, and if I'm the one who does the breaking up, my image will be destroyed."

I feel claustrophobic listening to Trey. He looks so angry and helpless, no trace of his usual smugness. "Have you talked to Kayla about this? I'm sure if she knew..." I realize what I'm saying and let my words trail off.

I look at Trey intently. "Go hike that trail! Sometimes you have to do something for yourself, regardless of what anyone thinks." I feel like I'm talking to myself, my fervor growing. "Stop letting Kayla dominate you. Maybe if you take back some control she'll start respecting you. At the very least, you'll get to do something you've always wanted to do."

Trey looks at me admiringly. "You're right. God, you make it seem so easy!" His eyes linger on mine. The air grows thick and my heart beats faster.

"How is it that you're so much younger than Kayla but so much more mature?"

My desire to see where this moment takes us conflicts heavily with my loyalty to Sean. I try to speak, but my throat tightens with emotion, my breath quick. Trey leans in, but a knock at the door breaks the spell. He stands, and I tear my eyes away from him, flushed.

"Oh my God, there you are!" Kayla bursts in and plants a kiss on Trey's mouth. I catch him eying me as they kiss. I get up and turn to Lauren.

"So," I say brightly, feeling flustered, "how's life as a protégé?"

"It's the best! Kayla's going to introduce me to her agent. We're all going to have lunch when she comes to L.A. She's giving me a list of exercises to do to improve my elocution, and she thinks I should sign up for an acting course at Shipley Studios."

"Wow!" I try to seem enthusiastic, but I'm distracted by Trey wrapping his arm around Kayla's waist.

"We've gotta run," Kayla says. "We've got an interview with *Cosmo*. Guess who's going to be on the cover in May!" She does a little dip, leaning backward, and Trey clutches her hard to ensure she doesn't fall. He's careful not to meet my eyes.

Kayla blows a kiss as she leaves, dragging Trey behind her. "Ta!"

Lauren closes the door and starts changing out of her costume. I pull wipes from a container and start to remove my makeup, thinking about Trey. I catch Lauren's eyes in the mirror. "What?"

Lauren raises her eyebrows. "You seemed less than enthusiastic about Kayla's plans to help me. You barely said a word." She puts her hand on her hip. "Don't you think I can do it?"

I snap out of my thoughts. "Of course! I wasn't throwing shade on your acting skills. It's just that Kayla gets caught up in something new and forgets about it after the shine wears off. I don't want you to get your hopes up."

"I may not be as worldly as you, but I'm not a complete hick, either. Kayla really does want to help me. She gave me her phone number, and we have a legitimate meeting with her agent next month. If I didn't know any better, I'd say you're feeling a little threatened by the idea of me becoming a star, too."

My jaw drops. "Lauren, that couldn't be further from the truth, I swear!" I grab her hands. "There's nothing I'd like more than for you to be a big movie star, if that's what you want. Maybe I'm a little touchy because Kayla screwed me over when she seemed to be a true friend."

I look at Lauren. "If you think she's serious, then I totally trust your judgment. I am behind you all the way. I promise."

Lauren's eyes brighten and she engulfs me in a big hug. "Thanks, Dani." We smile at each other in the mirror and Lauren says solemnly, "And I will totally thank you in my Oscar speech."

We burst out laughing.

43

Hours later, I'm alone in our suite talking to Sean. Kayla insisted on taking Lauren out to dinner so they could strategize. Martin, refusing to let Kayla lead another one of his charges down the path of moral decay, insisted on chaperoning. Alexi is eating dinner in his room. For a short time, I'm alone—no one to please, no one watching me. It feels amazing!

There's a knock on the door. "Dinner's here."

"Call me later when you're finished," Sean says. "I have to get home anyway and take care of Grandpa while Mom's on a conference call. *Bon appetit!*"

I blow a kiss and toss my cell onto the couch. Another insistent knock on the door makes me jump.

"I'm coming!" I call, annoyed.

I open the door. "Sorry, I..."

Trey is standing outside the door, looking furtively down the hall.

"Can I come in?" he whispers urgently, entering without waiting for me to answer.

"Uh, sure." I step out of the way as he brushes past me.

"Kayla's not here," I say. "She's out with Lauren."

"That's why I came. I had to see you."

Trey sits on the couch. I check my cell, making sure Sean's not still on the line. I perch on the far side of the sofa. Trey gets up and paces the room. He picks up a decorative glass ball from the coffee table and spins it in his hands.

"I can't stop thinking about what you said this afternoon." His words tumble out, his mood swaying between excitement and anger. "I'm seeing everything in a whole new light, and I just want to start living my life, like, *right* now!" He slams the ball on the table, cracking it and leaving a dent in the wood.

"Oh my God, Trey!" I pick up the broken ornament, careful not to cut myself. I toss the pieces away. I rub at the mark, but it won't disappear

Trey grabs my hand. "Sorry, Dani, I'm acting like a madman. But you've shown me the way to unlock my life. I've got to start living for me!" He drops my hand and wanders away, lost in a chaotic haze. The more he talks, the more I notice his words are slurry, running together.

"I'm quitting the show. I'm done with acting. I'm going to hike the Appalachian Trail, and then maybe I'll motorcycle across Asia or somewhere exotic. Maybe write a memoir about my experiences."

"What?" I say, horrified. Trey seems to be having some sort of existential crisis that I, at sixteen, am completely unprepared to handle. "I said take some time to go on a hike, not flush your career down the toilet!"

Trey seems to snap out of whatever hysterical mindset he's in and stops, confused. "But you said I should take control of my life."

"I meant you should stand up for yourself more. I never said to trash your only source of income. You'll never get hired again if you quit the show on a whim and give the finger to all your fans."

Deflated, Trey sits on the couch, sweaty and disheveled. "Maybe I need to give this a beat. I *have* been drinking a lot since we talked."

The doorbell rings, and I jump up. "That's room service." I don't want the waiter to see Trey, so I flap my hands uselessly. "Can you hide or something?"

Trey rolls off the couch and crouches behind it. I stop the waiter from wheeling the cart in and get rid of him as quickly as I can. As I push the cart over to the couch, Trey pops up, swaying as he stands.

"Oh man, I'm starving. Mind if I have some?" He grabs a handful of fries and shoves them in his mouth.

"Uh, help yourself."

Trey sinks onto the couch. I cut the burger in half and offer it to him, and he devours it noisily.

My phone pings. Lauren's sent a photo of her, Kayla, and Martin at dinner. Everyone looks ecstatic except Martin, who looks like he sucked a lemon. I show it to Trey, and he stares at it morosely.

"What am I doing, Dani?"

"I don't know. You seem really unhappy. But quitting the show is crazy. I don't think alcohol and major life decisions go together."

I pour him a glass of water and he gulps it down. He wipes his face with a napkin and fixes his hair. He looks relatively normal again. He stares into my eyes, searching for something. I try to meet his gaze, but his look is so hungry it makes me feel uncomfortable.

"We really connected this afternoon," he says sadly. But drinking too much, coming here, and making an ass out of myself...I've screwed it up, haven't I?" He looks at me longingly for a moment and pats my hand. "I'd better get out of here before Kayla comes back and sees me." He gets up. "I'm still serious about changing my life. But you're right. I don't have to be so extreme about it."

I wonder if he really believes what he's saying or if he's just plodding along the path Kayla carves for him like a domesticated donkey.

"Is it OK if I text you now and then? I really like talking with you."

"Sure," I lie. *I really don't want to be involved with any of this, but he seems so sad.*

"Thanks." Hand on the door, he turns to me. "And even though I'm going to start standing up to Kayla, you won't mention any of this to her, will you? She won't understand, and I don't want to deal with her getting upset."

"OK."

"Thanks." Trey looks at me and touches my cheek wistfully. I melt a little, his crazy ranting momentarily forgotten. His eyes are liquid gold, and in a brief moment I'm swept up by the thought of this Hollywood idol wrapping his arms around me and kissing me deeply, searchingly, as if all the answers he's seeking are in me. My breath quickens, and I stare at his full lips, mesmerized.

"If I'd only met you instead of Kayla when I was fifteen. I can't help thinking how different things would have been." He sighs and opens the door, making sure no one is in the hall, and leaves.

Trey's words rocket around my head, and the place where he touched my cheek tingles. I'm restless, an intense throbbing at my core makes it impossible to think straight. It's all I can do to stop myself from racing down the hall after him. I go to the window and stare out at the city lights, allowing my mind to play out the fantasy of Trey and me together in my suite.

I'm dizzy with distraction by the time Lauren and Martin return. Lauren gushes about Kayla as we get ready for bed. I'm grateful for her excitement because she's so consumed with Kayla, she doesn't notice my silence.

A text from Sean brings me back to reality. *Crap, I forgot to call him.*

Thinking about Sean and what a stable and loyal boyfriend he's been helps me shove all the heat I felt with Trey out of my mind, though my body takes a little longer to forget.

44

Back at the compound, we start recording my third album, *Queen of Harts*. All the people who helped make the EP and first album are back, and I imagine this is what it must feel like to return to summer camp and see old friends. Not that I would know, because I was never allowed to go, but still, it feels nice.

School work is on hold because my life revolves around recording and resting my voice. I get the feeling Regina has given up on me. She still sends assignments, but I don't get flak if they're late or I don't turn them in. Martin's been so busy with his business he hasn't noticed, and I'm sure as hell not going to say anything.

I'm grateful for the rigorous schedule because it gives me a chance to focus on singing and not on the distractions in my life. Trey's been texting me almost daily, sharing plans for his hike, inspirational quotes, photos of yoga poses he's mastering on his quest for a "new Trey." He's growing his hair out and now has a tiny man bun; he's swapped coffee for green tea and wears a leather necklace with some sort of Buddhist symbol on it in diamonds. His whole Instagram account is #blessed with photos of him and his tiny man bun living at a higher spiritual frequency.

It's weird that he's texting me all this stuff. It's so personal that it feels like he should be sharing it with Kayla, not me. But she thinks that yoga and meditation are a bunch of crap, and she keeps threatening to cut off his man bun in his sleep. She's been texting me a ton lately, too, venting about Trey while humblebragging about how she's mentoring Lauren.

Lauren's been M.I.A. in the weeks since we got back from Chicago. She's spent every dime she's saved on an acting course at the Shipley Studios. She's been reading Shakespeare, biographies on all the great actors, and trying out a new accent every time we talk. I keep reminding myself how much Lauren supported me while I was trying to make it, so I bite my tongue when she calls me up with an awful Cockney or Russian accent. Sean says Tom's losing his mind with all the acting crap, and I can't help but wonder if this is driving Tom faster into Zoe's waiting arms. Lauren has barely mentioned him lately except to say how he's not supporting her, and he doesn't understand her "talent."

Despite recording, we're still shooting the RYB videos on the weekends, but now we're doing it in a legit video studio. I'm getting amped for the gym opening.

But the thing I'm most excited about is going to the Grammys. Martin and I have been invited to sing "Try and Stop Me," since we're nominated for best pop duo performance.

REVOLUTION! will join us on stage, and we'll do a cool mash-up of all their biggest hits. It's been a trip to meet his old bandmates. The stories of Martin as a teenager do not disappoint!

***

Thank God the wardrobe room is on the first floor, or I'd kill myself walking down the stairs in the gown Petra made for the red carpet! It's a huge tulle tiered princess skirt in navy blue, and it's at least four feet wide! The tulle corset bodice is covered with individual lace flowers and ties in the back with a trailing navy silk ribbon. Skin peeks out in between the flowers, and it looks both classic and incredibly sexy. Givenchy loans me a diamond-encrusted tiara band, diamond bracelet and earrings, and the whole look is finished with navy opera gloves.

A wolf whistle splits the air. I turn and see Martin dressed in a stunning yellow tuxedo, from his bow tie to his custom leather shoes. He's as bright as the sun, and my eyes hurt if I look at him too long. Brett trails behind Martin in a handsome but arguably plain black tuxedo.

"I tried to tell him he looked like Big Bird," Brett says, "but he wouldn't listen."

"You wouldn't know high fashion if it slapped you in the face," Martin retorts.

Sean appears in the doorway, smiling. He's in a navy-blue tuxedo and looks absolutely gorgeous. He tries to wrap his arms around me, but my massive skirt won't let him get close.

"Now I love that dress even more! Nice job, P!" Martin high-fives Petra.

They load me into the car. Martin, Brett, and Sean squeeze together on one side while my dress takes up half the town car. Terrance and Jenner must drive separately because of my dress. Getting out of the car is a team effort, but I'm not the only one with intricately constructed fashion, so I don't feel too embarrassed.

People shout my name as Sean escorts me on the red carpet, cameras flashing. I stop for a few interviews and Sean ends up fielding a bunch of questions about the whole *Second Chance* debacle.

He smiles at me as we head into the pre-show reception where all the stars are milling about, several clapping Sean on the back. "I know I'm not a fan of the press, but I gotta admit, this is totally cool. I feel like a celebrity."

Sean stops mid-sentence and I follow his gaze to Kayla and Trey, who are surrounded by photographers and screaming fans. Kayla is gorgeous and practically naked in a skintight, nude catsuit, preening for camera flashes. Trey is clad in a saffron linen suit and sandals like a Buddhist monk going to a business meeting—all prayer hands and nirvana. Apropos of nothing, he effortlessly stands on his head for the photographers, who go wild. Kayla rolls her eyes jokingly, trying to hide her annoyance.

Sean's voice hardens as he watches them. "It's easy to get caught up in it and forget who you are." He gives my hand a squeeze.

"Dani!" Kayla screeches and the photographers go wild. We haven't been seen in public together since London and the press swarms around us, flashes strobing as photogs snap a million pictures. Sean groans and

I plaster a smile on my face as Kayla and I air kiss. Trey gives us prayer hands and a small bow. We don't know what to do, so Sean and I mimic him. The photographers eat it up.

Kayla leans close to Sean, running her fingers up his lapel collar, seductively. "Sean, you look delicious!" She eyes him meaningfully and anger ripples through me. But the whirrs and clicks of the cameras remind me to play it cool and keep smiling.

She purrs, "You definitely don't look like a high school kid."

He smiles warmly, taking her hand off his and patting it firmly. "Ah, but that's just what I am, Kayla."

She gives him a smile that doesn't quite reach her eyes. I do a mental victory dance at his self-deprecating rebuff.

It's like I can see Kayla's mind working, reaching for another tack; she doesn't like it when people don't adore her, especially in front of a gaggle of cameras. "I see you two patched things up after London. It was cute how Dani made that little song for you. You're lucky that someone with such a demanding career takes the time to do something like that. But I guess she killed two birds with one stone: she calmed your ego and made a few hundred thousand at the same time."

I glower at Kayla, but my anger disappears when Sean kisses my cheek. "Don't I know it! I feel like the luckiest guy in the world to have Dani as my girl."

Kayla flashes a brilliant smile for the cameras capturing every second of our exchange. But I know she's incensed because her nostrils flare in an unattractive pig-like way.

I don't know why she's coming after me, but Sean's refusal to take the bait must be killing her.

"Well, enjoy it while you can. Stars like Dani often get bored when they're not dating someone on their own level. Most pre-fame romances don't last once someone makes it."

"A lot depends on Dani staying true to herself." Sean squeezes my hand. "Shall we go?"

As we exchange air kisses goodbye, Trey whispers into my ear. "Sorry about that. Kayla saw my texts to you, and she's pissed. Watch out."

I blanch. I let Sean pull me along through the crowd as he follows Martin to our seats. *What if Kayla tells Sean that Trey and I have been texting? Does she know he showed up at my hotel in Chicago? I put up such a fit about Zoe's flirting, but Sean never even texted her. There's no excuse for me texting Trey for weeks and never mentioning it. I've got to keep Kayla away from Sean.*

With anxiety twisting my stomach into knots, we find our seats for the ceremony.

***

I'm so preoccupied, worrying about all the ways a spiteful Kayla can blow up my life, that I don't hear the announcement for Best New Artist. I don't realize they've announced the winner until Martin snatches me up in a hug and screams in my ear, ripping me out of my thoughts.

"Oh my God, I can't believe it!"

Martin shakes me so hard, it's disorienting. Sean jumps up, clapping like a crazy person. Jenner and Terrance thump each other on the back, and people pat me on the back, congratulating me. In a daze, I look up and see my name and face on the huge screens suspended on either side of the stage. My knees buckle, and Martin's strong arms catch me and set me on my feet.

Trembling, I slowly make my way to the stage in a trance, careful not to trip on my enormous skirt. I stare out into the auditorium as I've imagined doing a million times before, but usually I'm holding a shampoo bottle in the shower. My cheeks quiver as I smile, the audience obscured by my tears. I spy Martin's banana yellow tuxedo through the blur, his bold style guiding me to my loved ones, anchoring me.

My first words come out strangled by the lump in my throat. "All my life, this has been the dream. Countless hours dancing and singing, rehearsing, missing parties and school." I choke up as my childhood flashes before my eyes—Jodi critical and overbearing, Geena supporting, Dad silent on the sidelines. I struggle to speak through my tears, overwhelmed. "I'm honored and I'm going to work even harder to show you how much this means to me. Thank you."

I step away from the mic as the applause thunders. I stop, panicked, and run back. "Oh my God, I totally forgot to thank everyone!" The audience laughs. "Martin Fox, Jenner Redman, Terrance Flemming, everyone at MEGA who took a chance on me. My family who stood behind me, Geena, Sean and Lauren, the TrueHart Nation"—deafening screams erupt from the upper balcony where they sit—"Everyone..." I look at the audience overwhelmed and at a loss for further words. I just nod. "Thank you!"

Music starts to play, drowning me out, so I walk off stage. *I just won a freaking Grammy!* I let loose a high-pitched scream of excitement and jump up and down as a throng of strangers crowd around me, talking and taking pictures. My entire body buzzing with excitement, I scan the surrounding faces, desperate to see someone I know.

Martin, Sean, Jenner, and Terrance break through the crowd, hugging and laughing together until a black-clad crew member sternly ushers us away. Jenner takes my Grammy and I reach for it, but Martin grabs my hand. "We need to get ready to perform."

***

The whole auditorium is on its feet for our song, the audience erupting into a frenzy when REVOLUTION! joins us on stage for the second half of *Try and Stop Me.*" We segue into a medley of their old hits and blow the roof off the house. The high energy continues as we snatch up Best Song and Album of the Year. It's a mind-blowing night.

I change into a much more practical one-shoulder black liquid sequined mini dress, and we take a limo over to MEGA's party. Jenner pops a bottle of champagne and Martin hands around glasses. Sean seems uncomfortable, but Martin reassures him.

"A sip won't hurt you." He hands me a glass. "We gotta toast Dani's first three Grammys with champagne. It's bad luck not to!"

Sean reluctantly takes the flute.

Jenner thrusts his glass into the air. "To Dani! For her angelic voice. To Martin, for training her so impeccably and trusting me after all these years. To Terrance, for his amazing lyrics and musical precision. And to *me,* for guiding us all to success. We truly make a wonderful team!"

We clink glasses and drink, talking over one another as we snap endless pictures.

MEGA's rented a Beverly Hills mansion for its after-party. Larger than life cut-outs of me line the silver carpeted driveway as we exit the limo. Everywhere I look, I see musicians and celebrities taking selfies with cardboard Danis. *It's so meta.*

Inside, the mansion is packed, and my songs are blasting. We make the rounds among the executives, shaking hands and posing for photos with their kids. After our obligatory schmoozing, Martin shoves a plate full of gourmet sliders at us.

"You've done enough glad-handing tonight. Go enjoy yourselves!"

Sean grabs the plate, and we make a beeline outside for an empty table by the pool.

"I'm starving!" I grab a burger. We lean into each other as we eat and watch the crowd.

We kiss for a few minutes, but I force myself to pull away as my body heats up. I catch my breath, looking into Sean's green eyes, then my eyes wander down to his full lips, lingering. I shake my head. "I think we'd better dance."

Sean stares into my eyes, and I melt even more as he whispers, "That's probably a good idea." He puts his hands on my hips and pushes me onto the crowded dance floor. We move to the fast-paced music, our hands wandering from each other's hips, faces, and shoulders. I can't stop smiling, the thrill of winning so many awards, being with Sean, surrounded by people who adore me. Jodi, Carlton, Kayla...everything I've been worrying about is forgotten as Sean and I move our bodies rhythmically, laughing and touching. I feel so free.

45

Grammy night really brings into focus what I should be concentrating on: being true to myself and appreciating where my talent is taking me. Living a simple and honest life, but without the showy yoga posing and prayer hands that Trey's touting. I've been getting too distracted by the negativity in my life. For the first few days after Grammys, I do just that. I throw myself into recording, really focusing on staying present in the studio. I spend less time on social media and more time on the phone with Sean, Lauren, and Geena. I find joy in sending thoughtful gifts to the people I love—a new laptop to Geena, theater tickets to Lauren, and Lakers tickets to Sean. I am calm and centered. I forgive myself for what Beau and I did to Carlton and put it behind me. After all, I can't move forward if I keep feeling guilty about the past.

As expected, Jodi tries to take credit for my Grammy wins, but I follow Martin's advice and ignore her. Eventually, the press will get bored and stop giving her airtime. Her importance to the world will fizzle and she'll fade out of my mind.

Riding down to the studio one morning, Martin hands me a newspaper clipping and I laugh. "I feel like I'm in an old movie." I shake the paper at him. "You know they put this stuff online, Grandpa? You can read articles and save trees."

"Har, har, very funny," Martin says. "It's a nice article in *The New York Times*. You're on the top ten list of the most influential young entertainers."

I read as the cart bumps along.

> *Dani Truehart, recent winner of three Grammys including Best New Artist, is a refreshing role model for young people. Despite a minor public incident during her tour last year, Miss Truehart has managed to steer clear of the partying curse that plagues so many young celebrities, instead reveling in a lifestyle of good clean fun. Too many young stars today feel the need to push the envelope, shocking their audience with their sexual power, railing against the constraints of society or pushing the bounds of their talent to prove they cannot be matched. Miss Truehart, free of the obsession of becoming a sex symbol or relentlessly re-inventing herself, is content with doing what she does best—singing lighthearted songs with clean lyrics that parents can approve of. While she's breaking no molds or social barriers, Dani Truehart is a consistent creator of infectious pop hits you can't get out of your head. She's proving to young girls the world over you don't have to sell out to be a hit.*

I look up, horrified, at Martin, who's beaming at me. "*New York Times*, baby! Congratulations!"

"Did we read the same article?" I screech. "According to this idiot, I'm not pushing the bounds of my talent, I'm not a sex symbol, and my songs are like ear worms you can't get out of your head."

Martin looks exasperated. "He didn't say 'ear worms.' He said 'infectious.'" Martin looks at me puzzled. "Your songs *are* infectious—that's why every single one has been in the top ten list."

A wave of petulance washes over me and I groan, frustrated. "Don't you get it? You know who doesn't change? Old people, boring people, people who don't know that they're irrelevant in the first place, so they keep doing the same thing over and over again, oblivious."

Martin parks the cart in front of the studio. "What the hell are you talking about? It says you're a success because you've consistently put out good, clean music, and you're not dressed like a ho. All the stuff, *may* I remind you, that I vowed to do as your guardian. You're putting out your third album and you're not even seventeen." He snatches back the article and gets out of the cart. "This is good news," he growls. "Get a grip, girl!"

He flings open the studio door and I stomp through. I drop my bag on the couch and flop down. Martin places his bag on the table, waving hello to the musicians in the studio.

"Tea?" Carlton walks over, offering two steaming mugs to Martin, steadily avoiding my eyes. Every muscle in my body tenses up. I haven't seen Carlton in months.

"Thanks," Martin says, a little coldly, and takes the mugs. "I'm surprised to see you here today."

Carlton nods, stealing a glance at me. I catch his eye briefly, and his gaze turns icy, so I look away. *Maybe I should have just let Jenner fire him. He can't be happy working like this, and I know I'm not happy seeing him. Maybe I'll talk to Martin about it...*

"The studio assistant didn't show up, so Jenner had me come in. I'll stay out of your way. Just a force of habit to bring you tea. You should probably get your own for the rest of the day."

"I think that would be best," Martin says with finality.

"We should be ready to go in a few minutes." Carlton scurries off.

"Sorry about that," Martin says. "I'm sure that was uncomfortable for you. You going to be OK today?"

Between the *Times* article and Carlton being here, the day is off to an utterly crappy start. A scowl settles on my face and don't know how to get rid of it. I shrug listlessly. "It's fine."

I imagine how others walking by might see me: pouty face, leggings, oversized sweatshirt. Just a cookie-cutter teenager, nothing edgy or original. I've become what I was worried about all those months ago when I talked to Lauren on my first night at the compound—a pre-packaged pop act. *My music follows a formula, my lyrics are mundane, and Jenner could get anyone to do what I do if they just fit in my costumes.* My thoughts reel out, exploring the many ways I'm so pedestrian, predictable, and unoriginal. One tiny paragraph in a newspaper has torn my world apart.

Martin nudges me. "Still obsessing about that article? It's a compliment, girl. You're *mainstream*, one of the most popular acts today. People will be singing your songs for years to come because they're *good*. You go trying to break molds and changing your personality every album, you're going to confuse your audience and burn yourself out. Just be happy."

The bungalow door bangs open and Beau walks in, pushing his sunglasses on top of his head. "Morning, all!"

Jenner pops his head out of the studio, all smiles. "We're ready!" He sees Beau. "Hey, stranger, what are you doing here?" Jenner's been Beau's number two fan behind Martin ever since the "Carlton incident."

Beau sits on the arm of the couch and helps himself to my untouched tea. "I haven't seen Dani in a while and thought I'd drop by."

Carlton comes out of the recording booth and hands Jenner a paper. I feel Beau stiffen. Carlton does a double take when he sees Beau and hurries away.

"Good to see you," Jenner says. "We're about to start recording. Why don't you grab a seat in the booth and see what we're up to?" He looks at me. "We're ready whenever you are."

I suppress a sigh and heave myself up. "Yup, let's go."

* * *

Today we're recording a song called "Rise Up," which is all synthesizer drums and keyboard; a very canned '80s sound with a fast-paced, toe-tapping beat. I've looked forward to recording this song for weeks, but now that we're ready to do it, it feels plastic and vapid. Everything about it irritates me.

With each run through, it's tougher to hide my disgust. Martin keeps trying to catch my eye from the booth, which I pretend not to see. I'm off key, missing my cues, and I can't find the heart to belt out the lyrics and nail the high notes. Midway through another horrible take, Terrance waves his arms at the band and stops the music.

"What is wrong with you today?" he snaps, frustrated. "You're late, flat as hell, and you have the unmistakable look on your face of a girl who's got diarrhea. What's the problem?"

Terrance hasn't spoken to me like that since we first met, and my back goes up. *Who does he think he is?* I notice Martin and Jenner tensing up. Carlton watching me from the booth only adds to my stress.

Sweaty and annoyed, I snap back. "My problem is this whole song feels like some stupid hero montage in an '80s movie." I slip into a fake excited voice and move my arms like I'm running. "Hey, kids, let's get together and save the world." I straighten up and give Terrance a withering look. "I think I'm a little beyond this empty pop sound at this point, don't you?"

Shock floods Terrance's face and he stares at me coldly. "You seemed fine with all of the other empty pop songs I wrote to launch your career." He looks to the booth, incredulous. "Two hit albums and she has the temerity to tell me that *she's* beyond *my* music?"

He turns back to me. "You'd better realize that just singing the songs I write doesn't make you a genius."

Jenner jumps on the mic as I put my hands on my hips. "Take a deep breath everyone. Let's calm down."

Terrance looks at the booth. "I don't need this, Jenner. I've been in this business far too long to let some overinflated windbag talk to me that way."

My temper flares, and even though I know I shouldn't say anything, just like Jodi, I can never seem to walk away from a jab. I clap back. "Maybe it's time you retire, Terrance. Hang up your cookie cutter and let someone with originality have a chance. I'm sure the world will breathe a sigh of relief."

"Dani!" Martin yells into the mic, and we all flinch at the feedback screeching over the speakers. The pain in my ears deflates my temper and I look up at Terrance regretfully as he flings on his jacket and storms out.

"Terrance!" Jenner cries and flees the booth, chasing after him. Terrance slams out of the studio.

Martin rushes in as the musicians awkwardly shuffle out. "Have you lost your damn mind! What the hell is wrong with you?"

Flustered, I run my hands through my hair. "I guess I'm just over the sound for this new album. It's all poppy and plasticky—no substance..." I trail off. I can't find the words to express my anger—my thoughts scatter like a pack of frenzied rats fleeing a sinking ship.

"I feel idiotic singing about fighting for rights and changing the world with happy synthesizers in the background. No one with any real life experience would buy this crap."

Martin groans. "I wish I could go back in time and kick my own ass for showing you that article! You're taking this thing way too seriously. And yourself, for that matter! You'd be exactly nowhere if it weren't for that gloriously freaky little man who can pull hit after hit from thin air."

He lays a hand on my shoulder. "Dani, you're a girl with a beautiful voice, but you have no idea of the talent and experience it takes to write songs like Terrance does. I'm ashamed you spoke to him that way. You're better than that."

I shrug off his hand and stare at him coldly, acutely aware that everyone is listening to Martin reprimand me. "I thought you were supposed to be on *my* side. You're my guardian after all. You wouldn't be here if it wasn't for me."

For a second, hurt washes over Martin's face. My stomach clenches, and I realize I've gone too far. But then his face hardens. "Correction—you wouldn't be here without *me*. If you don't get your head on straight, I'll pull you from this world so fast it'll make your head spin. By the time you go to court and get yourself emancipated from me, your wave of popularity will have stalled. I guarantee that you won't be able to pick up your career as it is right now without this team of industry legends propping you up. You don't believe me? Just try it."

He turns around and leaves, not waiting for an answer. My temper has completely burned itself out, leaving only a smoldering glow of resentment toward the controlling and demanding adults all around me.

Beau walks in. "You OK?"

I shake my head. "Jeez, I feel like an idiot for losing it." I clench my eyes shut. "I hear what Martin's saying about me needing everyone. But that article..."

"The one in the *Times*?"

"Yeah, it really got me thinking. I don't want to be this bland, formulaic singer. I want to be unique. But I'm stuck recording these stupid songs that MEGA's already approved. The album is due to drop in April." Silence plays out as I think.

I sigh. "I guess it's not the end of the world. Every song Terrance has written *has* been a hit. I should just suck it up and finish this album. Maybe look at some different songwriters for the next album? I'll be eighteen by then. I can start making my own decisions."

"I get what you're saying about wanting to break out of the mold MEGA has you in, but your delivery sucks, Truehart."

I tap my fingers on the piano, trying to fill the silence. Justifications rattle around my head as I watch Jenner, then the band, and finally Martin and Terrance file into the bungalow. An icky feeling washes over me.

I look at Beau. "You're right." He squeezes my hand.

"I've gotta go, but you can totally do this." He throws me a wave as he leaves.

Everyone settles in and I approach Terrance at the piano. "I owe you an apology." I take a deep breath. "I was upset about an article Martin showed me and I just kinda lost it. I took it out on you, which was wrong. I didn't mean a word of those awful things I said. Please forgive me." I hold my breath.

"Thank you." He meets my eyes, but the usual warmth and friendliness is gone. "Let's move on."

It's not the reaction I expected. Normally if I mess up, people accept my apology. *Maybe Jenner can talk to him and smooth things over.*

I look around the studio. "I'd like to apologize to all of you. I embarrassed myself as well as everyone here. I know I wouldn't be here without all of you."

Martin nods once, his unhappiness coming through in waves from the booth. The musicians murmur and shuffle uncomfortably, picking up their instruments, eager to move on.

"Well, all right!" Jenner's falsely cheery voice comes over the intercom. "A bumpy start to the morning, but that's what happens when you're family. Sometimes you lose it. Thank you for the apology, Dani. Let's keep going."

We forge ahead through the rest of the day, but the whole vibe in the studio has changed. I try to sing perfectly and be as agreeable as possible. But Terrance has fully retreated from our normal friendly banter, giving my notes to either Jenner or Martin and avoiding eye contact. I swing from guilt to anger, irked that Terrance can't get over it. *I've seen him be rude to strangers all the time. For weeks he treated me like garbage when we first met and now just because I freaked out on him once, he's completely writing me off? What a hypocrite!*

I break down in the afternoon and text Beau. As much as I want to be good and not drink, a day groveling to a pouting Terrance has put me over the edge.

"It's not the best session we've had, but we've definitely got a song here somewhere. Let's call it a day and hit it again tomorrow." Jenner looks wrecked after a day of managing Terrance and me.

I throw Jenner a sincere smile and mouth "Sorry." He smiles back.

I take a deep breath and approach Terrance as he packs his bag.

"I know everything I have is because of you, Martin and Jenner. I'm sorry about what I said."

Terrance sighs heavily. "I've always known you to be a sweet, kind person. I don't know if that is really how you are, or if you're more like the self-centered diva you showed me this morning. It's going to take some time before I figure out which one is the real you."

I struggle to keep my annoyance in check. He grabs his bag and leaves. I flop onto the couch in the waiting room. Martin and Jenner sit across from me. I know what's coming, so I wait. Jenner begins.

"Going on tour, working on your third album, a staff of adults waiting on you hand and foot—I get how you feel justified in what you said this morning. But it's extremely important for you to understand that you did not create your success alone. Every step of the way, I've tried to treat you with respect and understanding. I expect you to do the same for everyone on this team."

Aggravated, I exhale through my nose, afraid I'll snap back if I open my mouth. His eyebrows raise.

"You disagree with what I'm saying?"

Martin watches me, his entire face closed. We've never been so at odds with each other. He's always been my champion. I feel a little lost and angry that he's not taking my side right now.

"No." Again, I find myself floundering, trying to explain why that article sparked my anger so much. "I know you guys have put me where I am, and I am grateful."

"Doesn't seem that way," Martin says under his breath.

Jenner holds up a hand at Martin. "That's not helping. Let Dani speak."

"Like I was saying," I glare at Martin, "I know I owe everything to you. But it feels like you guys are making all these decisions, and no one is consulting me. It's 'Dani, go here, wear this, sing that.' I'm going to be seventeen in a few months, but you guys are still treating me like a child. I feel like Jodi's in charge all over again, and I don't have a say in anything. I'd like to put my mark on my career, and I don't feel like I have that chance."

Martin sits up to respond, and Jenner holds up his hand again. "When you got overwhelmed on tour, we adjusted your schedule and scaled back appearances to reduce your stress. You wanted your boyfriend to visit on tour, we made that happen. We helped you write a song and produce a video when you two had an argument. You cannot accuse us of not considering your feelings. Being treated like an adult requires acting like one. If you disagree with something, you need to tell us and give us a chance to work things out. You can't stay silent and then blow up because we can't read your mind."

The bubble of anger in my chest threatens to explode. I resent having to sit here, being lectured like a naughty child.

Jenner continues, "What is it you want?"

What do I want?

Is all my anger coming from that stupid article, the songs I can't stand, or does it lead back to all the other stuff I've been carefully avoiding—Jodi, Carlton, drinking. The more I ignore everything, the unhappier I feel. The unhappier I feel, the more I lash out and drink. Everything seems like such a twisted knot of a problem. I can't figure out where to begin to unravel it all and get to the root of it.

Jenner's staring at me expectantly as my thoughts jumble together. Finally, unable to articulate my feelings, I throw out the first thing that comes to mind. "I don't like the songs on this album. I can't imagine doing a whole tour with this music."

Jenner shakes his head, but Martin stares at me intently. I can tell he's not buying it, so I focus on convincing Jenner.

"Really, that's it? All this over some stupid songs?"

I nod. "I should have said something earlier. But everyone seemed to love the songs, and I knew we were under the gun to get this album locked down after we got back from tour. I thought I'd be OK with them...but I hate them."

"OK," Jenner says. "Well, unfortunately, we can't start over now. But you'll have three albums of songs to work with on the next tour, plus, hopefully, some new material."

"Thanks, Jenner. I'm sorry I didn't say something sooner."

The studio telephone rings, and Jenner gets up. "I'm glad we had this talk. We good now?"

"Yes." He leaves, and Martin continues to stare at me. I look away, uncomfortable.

"There's something going on with you. I wish you'd tell me."

I shake my head. "Just over-scheduled and tired. It's hard to record music you don't like day after day." I get up and sling my bag onto my shoulder. "Ready?"

Unmoved, Martin continues to watch me. I fidget with my hair self-consciously.

"I can't help you if you don't tell me. We've got so much coming up—the album, the gym opening, and another tour. I need you at one hundred percent. Just tell me what it is, and we can work through it."

I see the lifeline Martin is throwing me from his place on shore as I bob in a cold, dark ocean, trying to stay afloat on my lies. *Confessing to Martin about Carlton and my drinking, imagining the disappointed look on his face, the legal trouble I could put all of us into...I'm not willing to risk that. I have to keep these secrets locked inside of me to protect myself and them.*

I just have to do a better job of keeping it together.

"Nope. I promise I'd tell you if there was something bothering me. I mean, the whole Jodi thing is still upsetting, but that's nothing new." Part of me is disappointed that it's so easy to lie to Martin. I always thought he knew me better than anyone else, that he'd never let me get away with anything. But in the end, I guess he's no different than anyone else. Eventually, everyone gets wrapped in their own life and forgets about me.

Martin gets up. "OK, I'll take your word for it. Remember, even if we disagree on something or I'm busy with RYB, you're my priority."

"I know." Tears come to my eyes, but Martin doesn't notice as he grabs his backpack.

"Let's go." He holds the door open to me, and I'm grateful it's dark as we drive back to the house. My tears are dry by the time we go inside.

46

The world feels like it is closing in around me. All I want to do is curl up in a ball and sleep. Or yell. Or run away. But I can't do any of those things because I have RYB videos to shoot or publicity photos to take. I have awkward recording sessions with a sullen Terrance to get through. I have Lauren, who is so wrapped up with Kayla that she barely talks to me anymore except to brag about Kayla's plans for her while I wait to see if Kayla comes after me for texting Trey. It's nonstop all the time.

Now that he's single, Dad drops by more often, which would be great, but all he does is complain about how difficult Mom is being about the divorce. She's fighting him on everything in hopes he'll give up and come home. But he seems to like his freedom and is fighting back for the first time in my life. I'm glad he's standing up for himself, but I'm tired of hearing about it.

I've taken to starting my day with a little slug of vanilla rum that Beau keeps me supplied with. It calms my chaotic mind and helps me get through the day. If I do it before I brush my teeth and make sure I eat before I talk to anyone, no one seems to be able to smell it on my breath.

The liquor is still burning my throat one morning when Martin bursts in. I throw a towel over the bottle on my nightstand and stand in front of it.

"We're not knocking anymore?" I snap.

Martin thrusts his phone in my face. "Knocking is the least of your problems." I pull my face back, self-conscious of my breath, and try to focus on the screen. His hand is moving around so much that I snatch the phone and sit on the couch. Martin stomps over and stands in front of me.

"Someone just sent me this. If we don't pay two hundred thousand dollars, they'll release this footage."

I watch a grainy video of Beau mixing jungle juice on the tour bus, then pouring it into a red plastic cup and me drinking from that cup. Over and over, different angles, different days, clips of Beau giving me drinks on tour. Then me drunkenly dancing in London, more drinks backstage with Beau, and finally the entire clip of my freak out on Terrance.

It's two minutes and seventeen seconds of humiliation. Proof for the whole world to see that I've been drinking for months. I tear my eyes away from the screen as the video starts again, playing an endless loop of my shame.

Martin is livid. He is so quiet, it's frightening. I'm used to Jodi and her emotional explosions. When she loses it, it's always been an excuse for me to walk away. But there's no walking away from this.

"Right now, I am not even going to address that you've been lying to *everyone* for months about drinking. You are in more trouble than you know because not only are you sixteen, but half your fans are underage, and their parents are going to *flip* if they see this. Not to mention that you've just handed Jodi an excuse to come after my guardianship, because clearly I cannot control you."

Martin takes a deep breath. I cringe, waiting for him to continue.

"Make no mistake, we *will* address your drinking later. But what I can't figure out is who on our team hates you so much that they want to bring you down."

It hits me as soon as he says it.

Carlton!

But how? He said he didn't know that I'd been drinking on the bus until the day he was fired. There's no way he had that club footage unless he pulled it from the internet. And he knows that Jenner wouldn't give in to blackmail without a fight.

I have to be careful. I don't want to say anything that's going to get me into more trouble. *Martin now knows about the drinking, but not that Beau and I lied about Carlton.* I shake my head. "I don't know who it could be. What are we going to do?"

Martin scrubs his face with his hands. "You're on lockdown until further notice. Either you're in the studio recording or you're here resting. No Sean, no Beau, no Lauren, and no phone."

He holds out his hand, and, reluctantly, I hand him my phone.

Martin takes another deep breath. "Now, I want you to be honest with me. How often are you drinking? Was it just to blow off some steam on tour? Or is this something I have to worry about?"

His face is a knot of anxiety, his initial anger transformed into pure worry. It breaks my heart. I'm tempted to come clean, but I'm sure what we did to Carlton will push Martin over the edge. *It's only one shot a day, I can stop if I want to. Now that the pressure-of-the-tour drinking is out in the open, I have one less thing problem to deal with. I'll do better now.*

"It's not something you have to worry about. I was really stressed about all the stuff Jodie was pulling and being on tour and everything. It was just to ease the pressure. I'm sorry." Tears spill down my cheeks. "I've been so stressed about hiding it from you all these months."

Martin gives me a hug and sighs.

"It happened to me, too. I drank on our later tours because there was so much stress and my family wasn't there to ground me. Luckily, the band broke up before things got too out of hand."

Martin rubs my back and gives me an understanding smile. "I get the stress, darlin', truly I do. But you need to lean on me for stuff like this. You're not ready to handle all these pressures on your own, and drinking definitely isn't the solution. Please let me help you."

I wish I could tell him everything. *But some things are just too big to share. Especially with Jodi looking for a chance to bring me down.*

"I promise I will."

"Good. It's been tearing me apart, wondering why we've been so off sync these past few months. But this explains it. I know I've been swamped with RYB, but you're my priority. I need to do better. I'm sorry."

"I'm sorry, too. I know I've been a teenage terrorist lately with my moods. I'll pull myself together and try to lighten up. And if you need me to pay for this person not to release the footage, I'm OK with that." I pause. "I have enough money to do that, right?"

Martin laughs. "You have enough money to pay off five hundred of these idiots. But Alexi's confident we can handle this without money exchanging hands. Blackmail is a felony after all, so this loser won't have a chance in hell once we figure out who it is."

Martin gets up. "See you downstairs. I'm going to tell your peeps you're working hard in the studio and won't be available for a couple of weeks. I don't want to open up an old argument with Sean about your drinking, and I *really* don't want your mama knowing about this if she doesn't have to. You cool with that?"

I nod, relieved. "I owe you one. Again."

***

I'm even more relieved when I get to the studio and don't see Carlton. I look around warily and Martin leans in. "I told Jenner I didn't think it was a good idea for Carlton to stay at the office from now on. Told him I thought it might have propelled your outburst yesterday."

"It definitely stressed me out having him here." Martin gives me a hard look and I nod, embarrassed. "I should have *told* you that when you asked me yesterday. I was trying not to cause a problem."

Martin snorts. "And look how well that turned out."

Jenner comes out of the booth. "I take it Dani's up to speed on recent events?"

Martin and I nod. I look sheepishly at Jenner. "I'm sorry."

"I am, too. This isn't ideal, to say the least. MEGA's working on overdrive to make this disappear before it hits the public. All you can do is lay low and finish up this album."

He looks at Martin. "And a little preemptive positive PR wouldn't hurt things. Maybe visit some sick kids or work at a soup kitchen?"

Before I can complain, Martin chimes in. "I think Drinky Dani here could use some time in the trenches to appreciate how good she has it compared to others." He turns to me. "Don't you?"

Seeing I'm in no position to disagree, I nod.

The three of us are tense and preoccupied throughout the session, but everyone else seems oblivious. I'm exhausted by the end of the day, but we're one song closer to finishing this album.

47

Two weeks later, the album is finished, our first wave of RYB videos and commercials are ready to go, and I spend every spare minute volunteering. I visit sick children in the hospital, sing for veterans, and serve food for the homeless. Everywhere I go, the TrueHart Nation shows up, giving each charity more enthusiastic volunteers for their cause. My social media is blowing up with my virtuous deeds.

Martin is forced to return my phone because everyone knows the album is finished. But he checks my phone nightly. *Thank God I got into the habit of deleting my texts with Beau in case I got caught!* Sean's busy studying for midterms, but we're talking as much as we can. Things are going well between us, especially since Martin helped keep my little secret from him. I've been doing my bit by walking the straight and narrow. Not one drink for two weeks.

Jenner's already planning my next tour, which is slated to start in June. Just thinking about hitting the road again makes me anxious, and I wish I could take a shot to take the edge off. But instead I've been distracting myself with schoolwork and learning to drive with Martin and Alexi. Martin took me to get my permit a few days ago, and I passed my test with flying colors. I'm practicing like crazy so I can take my test in a few months.

Late one afternoon I'm in the kitchen finishing up some work with Regina when Jenner, Martin, and Alexi walk in looking grim.

"I think that's enough schoolwork for today." Jenner smiles at

Regina. "Martin says Dani's been making some real headway in her classes."

Regina throws me a smile as she stacks up her books. "I was worried because she got really behind on tour. But these past couple of weeks she's been on fire." She gets up. "See you tomorrow?"

"Sure." I push aside my books as the guys sit down. Watching them avoid my gaze, I take a guess why they're here. "You found out who sent the email"

They nod in unison.

"Who?"

Martin sighs. "It's Beau, honey."

I cannot believe what I am hearing.

"But that's impossible! He was *in* the videos making the drinks. So now he's implicating himself serving a minor? That doesn't make any sense." Instinctually, I grab the necklace he gave me and look at Martin imploringly. "He's my friend. It's got to be someone else."

Martin squeezes my hand. "I felt the same way at first. But when Alexi showed the identifier embedded in the video, it came from Beau's phone. And the IP address he used to send the email also came back to a dummy account set up on his phone." Martin shakes his head. "If you hadn't corroborated his story about Carlton, at this point I'd have bet he made that up, too. He fooled us all."

My mind races, thinking back to the paparazzi showing up unexpectedly in Florida and all over Europe, how Beau always had my back, saved me from Carlton squealing about my drinking...could he really have been setting me up all this time? My head swims with questions and doubt.

"I have to talk to him."

"No way!" Jenner interjects. "Alexi and I will handle it from here. Martin's going to take you out for a bit while we head down to the dance studio and handle Beau."

Martin gets up. "Come on."

Martin takes my hand and pulls me gently out of the kitchen. I turn to see Jenner and Alexi heading down toward the studio. I imagine them interrupting dance rehearsal, accusing Beau of blackmailing me, and escorting him off the property. What I can't imagine is his reaction. Anger at being caught or surprise at being accused?

Martin bundles me into his waiting car and pulls out onto the highway. I stare out the window numbly, not knowing how to process this. Martin lets me be and drives into the city. We stop in front of a sprawling modern condo complex in mid-city. A valet hurries to open our doors, and I brace myself for the unwanted reaction I always get when I walk among the "normies." But this guy just nods at me and acts as if he doesn't know who I am.

Martin smiles. "Feels nice to be treated like regular people, doesn't it?" He takes my hand. "Come on."

A doorman opens the hulking glass and metal door, and we enter a luxurious lobby with marble floors. Mid-century modern chairs and coffee tables in bright colors are scattered around the foyer, complimenting the stark polished concrete walls. Abstract mirrored wall hangings that catch the light and a massive flower arrangement on a center entry table brighten the muted color scheme.

"Mr. Fox, good to see you." A young man in a blue suit steps out from behind the desk and shakes Martin's hand. "Your keys." He hands Martin an envelope.

I give Martin a quizzical look as he smiles at the concierge. "Thank you, Sam." We step into the elevator and Martin hits the penthouse button. The elevator quietly whisks us up.

"Are you going to tell me what's going on?"

The door opens into a hallway, the sunlight pouring in from several skylights and a large window at the end of the hall. Two doors on either side of the passage and a decorative table and mirror are the only things in the hallway. He fishes out a key from the envelope.

"Things are getting more serious with Brett and me. I told him I wouldn't move in with him until my guardianship was over." He unlocks the door. "However, his lease was coming up and we thought we might as well get a jumpstart on things." He beams at me as he opens the front door. "Welcome to our new home!"

I gasp as we enter. Warm honey-colored wooden floors awash in sunlight stretch out before us. A large terrace with a small lap pool and outdoor kitchen overlook the city below. We tour the condo—three bedrooms, an office, a large gourmet kitchen, and three luxury baths. It's amazing.

I gape at Martin. "When did you decide all this?"

"We've been talking about it for a while. But things between you and I got a little weird recently. Then Brett freaked out about the possibility of the blackmail video being released. I was doing a lot of damage control on that front."

"You never told me Brett was worried about the video."

Martin winces. "Yeah, well, I didn't want to make you feel bad. Truth is that for a minute he wanted to pull you as spokesperson, but he came around." Martin rushes on, waving a hand around the room. "This is all for the future. Brett will move in here next month, I'm with you for another year, and then we can decide what you want to do."

"To do?"

"You can't live in Jenner's house forever, honey. Eventually you're going to have to move on—live with your dad, get your own place."

"Oh." *I'd just assumed things would stay the same...* "Of course. I can't believe I never thought about this before. So stupid!"

"You're not stupid. I always assumed you'd want a place of your own, a little more freedom. But I'm sure Brett would be OK if you moved in with us for a bit." Martin's tone is less certain than his words.

"Oh God! Talk about a third wheel! I'm sure the last thing Brett wants is me hanging around while you set up house and plan a wedding." I flutter my hand and force a smile. "No, I'll figure something out."

My cheeks begin to quiver as I try to maintain my smile. *This day's just gone from bad to worse; first Beau, now having to figure out where I'm going to live next year. Every day it seems like something monumentally disastrous is happening. I don't know how much more I can take.*

Martin snaps his fingers. "Oh my God, I'm a genius!" He whips out his phone and steps outside to make a call. I wander around the empty rooms, feeling hollow and pointless.

"Dani!" Martin's voice echoes through the condo a few minutes later. "I've got the perfect solution."

He drags me into the hall as the elevator doors open. Sam steps out, jangling keys. "It's still filled with the previous owner's things, but you can get an idea of the space. The price is as we discussed last week. The owner's children are looking for an expedited sale. It's not listed yet, so you should decide quickly."

Sam unlocks the door across the hall from Martin's condo. We stare into an old lady paradise—stuffed to the gills with moving boxes, cat figurines, and bad oil paintings. The acidic stench of cat pee greets us, and Sam clears his throat. "The owners will clean the apartment to, uh, remove any lingering odors."

Sam nods.

If you look past the clutter and stink, the condo is a mirror image of Martin's and Brett's place.

Martin leans in and whispers excitedly. "We could be neighbors! I'd only be a few steps away. You could have your own space, maybe your dad moves in? Who knows?"

I nod my head, warming to the idea. "I can afford it?"

"You can buy it today and not miss a beat."

I smile, my excitement building. "Done!"

Sam smiles and shakes my hand. "Welcome to The Wilshire, Miss Truehart!"

***

Things are moving so fast I feel untethered and out of control. One minute I'm sitting at the kitchen table doing math. The next minute I find out one of my closest friends is blackmailing me and I'm buying a condo.

By the time we get back to the compound, Beau is gone. Jenner said he denied everything. But Alexi found the email and video on his cell and in his cloud. Devastated doesn't begin to describe my state of mind.

He tried to shake me down just like Jodi. Can I trust anyone in my life?

I FaceTime Sean and realize I can't tell him about Beau being fired because I'll have to explain the whole blackmailing/drinking thing, so I don't mention it, which feels like lying. Lying by omission, my grandma calls it, and I finally understand what she means. Instead, I tell him about the condo.

"I can't believe you bought a freaking condo." Sean's eyes bug out. "That's insane!"

"I know. But I had no idea that once I turn eighteen, Martin was planning on moving in with Brett. And he's right...I guess I can't live at Jenner's forever. I just never really thought about it. Brett isn't going to want me living with them, especially if they get married...so living across the hall from them makes the most sense."

"I guess. But living on your own is such a huge step."

"You'll be doing that next year when you go to college. Is that any different?"

Sean is quiet. "I guess you're right. It just seems like the changes you're going through are getting bigger and bigger. I remember you getting your contract seemed so huge, now a year later you're buying a condo. It's just hard to process."

"I know," I say quietly.

"You OK?"

I shrug. "Like you said, everything seems to be changing in such big ways so quickly...my parents are getting divorced, Geena's in college, Lauren's becoming an actress...(*Beau's blackmailing me, I want a drink, I'm keeping secrets from you, from Martin, from everyone*)...it's a lot."

"If anyone can handle it, it's you, rock star. You got this."

I muster a smile. "Thanks."

"OK, I gotta hit the books. Talk to you tomorrow?"

"Sure." *I wish my biggest worry was midterms right now.* I lose myself imagining what life would be like if I'd blown my audition with Jenner. Jodi would have made my life a living hell, but everything else would have been so much easier.

My phone pings with a message from Beau.

B: We need to talk

I know Martin would advise me to ignore him, but I'm too hurt and angry to keep quiet.

D: YOU TRIED TO BLACKMAIL ME!
B: I didn't, Dani, I swear
D: Explain the videos & email on your phone??
B: I can't. But you know I couldn't pull this off. And why would I show myself pouring you a drink?

It's a valid point and my conviction falters for a moment. The idea that Beau's spent months calculating this deception is too devastating to believe. But all the evidence Alexi uncovered can't be explained away and a fresh wave of anger engulfs me.

D: I can't believe I trusted you! You're just like Jodi
B: I did NOT do this. We need to tell Jenner what we did & have him investigate Carlton
D: Are you nuts? I'm already in trouble for lying about drinking. If I tell them we set Carlton up, I'm dead. Besides, everything came from your phone!

I hesitate before I send the next text but only for a moment. I realize it's the only way I can keep Beau from spilling his guts.

D: You tell anyone about Carlton–I'll deny it. My word against yours, just like you said to Carlton. Only now you're the one who's lost all credibility. I have to protect myself. I can't believe you'd do this to me. I really loved you as a friend.

Frustrated, I block his number and delete the texts. There's nothing more I can say, and he's talking crazy if he thinks I'm going to tell Jenner what we did to Carlton. He's just trying to take me down with him, and I'm not having it.

For the first time in weeks, I take a nip from my bottle of rum. I'm going to have to make this one last now that Beau isn't around to replenish it.

48

Weeks zip by, and while I miss Beau a lot at first, slowly, he fades from my mind. Bronwyn steps up as dance captain, and Jenner hires a random dancer to take Beau's place. Rehearsals are less fun than they were when Beau was around, but soon we're all in sync, prepping new numbers for the release party and the tour.

Serena returns to the compound to choreograph for the tour. I try to avoid her because I suspect she'll see right through my smoke and mirror act, place her finger firmly on my issues, and hold me accountable. She keeps arranging one-on-one time with me, which I either cancel or miss. But it's only a matter of time before I have to meet with her. I'm dreading it.

The RYB grand opening is amazing! They open the gym with a huge charity event, filling the parking lot with a worldwide RYB online class. TrueHarts around the globe make the event a success. Brett's already gotten calls to open franchises in London, Tokyo, and Paris. Everywhere we go, we see billboards with my face for RYB or my new album. It's crazy that I'm everywhere all at once!

Jenner has me doing the same circuit of PR that I did when my songs started dropping for my first album—morning news shows, Laker games, etc. I'm still doing volunteer work because it's such a positive PR bump that MEGA insists that I keep it up.

About a week after the RYB opening, I head downstairs earlier than usual. Every few days I try starting my day without a shot. Magda is in the kitchen, chopping up fruit.

"Morning, *lanv*. You're up early."

I give her a hug, stealing a piece of cantaloupe. "Thought I'd go out for a run."

"Is Martin going with you?"

I smile. "Sleeping beauty is still resting."

She pauses her chopping and looks at me. "I don't think you should go alone."

"I'm only going to the jetty. Jenner has cameras the whole way there, and I've got my phone."

She shrugs non-committedly and resumes slicing.

"I'll be fine!"

I put in my ear buds and run down the path to the beach. It's a brisk, foggy morning, colder than I expected it to be, but I'll warm up once I get moving. I lose myself in my strides, the salty air stinging my nose. I dodge waves that threaten to soak my shoes as they come rushing into shore.

Every few minutes a troubling thought about Beau or the lies I've told emerges, and I shove it to the back of my mind. These thoughts seem to surface more often, like a pot of water threatening to bubble over. I wonder how long I can keep ignoring them before they spill over into everything. I shove that thought away, too, determined to enjoy my run.

I come around to the jetty and spot a flash of color leaning up against a rock. I tense up. While Jenner's compound has a private beach, the jetty is public property, and anyone can use it. But it's so remote, it's usually deserted. Uncomfortable, I turn to go home and see the person waving and running toward me. I pick up my pace, and glance back to see the figure closing in. I stop when I realize who it is.

Jodi.

I haven't seen her in months. Her expensive hair extensions are gone, and she's got about three inches of dark roots along the part of her platinum blonde hair. She's running as fast as she can, but her enormous breasts make her gait awkward. She waves wildly at me, and when I pull out an ear bud, I hear her screaming my name.

She gasps dramatically as she approaches. "I thought you were going to make me chase you all the way to the compound. Thanks for taking pity on your dear old mom."

I cross my arms. "How did you know I'd be here?"

"I didn't," she says, breathing heavily. "I remember you once mentioned you like a morning run on the beach. I've been coming here for weeks trying to catch you. Everyone's turned their back on me. I have no money, soon I'll have no home."

I look at her coldly. "You brought this on yourself."

She shrugs. "We can agree to disagree on that. I'm not here to fight. I haven't seen you in so long. I just wanted to make sure you're OK. From what I've seen, you're not doing so well."

I look out at the choppy waves and shiver as the wind cools my sweat. "What do you know? You haven't talked to me in months."

I look back at her, but my confidence evaporates when I see her holding up her phone, playing the blackmail video.

She smiles smugly. "A guardian angel sent me this. I wish I knew who it was so I could thank them. Someone's got to do something about your drinking problem. If Martin can't handle parenting you, maybe it's time I get my old job back."

Blood pounds in my ears and I become lightheaded. Jodi feigns concern, putting a hand on my shoulder. "You feeling OK, hon? You look a little faint."

I shrug off her hand and wipe my clammy brow. A deep breath of the salty air slows my hammering pulse. "What do you want?"

Jodi puts her phone away. "I want my life back. I know I can't expect you or your sister to come back home, but I know if you told your dad you thought we should get back together, he'd consider it."

"What?"

"And I've grown accustomed to living a certain way—my hair extensions, a housekeeper, not having to work. I think I'd like to resume my former lifestyle, courtesy of *you*, of course. Maybe we could even have a reunion in the media so I can start making appearances again. Once I start making money on my own, I won't need as much from you."

Her demand winds me like a punch to the gut and anxiety squeezes my heart.

"Now there's no reason to involve anyone else in this little proposition. If you tell Martin, I'll have to go after him for being a negligent guardian, then the courts will get involved." She pulls out her phone. "Evidence will be submitted. I'm sure you'd hate for Martin and his boyfriend's new business to fail because their spokesperson is caught up in an ugly scandal?"

She's thought of everything.

My ears start ringing, and bile rises in my throat. She has me cornered.

"No," she continues, ignoring my quiet panic. "I think it would be best for you to take care of this on your own." She slips a piece of paper into my pocket. "Here's my banking information. I think ten thousand a month should cover things. I'll expect the first deposit in a week."

"But I don't have access to my money. Martin runs it all."

Jodi shrugs. "You'll figure it out. You're a smart girl. Like mother, like daughter." She blows me a kiss. "Good to see you, sugar. You look thin—told you a diet was just what you needed to make it. Mama always knows best. 'Bye."

She stalks off confidently. I stare numbly after her. I whip out my phone and call Beau.

"Dani, I'm so glad you called."

"How could you send that to her? She's going to release it. She's going to ruin everything!"

"Who is?" Beau sounds bewildered. "What are you talking about?"

"Jodi! She has your video and now *she's* blackmailing me. If I don't pay her, she'll release the video to the press and sue to end Martin's guardianship. It could ruin RYB!"

"Christ! You've gotta tell Jenner about this. I didn't do it, Dani. I swear."

"What am I going to do?"

"Tell Jenner. I'll call him right now with you if you want."

"NO!" The wind blows into the phone. I can't hear what Beau says over the static. "Never mind, I'll figure it out myself." I hang up.

***

I drag myself back to the compound, unable to find a solution. All my money is locked up in a trust monitored by Martin. I don't want to ruin Brett and Martin's happiness over the RYB opening with this bombshell. *If I can just figure out how to make the first payment, maybe I can buy some time.*

My phone buzzes with a text from Trey.

Trey!

He's in town shooting promos for his new line of yoga wear. I'm pretty sure I can ask him to loan me the money without any questions. I race up to my room.

> *D: Morning! How's it going?*
>
> *T: Namaste, Dani. All's good*
>
> *D: Can we meet up if you're not too busy? I need a favor*
>
> *T: Sure. Finishing up a retreat in SB. I can swing by on my way back to town. Everything OK?*
>
> *D: Yeah, just need a friend*
>
> *T: I'm your man. See you around 4*

I feel extremely slimy for hitting up Trey for money. I should tell Martin like I promised. But is it wrong if I'm trying to protect him?

***

It's a tense day as I wait for four o'clock to roll around. I beg off dance rehearsals, claiming exhaustion. Martin sets me up by the pool with some magazines, a blanket, and hot tea.

"I have to run into the city to meet the decorator and sign some papers. Then I was going to stop by the gym and take Brett to dinner. But if you want, I can cancel all that."

"I'm just a little run down. I'll be fine."

He plants a kiss on my forehead. "Take care and get some rest."

About twenty minutes after he leaves, Magda brings out Trey. I put an eager smile on my face, determined to get Jodi's money.

"Dani!" He gives me a warm hug, his hand lingering on my waist a moment too long. "I've been dying to catch up with you." Trey launches into a long monologue about the success of his clothing line and his upcoming contract negotiations for *The Fleetwoods*.

"With my clothing line taking off and Discovery covering my trail hike this fall for a special, I feel like now is the time to make a break from the old me. Let *The Fleetwoods* go and really evolve to the next level of my life."

I try hard to listen sincerely and not roll my eyes.

"Can you afford to quit the show?"

He laughs. "Of course! I've got a great financial advisor. He's really set me up for success."

Seeing my opportunity, I leap into action. "See, that's the thing, Trey. I don't have one yet. All my money is locked up in a trust."

His eyes grow wide. "Oh yeah, that's a bummer. But it keeps you from blowing it all on stupid stuff."

"True, but it does leave me in a bind if I want to do something, especially if it's a surprise for someone." I pause. "There's a meditation retreat up north I want to surprise Martin and Brett with, to thank them for letting me be the RYB spokesperson."

Trey lights up. "The one in Big Sur? It's amazing. Seriously, life changing. They'll love it."

I look chagrined. "Only problem is that I don't have access to my money."

Trey nods knowingly. "You need a loan. Of course! Happy to help. Anything to turn someone onto the miracles of meditation. What do you need—a credit card, money transfer?"

Yes!

"A money transfer would be great." I reach into my pocket. "Here's the info."

Trey whips out his phone and glances at the paper. "I just need the name on the account."

"J. Truehart."

I'm worried he's going to ask what the J stands for, but he doesn't.

"Done. You can pay me back later." His smile has a weight to it that makes me uncomfortable. "I know you're good for it."

He glances at his watch. "I gotta jet. Got a meeting in town at six." We get up, and he gives me another hug that lasts a little too long. His hand traces my arm as we separate and kneads my hand.

"I'm so glad you reached out. It makes me feel good to know you chose to turn to me for help. I hope this is the beginning of a new chapter in our friendship." He leans in, and I pull back. "I really want to be there for you. Any way I can."

I'm completely skeeved out, but he did just loan me ten thousand dollars, so am I really in a position to slap him? "Uh, thanks again, Trey. Say hi to Kayla."

"Kayla, yeah, right." He seems to remember himself and nods. "*You* say hi to Sean. See you next week at the party."

He leaves, and I feel about as cheap and dirty as it gets. I just flirted with a guy and borrowed money to pay off my blackmailing mother. A new low for me.

49

I'm grateful that *The Queen of Harts* release/birthday party falls on the night before Sean has a big presentation in class. It counts for half his grade, and he feels awful he can't come. But I can't bear to face him with all the stuff I've been dealing with. Tonight of all nights, I need to blow off some steam, and it'll be easier to do that if Sean isn't birddogging me.

Crews have been working for days to get the compound ready. The theme is "Mad Hatter Tea Party." If I weren't so stressed, I could enjoy the decadent splendor of it all. Oversized teapots, teacups, playing cards, and whimsical flower arrangements dot the grounds. Tables laid with pastries and finger foods on the terrace overlook the swimming-pool-turned-dancefloor. Pink and purple floods light the grounds, twinkle-lights sparkle high in the treetops. The palm trees are decorated like lollipops and candy canes, and the DJ is dressed like the White Rabbit. Everyone is supposed to come in costume, which will be a trip.

Petra has worked up a sexy little Alice in Wonderland costume with a short blue dress, white over-the-knee stockings, and a tiara with hearts on it. Martin and Jenner are dressed as Tweedledee and Tweedledum, their foam stomachs bringing a smile to my sour face when I see them by the pool.

"You guys look awesome!" I poke Martin in the belly.

He laughs and rubs his stomach. "Brett's sorry he couldn't be here.

He's putting in long hours at the gym, making sure everything's going smoothly."

Trey, Kayla, and Lauren come over. Kayla is dressed in a pink-and-purple-striped catsuit with fake whiskers stuck to her cheeks. A pink and purple wig with cat ears leaves no doubt about who she is.

"Kayla," Martin says, "you're a perfect Cheshire cat."

"Meow." She purrs seductively. She is working hard to ignore me.

Lauren is dressed as a brown dormouse. Cute but frumpy enough not to steal Kayla's thunder. I'm sure Kayla picked it out for her. I give her a hug.

"I didn't know you'd be here. Is Tom here, too?"

"Nope. Kayla's going to introduce me to some industry people tonight, so Tom decided to stay home. He wants nothing to do with my acting career. Says I'm being an idiot." She snorts. "Loser."

Martin and I exchange a glance at Lauren's attitude, but she doesn't notice because she's scanning the crowd.

"Dani!" It's Trey dressed as a millennial Mad Hatter in skinny plaid pants, a vest with no shirt, and a comically large pocket watch hanging from a chain, with an oversized top hat over his flowing locks. "Long time, no see."

He winks and pecks my cheek, but Kayla is too busy surveying the party to notice.

"Shall we do a round?" Kayla grabs Lauren's hand and drags her away without waiting for an answer. "Ta!"

"Unfortunately, I have to make the rounds as well. Trey, enjoy yourself. Dani, I'll see you in a bit for the performance." He leaves as Martin's cell pings.

"Excuse me, that's Brett." He hurries off leaving Trey and I alone.

He gives me the once over. "You look incredible." He leans in and I can smell alcohol on his breath. "Been thinking about you all week."

I step back and almost bump into a waiter dressed as a playing card carrying a tray of drinks. "Do a little pre-partying at home, Trey?"

He shrugs as he picks two drinks up and holds one out to me. "A toast on your birthday."

"My birthday is next week."

He grins and shoves the glass at me. "Minor detail." He nudges my shoulder. "Let's have some fun tonight. I need it."

I look around.

He leans in and whispers conspiratorially, his breath sour. "Don't worry, Martin and Jenner aren't here."

As much as he grosses me out, temptation overwhelms me. I take the glass and we toast. The drink is cool, fruity, and instantly calms my nerves. Trey licks his lips devilishly and reaches out to wipe away a drop of liquid from my lip, his eyes lingering on my mouth. It's too intimate a move for me. He notices my discomfort and looks away.

He steals a tray of drinks from a passing waiter. "Now it's a party."

Against my better judgment, we move to a more private area in the garden, finding a gilded sofa among the hibiscus bushes. I just need a few minutes to relax before the party gets into full swing. We help ourselves to another cocktail while Trey tells me about the huge fight that he had with Kayla on the drive over. "She thinks she owns me. I can't stand it anymore, Dani."

He takes my empty cup and hands me another cocktail. The drinks are hitting me, and Liquid courage from the cocktails eggs me on. "She doesn't own you! You're your own man."

"I am!" He sways drunkenly.

I point to my chest. "And I'm my own woman! No one owns me. Not my mom, or Jenner, or MEGA. With the TrueHart Nation behind me, I can do anything I want."

"The TrueHarts are loyal. They'll always adore you. Just like I do." Trey plops down next to me, splashing his drink on me, leaning in to caress my cheek.

I push him away, and he stares forlornly into his cup. "Kayla won't let me quit the show. She said no."

I squint at Trey, my posture loosening the more I drink. "She can't say no!"

His shoulders drop and he tilts his head. "I *knew* you'd understand! You always get me."

Guilt creeps over me and I try to wash it away with another sip. "Sean would be furious if he saw me drinking with you." I try to tap Trey's nose and miss, nearly poking him in the eye. "He doeshn't trusht you." I look at Trey, blurry from the drinks, and turn away, whispering to myself. "He shouldn' trusht me. I'm the worsht girlfriend."

Trey puts his arm around me. "No, you're naw, baby. You're amasin'. That boy doeshn't know what he hash. You need a man to really appreshiate you."

"You're only two yearsh older than Sean. Whadda you kno'?"

Trey leans in and kisses me. It takes me too long to realize what's happening before I pull away, shocked. "Whad are ya doing!" I push him away, almost falling over in the process. "I've gotta go."

"Dani, wait!"

I turn around to leave only to see Lauren staring at me, mouth agape. *Oh my God!*

I stop abruptly and Trey bumps into me, almost knocking me over, spilling his drink all over my back.

I point as Lauren runs away. "Lauren shaw you kiss me."

"Dammit!" Trey pushes me forward. We chase after Lauren, stumbling into people. I run right into Jenner, practically bouncing off his foam stomach. He catches me before I fall.

"Hey! Easy there. What's the rush?"

It only takes a moment for Jenner to take in my punch-splattered costume, smeared lipstick, and disheveled hair to know what's up.

"Are you kidding me, Dani? You're supposed to perform in thirty minutes."

I pull my eyes off of Lauren, as she runs inside the house and try to focus on Jenner. He steps toward Trey menacingly.

"How much did you let her drink?"

Trey stumbles for an answer.

"Don't lie to me, you little jerk! How much!"

"Two, maybe three?"

Jenner curses and takes my arm. "Come on, I've got to get some coffee in you before Martin sees you."

Trey tries to follow, but Jenner stops him. "You, out now. I don't want to see you around her again."

I try to pull my arm away. "Jenner, isn't Trey's faul'. We're jusht talkin'. I only had two punshes, I'm fine." *Was it two or was it three?*

In my head, my words come out perfectly clear, but I can tell by the look on Jenner's face that I'm drunker than I think. He sighs. "Guess you won't be performing tonight. Not a good look with all the MEGA execs here, but it'd be worse if you vomit on stage." He steers me toward the house and whispers, "Put a smile on your face and *don't* say a word."

He plasters a smile on his face, and I do the same, trying to look as normal as possible. I nod as I pass people, but the looks I get back make it clear I'm not pulling it off as seamlessly as I hope. I stumble up the steps, and Jenner plops me at the kitchen island. The smell of food makes my stomach roil.

"Coffee, now!" he barks at a random waiter who scrambles into action.

He hands me an open bottle of water. "Drink."

Suddenly I'm parched and down the whole bottle. My stomach lurches again, but luckily the water stays down. Jenner places a cup of coffee in front of me. "Don't move. I'm going to tell the execs that you've got a sore throat and won't be able to sing. A quick walk on stage, you blow out your birthday candles, and then you sit in a chair and try not to embarrass yourself or me for the rest of the night. Do you understand?"

I nod.

He storms off, and I sip the scalding hot coffee. It sobers me up some, clearing my vision a little, but I'm still drunk and feeling extremely loose.

Trey peeks in from the hall. "You OK?"

"Jenner's on the terrace. He'll be back in a minute."

"We gotta find Lauren before she gets to Kayla." The urgency makes Trey's voice shrill.

Lauren!

I'd completely forgotten about her. "An' before she tells Sean! Go fin' her."

Trey looks uncomfortable. "What if Jenner sees me? I don't wan' him to make a scene kicking me out."

"Kayla'll make a bigger scene if she fin' out you kissed me. Idiot! Now look at the mess we're in."

I see a blur of brown shoot out the front door and point. "Is tha' her?"

Trey spins around. Seeing Jenner tied up talking to a MEGA exec, I sneak out of the kitchen.

"Lauren!" I chase her out the front door, Trey follows behind me.

"Wait, Lauren. I cahn explain!"

"I don't want to hear it!" She checks her phone, looks around, starts walking toward an oncoming Uber.

I grab her hand and lower my voice. "It's not whad you thin'."

She rips her hand away from me, yelling. "Really? Because it looks one hundred percent like you're making out with Kayla's boyfriend. What do you think she's going to say? Or Sean?"

I look around, grateful the party is in full swing and that there's only one or two valet guys hanging out front. "It's not like tha' at all. If you'd jusht calm down for a second."

Lauren whips open the Uber door and looks at me, disgusted. "I don't know who you are anymore. The Dani Truehart I know would never cheat on her boyfriend or kiss another girl's guy." She gets in and slams the door. The car starts to pull away but stops. Lauren's window rolls down. "And if you think I won't tell Kayla or Sean, you've got another thing coming. I'm not covering up for you. So you'd better tell them both now."

Her car leaves, and Trey comes up to me. "We've gotta go af'er her. She can't tell Kayla."

My heart races as I try to figure out what to do.

"Come on, Dani, we gotta go." He paces back and forth.

"I cahn't jus' leave. I gotta go tell Mart'n, get Alexi to drive ush."

Trey grabs me. "We don't haf time. She's prolly calling Kayla from the car."

"Dani!" Jenner bellows from the front door, Carlton trailing behind him. *Great! Carlton's all I need right now.*

"I told you to stay put!" He spies Trey. "And I told you to leave."

"Come *on*, Dani." Trey wheedles, inching toward a convertible Mercedes parked by the steps.

"Dani, get inside *now!*" Jenner barks, storming down the steps.

I put my hands to my temples, my head buzzing and stomach churning. "Can ef'ryone jus' stop yelling at me for a sec?"

Jenner keeps coming at me, rage distorting his face, dressed in that stupid costume. It seems like a nightmare, and I turn away.

"This is serious, Dani. Stop acting like a child and get in the house."

Suddenly, I snap. "Jus' leave me alone! Both of you! I jus' need a minute to think!"

I stumble around, looking for someplace to escape, panic building in my chest. My eyes land on the convertible. I pull open the door and sink into the seat. "I jus' need ta sit down for a sec."

"Dani, get out of that car."

Exhausted and nauseous, it's hard to talk. "I'm not goin' anywhere, I jus' need to think."

Jenner rushes over and tries to pull me out, but his touch enrages me. Suddenly, I'm alert as a rabid dog.

"I jus' wanna sit!" I twist to pull my arm away. "Why are you always tellin' me what to do?"

My arm slips from his grasp and, before I know what I'm doing, I start the car and put it in gear. He tries to stop me but has to jump out of the way before the open door hits him.

"Dani! Stop!" Jenner tries to grab the door, but the car keeps rolling forward. In an instant, Trey jumps in, legs hanging out the passenger window, and presses the gas pedal with his hands. The car jerks forward.

"Go!" he yells.

As if in a dream, I grab the wheel before we hit a palm tree, my door slamming shut. I drive up the curving driveway, ping-ponging between bushes and trees, scraping the sides of the car. I scramble for my seatbelt and pull it across my chest. Trey laughs wildly as we peel out onto the coast highway.

"Punch it! We can catch Lauren!"

I blink wildly, hair blowing in my face as we race down the dark highway. We're so far out in Malibu, we don't see any cars. The cold air clears my head enough to realize how drunk I really am. Bright flashes blind me, and I lose control for a second as Trey laughs again, pushing his face next to mine, taking a selfie.

"Best exit to a party ever, D! You never disappoint!" He smashes a kiss onto my cheek, snapping another photo.

I shove his face out of the way blinking rapidly, phantom spots from the flash dazzling my vision. "You idiot, this isn' funny! I'm inna lotta trouble now. Pu' on your seatbel'! I gotta get off tha road." I start to pull over, but Trey jerks the wheel and veers the car back onto the highway.

"No, you need to catch Lauren." He puts on his belt.

"Stop! We're never gonna catch her. Even if we do, she won' talk to us. Just lemme pull over. We're gonna get into an accident."

Trey jerks the wheel again, and I turn it sharply to the right. Too sharply.

The headlights slice through the night as the car careens onto the shoulder at full speed. A ghostly visage comes into focus, the eyes and mouth three perfectly round 'O's as an unfortunate nighttime cyclist appears out of nowhere.

I scream, slamming on the brakes. I close my eyes and turn the wheel sharply to the left, trying to avoid the bicycle, praying with all my might.

With a sickening crunch, the world fades to black.

TO BE CONTINUED IN BOOK THREE
FALLING STAR

Acknowledgements

This is my favorite part of writing a book. I don't think I'll ever grow tired of thanking all the wonderful people who support me. Being a writer is a solitary process, but I am grateful for all my friends and family for keeping me grounded, making me laugh and encouraging me to keep going.

This entire book was written during the pandemic after the loss of my mother and my good friend, Neena. With my world turned upside down, I didn't know how to put one foot in front of the other, and I wasn't sure if I would be able to write another book. Dani Truehart got me walking in the land of the living again. For that reason alone, this will always be a special book to me.

Many thanks to my wonderful agent, Diane Nine of Nine Speakers, Inc. Thank you for being an ear, a guiding hand, and a shining light throughout this process.

A mountain of gratitude to Rand-Smith Publishing. I appreciate your time, energy, and your belief that I could deliver a series that people would want to read. And thank you for teaching that there is only one space between sentences.

Craig and Liam – thank you, thank you, thank you for being the best family a person could have! I love you both more than I can say. I could never have started or finished this book without your support, patience and the many inspirational Lego creations left on my writing table. Thank you for letting me pursue my dream. I am always here to do the same for both of you. There's no place I'd rather be than hanging out with you two. Turn up the *Christmas Can-Can*! *Yah Mo Be There* for you both, always.

To my big sis, Christina Dicker – you are a real-life rock star! Thanks for reading my book a million times, for helping me through the dark days we've recently shared and for making me laugh when I needed it the most. I'd be lost without you. We've come so far together and I'm grateful to have you as my sister and best friend. Love to Josh, Eva, and Claire!

James Perez-Gillespie – my brother from a different mother! Your writing skills are only surpassed by your enormous heart. Your friendship has helped me through good times and bad and innumerable rough drafts. I know Solie and Diane are watching over us with big smiles on their faces. Onward and upward.

Debi Tarvin – beta reader extraordinaire and stellar first soprano. I appreciate all the hours you have spent grappling with my grammar and reading my books. Thank you. I miss singing with you.

A big shout out of gratitude to Elaine and Bill Kwasniewski and the Atwood family. I hit the jackpot with my in-laws. Thank you for your constant support.

Finally, a heartfelt thank you to everyone else who has helped in countless ways: my amazing grandmother Barbara Martin and Trino Alvarez for taking my beautiful author photo. My wonderful group of friends – Andrea S., Amber N., Heather A., Kristen G., Suzi M., Kelly B., Hillary S., Hannah A., Tatiana C., The Let's Get Lit(erature) Book Club, MomsNext, everyone at OLF and many more. Your friendship and support mean the world to me, and I am blessed to know each of you. And I can't forget Phoebe who is the best writing buddy I know.

There's so much to be grateful for in life if you know where to look. Every step of the way these past two years, I have tried to focus on the blessings in my life and that has made the hardships much easier to deal with.

Chase your dreams because the clock is ticking.

CPSIA information can be obtained
at www.ICGtesting.com
Printed in the USA
LVHW081533011121
702132LV00019B/109

9 781950 544349